HALO

SILENT STORM

DON'T MISS THESE OTHER THRILLING STORIES IN THE WORLDS OF

Halo: Renegades
Kelly Gay

Halo: Silent Storm
Troy Denning

Halo: Bad Blood
Matt Forbeck

Halo: Legacy of Onyx
Matt Forbeck

Halo: Retribution
Troy Denning

Halo: Envoy
Tobias S. Buckell

Halo: Smoke and Shadow
Kelly Gay

Halo: Fractures: More Essential Tales of the Halo Universe (anthology)

Halo: Shadow of Intent
Joseph Staten

Halo: Last Light
Troy Denning

Halo: Saint's Testimony
Frank O'Connor

Halo: Hunters in the Dark
Peter David

Halo: New Blood
Matt Forbeck

Halo: Broken Circle
John Shirley

***THE KILO-FIVE TRILOGY* | KAREN TRAVISS**

Halo: Glasslands

Halo: The Thursday War

Halo: Mortal Dictata

***THE FORERUNNER SAGA* | GREG BEAR**

Halo: Cryptum

Halo: Primordium

Halo: Silentium

Halo: Evolutions: Essential Tales of the Halo Universe (anthology)

Halo: The Cole Protocol
Tobias S. Buckell

Halo: Contact Harvest
Joseph Staten

Halo: Ghosts of Onyx
Eric Nylund

Halo: First Strike
Eric Nylund

Halo: The Flood
William C. Dietz

Halo: The Fall of Reach
Eric Nylund

SILENT STORM

TROY DENNING

BASED ON THE BESTSELLING VIDEO GAME FOR XBOX®

G

GALLERY BOOKS

New York | London | Toronto | Sydney | New Delhi

Gallery Books
An Imprint of Simon & Schuster, Inc.
1230 Avenue of the Americas
New York, NY 10020

This Gallery Books trade paperback edition July 2019

Manufactured in the United States of America

10 9

Library of Congress Cataloging-in-Publication Data is available.

ISBN 978-1-5011-3838-6
ISBN 978-1-9821-2315-4 (pbk)
ISBN 978-1-5011-3839-3 (ebook)

For Ross and Ashley
The future is yours

HISTORIAN'S NOTE

On March 1, 2526, approximately one year after the loss of Harvest during humanity's first contact with the Covenant, Vice Admiral Preston Cole arrived to counterattack with the largest fleet in human history. In his bid to reclaim the colony, the forty warships of Battle Group X-Ray squared off against a single Covenant super-destroyer—and lost thirteen vessels before finally overcoming the staggering power of the enemy ship. Now, with a handful of colonies already fallen to the Covenant invasion fleet and many more worlds in its path, the United Nations Space Command is pivoting to a new strategy—and scrambling to stop the greatest existential threat humanity has ever faced.

HALO®

SILENT STORM

CHAPTER 1

0342 hours, March 5, 2526 (military calendar)
UNSC *Razor*-class Prowler *Starry Night*
High Equatorial Orbit, Planet Netherop, Ephyra System

The distant slivers of five alien spacecraft burst from Netherop's pall of brown clouds and climbed into orbit on tails of white-hot propellant. The attack plan was to match velocities with the vessels, then have a squad of Spartans go EVA and follow them into their mothership's hangar. But the aliens were traveling about twenty times faster now than when the *Starry Night* had spotted them just fifteen seconds earlier, and John-117 didn't know if a *Razor*-class prowler could match that kind of acceleration.

There were a lot of things John didn't know about this operation, like whether the alien craft were reconnaissance boats or superiority fighters, or whether their mothership was a survey frigate or an assault corvette. He didn't know the size of the vessel's complement, or how many of them would be trained for close-quarters combat, or why the Covenant might be interested in a greenhouse planet that had probably cooked its native population a hundred centuries before.

What John *did* know was that the aliens were the enemy, and today they were going to die.

He continued to watch the five spacecraft via a tactical monitor mounted high on the drop-bay bulkhead, and a crisp female voice sounded over the *Starry Night*'s internal comm net.

"Brace for acceleration. The inertial compensator won't handle what we're throwing at it."

"Acknowledged."

John and his eleven Spartan companions lowered their center of gravity against the prowler's acceleration. A moment later, they began to hear muffled clangs and thumps as poorly secured equipment slammed into nearby bulkheads. "How long until we catch the targets?" he asked.

"It depends."

When she failed to elaborate, John said, "That's not an answer, ma'am."

He tried to keep the impatience in his voice to a minimum. Halima Ascot might have an informal manner, but she was still a captain in the United Nations Space Command, and he was just a fifteen-year-old petty officer first class. Not that his age mattered. The date-of-birth had been falsified in the service records of all Spartans, and no one in the *Starry Night*'s crew had reason to believe any of them were younger than nineteen.

Besides, John and his fellow Spartans were no ordinary fifteen-year-olds. At age six, they had been conscripted into a top-secret program to develop bioengineered super-soldiers. The intention had been to use them against a massive colonial Insurrection that threatened to shatter humanity's young interstellar civilization, but priorities had changed when the Covenant appeared.

That was the life of a Spartan. He went where he was needed, he didn't complain, and he killed whatever he had to. It was that simple.

Deep down, John knew he had been wronged when he was taken from his family at such an early age—that he should have hated his abductors for robbing him of a normal childhood. But he didn't. They had molded a schoolyard bully into a soldier, then forged him into the leader of the finest fighting unit in the UNSC. He was grateful for that.

And he was damn proud they had chosen him.

When Captain Ascot did not acknowledge his point, John added, "We need a little warning before deploying, ma'am. Once we activate our rebreathers, we'll only have ninety minutes of air."

"I'm aware of that, Petty Officer," Ascot said. "Which is why this drop may be no-go. The mothership is on the far side of its orbit right now."

This meant it would be hidden from the *Starry Night*'s surveillance systems until both vessels were on the same side of the planet again, but that was hardly a cause for concern. The *Starry Night* had been observing the Covenant vessels for more than a day, and the mothership had never been visible for longer than twenty minutes out of every hour.

"So, situation normal," John said. "I don't see the problem."

"Orbital mechanics," Ascot said. "You can't just go faster and make the rendezvous—try that, and your whole squad will end up flying out of orbit."

"Right." John had studied classical mechanics in the physics courses during his third year of Spartan training. But that had been five years ago, when he was only nine, and he had been more interested in tactical theory than Newton's laws of motion. "We have to drop into a lower orbit and catch up, then sync orbits and begin proximity operations."

"While staying hidden behind the alien spacecraft," Ascot said. "In their current orbit, it's going to take seventy minutes just to sync. After that, you still have to last through proximity operations, then sneak aboard and capture a five-hundred-meter ship full of LGMs."

LGM stood for little green men, a slang term that could be traced

back at least as far as the unidentified flying object reports of 1950s Earth. Because one of the Covenant species averaged only a meter and a half tall, some analysts in the Office of Naval Intelligence believed the enemy might actually have visited Earth in the past. But John knew better. If the Covenant had *ever* been to Earth, it would be a glassed-over wasteland by now.

"We can handle it."

John hoped he sounded more certain than he felt. On the one hand, he and his fellow Spartans were the deadliest soldiers mankind had ever created. On the other, humanity had not even been certain that aliens really existed until the violent first contact with the Covenant. So there was no getting around it—at best, John and his assault squad were only somewhat prepared for what they were about to attempt.

But he didn't dare admit that. If he wanted his team to fight with confidence, he had to project confidence at all times.

When Ascot did not respond to his reassurance, John decided to double down. "Really, ma'am, we'll be fine. Spartans work fast."

"Nobody works that fast," Ascot said. "Look . . . you'll have no more than a fifteen-minute margin. If anyone runs out of air during the boarding action, there's nothing the *Starry Night* can do to help."

"I appreciate the concern." John did not let her caution shake him. The SPARTAN-II program was so highly classified that even prowler captains did not know the full capabilities of the super-soldiers they ferried into battle. "But once we're aboard, rebreather time won't be a factor. The mothership's atmosphere should support human life."

"There's a big difference between *should* and *will*."

"The odds are with us. You've seen the intelligence summaries. Only one Covenant species *doesn't* breathe oxygen."

"Only one species that ONI is aware of," Ascot replied. "We both know there could be a dozen more that breathe anything from hydrogen to cobalt. The UNSC has a lot to learn about the Covenant."

"Yes, ma'am. That *is* the reason for the operation."

"Careful, Spartan," Ascot said. "A pissed-off prowler captain has about two hundred ways to make your life miserable."

"I apologize, ma'am." John didn't like begging for permission to carry out a mission assigned to him by the chief of the Office of Naval Intelligence's Section Three, but as the commander of the *Starry Night*, Ascot was in charge of the mission until the Spartans left her vessel. "I still think we need to take the risk."

"I know you do."

Ascot's tone was sympathetic. The UNSC knew almost nothing about the enemy. If the Spartans could capture a Covenant vessel, the scientists of ONI's Section Three Materials Group should be able to reverse-engineer the technology and learn the secret of the enemy's superior slipspace drives and nearly impenetrable energy shields. They would also attempt to discover the true capabilities of the aliens' advanced weaponry, and perhaps even uncover a few hidden vulnerabilities. With a little luck, they might even figure out where the aliens lived out there—and why they wanted to eradicate humanity.

"But it's my call," Ascot continued. "And I need to be sure you understand the risks. We're working at the edge of your armor's capability, with more unknown variables than we can count. If something goes wrong, there won't be much chance to recover."

"If you're saying we'd be on our own, Spartans are trained—"

"I'm saying the *Starry Night* will do everything possible," Ascot said. "But we're limited by orbital mechanics. It might be smart to wait for an opportunity that's not quite so marginal."

"With all due respect, ma'am, I disagree." As much as John wanted to accept her recommendation, he didn't even consider it. The longer they waited, the more likely they were to run into a mission-killing complication—and the more his private doubts would eat away at him. "We've been here a day already, and our luck won't hold forever. Sooner or later, an enemy patrol will spot the *Starry Night*, or a second Covenant vessel will arrive, or the enemy commander will decide it's time to move on. I can think of a dozen things that might go wrong if we don't go now."

Ascot fell silent for a moment, then finally sighed. "So can I." There was a low murmur while she consulted with someone on the bridge; then she said, "Very well, Spartan. You're cleared to move forward. Slingshot maneuver in five minutes."

"Affirmative," John said. "And thanks."

"Don't thank me, son. This isn't a favor."

She closed the comm channel, leaving John to hope he was making a sound decision. His best friend, Samuel-034, had died a few months earlier during the boarding action that had inspired this one, and John was still trying to figure out what had gone wrong.

The UNSC's entire complement of Spartans had been aboard a modified Pelican dropship, ascending toward an orbital rendezvous above Chi Ceti IV, when they spotted a Covenant warship moving to attack their transport frigate. The vessels had savaged each other earlier, and it was clear the UNSC frigate would not survive another engagement. John ordered the company to go EVA and board the enemy ship.

He'd told himself he had no choice, that the desperate assault was the only way to prevent all thirty-three Spartans from being trapped on a soon-to-be-occupied world. And that had probably been true.

But the whole reason for going to Chi Ceti IV had been to outfit the Spartans in their new, state-of-the-art Mjolnir power armor. The automatic neural interface, performance-amplifying circuitry, and titanium-alloy shell had made them feel almost invincible, and John had been as keen as anyone to test the new armor in action. So when the Covenant ship reappeared, he hadn't hesitated to commit his entire force to an impromptu boarding action.

The risky attack had worked—though just barely. John and two companions, Samuel-034 and Kelly-087, had intercepted the vessel and boarded through a breach in the combat-battered hull. They had managed to plant a trio of Anvil-II warheads near a power core, but not before a lucky plasma bolt found a soft spot in Sam's armor and ruptured the pressure seal beneath.

The only way to flee the ship had been to jump back into space, where Sam would decompress inside his armor. Rather than condemn his friend to such a slow and agonizing death, John had ordered Sam to stay behind and guard the warheads until they detonated.

The decision continued to haunt John in his dreams, and that troubled him. He had seen many soldiers die, both in training and in combat, and suffered no self-doubt. But Sam had been under his command, and John could not help believing that had he been better prepared—and not quite so reckless—his friend would be fighting at his side today.

John didn't see what he could have done differently—there had been only moments to plan and no opportunity to marshal ordnance—but he was not about to make the same mistake twice. This time, the Spartans were carrying emergency patching kits and extra thruster packs and locator beacons . . . equipment for just about every foreseeable contingency.

And still he worried, thanks to the UNSC's lack of knowledge about the enemy. Almost literally, John was leading his Spartans into battle blind, and everything in his training told him that was a recipe for disaster.

But they had to try.

John turned toward the interior of the drop bay. Including him, there were twelve Spartans prepared to launch, all looking vaguely robotic in their angular helmets and bulky Mjolnir power armor. In an effort to optimize each Spartan's individual field competencies and test skunkwork modifications, their armor's titanium alloy frame had been temporarily modified, each of them bearing distinctive features. And to avoid enemy sensors, their plating sets had been tinted with the same refractive coating that helped conceal the UNSC's prowlers.

Whether the precaution would work against the aliens was little more than an educated guess. The only thing the UNSC knew about Covenant sensor technology was that in the active mode, it radiated across a broad array of the electromagnetic spectrum. In theory, the apparatus *had* to operate on the same general principle as human sensor systems—by emitting a signal and looking for reflections bounced off an unseen object—but that was really just an assumption. For all anyone in the UNSC knew, the alien transmissions could be the byproduct of some quantum-scanning technology that humanity had not yet imagined.

Another good reason to capture an enemy ship.

The illumination in the drop bay dimmed from white to pale purple, an indication that the *Starry Night* was three minutes from start-of-maneuver. The darker light would be less noticeable when the jump hatch opened to discharge the Spartans, and the time buffer gave their eyes a chance to adjust to the darkness.

"Final check, everyone," John said. The Spartans had already examined their systems twice since entering the drop bay, so this was more of a focusing ritual than an actual equipment inspection. "Make sure you give your partner a careful lookover. No loose straps or partial mag-clamps."

Inside his helmet, a chain of LEDs flashed green as the eleven other Spartans acknowledged the order. John ran through his own checklist—weapons loaded and safe, suit integrity good, rebreather operable, thruster canisters charged, directional nozzles responsive, attachments secure, quick release functional—then turned to his inspection partner, a dry-witted Spartan named Fred-104. John began a visual check, confirming that the seams on the outer shell of Fred's armor remained tight, that the refractive paint was unblemished, the weapons attachments were solid, and the thruster harness sat flush beneath the fission reactor.

John gave Fred's shoulder an all-good thump, then turned to await his own inspection. By the time he felt the all-good on his own shoulder, five LEDs were glowing green on the squad-status bar inside his helmet. The first three represented the other three members of John's own Blue Team. The fourth represented the four members of Gold Team, led by Joshua-029, and the final light represented the four members of Green Team, led by Kurt-051. Twelve souls in all, ready to be hurled through space like human slingshot pellets.

"This intercept will be a lot easier than at Chi Ceti IV," John said. "But if you miss the target, break orbit and power down, then settle in—"

"And conserve your air," Kelly-087 interrupted. A member of John's Blue Team, she was the fastest of the Spartans, as quick mentally as she was physically. "You said that already. Twice."

"Just making sure everyone remembers."

"Don't trigger your locator beacon until the battle is over," Linda-058 added. Normally quiet and reserved, she was the best sniper in the Spartans—and also on John's Blue Team. "We remember."

"Yeah, what's up?" Kurt asked. A natural people-reader who made friends easily, he was plainspoken and direct. "What are you so worried about?"

"I'm not worried," John said. In most units, such banter would have been borderline insubordinate. But the Spartans weren't most units. They had been training together since childhood, and they were as much family as comrades-in-arms. John would have been worried if his squad *didn't* feel comfortable speaking freely with him. "I'm just confirming procedure."

"Not much to confirm," Fred said. In addition to being John's inspection partner, he was the squad's backup leader and Blue Team's fourth member. "Sneak aboard the alien ship and kill everything that's not a Spartan. If things go bad, stay out of sight until the fight's over, then call for rescue. It's a simple plan."

"I guess so, when you break it down that way," John said. Nobody had mentioned the five prowlers standing by for rescue operations, but he could see that his reminders were only making the squad nervous. "Sorry for overbriefing, everybody. I just want us to be ready for surprises. What we know about the aliens would fit in a bullet casing."

"And there's our advantage," Joshua said. "We know that we *don't* know, which makes us careful. But the aliens may have been studying humanity for a while. They'll think they know more about us than they do, and that makes them vulnerable."

"Hadn't looked at it that way." It seemed a stretch to claim that ignorance was an advantage, but John appreciated the out Joshua was giving him. "Good point. The aliens have no idea how hard we're about to hit them. Any questions?"

A chain of status lights blinked red inside his helmet.

"Okay then," John said. "Captain Ascot is right about working on the margins, so stay off your rebreathers until we're clear of the hatch. We may need every second of air we can save."

The alert lamps on the drop-bay bulkhead changed from red to amber, and Ascot's crisp voice sounded over the *Starry Night* comm net.

"One minute to maneuver."

John and the other team leaders stood shoulder-to-shoulder in front of the jump hatch. Their team members lined up in columns behind them, each one grabbing the thruster pack of the Spartan ahead. Even with their physical enhancements and the Mjolnir's mechanical strength multipliers, they would never hold fast through the wild acceleration of the slingshot maneuver. But that wasn't expected. John just wanted to keep the members of each team close enough to support each other if an emergency arose.

The alert lamps began to blink.

"Thirty seconds," Ascot said.

"Begin comm silence," John said.

He had barely voiced the order before his Mjolnir's onboard computer shut down all external communications. It was reacting not to his words, but to the intention that had given rise to them, accessing his thoughts via the neural lace implanted at the base of his skull. The interface allowed him to manipulate a half-ton of power armor as effortlessly as his own body, and to keep track of his fellow Spartans by merely thinking about them. Yet even after using it for the last few months, he still found it unsettling at times—especially when a targeting reticle or status readout appeared on his heads-up display before he had consciously summoned it.

The alert lamps flashed green as the *Starry Night* swung into the slingshot maneuver. Control of the mission had now passed to John—though that was, for the moment, a meaningless distinction. For the next few seconds, their fates would be determined by the laws of classical mechanics, and he could not have called off the launch had he wanted to.

John's weight sank and shifted aft. The alert lamps stopped flashing, then the jump hatch split down the center and retracted into the hull, creating an exit portal four meters square. The bay had been left pressurized so the decompression would augment their acceleration.

He felt the push of escaping air and jumped.

John saw five white needles shining bright against the brown crescent of Netherop's horizon, more or less where he expected to find the propellant tails of the Covenant spacecraft. He began to experience the full force of the slingshot maneuver's thirty-g acceleration. Even with the hydrostatic gel inside his Mjolnir pressurized to protective levels, his vision narrowed and his chest hurt, and the back side of his body ballooned with pooling blood.

For a few heartbeats, the shining tails of alien propellant remained fixed in the center of his faceplate, growing longer and thicker as he began to overtake them. In his HUD's motion tracker, he saw the three other Spartans of Blue Team lined up behind him in an undulating column, everyone struggling to hold fast to the thruster pack ahead, but still together after the initial furious acceleration. Gold and Green Teams were already beyond his motion tracker's range, so he could only hope that their launch had gone as well as Blue Team's.

Then the propellant tails started to drift across John's faceplate, as did Netherop's brown horizon, and he realized he was entering a roll. He felt his center of mass change as the Spartans behind him finally yielded to the minute variances in their launch vector and released their holds on each other. His roll accelerated, and stars began to streak past his faceplate in a dizzying blur. He checked his HUD and saw Blue Team drifting apart in a long arcing curve.

No matter. The assault squad had always intended to approach the target in loose formation, as it was easier to spot a group clustered together than one scattered across several kilometers of space. All John had to do was bring himself under control and continue toward the Covenant spacecraft.

The thought had barely formed in his mind before a waypoint marker appeared and began to gyre around the edges of his faceplate. He focused on it and began to feel dizzy.

And light-headed.

It had been seven seconds since he leaped from the jump bay, and he still hadn't activated his rebreather. He might be getting a buildup of carbon dioxide.

The rebreather light activated in his HUD, and the dizziness faded as fresh air flooded his skinsuit. John felt refreshed. Although there was something creepy about a suit of power armor that seemed to know what he was thinking before he did, it *did* spare him the necessity of managing suit-systems when he had more important things to worry about.

John activated his thrusters with a thought and began to expel tiny bursts of propellant, being careful to fire against the movement of the waypoint marker and keep working it back toward the center of his faceplate.

It took only a few seconds to reach equilibrium. By then, the alien propellant tails had vanished from sight, and he had to remind himself that Covenant spacecraft were subject to the same laws of motion as human ships. Once they reached the desired orbit, they had to shut down their engines. If they kept accelerating, they would only climb higher and eventually break orbit altogether.

John would have liked visual confirmation that the Covenant was on the expected trajectory, but that wasn't going to happen. The Spartans were still eighty kilometers from their targets, much too distant to spot the dark sliver of spacecraft roughly a dozen meters long and with cold engines.

Knowing his squad would not show up in his HUD—the motion tracker had a maximum range of twenty-five meters—John increased his faceplate magnification to its highest setting, then used his thrusters to begin a slow roll and start locating his Spartans.

Initially, he saw only a dark blur obscuring a distant field of stars. But when he rolled toward the planet, their forms were more distinct—tiny human-shaped figures silhouetted against the brown disk of Netherop's clouds. If an enemy patrol happened to pass by in a higher orbit, there was a chance the pilots might glimpse the little shadows and realize what they were seeing.

But that seemed unlikely. The aliens would be even farther away from the tiny figures than John was, and they would be looking for spacecraft, not humans in airtight armor.

It took a few minutes to locate the twelfth squad member, but once he had, John felt an immense wave of relief. Given the number of missed intercepts at Chi Ceti IV, he had expected at least a couple of Spartans to be out of position by now. But his concerns had been unwarranted. In their new Mjolnir, with time to plan and marshal resources, the Spartans could not fail.

And John wouldn't let them.

CHAPTER 2

0402 hours, March 5, 2526 (military calendar)
Spartan Extra-Vehicular Assault Squad
High Equatorial Orbit, Planet Netherop, Ephyra System

The alien spacecraft were growing more visible by the second, five dark slivers silhouetted against the curve of Netherop's dingy horizon, swelling into thin black blades as the assault squad descended on them from above and behind. The Spartans were diving into Netherop's gravity well at a shallow angle, traveling thirty-three thousand kilometers per hour relative to the planet—and at that kind of speed, reaction time didn't exist.

Were someone to cross paths with a meteorite or a hunk of Covenant jetsam, there would be no opportunity to evade. By the time the object appeared on the motion tracker, it would have punched through the Spartan's armor, passed through the body, and already be a dozen kilometers away.

Yet there was no sense of motion. The Spartans had stopped accelerating, so it felt like they were motionless in space. The vestibular fluid in their ears was still, and their organs were floating free in their torsos. Only the rapidly expanding cloud swirls on Netherop hinted at their true speed—the clouds, and the vessels stretching from thin little blades into thumb-length crosses.

As the silhouettes continued to swell, their forward-swept wings and twin nose-cannons grew apparent. John recognized them as an ex-atmo variant of a single-pilot fighter that UNSC pilots had nicknamed "Banshees." Banshees were not especially deadly in combat, but the enemy used them for everything from atmospheric patrol to orbital interception, depending on the variant deployed, and they were a high priority on the Covenant equipment capture list.

But then again, what wasn't?

The Covenant had made "contact" with humanity more than a year ago, when it happened upon a shipping lane near the planet Harvest. A local attempt to negotiate peace erupted into open warfare, with the aliens initiating a planetary bombardment and blocking all communications with other worlds. So superior was the enemy's technology that the Colonial Military Authority did not even learn of the conflict until nine months later, when the CMA *Heracles*—the sole survivor of a mission to investigate the world's sudden silence—limped home with a message from the aliens: *"Your destruction is the will of the gods, and we are their instrument."*

FLEETCOM received the declaration on October 31. The following day, the Unified Earth Government mobilized the UNSC, the CMA, and all other military services against the alien menace. The Spartans were deployed on the second of November, and by the twenty-seventh, Samuel-034 was dead.

The UNSC had been on a full war footing for four months now, and so far it continued to reel. The alien foes had superior weaponry, superior mobility, and superior intelligence, and they were using all three to good effect, emerging from slipspace to destroy support bases and ambush convoys, to knock shipyards from orbit and bombard civilians with hundred-meter plasma beams. The UNSC had to find a way to eliminate the Covenant's advantages—and so far, John's assault team was its best hope. Perhaps its only hope.

The waypoint marker in John's HUD flashed yellow. He activated his thrusters and began to decelerate, flattening his angle of descent until he entered orbit. The Banshees were clearly visible in his faceplate magnification against the pearl haze of Netherop's mesosphere. They were still a couple of kilometers ahead, too distant to offer protection from any mass-discerning sensor systems the mothership might employ.

Not that John actually *knew* the Covenant employed mass-discerning sensor systems. It was simply a theoretical possibility the UNSC's own scientists were exploring. But given the enemy's technological superiority, it seemed wise to be cautious.

He took a few moments to do another visual head count. When he was sure that everyone was in position, he used his thrusters to nudge himself into a slightly lower orbit.

The other Spartans followed his lead, and they began to creep toward the targets. This was the most dangerous phase of their approach. They were close enough to be spotted visually if a pilot happened to look back and had the right angle. Under different conditions, it would be smart to move in as fast as possible. But closing the distance more quickly meant dropping lower, which would make the Spartans even *more* visible. Better to stay behind the Banshees and hope for the best.

After forty minutes of inching closer, the Spartans remained undiscovered. The silhouettes of the craft had swollen to the size of a head, and the lines of their drooping wings were thickening into three-dimensional forms. John brought up a mission projection on his TACMAP and saw that the Covenant mothership would appear above the planetary horizon in eight minutes. After that, Netherop's bulk would no longer shield the assault squad from the vessel's sensor umbrella. In theory, the Spartans would remain as undetectable to the aliens as the *Starry Night* and her sister prowlers. In theory.

John extended an arm above his head, signaling the squad to form on him, then dropped into a lower orbit and began to quickly overtake the Banshees. His Spartans closed up, grouping themselves by team, but taking care to maintain a spacing of a hundred meters. That was tight enough to support each other if necessary, but far enough apart to avoid presenting an eye-catching cluster of dark forms—or a massed target that could be taken out by a single plasma strike.

After nine additional slow minutes, the Spartans were finally close enough to make out the knobby equipment pods at the tips of the Banshees' drooping wings. John raised his hand and, closing his fist, made a twisting motion. The squad tightened formation, arranging itself so that there were at least two Spartans fifty meters below each spacecraft.

John raised a thumb and used his thrusters to ascend into orbit behind the leftmost Banshee. Fred climbed into position beside him, with Linda and Kelly behind the next spacecraft over, while Green and Gold Teams slipped into place behind the other three craft. The aliens maintained their formation.

So far, the mission was going flawlessly. But John wanted to be ready, in case that changed.

He unlimbered the M99 Stanchion Gauss rifle magclamped across his back and made sure there was a round in the chamber. While M99s were normally used as extreme-range sniper rifles or antimatériel weapons, their accuracy and recoilless firing mechanisms made them ideal weapons for zero-g infiltration operations, and he had equipped half the squad with them. The other half was carrying M41 rocket launchers. The M41s were less accurate than M99s, but they had more combat applications, and like the M99s, they could be fired without sending a weightless gunner into an uncontrolled spin.

The Covenant mothership now materialized above Netherop's

horizon. Just visible through the planet's thick corona of atmosphere, the vessel appeared as a hazy gray drop not much larger than a pinhead. But John knew from previous observations that it had a long, tapering tail that curled down into an open hook.

If the Banshees followed prior procedure, they would return to a maintenance hangar located in the interior of the hook. After being serviced, they would be moved out of the hangar and suspended beneath the elongated tail, ready for immediate launch.

John suspected the trickiest part of the assault would be advancing through the tail. It was an obvious choke point that would be sealed at the first sign of trouble—which meant the Spartans either had to board forward, or capture the hangar without allowing an alarm to be raised.

At least they had options.

They remained behind the Banshees and continued to close, the mothership's tiny shape growing longer and darker as it slowly drifted higher above Netherop's horizon. The ONI analysts aboard the *Starry Night* had measured the vessel's length at 550 meters and its horizontal and vertical beams at 110 meters—about the size of a UNSC light frigate. A standard complement for a human warship that size would be about 250 crew plus the same number of combat personnel, but there was no guessing how many aliens might be crammed aboard such a vessel.

The mothership passed out of sight in front of the Banshees, and John signaled the assault squad to slip in tight, within a few meters of the spacecraft. When the mothership emerged from behind the Banshees again, it would be above the Spartans relative to the planet, and he didn't want a lucky alien to glance down through a porthole and see a dozen humans silhouetted against Netherop's brown clouds.

John and Fred stopped about two meters behind their target Banshee, positioning themselves just outside the tail stabilizers. This close to the mothership, the craft could probably sync orbits without firing its main engine—but John wasn't taking chances. As tough as the Spartans' new Mjolnir armor was, he was not eager to see how the outer shell would hold up against a plume of white-hot propellant.

It was a precaution John was glad he had taken when the Banshees raised their noses and ignited their engines for a half-second burn. The Spartans climbed after them, but thruster packs were no match for main engines, and the Banshees quickly pulled away. A moment later, the mothership appeared over them, a huge, tear-shaped darkness looming against the starlit beyond.

The Banshees used their maneuvering jets to bleed off excess velocity and sync orbits, then brought their noses down and positioned themselves about fifty meters beneath the belly of the mothership—no doubt awaiting authorization to dock.

All five were facing aft, toward the interior of the hooked tail, and the pilots could not see the Spartans climbing back into position behind them. Beyond the spacecraft, the mothership's belly was as dark as a closet, suggesting it lacked any viewports or observation bubbles through which the assault squad might be spotted. But the mouth of the maintenance hangar was a bright, flat-bottomed oval facing forward, and although John was still too far below to see inside, he knew there would be plenty of crewmembers looking toward a flight of arriving Banshees.

John raised a fist to bring his assault squad to a halt, then lifted his index finger and made a circling motion. The Spartans began to tighten their formation and prepare for boarding action.

One by one, the Banshees rose into the docking hollow beneath the mothership's tail, then drifted through the hangar mouth. A faint shimmer suggested the presence of some sort of energy barrier.

John waited until only the last craft remained, then gave the thumbs-up. Being careful to remain near the tail of the craft, the squad rose alongside the Banshee, their weapons shouldered and off-safety.

As more of the hangar interior came into view, John found himself looking into an oblong vault thirty meters deep and twenty wide. Lit in ambient blue-white light, it had an arched overhead and bulkheads lined by curved alcoves filled with equipment and supplies. It was bustling with the tall, vaguely avian aliens that the UNSC had nicknamed "Jackals." There were also a half dozen winged, insectile creatures, and two of the short, mask-wearing bipeds known as "Grunts."

The last Banshee began a leisurely drift toward the hangar mouth, an indication that the Spartan assault squad remained completely undetected. With any luck, John and his teams would soon be the proud new crew of a Covenant frigate . . . or whatever the analysts decided to call it.

John motioned Fred and Kelly forward to deal with the pilot, then shouldered his M99 and placed the scope in front of his helmet. An aiming reticle appeared on his HUD, and he scanned across the hangar, selecting his target. He was the third sniper from the left, so attack-by-surprise protocol dictated that he take the third high-value target from the left. And standard priority was clear: commanders, comm techs, countersnipers, high-mobility personnel, heavy weapon operators, everyone else. The challenge with the Covenant was that humanity hadn't engaged them long enough yet to learn the nuances of those roles or how they related to the species and armor. They would just have to leverage what little available intel and speculative theories they had at their disposal.

John didn't see any obvious commanders or comm techs, so he set his sights on number three, one of the insect-aliens—he thought of it as a Drone—then nodded. He waited a one-count, let out his breath, and fired.

A faint glow flashed along the M99 as the electromagnetic coils charged and drew the projectile down the barrel; then the Drone's body erupted into a spray of blood and chitin. John shifted to the next target inward—one of the Grunts—and fired again. This time, there was an orange ball as the creature blew apart in flames.

John looked away to check on the final Banshee. Fred was holding the edge of the cockpit with one hand and using the other to drag the tall pilot out through the shattered canopy. Kelly was on the opposite side, holding herself in place while firing M6 pistol rounds into the alien's techsuited chest.

When John turned back to his targeting reticle, he spotted a pair of similar aliens moving toward an alcove at the back of the hangar. Like the pilot Fred and Kelly were attacking, these were taller and more powerfully built than Jackals, with strong shoulders and compact, oblong heads. They wore the same sinewy techsuit as the other pilot and seemed to have a proud gait to their movements, which told John they likely held some level of leadership. He took them out with two quick shots, then looked for more targets. Finding none, he tossed the M99 aside—flinging it toward Netherop proper so it would drop out of orbit and burn up during atmospheric entry—then reached back and pulled his MA5K carbine off its magnetic mount. He checked to make sure the sound suppressor was still attached, then activated his thrusters and led the way into the hangar.

His HUD system flickered and dimmed as he passed through the energy barrier and entered the ship's artificial gravity field, but it returned to normal the instant his boots hit the deck. John noted the phenomenon without letting it worry him. Mjolnir armor was supposed to be shielded against electromagnetic interference, but ONI clearly had a lot to learn about the alien technology, and the glitch might reveal something useful to the science jockeys in the Section Three Materials Group.

The rest of the assault squad appeared on John's HUD, and the Spartans quickly swept the hangar, putting two rounds into the head of any alien that remained in less than three pieces. Several Jackals had turned toward luminous ovals set into the hangar bulkheads, but they had all died well short of their goal. If they had been trying to sound an alarm, it seemed unlikely they had succeeded.

The same was true for the pilots of the Banshees. Three of them had perished with their helmets under their arms, which would have prevented them from accessing any comm systems that might be integrated into their techsuits. The fourth pilot—the last to enter the hangar before the Spartans launched their attack—had taken an M99 round as he raised his canopy, and now his head and helmet were splattered all over the cockpit interior.

John could hardly believe it. The entire Spartan assault squad was inside the hangar, and the enemy did not yet know it had been boarded. Missions just didn't go this well.

CHAPTER 3

0502 hours, March 5, 2526 (military calendar)
Unknown Covenant Frigate
High Equatorial Orbit, Planet Netherop, Ephyra System

With a quick check of his HUD, John confirmed that the atmosphere in the carnage-strewn hangar was breathable—which was a good thing, since he had just fourteen minutes of rebreather capacity left. The Mjolnir's onboard computer anticipated his next request by shutting down his rebreather, and warm, acrid air began to flood into his helmet.

He activated his suit's external speaker, going to voice comm. "External air, everyone." Their own rebreathers would recharge as new air ran through the Mjolnir's filtering system. "Gold Team, execute the equipment dump. Include a couple of those four-jawed pilots. I don't know if the xenos have dissected any yet."

He was talking about the xeno-scientists of Section Three's new Beta-3 Division, a fast-growing ONI unit dedicated to analyzing and replicating Covenant technology.

Joshua-029's status light flashed green in acknowledgment; then he and the rest of Gold Team began to retrieve different types of weapons and tools. Once they had packed the Banshee cockpits full, they would close the canopies and push the spacecraft out of the hangar for recovery by the support prowlers. It would tie up Gold Team for a while, but John had insisted on it as a hedge against mission failure. That way, even if the assault squad could not capture the ship, the UNSC would still get *something* worth analyzing.

John took Blue and Green Teams to an oversize iris hatch at the back of the hangar. The bulkhead around it was cratered with strikes from M99 rounds that had passed completely through their targets. But none of the projectiles had penetrated the ship's thick armor and actually breached the hull.

John was still looking for a control pad or mechanical release when the hatch leaves suddenly retracted—and revealed a pair of Jackals coming from the opposite direction, descending a gray-blue passageway that curled down the vessel's hooked tail. They were clucking and squawking at each without paying much attention to where they were going. John stepped through the hatch and put a round through the head of the one on the right. Fred followed and took the one on the left.

Both Jackals flew backward and landed on the deck, and the hatch closed behind the two Spartans. Guessing that it responded to proximity, as had the hatches aboard the Covenant ship Blue Team had boarded at Chi Ceti IV, John sent Fred to secure the passageway ahead, then tossed one of the bodies back toward the hangar.

The hatch opened, and the rest of Blue and Green Teams stepped through.

"Green Team, secure all compartments and intersections as we move forward," John ordered.

John hurried after Fred, who had already vanished around the curve of the passageway and was almost beyond the range of the motion tracker on John's HUD.

As they advanced, John was surprised by the simple sensation of walking. Although the passageway curled steeply upward as it followed the curve of the mothership's hooked tail, it always felt like "down" was beneath his feet. Clearly, the aliens' control of artificial gravity was a lot more refined than humanity's.

Big surprise.

After fifty meters, they reached the top of the vessel's hooked tail. Instead of flipping pedestrians upside-down, the passageway ran through a ninety-degree twist, shifting the deck to what seemed like it should be a bulkhead. Then it ran through another twist, so that now it had the same orientation as the hangar deck below.

The assault squad was still in the mothership's tail, but as they hurried forward, more iris hatches began to appear in the adjacent bulkheads. The first hatch opened automatically as they approached, and Kurt stepped inside. He fired a few rounds, then stepped back into the passageway. "Supply locker."

Blue Team continued up the passageway on its own. Green Team followed, their sound-suppressed rifles coughing softly as they cleared compartments. After fifty meters, the iris hatches were replaced by tall, swinging hatches that did not respond to proximity. And there were a *lot* of those entrances, spaced every few meters.

"This is dangerous," Kelly said. She looked back down the passageway toward Green Team, which was lagging about thirty meters behind as they paused to clear each compartment. With that much gap, someone could step out of an uncleared compartment between the two teams and wreak havoc by forcing them to fire toward each other. "You want me to blow the ones that don't open?"

She had a fifty-meter coil of breaching cord in one of her cargo pouches, and it would take only three seconds to place it and blast open each hatch. But John counted twenty hatches, and that meant delaying their advance by a full minute.

John paused for a second, thinking about where they were in the ship and how that might be related to the change in hatch style. But mostly he found himself trying to decide whether it was more dangerous to risk splitting up, or to give the enemy an extra minute to trap them in the tail of the vessel. Either way, if something went wrong, he would get someone killed.

"John?" Fred urged. "We're seventy seconds into the mission—"

"Keep going," John said. If they were still in the tail of the vessel, that meant they had to be in the narrowest part. "Nothing's coming out of those hatches."

Blue Team continued to advance, but Kelly asked, "You sure about this?"

"Sure enough," John said. He *wasn't*, not when he was risking the lives of his Spartans, but he had to make a call. "We're above the Banshee racks. Those hatches are sealed because they serve airlocks."

Kelly didn't reply for a moment, then said, "You're smarter than you look."

"That's a relief," Fred said. "But let's watch our six anyway."

"On it," Linda said. "I'm smarter than John looks too."

"Thanks, team." John was not offended by the banter. In fact, he was glad to hear his team joking and easing the tension. "When we get back, you're all volunteering to swab the hold."

The declaration was greeted with snorts, and they continued up the passageway toward an oversize iris hatch that John figured opened into the main body of the ship. Until now, the mission had depended on speed and stealth, but once they crossed that threshold, success—and survival—would depend on shock and firepower. A dozen paces from the hatch, John called a halt so Fred could shoulder his rocket launcher and everyone else could open their grenade satchels—then his helmet speakers popped as someone went active on the prowler squadron's comm net.

"Contacts! Two adrift—make that three—with no power." The voice

was excited, male, and speaking English with an unfamiliar Outer Colonies accent. *"It has to be the assault squad, dumping—"*

"Close transmission!" a second voice interrupted. *"You're not internal. This is SQUADCOM!"*

"SQUADCOM?" the first voice said. *"Oh, sh—"*

The voice cut off in midsentence, no doubt because he had realized his mistake and closed the channel.

"What the hell?" Kelly demanded. "Are they *trying* to blow—"

"We'll figure it out later." It was hard to imagine a Prowler Corps crewman deliberately undermining the mission, but mistaking the squadron comm net for an internal channel was *not* an easy error to make. "Keep moving."

John waved Kelly toward the hatch.

Kelly stepped forward. The hatch remained closed.

"Not good," Fred said. An alien voice began to bark orders from a bulkhead speaker. "Might even call it a mess."

"But just a little mess," John said. "We can still do this."

Fred tipped his helmet toward John. "Did I say we couldn't?"

"No." It had not been Fred he was trying to convince, John realized. Irritated by his doubts, he turned to Kelly and said, "Blow it."

Kelly was already pulling the breaching cord from its cargo pouch. "I'll give it a little extra, in case there's a reception committee on the other side."

"Affirmative," John said. "Fred, be ready. Both tubes."

Fred's status light flashed green. "Is there any other way?"

The M41 SPNKR had a disposable double-tube loading system, so two rockets could be fired in quick succession—a feature that often proved useful against enemies lying in ambush.

At least, that's how it went in mock battles against human enemies.

John pushed his doubts aside and activated TEAMCOM. "Comm silence lifted," he said. "The aliens know we're here."

"No shit," replied Daisy-023. Gold Team's infiltration specialist, Daisy was probably the most intractable of the Spartans. "If we get out of this, I'm gonna find the dumbass who gave us away and rip his—"

"After the mission," John said.

"Seriously?" Daisy asked. "You're okay with that?"

"All I care about is the mission," John said. "Let's do that first."

John was reacting to this setback as he had been trained, swiftly and forcefully. But in the back of his mind, he was asking himself how many of his friends would die because of the sensor operator's mistake, and he could not help wondering whether he should abort while he still could.

Kelly said, "Stand clear."

Fred dropped to a knee five meters from the hatch, while John backed up against the side of the passageway alongside Kelly and Linda. After a quick glance to confirm everyone was in position, Kelly detonated the breaching cord. The hatch vanished behind a curtain of smoke and blast flash, and a dull clang echoed through John's helmet as the pressure wave slammed it against the bulkhead.

An orange streak filled the passage as a Special Warfare M21 antipersonnel rocket shot past. Half a second later, a loud boom shook the deck beneath John's feet. A plume of black smoke billowed back through the hatchway, bolts from enemy plasma weapons already flying out of it.

At least he could stop wondering when the mission was going to take a bad turn.

John reached for a grenade, and Fred rose to his feet and fired his second rocket into the smoke at a slight downward angle. The deck shuddered with another explosion, and the spray of plasma bolts dwindled to a stream.

John thumbed the primer slide on his grenade and pitched it down the stream of bolts. A smaller bang followed, and the plasma fire ended.

He stepped through the open hatch and found himself in the ship's main passageway, a broad, smoky corridor lined with burned and mangled bodies. All of the casualties appeared to be species he had already seen. Most were Jackals, but a few were the same as the Banshee pilots—tall, powerfully built saurians with compact heads and jaws with four mandibles. Unlike the pilots, however, these wore thick, contoured armor and sleek, oblong helmets with a long, sharply-pointed neck guard. And three of the aliens were the same vaguely man-sized creatures they had encountered in the hangar. They resembled insects with undersize wings, four limbs, and five lanky body segments.

Most of the aliens were unarmored, with no weapons larger than a sidearm, so John guessed they had been an improvised force of officers and support crew. Some were still writhing, and others lay with a plasma pistol in hand or nearby, so he put two rounds into the heads of all of them. The last thing he needed was a handful of wounded survivors attacking from the rear.

John glanced at his HUD. The rest of Blue Team was in position immediately behind him, and Green Team was about halfway through the tail. He started up the passageway at a sprint. Blue Team's objective was to capture the bridge, which the xeno-engineering analysts aboard the *Starry Night* had assured them would be located high in the mothership's bow. John suspected the analysts were just making an educated guess, but that was okay—he would have figured the same thing.

Green Team stepped through the blown hatch behind them, then immediately split down intersecting passageways, searching for a route below. Their assignment was to secure the engineering deck, and the location of the thrust nozzles almost guaranteed it would be in the belly of the vessel.

Gold Team would provide tactical support, coming in from the hangar to eliminate pockets of resistance and launch rear-attacks on enemy units that attempted to ambush either Blue or Green Team. Given past engagements with the Covenant, prisoners seemed unlikely, but should any aliens choose to surrender, Gold Team would also be charged with securing them.

Blue Team met little resistance as it advanced, eliminating perhaps fifty aliens who attempted to flee down intersections or take shelter in nearby compartments. By the time they had traveled three hundred meters, the ship appeared deserted—a sure sign that the enemy was organized and aware of their location.

The main passageway ended fifty meters ahead, at a double-width, horizontal-oval hatch with a seam across the center. As they approached, John saw that the deck to either side was shiny with wear—probably from feet moving back and forth as a pair of sentries repeatedly entered and left attention.

John signaled Kelly to blow the hatch, then sent Fred and Linda back down the passageway to take covering positions. The Covenant was most likely to attack as the Spartans advanced into the hatchway, but it would also be sound tactics to hit them from behind before they blew it. As Kelly placed the breaching cord, John activated TEAMCOM.

"Blue Team preparing to storm possible bridge approach." The aliens would probably capture the transmission, but their chances of breaking TEAMCOM's double-encryption protocols were nil. "Green Team sitrep?"

"On third deck and still laying below," Kurt reported. "Meeting moderate but steady resistance from Jackals and those flying roach guys."

"Designate flying roach guys as Drones," John said. "How long before you take the engineering deck?"

"No idea," Kurt replied. "We haven't found it yet."

"Keep looking," John said. "And keep me posted."

"Affirmative."

"Gold Team?"

Before Joshua could respond, the hatch split across its centerline and retracted to reveal a large gray shaft. A trio of white fiery spheres came flying out at an angle, and John realized the enemy had chosen a counterattack tactic so crazy he hadn't anticipated it: head-on assault.

"Grenades—go go go!"

Shoving Kelly ahead of him, he hurled himself through the hatchway . . . and found himself in a metal-walled shaft about four meters in diameter. They began to drop, not falling, but being drawn gently downward by an invisible force that had to be some kind of grav tech. Unexpected, but not necessarily a disaster.

The hatch clanged shut behind the two of them, and a trio of muffled booms sounded out in the passageway.

Sparks began to flash along the grav tube walls. A projectile deflected off John's shoulder armor, and he checked his motion tracker. Five hostiles were clinging to the wall twenty meters behind him—which meant *above* him, since he was descending the grav tube face-first. He rolled onto his back, then felt more impacts as two more projectiles burrowed into his titanium breastplate.

Still wasn't a disaster, but getting closer.

A line of the saurian aliens was hanging above the closed hatch, each clinging to a built-in utility ladder with one hand and firing some sort of Covenant carbine with the other. Sooner or later, one of them was bound to hit a soft spot in his armor, just as they had Sam's. John raised his MA5K and emptied the magazine, running a line of fire straight up their column.

His rounds deflected off some kind of personal energy barrier, ricocheting around the grav tube and coming back at the aliens' flanks and deflecting again. The energy shields seemed to flicker out after multiple hits, but these guys were clearly elite warriors who knew how to maintain fire. When a lucky ricochet finally caught one of them in the throat, the four survivors stepped away from the ladder and began to descend after John and Kelly. Still standing upright, they arranged themselves into a circle and began to fire down through the center of their formation.

Kelly opened up, squeezing off targeted three-round bursts. She caught one of the aliens under the mandibles and filled his helmet with gore. John ejected his ammo magazine and reached for another, enemy rounds still impacting his armor, mostly glancing off, but some burying themselves deep in the titanium shell.

A little deeper, and it *would* be a disaster.

Above the enemy, the blast of a breaching charge launched the hatch itself into the grav tube. Fred and Linda stuck their helmets through the opening and poured targeted fire from above. The head of one alien erupted into a purple spray. The surviving pair adjusted to the situation instantly, one raising his weapon to meet Fred and Linda's attack, the other continuing to lay fire on John and Kelly.

A heartbeat later, John's stomach flipped, and the invisible force drawing them *down* the grav tube reversed direction and began to carry everyone—aliens included—back *up* toward the blown hatch. As the aliens rose past it, they stopped firing and pulled dark orbs from their belt pouches.

John and Kelly both yelled "Grenade!" over TEAMCOM. John slapped the new magazine into his MA5K and opened fire, but the orbs had begun to glow with white flame, and the two aliens were already throwing.

Fred and Linda spun away, and the grenades flew through the opening into the main passageway. In the next instant, the two Spartans reappeared, leaping into the grav tube feet-first. They immediately raised their weapons and began spraying rounds at the enemy above them.

The grenades detonated, a searing white brilliance pouring through the hatch and filling the shaft, and John lost sight of the pair. His own ascent slowed briefly as a concussion wave hammered him from above; then he and Kelly were rising past the open hatch.

The passageway beyond was lined with dead enemies, clustered in four groups, all armored and armed with Covenant carbines. They were facing all directions, a sign they had died surprised and confused. Beyond them, Gold Team was advancing down the passageway, Joshua and Daisy leading the way with M301 grenade launchers slung under their MA5C assault rifles. The other two members were hanging back, ready to eliminate any more of the Covenant who made the mistake of thinking they could sneak up on a Spartan.

Then John was past the hatch, still ascending the grav tube next to Kelly. The clatter of small-arms fire above fell silent, and he looked up to find Fred changing his magazine while Linda continued to aim her BR55 upward. The grav tube beyond was too littered with hatch doors and dead aliens to see what awaited Blue Team at the top of the shaft, but amazingly enough, it still appeared possible to capture this ship.

John went back to TEAMCOM. "Gold Team, sitrep."

"Main deck under control," Joshua reported. "Eliminated maybe two hundred targets. No casualties."

"How's your ammo holding up?"

"About half down," Joshua said. "But Naomi has figured out those hinge-head rifles. We'll be okay."

Naomi was Naomi-010, one of the Spartans' more resourceful soldiers and a near-genius with any sort of equipment. By the age of ten, she had been a master armorer who was refining and modifying every infantry weapon the Spartans used, and currently she was the only one on the squad who seemed to completely understand the theory behind the Mjolnir's reactive circuits.

But John had never heard of such a weapon designation. "Hinge-head?"

"The big ones with the four jaws," Joshua said. "The ones that know how to fight."

The tall saurians, in other words.

"Now designated Elites," John said. "Take Gold Team and lay below. Disrupt any counterattack preparations—especially those led by Elites."

"Affirmative."

Gold Team moved out of motion-tracker range and vanished from John's HUD. The clang of colliding metal drew his attention overhead, where a jumble of twisted hatch-sections and dead Elites were pinned against the top of the grav tube. To their left—on the side opposite the utility ladder—hung a single-width hatch, a vertical oval with a split down the center. A second utility ladder descended beneath it, each rung slightly offset so that it angled around the shaft wall to join the first.

"Shouldn't that hatch be open by now?" Kelly asked. "If it's activated by proximity, all those dead Elites—"

"It's overridden!" John reached over and caught hold of a ladder rung. "Grab—"

The gravity field reversed polarity and jerked John downward, and the order came to an abrupt end. His arm straightened, and his elbow hyperextended and erupted in pain. He held on anyway, his Mjolnir armor's force-multiplying circuits droning as he fought the grav tube's pull. Fred and Linda dropped past and shot down the shaft, their outstretched gauntlets clanging off the ladder rungs as they tried to grab hold. Kelly was somewhere below them, already beyond motion-tracker range.

A new contact appeared on his HUD. John looked up and saw the hatch door splitting open, an armored hand reaching into the seam from either side. Both held dark orbs. Grenades.

More grenades.

John opened fire, raising his MA5K one-handed and running a

burst up the widening seam. The first rounds were deflected by energy shields, but he managed to hit both grenades as they ignited in white flame and were released. He managed to send one tumbling back toward the enemy. The second fell to the deck, then rolled into the grav tube and was sucked down the shaft.

"Incoming!" John warned over TEAMCOM. "Gren—"

The detonations filled the tube with white heat, one blast boiling up the shaft from below and the other spraying through the half-open hatch above. John's HUD flashed to static, and the first blast wave ripped one side of the ladder from the wall. The second wave nearly impaled him on its broken rungs.

John's grasp remained secure, even when the rung in his hand snapped on one side and bent downward. He jammed his boots onto the ladder, slapped his MA5K onto its magnetic mount, and began to climb the offset rungs—the few that remained—ascending toward the mangled wreckage of the hatch.

"Blue Team, report!"

"Gel-locked, but uninjured," Fred responded. "Lying in the bottom of the grav tube. Should be operational once the pressure bleeds off."

"Same as Fred," Linda said. "Condition good."

"Under them both." Kelly's voice was thin with anguish. "Also gel-locked, but I have torso pain and blood in my underarmor. Must be a compound rib fracture."

John felt his gut clench. Compound rib fractures were dangerous, even for Spartans. With the jagged end of a bone moving around inside the chest cavity, something as simple as a deep breath could puncture a lung or lacerate the heart.

"Copy," John said. "Fred, get her out of the grav tube. I don't want her getting slammed around any more."

"I can take care of myself," Kelly said. "I don't need a babysitter."

"And *I* don't need an argument. Clear?"

"Affirmative. But you're being . . . overprotective."

By *overprotective*, John knew Kelly meant *jerk*. But if it kept his Spartans alive, John was okay with being an overprotective jerk. He was under the hatch now, and could hear the chattering of alien voices coming through the gap between its twisted halves. He poked his head up above the deck and glimpsed a relatively small oval compartment beyond, with a high dome overhead and a two-tiered bank of instrument consoles arranged in a semicircle around a central commander's throne.

The consoles were manned by busy Elites, most uniformed in white tabards striped by blue diagonals. But at least three armored Elites were pointing alien carbines at the hatch, and when they saw John peering through the gap, they opened fire.

Already ducking out of sight, John grabbed a pair of fragmentation grenades from his satchel and thumbed the arming sliders.

"Hold fast, Blue Leader," Linda said over TEAMCOM. "I am unlocked and climbing. I'm with you in sixty seconds."

Sixty seconds was forever in a firefight, but with the hatch jammed open, John could probably hold his position that long. What he couldn't do was prevent the enemy from tossing more grenades into the grav tube—and that meant Linda's chances of getting blown up were about the same as her chances of reaching him alive.

"Negative." John brought his arm up and tossed his grenades through the half-open hatch. "Vacate and support Green Team. I've got this."

"Alone?" Linda asked. "That's insane. You need support."

The ladder shuddered with the double-thump of the grenades detonating on the bridge, and a cone of flame and shrapnel shot from the half-open hatch and flashed across the tube above John's head. He was already drawing two more grenades from his belt satchel.

"The grav tube is a kill zone." John thumbed the arming sliders and tossed the grenades through the hatch, this time trying for a higher arc that would carry them toward the front of the bridge. "Vacate. That's an order."

Another pair of detonations shook the ladder. John poked his head up again and found the bridge littered with Elites, some broken and dead, some still writhing in pain, all torn and bloody. Here and there, a slender saurian head showed above an instrument panel, its beady eyes fixed on the hatch.

In the center of the compartment sat the commander's throne, its back panel warped and blackened from a grenade detonation. On the right side, a jagged limb hung above an armrest filled with glowing toggles and glide switches. On the left side, a leathery forearm in singed cloth lay stretched along the armrest, a pair of long alien fingers scratching at a boxy yellow cover about half the size of a human palm.

It looked like a safety cover.

John reached into the opening, grabbed a hatch panel, then hauled himself onto the top rung of the utility ladder.

The fingers on the commander's throne found what they were scratching for, and the yellow safety cover retracted into the armrest. A holographic keypad appeared in its place, and the fingers began to fly over glowing symbols.

John drew his M6D sidearm and put a round through the Elite's upper arm. The fingers touched another pair of symbols, and the keyboard vanished. A yellow blister—likely some kind of control button—rose out of the armrest.

John put a second shot through the elbow, but the hand was already descending toward the blister. The round blew the Elite's forearm half off and sprayed purple blood across half a dozen instrument consoles, but the alien retained adequate shoulder control to draw its arm back toward the chair. Its hand landed atop the yellow bubble, the heel of its palm coming down hard enough to punch it back down into the armrest.

The ship did not self-destruct.

Instead, the commander's hand remained atop the blister, and an ambient green light rippled through the bridge. A trio of hidden panels retracted into the outer bulkheads, revealing open iris hatches on the three forward sides of the bridge. Elite survivors began to rise from behind their instrument consoles and spring toward the hatches, obviously less afraid of John than of what their commander had just initiated.

Bad mistake. The last thing ONI wanted was survivors providing firsthand accounts of the Spartan boarding action. John opened fire with his M6D, blowing holes through Elite chests with .50-caliber nickel-plated rounds, and activated TEAMCOM.

"Green Team, sitrep?"

"Assaulting the engineering deck now," Kurt-051 reported. "We're going to take it, but it's too easy. Something's wrong."

"Like all hands abandoning ship?" John asked.

"Not the Drones," Kurt said. "They're staying to fight. But everyone else—"

"Break off and get out *now.*" John's M6D locked open as it ran out of ammunition. "Gold and Blue Teams, you too."

"What happened?" Linda asked. "I can be on the bridge in thirty seconds. Maybe less. We can still take the ship."

John holstered his sidearm and thought about it, pulling the MA5K off its magnetic mount. There were no aliens left to throw grenades down the grav tube, so it wasn't a kill zone any longer. But if he was right about that blister on the commander's armrest, he'd still be putting her at risk—for no reason. The bridge was already John's. All he had to do was walk in, secure the wounded, and make certain the commander's hand did not leave the blister.

John muscled the hatch panels apart and, shoving the MA5K through ahead of him, quickly checked the adjacent corners for ambushers. Seeing only pieces of dismembered Elites, he stepped onto the bridge and finally replied.

"Negative, Linda." John switched to SQUADCOM so that Halima Ascot and the rest of the prowler squadron would hear his report. "The alien commander has his hand on what looks like a dead man's switch. I think he's trying to give his crew a chance to abandon ship before he self-destructs."

"That's supported by what we're seeing from our position," Ascot replied. *"There are escape capsules dropping everywhere."*

"I think I can secure the switch," John said. "But I want the rest of the assault squad off the ship, just in case."

"Affirmative," Ascot said. *"The squadron is already moving to sync orbits."*

"We heard." John did not elaborate on the trouble the sensor operator's mistake had caused his Spartans. That would come later, during the debrief—and, if he had anything to say about it, right before the court-martial. "Team leaders, let me know when you're clear."

"Green Team clearing now," Kurt reported. Once clear of the ship, the Spartans would drop into a preassigned orbit and await pickup by a prowler. "Rebreathers recharged to seventy percent, beacons on."

"Gold Team right behind him," Joshua said. "Rebreathers recharged to seventy-five percent, beacons on."

"Blue Two and Three commandeering enemy escape capsule," Fred reported. He was Two, Kelly was Three. "Three's pressure seal is compromised. We'll try to repair, but check for friendly beacons before you open fire on any escape capsules."

"Affirmative," Ascot said. *"And good luck."*

Only Linda had not reported. As he waited for her, John began to shoot wounded aliens—when he made his move to secure the commander's dead man's switch, the last thing he wanted was a still-capable Elite ambushing him.

By the time John had finished and reloaded both of his weapons, he still had not heard from Linda. It wasn't like her to disobey an order, but he glanced back down the grav tube just to be sure.

Empty.

"Linda? What's the holdup?"

"Drones," Linda said. "An entire nest, herding me like a damn sheep. They do *not* want me to leave."

John cursed himself—she would probably have been better off joining him on the bridge after all.

"What's your situation?" he asked. "I don't think I can wait much longer—I don't know whether this commander is dead or alive, but his hand could come off that dead man's switch any second."

"Go," Linda said. "I'm almost in the hangar. They can't stop me then."

"Affirmative."

John gathered himself to leap across the bridge—then thought, *Drones*. They could fly.

He stepped through the hatch and spun right, bringing his MA5K up, and, sure enough, saw a Drone trying to track him with a plasma pistol. He brought it down with a quick burst, then spotted another on his motion tracker, dropping down behind him.

He threw himself to the floor, rolled toward the commander's throne, and came around firing. The Drone dropped to the deck in two pieces, and John rolled again, bringing a knee under and springing up, already stretching for the armrest.

The throne spun away from him, whirling around in a three-quarter circle, the bloody hand still resting atop the yellow blister. John found himself looking over his shoulder into the pain-clouded eyes of the Elite commander. The alien's head was cocked as though it could not quite understand what it was seeing—or could not quite bring itself to believe it. Its mandibles opened in a four-pointed star that might have been scorn . . . or laughter . . . then it twisted its shoulders and dragged its hand free of the armrest.

John did not wait to see the yellow blister rise. He dived for the nearest hatch and felt the ship rumble as he bounced off the edge and landed inside a spherical escape pod lined by crash couches and safety harnesses. He spun to his knees and lurched back toward the entrance, hands slapping at everything that could possibly be a control panel—and hoping Linda was clear of the hangar.

The hatch closed, and in the next instant, he began to ricochet around the interior, his Mjolnir armor going into gel-lock as the Covenant ship outside flew apart in a cloud of flame and metal and his escape pod tumbled away.

CHAPTER 4

0840 hours, March 7, 2526 (military calendar)
UNSC *Valiant*-class Cruiser *Everest*
Deep Space Transitional Zone, Dynizi System

The elevator made its first stop, and the doors opened to reveal a double-width passageway with a spotless deck and a recently painted overhead. The bulkheads were lined with life-size holographs of great naval commanders, dating all the way back to Themistocles and Lysander. Across from the elevator stood a pair of sentries uniformed in service dress blues and armed with MA5B bullpup assault rifles.

Staff Sergeant Avery Johnson stepped to the back of the car, making room for new riders, and assumed proper posture in case they happened to be officers. Which seemed likely, since the Navy did not post armed guards to secure access to crew decks. Even more telling was the sweet air beginning to drift in from the passageway. No ventilation chief wanted a bridge officer yelling at him about moldy ducts and musty scrubbers.

But no one boarded. The sentries glanced toward Avery, but did not otherwise acknowledge his presence. The doors remained open, giving him time to study the holograph directly across from the elevator. Situated between the two sentries, it depicted a pointy-bearded Korean warrior in a conical helmet and knee-length hauberk. He didn't recognize the Korean's image from memory, but the information at the bottom read *Admiral Yi Sun-sin, who defeated a Japanese fleet of 133 ships with just 13 ships at the Myeongnyang Strait in 1597.*

Avery hoped the UNSC had a few admirals like Yi Sun-sin. The odds facing humanity right now were a lot worse than ten to one.

After a moment, he realized the elevator had not stopped to admit new riders. He glanced over at the control panel and saw that he had arrived at Level Nineteen, the destination selected for him when he was ushered into the car. He hadn't noticed at the time, but Levels Thirteen through Twenty could only be accessed via biometric thumb-scanner. Levels One through Twelve could be reached by simple touchpad. There was another thumb-scanner at the Hangar Deck level, then the touchpads began again, increasing in number from First Deck through Thirty Deck.

Avery had been aboard enough large vessels to know this was standard ship layout. The Hangar Deck was always considered Zero Deck. Everything above the hangar was a "level," rising from one to as high as necessary. Everything below the Hangar Deck was "belowdecks," starting at First Deck and descending through Second Deck, Third Deck, etc. What he did *not* know was why he had been sent to a command level of what seemed to be one of the largest vessels in the UNSC Navy.

Just three minutes earlier, Avery had stumbled out of a transfer shuttle and descended the boarding ramp onto a hangar deck the size of a small city. Still groggy and shivering after a three-week slipspace jump, he had been far from his usual handsome self—his black mustache had gone from close-trimmed to unkempt and spiky, while his brown skin had been dry and itchy—and waiting for him at the base of the ramp had been a burly lieutenant with a Hangar Boss insignia above her pocket.

"Staff Sergeant, you look like something I just scraped off my boot heel." She was tall and broad-shouldered, with black lip-gloss and blond hair pulled into a bun. "Have you been drinking?"

"I wish, ma'am." Avery came to attention. "It's just cryofog. They pulled me out of a sleep tube about five minutes ago."

The lieutenant wrinkled her nose. "That explains the smell." She crooked a finger and turned away. "This way, marine."

Avery had followed her across three hundred meters of deck to an elevator bank. She'd reached inside an open car and thumbed the control panel, then pointed him inside.

"Welcome aboard, Sergeant Johnson."

Avery had still been so foggy-headed that he had not thought to ask where he was going—or even what ship he was aboard. His original orders had called for him to join the 11th Marine Force Reconnaissance/ODST Battalion at Neos Atlantis, then ship out to fight aliens in the Outer Colonies. But instead of awakening in orbit above the planet's familiar green ice ball, he had emerged from cryosleep to find himself aboard the UNSC transport schooner *Santori*, in the middle of a major battle fleet so far out in deep space he couldn't even tell which star was the local.

His first assumption was that the 11th Recon had left Neos Atlantis early, and his transport had been diverted to join them in transit. Now he was beginning to wonder. When a marine staff sergeant boarded a ship to join a combat unit, he wasn't usually received on a command level.

Finally, the sentry on the left asked, "Something wrong, Sergeant Johnson?"

"Possibly." Avery was a little surprised to be addressed by name, since he had not seen her gaze drop to the name tag on the breast of his combat utilities. "Where am I?"

"The Flag Deck." An attractive petty officer second class, she had pale skin, hazel eyes, and short red hair barely showing beneath her white-and-blue bucket cap. "You think we put on these dress blues just for you?"

"Never crossed my mind." It was beginning to sound like Avery was in the right place after all. He stepped out of the elevator, then asked, "The Flag Deck of what vessel?"

The sentry narrowed her eyes and glanced toward Avery's name tag, apparently confirming that he was who she thought he was, then said, "You're aboard the UNSC Super-heavy Cruiser *Everest,* flagship of Vice Admiral Preston J. Cole, commander Battle Group X-Ray."

Damn. Preston Cole had been a decent battle commander twenty years ago, before the Office of Naval Intelligence identified his second wife as an insurrectionist spy and forced him to retire. Over the next several years, the gossip vids had mentioned a couple of short marriages and bitter divorces, and Avery seemed to recall something about a long hospital stay for a double organ transplant. If FLEETCOM was reactivating guys like *him* and giving them command of frontline battle groups, the UNSC was in worse trouble than Avery thought.

He grunted, then asked, "And I'm here because . . . ?"

"I have no idea." The sentry looked him over from head to foot, then arched a brow. "Only thing I can figure is there's more to you than meets the eye."

"On occasion." Avery wasn't sure whether she was flirting or putting him down, but he was a noncommissioned officer and so was she, so he didn't see anything wrong with finding out. He grinned and added, "I could tell you about it over coffee."

She almost smiled back. "You'd have to shower first."

"I can do that."

The second sentry, a smooth-faced petty officer third class with puffy cheeks and pale hair, cleared his throat.

"Sergeant Johnson, the admirals aren't known for their patience." He extended a hand down the passageway. "It might be wise to arrange your date with Petty Officer Anagnos on your way out."

Avery gave Anagnos an apologetic shrug, then glanced down the passageway past the holographs of a dozen ancient naval commanders. At the end, he saw a set of double doors. On the left-hand door was a large brass plaque that read CHESTER W. NIMITZ. On the right-hand door was a plaque that read SECURE CONFERENCE SUITE.

"Son, did you say *admirals*, as in *plural*?"

"That's right, Sergeant."

Avery groaned. "I was afraid of that."

Wondering what he'd done wrong this time, he picked up his duffel bag and started toward the doors. Along the way, he passed holographs of Marcus Agrippa, Oliver Hazard Perry, and Isoroku Yamamoto. Between the three of them, they had saved Rome at Actium, won control of Lake Erie during the War of 1812, and crippled the United States Pacific Fleet at Pearl Harbor. With any luck, their ghosts would be among the admirals waiting in the Nimitz suite, because the way the war with the Covenant was going so far, Preston J. Cole would need all the help he could get.

As Avery approached, the doors parted and slid aside. Beyond the threshold stood a young ensign in dress blues, his jaw set and his hands clasped behind his back. Avery stepped through the doorway into a rectangular compartment with a waiting area on one side and a galley on the other, then dropped his duffel bag next to his leg, came to attention, and saluted.

"Staff Sergeant Avery Johnson reporting as . . ." He hesitated, realizing that he hadn't actually been *ordered* to report, then said, "As directed."

The ensign returned his salute smartly, then reached for Avery's duffel. "Let me stow that for you, Sergeant. You won't be bunking here."

"Thank you, sir." Avery allowed the ensign to take the bag, then said, "My personal weapons are in the duffel, unloaded or sheathed."

"You're a squared-away marine. May I offer you anything from the galley? Coffee or a sandwich?"

Avery shook his head, then added, "Nothing, thank you. Unless you have some odor neutralizer handy. I'm coming straight from the cryotube."

The ensign—his nameplate read A. TISCHLER—gave a wry smile. "I'd never have guessed." He dropped the duffel behind a counter, then took a bottle of Rejuverol from the beverage cooler. "No worries. They knew what they were getting when they told Lieutenant Ruta to send you straight up."

"What's their hurry?" Avery asked. "Nobody's bothered to tell me what I'm doing here."

"I wish I knew, Sergeant." Tischler pushed the bottle of Rejuverol into Avery's hand, then stepped over to an interior door and pressed a thumb to a biometric scanner. "No need for introductions. They already know who you are."

The door slid aside. Avery stepped through, then came to attention and brought his hand up in a salute. He found himself in a large compartment with a holographic star map at one end and a conference table at the other. On the far side of the table sat two gray-haired officers with the triple stars of vice admirals on their collar tips. One was a haggard-faced man in his midfifties, dressed in a white service uniform with no jacket and the name P. J. COLE above his breast pocket. The other was a hollow-cheeked man in blue camouflage utilities with no unit patch, name tag, or service badges—a not-so-subtle hint that he was from ONI and therefore not to be screwed with.

Across from them sat a slender woman in a white lab coat. She had her back to Avery, so all he could tell about her was that she had collar-length chestnut hair and was completely unintimidated by vice admirals. She was wagging a finger in their direction, pumping her arm up and down and lecturing the pair like schoolboys.

". . . can't defeat an enemy it doesn't understand, Admiral," she said. "We *must* try again."

"To what effect?" the ONI admiral demanded. "You said yourself it might be a year before the Materials Group understands the alien technology."

"Wars rarely end in a year."

"This one might be an exception, Dr. Halsey." As Cole spoke, he flipped Avery a return salute, then pointed him toward the empty chair at the head of the conference table. "The UNSC has two choices at the moment, one rotten and the other lousy. Either we engage the enemy right now and start losing fleets in battles we have no chance of winning, or we mass at strong points and let the enemy glass everything else."

Glassing was a relatively new term to Avery, but one that had already grown much too familiar. It referred to the results of an alien plasma bombardment, which struck a planet's surface with so much heat that the silica in common dirt fused into glass. It seemed to be the Covenant's favorite method of reducing human worlds to uninhabitable wastelands.

"I should think the answer is obvious," Halsey said. "We mass at the strong points. It will take the Covenant *at least* two years to locate all of our undefended worlds, and by then the Materials Group will have reverse-engineered—"

"Catherine, FLEETCOM can't *do* that," said the ONI admiral. He was referring to Fleet Command, which oversaw the deployment and combat operations of the entire UNSC Space Navy. "We'd be leaving hundreds of worlds defenseless. We'd be condemning billions of colonists to death by plasma incineration."

"And if you commit prematurely, you will lose every fleet you send—and leave hundreds of worlds defenseless anyway." The woman paused and watched Avery ease himself into the chair Cole had indicated, then looked back to the ONI admiral. "I think you need to make FLEETCOM understand that, Admiral Stanforth. There is nothing you can do to save those people—not until I can give you the tools you need to fight."

In his chair at the head of the table, Avery sat ramrod straight and wondered what the hell he was doing there. He'd never heard of the Materials Group, or Dr. Catherine Halsey, or ONI Vice Admiral Stanforth—which, in the tradition of clandestine services everywhere, probably meant he didn't want to. Even more confusing, both admirals were talking to Halsey as though she had equal say in their decisions.

Which didn't make any sense. Now that Avery was sitting adjacent to her, he could see that Halsey wasn't even military. Beneath the lab coat she was wearing a form-fitting jumpsuit that had more in common with a laboratory clean suit than a uniform, and in her piercing blue eyes there was a stubbornness that would have been disciplined out of her the first week of boot camp.

After a moment, Cole leaned forward and braced his forearms on the table. "Point taken, Dr. Halsey," he said. "But if FLEETCOM decided to pursue your plan—"

Avery snorted at the absurdity—he was so shocked it just came out—then swallowed hard as three heads swiveled in his direction.

"Pardon me." He opened the Rejuverol he had been given by Ensign Tischler. "Something just went down the wrong pipe."

Stanforth smirked. Cole merely frowned and looked back across the table, leaving Avery to wonder if the reactivated admiral's instincts could really be so rusty that he would consider Halsey's plan. The minute the UNSC began to abandon planets and mass at strong-point worlds, the Outer Colonies would go into full rebellion, and the UNSC would have two wars on its hands. Not to mention billions of dead civilians. No commander could accept that kind of casualty figure.

But Cole seemed determined to entertain the idea. "*If* we could persuade FLEETCOM to pursue your plan, Dr. Halsey, how can we be sure the aliens will go after undefended targets first? Why not destroy our strong points, then locate and eliminate the defenseless worlds at their leisure?"

"That's hardly an efficient invasion strategy," Halsey said. "The most effective way to advance is shock penetration—bypass strong points to secure easy victories and seize enemy territory, then bring up heavier units to reduce the strong points in a more measured fashion. That's been optimum infiltration strategy since Oskar von Hutier used it in Operation Michael in 1918."

"But have the *aliens* studied Operation Michael?" Cole asked. "More importantly, could they know a better way?"

Stanforth nodded. "Technology dictates strategy," he said. "And since we don't understand their technology—"

"We can't anticipate their strategy. I see that." Halsey was quiet for a minute, then said, "And it's all the more reason to attempt another ship capture."

Ship capture. Avery had a sinking feeling he'd just heard the real reason he was here. Earlier that year, he'd actually boarded a Covenant vessel near the planet Harvest, then ended up fighting a protracted surface battle against a company of alien warriors. There were probably only a handful of marines in the UNSC who could say the same thing, and that made Avery a pretty good choice to lead a suicidal boarding action.

But Stanforth vehemently shook his head. "Another capture attempt is too risky," he said. "It keeps the assault squad aboard too long. We're lucky we didn't lose our Spartans at Netherop."

"It wasn't luck, Admiral," Halsey said. "It was training and capability—and the mission was not a total failure. I've already ascertained a great deal from the captured Banshees. We're still learning how to operate them, but I can tell you that, despite the lack of instrumentality and the enigmatic architecture, the drives and even the weaponry don't seem as effective—"

"Yes, that's great," Cole interrupted. "But is it going to help us *this* year?"

Halsey hesitated, then said, "It's a mistake to focus on the short term, Admiral."

"The short term is all we have." Cole sank back in his seat, and his tone grew firm. "Dr. Halsey, I'll get you an alien ship if the chance presents itself, but capture can't be our prime objective. We lost thirteen vessels taking Harvest back—against one Covenant defender. If we don't blunt the Covenant advance, the Outer Colonies will be so many glass marbles by this time next year."

"I'm afraid I agree, Catherine," Stanforth said. "It's the only way to buy the time your group needs to give us a fighting chance."

Halsey sighed, then reluctantly nodded. "I'll support the operation however I can, naturally." She turned to Cole. "I look forward to hearing your plan."

"So do I." Cole's gaze slid toward Avery. "As soon as we develop one."

Avery's stomach clenched. He hadn't even heard that the UNSC had counterattacked at Harvest—much less what it had cost them. "You're asking *me* for input, sir?"

"You see anyone else in this compartment who looks like he's been trading fire with aliens on a regular basis?"

Avery glanced around the table for form's sake, then said, "No, sir."

"Then now's the time to speak up, Sergeant," Stanforth said. "I didn't forge those transfer orders so you could sit on your hands. Tell us what you think."

Avery hesitated a moment, trying to decide whether turning to a noncom for advice made the two admirals smart or desperate. In either case, he had to answer—and not only because he was being ordered to. Unless he spoke up, he would never be able to complain about a commander's stupid battle plan again.

"All right, sir. What strikes me first is that while the enemy's technology is *very* superior to ours, their soldiers *aren't.*"

"Elaborate on that," Cole said.

"I assume you've all read the incident reports from the initial contact at Harvest?"

Stanforth nodded.

"Then think about what happened there," Avery said. "Sergeant Byrne and I killed five Jackal raiders, then fought our way aboard their ship. The only reason we didn't take it is because their captain self-destructed it to avoid capture. Later, we fought off a company of Brutes and Grunts at the Harvest Botanical Gardens with a platoon of half-trained militia. And over the next few weeks, we managed to evacuate the planet right under their noses. So, the Covenant may have better equipment, but from what I've seen, they're inferior soldiers."

"Interesting," Stanforth said. "And your impressions of the different species?"

"The Brutes are ferocious," Avery said, "but not as clever as they think they are."

"I'm sorry . . . Brutes?" Cole asked.

"The big ape-looking ones," Avery said. "They seem to like hand-to-hand combat, where their strength is an advantage. The Jackals are cunning, but not very brave. The Buggers—"

"Buggers?" Stanforth asked.

"I believe he means what John is calling the Drones." Halsey turned to Avery. "Those flying insectoids?"

"Sounds right," Avery said. "Whatever we call them, they're unrelenting, but easy to misdirect. And the Grunts . . . well, the Grunts are mostly dangerous because they get in your way."

"What about the tall saurians?" Cole asked. "Those are the ones that worry me."

"I don't believe Sergeant Johnson fought any of them on Harvest," Stanforth said. He turned to Avery. "They're some kind of leader class, larger and stronger than the Jackals. They might be comparable to our Orbital Drop Shock Troopers—smart, tough, and disciplined."

"In other words, the ones we kill first," Avery said.

Stanforth smiled, then looked to Cole. "I like him."

"He's confident," Cole replied. "That's good."

Avery was there for more than a debrief, he realized. He was being tested for an assignment he might not want. "With all due respect," he said. "If there's something I should know—"

"And observant too," Halsey interrupted. "You could do worse."

"Worse than what?" Avery asked. "What exactly are we talking about here?"

"Relax," Stanforth said. "We don't really know yet ourselves."

"But they want a veteran on the team who's actually fought the Covenant," Halsey said. "And there aren't many of you available. The Covenant is very thorough that way."

"What team?" Avery demanded.

"At ease, Sergeant." This time, Stanforth's words were an order. "So far, it's just a planning team."

Avery relaxed . . . a little. "But I don't know naval tactics, sir," he said. "I'm an infantry marine."

"You were also an ORION project volunteer," Halsey said. "Which makes you an ideal addition for this assignment."

"ORION project?" Avery repeated. That had been a top-secret Naval Special Warfare program to create biologically augmented super-soldiers to fight the Insurrection. As a participant, Avery had acquired his Orbital Drop rating and developed top-notch sniper and close-combat skills. But the program had been shut down almost twenty years earlier, when its results failed to justify the cost. "I have no idea what you're talking about."

As one, Stanforth rolled his eyes, Cole looked annoyed, and Halsey pursed her lips.

"Okay . . . *maybe* I've heard of it," Avery said. Even *that* was more than he was supposed to admit under the ORION project's ultra-classified protocols. But he was beginning to think that of all the people sitting at the table, *he* was the one who knew the least about the ORION project. "What's the assignment?"

"You keep asking that," Stanforth said. "And I'm telling you, we still don't know. Really."

"Sorry, sir," Avery said. "I'm a little confused."

"I'll try to clear that up," Cole said. "The Covenant ships are protected by energy shielding that nothing short of a nuke or a Mass Accelerator Cannon can penetrate in one shot. Since their vessels are faster and more maneuverable than ours, that's a problem."

"Because you never get more than one shot," Avery surmised.

"Sometimes not even one," Cole said. "To make matters worse, their plasma beams cut through our Titanium-A armor like it's paper."

"And their pulse lasers are damn near as bad," Stanforth said. "So we're trying to find a way to fight that doesn't involve fleet-to-fleet engagements."

"Given your special operations background, Sergeant," Halsey said, "and your creativity in improvising during the Harvest evacuation, I thought you might be an asset."

Avery nodded. "I can definitely bring some asymmetric whoop-ass to your game," he said. "Mines, decoys, logistics sabotage, provision poisoning, false signals . . . just give me a couple of prowlers and fifty good ODSTs."

"All good ideas," Cole said. "And we're already implementing most of them."

"We want to add you to something that's a bit more hard-hitting,"

Stanforth said. "Something with the potential to rock the enemy back on their heels."

Avery didn't like it when officers said *potential.* That meant they were gambling big. And when officers gambled big, jarheads died.

"Okay, I'm listening."

"As you've noted yourself, the aliens themselves aren't as good as their technology," Stanforth said. "We have a special unit that's taken advantage of that to board a couple of enemy vessels."

"The capture attempt you were discussing when I arrived," Avery said. "The *failed* capture attempt."

"The vessel was still destroyed," Stanforth said. "As was a frigate-size ship the first time the team tried this."

"It's our single most effective tactic, from all that we've seen," Cole added. "We'd like to try it on something bigger."

"*How* big?"

"As big as we can find," Stanforth said.

"Don't worry." Cole flashed a grin. "You'll have nukes."

Avery was not amused. So far, Cole struck him as an admiral who had probably been a pretty good commander in his day, but hardly someone special enough to drag out of retirement.

"Nukes are fun," Avery finally said. "But I haven't volunteered for anything yet."

"You will," Stanforth said. "You always do."

"After twenty years," Avery said, "maybe it's time I learned my lesson. Sir."

"Not yet." Stanforth leaned in and locked gazes with Avery. "You don't want to miss this one, Johnson. You'll be part of a team that's going to save the human race . . . and I'm not exaggerating."

Avery grunted and wished he had a cigar right now. He always thought better when he was chewing on a Sweet William.

After a moment, Avery said, "Something as big as you're thinking will be protected by a fleet. We can't just rush in and drop a boarding party."

"That's why we want your experience on this operation," Cole said.

"And your creativity," Halsey added. "I imagine you'll need to develop new infiltration tactics for each mission."

"*Each* mission?" Avery echoed. "You intend to do this more than once?"

"Certainly," Halsey said. "You don't expect to stop the Covenant by destroying one ship, do you?"

"I suppose not." Without being aware of it, Avery pulled a Sweet William from his breast pocket and jammed it, unlit, between his teeth. "What's our force?"

"The primary force will be an ODST space assault battalion," Cole said. "The 21st."

Avery smiled. "Colonel Crowther's Black Daggers," he said. "That's a good unit."

"The best," Stanforth said. "But you'll be attached to a special squad of twelve Spartans."

"Spartans?" Avery chomped his cigar. He had heard Stanforth use the term earlier, but he'd assumed that a Spartan was a designation for a new kind of special operations soldier. Now it was beginning to sound more like a unit. Or maybe some sort of advanced infiltration craft. "What, exactly, is a Spartan?"

"Show him, Catherine." Stanforth glanced toward Avery. "Your security clearance just rose three levels, Sergeant."

Avery nodded, and Halsey withdrew a portable holopad from the pocket of her lab coat. She placed it on the table in front of Avery, then touched the activation tab.

The meter-tall hologram of a heavily armored form appeared above the pad. With a blocky helmet, mirrored faceplate, and bulky outer shell, the figure looked more like a robot than a man. Had there been integrated cannons to add firepower and a few extra limbs to facilitate movement, Avery would have assumed he was looking at a prototype war android. But the Spartan had only two legs, two arms, and a single helmet with a forward-looking faceplate, so there had to be a human inside.

"Impressive," Avery said. There were no other figures in the hologram to provide scale, but judging by the size of the MA5K assault carbine affixed to the magnetic mount on the back of the armor, the Spartan had to be well over two meters tall. "But it's going to take more than twelve soldiers in fancy armor to do the job you're talking about."

"The Mjolnir power armor is the least of their assets, Sergeant Johnson." Halsey's voice was proud. "The SPARTAN-II program succeeded where the ORION project failed. They *are* what you were meant to be."

"This old failure has been getting the job done for two decades." Avery didn't appreciate being called a dud, but at least he was beginning to understand why the admirals treated Halsey with such deference. "But go ahead and brief me anyway."

"No need to take offense, Sergeant Johnson. The ORION project failed *you*." Halsey left the hologram of the Spartan standing in the middle of the table. "Each Spartan was selected at a young age for intelligence, physical prowess, aggressiveness, and emotional resilience. They were, almost literally, born to be soldiers. After conscription, they trained for eight years to become the most elite warriors humanity has ever seen."

"So why am I only hearing about them *now*?"

"Ideally, they wouldn't have been fully deployed for another two years," Halsey said. "But when the Covenant appeared, we had to accelerate the program."

"So you were going to train them for a *decade*?" Avery asked. "Talk about overkill."

"Not for what we intended," Halsey said. "The extra time would have given me an opportunity to fine-tune their biological augmentations and develop some custom enhancements. But no matter. My Spartans are still stronger, faster, more resilient, and more capable than any soldier you have ever seen."

"I don't doubt it," Avery said, remembering the long course of biochemical enhancement injections he had endured during the ORION project. It had been an agonizing experience filled with confused, hormone-induced rages—and, given the apparent size of the Spartan in the hologram, he could only marvel at the anguish the man must have endured during his own augmentation process. "But if these Spartans of yours are so great, why do you need me?"

"First, you have some understanding of what they've been through," Halsey said. "Second, you have something they don't—twenty years of combat experience."

"Exactly," Stanforth said. "These kids are top-notch soldiers, but they're still fifteen."

"Fifteen?" Avery said. "Doesn't that make them child—"

"They are *not* children," Stanforth interrupted. "Get that notion out of your head, Sergeant. Do I make myself clear?"

Avery swallowed. "Yes, sir." He had done enough work for ONI to understand that the admiral was telling him not to ask questions that the Office of Naval Intelligence didn't want answered. "I only meant to inquire about their, um, level of training."

"Second to none," Halsey said. "They entered boot camp at age six and earned every combat rating by age eight—"

"You might say they attended an elite military academy," Stanforth said. "Not so different from Corbulo Academy or Luna OCS."

Halsey grimaced and looked away. "Yes. You *might* say a lot of things," she complained. "That doesn't make the Martian Elementary Education Complex the equal of the Perimeter Institute for Theoretical Physics."

"My apologies, Catherine." Stanforth looked more amused than regretful. He turned back to Avery. "The important thing is that, on paper, the Spartans are every bit the soldier you are. They just need someone who understands the intangibles that can't be taught on a training mission—someone who has a few tricks up his sleeve."

"In other words, a sergeant," Avery said.

"Exactly," Stanforth said. "Just not a sergeant who gives orders."

Avery scowled. "Are you looking for a sergeant or a nanny?"

"More of a big brother," Stanforth said. "They already have a squad leader they trust, and you'd never replace him."

"He understands their capabilities in a way you never will," Halsey added. "They've been training together so long their communication seems almost telepathic at times."

Avery gnawed on his cigar and wondered if he dared say no. The last thing he wanted was to play babysitter for a squad of new boots. But he wasn't aware of any admiral who appreciated being told no—and ONI admirals did not play nice. If he turned down this assignment, he had a feeling his next one would be guarding snowballs on Venus.

Finally, Avery sighed. "If I'm that important to the operation, how can I refuse?"

"Exactly." Stanforth flashed a tight-lipped smile. "You can't."

CHAPTER 5

0558 hours, March 8, 2526 (military calendar)
UNSC *Point Blank*–class Stealth Cruiser *Vanishing Point*
Deep Space, Polona Sector

Even on a vessel as large as the UNSC stealth cruiser *Vanishing Point*, John-117 was too tall to stand upright inside the tactical planning center. He must have been an astonishing sight, because as he followed Dr. Catherine Halsey toward the conference table, all eyes swung toward him and remained fixed there. He was wearing his khaki service uniform rather than his Mjolnir armor, but in cramped spaces like the TPC, standard clothing only seemed to emphasize his size.

Dr. Halsey took the first open chair, but John stopped two steps from the table and drew himself into a hunched-over version of attention. There was more brass in the compartment than he usually saw in a month, with Vice Admiral Preston Cole standing at the far end of the table between Halima Ascot and a marine colonel John didn't recognize.

Seated at the table, three chairs from the end, was a grim-faced staff sergeant with dark skin and a short-trimmed mustache. He was pretty old—about forty, John guessed—with crow's-feet around his eyes and permanent frown lines flanking his mouth.

The colonel wore the flaming-skull ODST crest on the breast of his combat utilities, and the Black Dagger emblem of the 21st Space Assault Battalion on his shoulder. The sergeant wore no unit emblem at all—an indication that he either had just transferred into the battalion or was attached to an ONI black ops unit.

Cole returned John's salute. "Have a seat, Petty Officer." He pointed to a chair next to the one Dr. Halsey had selected. "No need to kink that thick neck of yours."

"Thank you, sir."

John slipped into the indicated chair and found himself directly across from the mustached staff sergeant. Above the breast pocket, the sergeant wore a name label that read A. JOHNSON, but John knew better than to assume it was the man's real name. It was exactly the kind of generic alias ONI might assign to an operator it didn't want to acknowledge.

Whatever his real name, the sergeant studied John with an air of unabashed appraisal, as though he couldn't quite decide whether John was a real soldier or just some oversize pretender. John didn't take offense. With clear blue eyes and thin brown eyebrows set in an oval face, John still looked like a teenager, and he knew that made him appear less capable than he was.

Cole waited until Ascot and the marine colonel had taken their seats, then nodded toward a control booth in the back of the compartment. "That's everyone."

The TPC's door slid shut, then a hush settled over the compartment and all eyes turned toward the admiral. Well, *almost* all eyes—Johnson continued to study John.

"Let's start with the obvious," Cole said. "We're holding this briefing aboard the *Vanishing Point*, rather than my flagship, for operational security. There are a lot of clever people aboard the *Everest,* and if they saw this group reporting to my conference suite, tongues would start wagging."

John looked around the table and realized Cole was right. The captain of a prowler squadron . . . the commander of a space assault battalion . . . a veteran black-ops sergeant. Even before he considered himself and Dr. Halsey, it seemed obvious to him that a force was being assembled to board another Covenant vessel. Probably a big one.

"Now, introductions." Cole gestured to Ascot. "Captain Halima Ascot, commander of Task Force Yama."

Ascot's eyes widened at the statement—a sign that the possibility had still been under discussion when John and Dr. Halsey entered the room. Recovering quickly, she tucked a lock of short blond hair behind an ear, then turned her gray eyes on the others.

"At this point . . . I don't know much more than you do," she said. "All I can add is that Task Force Yama will be an all-prowler force consisting of three squadrons of *Eclipse-* and *Razor-*class prowlers, each led by a *Sahara-*class prowler. The *Vanishing Point* will serve as our logistics-support ship."

John frowned. Three squadrons was overkill for a capture mission—even if they *were* prowlers. Stealthy or not, that many vessels would raise the boarding party's chances of being spotted as it moved into position.

Cole extended a hand toward the marine colonel. "Colonel Marmon Crowther, commander of the 21st Black Daggers Space Assault Battalion."

"Thank you, Admiral." A short and slender man of about fifty, Crowther had black hair, olive skin, and eyes the color of blued steel. "The Black Daggers consist of eight hundred elite Orbital Drop Shock

Troopers, trained and equipped for zero-g operations. We have yet to engage the Covenant, but last year alone we stormed and seized eighteen insurrectionist facilities in locations ranging from low planetary orbit to deep transitional space. With advice from those who *have* fought the aliens before, I'm sure we'll be able to adapt our tactics to the mission . . . whatever it may be."

Cole motioned toward the sergeant across from John. "Sergeant Avery Johnson, special tactics sniper. He was training the colonial militia on Harvest when the Covenant arrived, so he's had plenty of alien-fighting experience."

Johnson nodded to the officers. "Honored to be here."

Cole gestured at Dr. Halsey next. "Dr. Catherine Halsey is leading the effort to analyze and reverse-engineer the alien technology. Seized equipment will go to her first, and you should try to fulfill her requests to capture specific items. For the UNSC to win this war, her work must succeed."

What Cole did not say was that, as the originator and chief scientist of the SPARTAN-II program, Dr. Halsey was somewhere between a commanding officer and a mother to all of the Spartans. She had personally selected John and many of the others, she supervised their general education and kept a careful watch on their military training, she had overseen their biological augmentations, and she was the one who had designed their Mjolnir power armor. Although she had no military rank, most of the Spartans viewed her as their cardinal authority and treated her with a deference and respect that on rare occasion exceeded even what they showed to admirals and generals.

When Halsey chose not to add anything to her introduction, Cole moved on and pointed to John.

"And last, we have Petty Officer First Class John-117. He leads a squad of power-armored NavSpecWar operators known as Spartans.

Their existence is classified top-secret, and you should emphasize to your subordinates that any mention of their unit to nonauthorized personnel will result in charges."

Cole had been careful to omit any reference to ONI or Section Three when he introduced John and Dr. Halsey. It made John wonder what the admiral had neglected to mention about the other people in the compartment. He glanced across the table and found Johnson studying him again, openly watching him in a way that seemed almost a challenge.

John met the sergeant's gaze and let his lips tighten in a faint smile. He had no idea what Johnson's game might be—but whatever it was, John did not intend to lose it.

"As of now," Cole continued, "you're all attached to Task Force Yama for the duration of Operation: SILENT STORM. Your objective is to intercept the Covenant invasion fleet, then board as many capital ships as you can and detonate small-yield tactical nuclear devices inside their hulls."

Ascot's jaw dropped, and Crowther's eyes bulged. Both looked at Cole as though he were a madman.

"I'm sorry, sir . . ." Crowther said. "Are you suggesting we launch our troops against the enemy like *missiles*?"

"I hope you'll be a bit more subtle than that," Cole said. "But anything you need to do."

Crowther's eyes shifted toward Ascot, but her gaze had grown distant, and John guessed she was thinking back to the tactical difficulties with the Netherop mission.

John found himself smiling broadly, the way he often did when he finally saw how to beat the opposition. "I think it's a fine idea, sir. The aliens will never see it coming."

"With good reason," Crowther said. He turned to Cole. "Admiral, it's difficult enough to sneak a single assault team onto a lone enemy ship. But using a whole battalion to board dozens of vessels in the middle of their fleet? I'm not sure it can be done."

"I didn't say you had to use the whole battalion," Cole said. "Any way you can get the job done will be fine."

Crowther refused to back down. "Sir, if I may speak freely—"

"You *have* been." Cole's glance slid toward John, then he continued, "You might want to include John in your planning sessions. From what I hear, Spartans are pretty good at doing what can't be done."

Crowther's expression clouded over, but he dropped his gaze and nodded. "If those are my orders."

"Your orders are to knock the hell out of the Covenant fleet any way you can." Cole paused, and his tone grew conciliatory. "Marmon, if the UNSC can't bloody the Covenant's nose here, the war is already lost. I need you to find a solution."

Halsey leaned toward Cole. "Then put John-117 in command. At least he believes in the mission."

Cole looked less surprised by the suggestion than John felt, and the admiral quickly shook his head. "We discussed this, Dr. Halsey. John's not ready to lead an operation of this scale."

Halsey turned to Crowther. "How many engagements have you and the Black Daggers fought against the Covenant?"

"That's not the point, Doctor," Cole said. "John's expertise is in small unit tactics. Commanding a battalion is seventy percent logistics."

"I'm sure Colonel Crowther will be happy to assist—"

"Dr. Halsey, the Black Daggers don't know me," John said. "They'll have more faith in their colonel."

Halsey shot him a scowl, but he pretended not to notice. She might be a brilliant scientist, but she was no soldier. She despised the chain of command, didn't understand how loyalty held a good unit together, and couldn't see that Crowther was only trying to make sure he wouldn't be sending his soldiers to die on a mission that had no chance of success. In the colonel's position, John would have done the same thing.

He turned to Crowther. "I look forward to serving under you, Colonel. Feel free to call on me if you have questions about Spartan capabilities or our experiences fighting the aliens."

Crowther's frown did not quite vanish. "I've been fully briefed on both, Petty Officer. I'm sure you and your Spartans will prove a vital asset to the operation."

It was not quite a promise to consult, but at least Crowther seemed to have some awareness of Spartan capabilities. Realizing he would only alienate the colonel by pressing for planning involvement now, John settled back in his chair—and noticed Johnson watching him again. This time, the sergeant nodded and looked away.

Cole allowed a silence to settle over the compartment, then braced his hands on the table and leaned forward.

"This is a desperate mission," he said. "There's no denying it. But the UNSC needs time to develop effective countermeasures against Covenant technology, and it's your job to buy that time. You need to make the alien commanders *afraid* of us. You need to convince them that humans are crazy, that anytime a Covenant fleet outruns its support or fails to consolidate its advances, we *will* find a way to make it pay."

"I get it, sir. Unconventional warfare," said Crowther.

"Think of *unconventional* as your jump-off point," Cole said. He drew himself upright again. "But I think we understand each other. Any questions about your objective?"

John shook his head, as did everyone else seated at the table.

"Good," Cole said. "Just so you know . . . currently, the Covenant's primary invasion fleet is glassing Etalan."

"Why?" Johnson asked. "If that's Etalan in the Igdras system, I was there on a recon once. It's ten million nomads living in a hundred thousand camps. The place is so poor they share underwear."

"That's the world, Sergeant. And I don't have an answer for you. Our analysts are still trying to figure out why the Covenant burns some planets and seems to ignore others." Cole paused, then added, "What we *do* know is that Biko is only a short slip away."

"And *that*'s where you think we should hit them," Ascot surmised. An agricultural world with insurrectionist leanings, Biko was orbited by three resource-rich moons and a handful of shipyards. "If the aliens bypass Biko, they're leaving us a potential operations base—in the middle of their invasion route."

"My thoughts exactly," Cole said. "The Covenant is unpredictable, but not stupid. They can't skip Biko."

Ascot pulled a datapad from her thigh pocket and tapped a few keys, then looked up. "We'll be there waiting."

Cole smiled. "I thought you might. Battle Group X-Ray will draw their attention by launching a high-intensity harassment campaign. It'll be the real thing, and when we can deal damage, we will. But our main objective will be to keep them thinking about us until Yama can slip in close for the gut stab."

"And afterward?"

"Disappear," Cole said. "And do it again."

"On our own initiative?" Crowther asked. He seemed a little surprised by the admiral's instructions. "No coordination?"

"Correct," Cole said. "If you succeed at Biko, our roles will be reversed—the aliens will be hunting Yama, and X-Ray will be gnawing at their heels. I don't want any indirect intelligence out there that might give you away, so go dark. No message couriers, point-to-point comms only, no friendly contact. Commandeer your provisions when you can. If you need to make a depot stop, show up unannounced, grab what you need, and take off fast."

"Understood," Ascot said. "When do we stop?"

"When you have to." Cole ran his glance around the table, pausing to make eye contact with each person present, then said, "You've all been on infiltration missions before, so you know the drill. Captain Ascot controls space operations. She's in charge until a jump-off. Once an assault force goes EV, Colonel Crowther controls everything but the prowlers themselves."

Crowther and Ascot nodded their understanding.

Cole turned to John. "John-117 will take orders from Colonel Crowther, but the Spartans report to him."

"Very good, sir," John said.

"Sergeant Johnson will serve as a training resource for the Black Daggers," Cole said. "But his superiors want him attached to the Spartans. His qualifications and experience are more suited to their style of operation."

Johnson tipped his head toward John. "Looking forward to working with you, Petty Officer."

"Same here, Staff Sergeant." It did not escape John's notice that Cole had been careful to avoid identifying Johnson's superiors—a sure sign of the sergeant's ONI background. "I'm eager to compare notes."

Johnson flashed a smile. "Should be interesting."

"Dr. Halsey has no direct authority over the mission, but like I said earlier, try to make her happy." Cole paused, then added, "And keep her safe. If she dies, so do the UNSC's hopes."

Ascot turned to Halsey. "Consider yourself confined to the *Vanishing Point*."

Halsey scowled. "That's not practical. I may need—"

"Whatever it is, we'll bring it to *you,*" Ascot said. "The *Vanishing Point* is the only vessel in Task Force Yama that will actually be *avoiding* the enemy."

"Put a control anklet on her if you need to." As Cole spoke, he kept his eyes on Halsey. "I'm serious about this, Doctor. If you even *think* about disobeying, Captain Ascot will ship you straight back to Reach. Clear?"

Halsey nodded reluctantly. "The anklet won't be necessary," she said. "I know my value to the UNSC better than you do."

Cole studied her for a moment. "I hope so." He shifted his gaze to the rest of the table. "Any questions on the chain of command?"

When there were none, Cole straightened his posture. "Then, good hunting."

John and his squad of Spartans spent the first part of the ten-day slip in the *Vanishing Point*'s mission preparation hold, training against the 21st ODST Space Assault Battalion. Both sides were armed with TLRs—tactical lockup rounds that signaled a target's armor to lock in position when struck. The initial exercises were simple zero-g combat scenarios with equal numbers on both sides, and at first John suspected Crowther just wanted to prove that his ODSTs were as good as Spartans. But as session after session ended with Black Daggers floating around in strike-locked armor, the colonel began to test the Spartans under more difficult circumstances.

Once, Crowther had the hold filled with floating obstacles, then ordered a four-Spartan team to recover a nonexistent ball while engaging an entire platoon of Black Daggers. Another time, he had all twelve Spartans defend a hatch against an assault that did not end until the hold was so packed with strike-locked ODSTs that no one could maneuver. By the third such test—a hostage-rescue scenario in which the "hostage" turned out to be a hostile impostor—John realized Crowther was just doing everything he could to understand Spartan capabilities.

Meanwhile, the Black Daggers were certainly earning John's respect. The Spartans began to suffer strike-locks at a mere five-to-one disadvantage, which was about half the normal ratio of the ODST companies they had faced while training back on Reach. When the disadvantage reached twelve to one, the Spartans could no longer be certain of prevailing—and that shouldn't have happened until the odds were twice that bad.

Then Avery Johnson began to lead the opposing units, and suddenly the Spartans' quick reaction time and ingrained training became liabilities. A team of Black Daggers would attempt to slip past a position, and when a Spartan moved to block them, an even larger force would appear on his flank. Or an assault would fail, and when the Spartans tried to pursue the retreating unit, they would find themselves under fire from all sides. Once, a sniper began to plink away relentlessly from the same position. Linda took him out with a countershot—and was immediately strike-locked herself by a storm of incoming fire.

John saw what Johnson was doing, of course—spending soldiers like coins to lure Spartans into exposing themselves. It was a tactic most special-ops commanders would never employ in live combat, if only because elite soldiers were so costly to train. But it was certainly one the aliens would use. John had seen them do it several times—most recently during the capture attempt at Netherop. The difference was that Avery Johnson understood UNSC special forces tactics as well as John did, and he was using that knowledge to trick the Spartans into mistake after mistake. John had to respect the man's ingenuity.

But it still felt like Sergeant Johnson was cheating.

By the fourth morning, John was growing frustrated with his inability to counter Johnson's tricks. The most effective tactic seemed to be sitting back and hiding until the sergeant ordered a mass advance, but even that only worked until the Spartans ran out of ammunition.

Besides, Spartans weren't garrison troops. *They* were supposed to be the ones attacking, and that was exactly what John was going to do.

Today, rather than relying on standard tactics that Sergeant Johnson would anticipate anyway, he intended to launch an immediate charge and disrupt the Black Daggers' plan before it could be executed.

Unfortunately, Colonel Crowther had other ideas. After breakfast, he ordered all assault personnel to report to the drop hangar and form by company. The hangar was inactive and draped in gloom, and in their black helmets and space assault armor, the ODSTs on the far side of the formation vanished into the murk—an effect that made the eight-hundred-member battalion look like an endless host of phantoms.

The Spartans were temporarily attached to the 21st rather than part of it, so they stood adjacent to Alpha Company at a right angle. Their Mjolnir remained tinted in the refractive coating applied before the capture attempt at Netherop, so they too resembled phantoms—twelve larger, bulkier versions of the Black Daggers. With them stood Avery Johnson, still looking very human in his customary field cap and green combat utilities.

Crowther and his female aide emerged from the gloom, both in black combat utilities. The aide called the formation to attention, and Crowther began.

"Your company commanders have briefed you on our mission, so you know our assignment is to board alien capital ships and destroy them using tactical nuclear devices. I'll be honest. When we were given this mission, I didn't believe it could be done.

"But over the last four days, the Black Daggers have convinced me I was mistaken. In exercises against the Spartans, you've demonstrated your ability to adapt to a ferocious and skilled adversary, and I'm confident you'll prove just as resourceful when we start killing aliens. In your work with Sergeant Johnson, you've learned a new tactical style I hope we never have to implement."

A chill ran down John's spine. He had assumed that Johnson's cold-blooded tactics were for exercise purposes only, but Crowther sounded like he was prepared to employ similar maneuvers in actual combat—and John wanted no part of that. It had been hard enough to leave Sam behind when there had been no choice; if he started sending his fellow Spartans to their deaths on purpose, he would lose all confidence in his own judgment.

Crowther clasped his hands behind his back. "Today we start integration exercises. One Spartan will be attached to twelve of the 21st's platoons." He flashed a wry smile, then continued, "They'll be the ones carrying the nukes."

A chorus of speaker-modulated chuckles rustled through the battalion, but all John heard over the Spartan TEAMCOM were gasps of disbelief. Not only was Crowther breaking up the Spartan units, he was assigning them to a transport role—using them to support the attack when they should be leading it.

"This will allow us to hit twelve separate targets," Crowther continued. "Assuming we can achieve even a fifty percent success rate, the invasion fleet will be hit hard. Any questions?"

The hands of a dozen Black Dagger lieutenants shot up, and Crowther began to answer queries about weapon load-outs, insertion methods, and command authority.

What *John* wanted to ask was whether Crowther had lost his damn mind.

If the Spartans were attacking separate targets, they wouldn't be able to support each other—and the efficiency of a Spartan team decreased exponentially each time a member was removed. Dr. Halsey estimated that a Spartan operating alone was only one-sixteenth as effective as a four-member team . . . and sixteen times as likely to get killed.

Had Crowther bothered to consult John before developing his strategy, he would have known that.

The questions continued to come, and John continued to fume. He had no intention of challenging Crowther in front of the battalion, but the colonel had completely ignored Admiral Cole's suggestion to include John in his planning sessions. Perhaps Crowther had felt slighted when Dr. Halsey pressed for John to be given command of the operation, or perhaps he was simply emphasizing that *he* was the one in charge. Either way, John no longer felt good about speaking against Dr. Halsey's suggestion. Clearly she had read something in the colonel's character that he had not.

As John considered how he should respond, Avery Johnson started to whisper from the corner of his mouth.

"You *can't* be happy with this plan, Petty Officer."

"Negative." John's whisper was a bit louder than Johnson's, as it was being transmitted through his helmet's external speaker. "But the colonel didn't ask my opinion."

"Didn't want to give you a chance to object." Johnson sounded pissed. "So you've got to do it *now.*"

"In front of everyone?" John shook his helmet. "I'll do it in private."

"It'll never happen, son—not until after he's gotten Ascot to sign off on *this* plan." Johnson was still whispering. "It's called *planning momentum*, and it's lost more battles than bad supply and poor terrain combined."

"When we're dismissed, then."

Crowther's voice rang across the deck. "Repeat that, Spartan."

John's gaze snapped back to center, and he found Crowther and the aide both looking at him. "Sir?"

"Repeat your question." Crowther's voice carried a note of warning. It was a breach of protocol to converse while at attention, so there was only one valid reason for John to be talking. "You *were* trying to ask something, weren't you?"

"Of course, sir." John found himself wondering if Johnson had been *trying* to get him to draw Crowther's attention. "Respectfully . . . Spartans are trained to work in teams, so I'm concerned about splitting us up. If we're all attacking different vessels, I don't see how we'll be able to support each other."

Crowther lowered his brow. "You *won't*, obviously," he said. "The Black Daggers may not have a Spartan's speed and fancy armor, but they *are* well-trained. After a few days of drilling, you'll find that a platoon of space assault troopers provides all the support you need."

"Real smooth, John," Kelly-087 said inside John's helmet. TEAMCOM was an encrypted Spartan-only channel, so there was no risk of being overheard. "Now the Black Daggers think we don't like them."

John ignored her sarcasm and tried for a graceful recovery. "The Black Daggers are very impressive, sir. I certainly didn't mean to imply they weren't."

"Still, they're not Spartans," Johnson said. He shot a smile at the Black Daggers. "No offense, people, but you know it's true."

John wasn't sure whether he was more surprised by the amused murmur from the battalion, by Crowther's nod of agreement, or by a staff sergeant who felt free to challenge a superior's plan in front of the troops. The command structure of special forces units was typically informal, but still. Avery Johnson was either an insubordinate madman—or a lot more important than he looked.

And Crowther was not making it easy to tell which. His eyes flashed anger, but when he spoke, his tone was conciliatory. "I don't think anyone would argue the point, Sergeant Johnson. Does something about my plan concern you?"

"Maybe just a little," Johnson said. "Maximizing the target list, I understand. But anyone can carry a nuke. Why assign that job to the big guns? The Spartans should be up front, leading the assault."

Crowther gave a thoughtful nod. "That makes sense, as far as it goes," he said. "But on unprecedented operations like these, the Black Daggers have been more successful—and suffered fewer casualties—when we lead with experience."

"I can see that, but the Spartans—"

"Are just kids," Crowther said. "I have troopers who've been Black Daggers longer than the Spartans have been out of diapers."

An electronic snort sounded from the first row of Spartans, and John turned to see a relatively small Spartan standing at a slight angle to the rest of the line. Her shoulders were squared toward Crowther, and her helmet was cocked at a disdainful angle. It was, of course, Daisy-023.

It was always Daisy.

John ticked his TEAMCOM toggle. "Daisy, stand down."

But Crowther was already striding across the deck, his gaze fixed on Daisy's helmet and his thin-lipped mouth twisted into a sneer.

"Tell me I'm wrong, Spartan . . ." He paused to read the number on Daisy's torso armor. "Zero-two-three. How old are you?"

Daisy leaned in. Though she was a little shy of two meters tall in armor, she still loomed a full head over Crowther.

"Our age doesn't matter, sir," she said. "Our training does."

"Not as much as your experience." Crowther craned his chin up to glower into her faceplate. "And you still haven't answered my question."

"Because she's not allowed to, sir." John stepped forward. "It's classified."

"I knew *that* when I found the falsified DOBs in your personnel jackets." Crowther turned to John. "If someone is going to alter your birth dates, they need to adjust the Paymaster General's records as well."

"I fail to see the relevance, sir."

"You and your Spartans started banking recruit pay eight years ago," Crowther said. "That means either you're all a hell of a lot older than nineteen—or you entered training when you were eleven."

John was happy to have his face hidden behind a faceplate, where his expression would not be visible. The truth, of course, was even worse than Crowther had surmised—but John was not about to tell him that. Under the UNSC's own Uniform Code of Military Justice, recruits had to be a minimum of eighteen years old, and Crowther clearly realized that the SPARTAN-II program had ignored those restrictions. Now the colonel was using that to pressure John into going along with his plan. It seemed odd behavior for a high-profile special forces commander, but what did John know? Spartans were not trained in political infighting.

"Someone changed the Spartan DOBs, John." Crowther's voice grew sly. "I think we both know why."

John allowed a moment of silence to hang in the air, then finally said, "I find it hard to understand why ONI does anything. It's probably best not to speculate."

"Is that supposed to be a warning, Spartan?"

"It's more of a suggestion, sir," John said. "ONI can get pretty protective of its secrets . . . as I'm sure you already know."

Crowther's eyes widened and his nostrils flared, a combination that made him appear fearful and angry at the same time—and suggested that he knew John wasn't bluffing.

It was Avery Johnson who finally broke the silence. "I'd like to offer a suggestion, Colonel."

Crowther's expression turned dark, but he nodded and spoke through a clenched jaw. "I'm always happy to listen, Sergeant."

"Glad to hear it, sir," Johnson said. "Let's attach a Spartan to each platoon, as you suggest, and spend the day in exercises. Then you and I and Spartan-117 can evaluate the results and decide whether that's the most effective order-of-battle."

The resentment drained from the colonel's face, and John's respect for the staff sergeant went up another notch. Johnson was giving

Crowther an out that didn't look like backing down—and when the three of them came up with a better plan, the colonel would be able to claim it as his own.

But Crowther didn't seem satisfied with a graceful withdrawal. He still needed a way to claim victory.

"One day of exercises isn't enough." He turned to John, then said, "I think we'd better make it three. How does that sound, Petty Officer?"

John gave a crisp helmet nod. "Whatever you think, Colonel," he said. "It's your battalion."

CHAPTER 6

0638 hours, March 12, 2526 (military calendar)
Charon*-class Frigate *Bellicose
Deep Space, Little Nelek Nebula, Grenadi Sector

The envoys sat hip-to-hip at the steel mess table, only a bit blurry-eyed from the welcome party a few hours before, the men freshly shaven and the women in light makeup or none at all. Most were dressed in what twenty-year-old Petora Zoyas privately called "Insurrection chic"—worn fatigues with cutoff sleeves or no collar or both, often with too many buttons undone and a flask cap peeking out of a breast pocket. The style was more statement than uniform, an assertion that they were warriors without being soldiers and didn't take orders from anyone—least of all the grim-faced former general standing at the far end of the *Bellicose*'s cramped wardroom.

Tall and lean with salt-and-pepper hair, Harper Garvin wore pressed gray slacks and a cream bush shirt with matching tie. There were no stars on his collar tips, but otherwise his attire could have been a United Rebel Front version of the Service B uniform he had worn as a major general in the UNSC Marine Corps. If he realized how his soldierly dress undermined his prestige in the eyes of the envoys he hoped to unite into a coalition, he showed no sign of it.

"Thanks to all for rolling out for an early meeting. I know it wasn't easy after last night's fun." Garvin paused for a round of chuckles that failed to come, then turned to the woman seated directly to his left. "And thank you, Captain Castilla, for hosting us."

Castilla dipped her head in acknowledgment. "I'm happy to do this, General." An almond-eyed woman in her late forties, Lyrenne Castilla was the commander and owner of the privateer frigate *Bellicose*. She had silky black hair, a high-cheeked face with a thin nose, and a sure voice that instantly commanded the respect Garvin was still struggling to win. "Our brothers and sisters in the Insurrection need to understand what is happening here in the Outer Colonies."

A general murmur of agreement rose. Everyone in the compartment had heard reports of the unsettling events: massive fleet movements . . . planets going silent with no explanation . . . unprovoked attacks by odd-looking ships . . . automated cargo pods full of half-dead refugees. But confirmed facts were in short supply, so the slip-space lanes were filled with wild rumors: the UNSC was annihilating insurrectionist-friendly worlds . . . an incurable plague was being spread by a fleet of research vessels . . . a host of rampant AIs had declared war on humanity. Most far-fetched of all was a claim that the UNSC had discovered a civilization of defenseless aliens and was trying to eradicate them.

But instead of turning their attention back to Garvin, who still seemed half-UNSC in his manner and dress, the envoys continued to look toward Castilla. She was a rebel legend, a female captain with a mysterious past who supplied a good part of the Insurrection by snatching cargo pods from transport routes. There were whispers that she'd once seduced and married a UNSC captain in order to spy on him, and she'd been pregnant with his child when forced to fake the destruction of her vessel after ONI had discovered her true identity. Petora didn't know how much of the story was true—few people did—but the *Bellicose* always operated under a false name to hide its identity, and there was a hardness in Castilla's patrician features that suggested she was capable of anything.

When Castilla realized the envoys were still looking at her instead of Garvin, she turned and fixed her own gaze on the general—a deft maneuver that left no room to doubt her support for his leadership. Presumably he had a few qualities not readily apparent to Petora.

"The floor is yours, General," Castilla said. "What are you hearing from your spy in FLEETCOM?"

Garvin's eyes widened, but if Castilla had revealed too much about his source, her mistake worked in his favor. The envoys finally began warming to him, regarding him with something approaching respect, and even Petora began to see him in a new light. Given the current uncertainty about what was happening in the Outer Colonies, good intelligence bought a lot of goodwill. In fact, Petora was counting on it.

"In brief," Garvin began, "humanity is under attack by an alien empire, an alliance of different species who call themselves the Covenant. At the moment, the invasion is limited to the Polona, Grenadi, and Vevina sectors. But their military technology is vastly superior to ours, and FLEETCOM has no expectation of being able to contain them."

The envoys studied Garvin in wary silence, until a square-jawed woman at Petora's end of the table asked, "You mean they're *real?*"

"The aliens? Of course they're real." Garvin furrowed his brow. "Considering what happened on Harvest, Ms. Ander, you should know that better than anyone."

Ander shook her head. "Our intelligence hacks didn't think that incident was really aliens attacking." Nanci Ander was the daughter of

Jerald Ander, who had been the secret leader of the Secessionist Union on Harvest until his assassination in 2502. "We thought it was a ruse to empty the planet so the Colonial Military Authority could recolonize it with a rebel-free population."

"That seems a little paranoid, don't you think?" asked Reza Linberk. A blond, blue-eyed woman with high cheeks and a delicate jaw, Linberk was just a few years older than Petora—and already the first deputy of the Venezian Militia. "Razing an entire planet to flush out a few insurgents is a bit over the top. Even the UNSC wouldn't go that far."

"You haven't seen what the Freedom League is fighting on Jericho VII right now." The speaker was Bahito Noti, a slender man with a dark complexion and fierce eyes. "We're not sure whether they're people or something else, but they're killing machines. They've just about wiped us out."

"Huge guys in power armor?" Petora asked. As the envoy for the recently established Gao Liberation Force, she had been instructed to secure a leadership role for her group in the developing coalition—and Noti had just given her the perfect opportunity. "Blocky helmets with mirrored faceplates, just about the fastest thing you've ever seen on two legs?"

Noti's brow rose. "You're fighting them too?"

"Fortunately, no," Petora said. "But the Gao Liberation Force has developed some intelligence on them. They're called Spartans, and they might as well be machines. According to our information, they're biologically enhanced humans who have been training together for years, and they've just been equipped with advanced power armor. Apparently, ONI considers a single soldier the equivalent of twenty-five ODSTs."

"How do you know all that?" Castilla's tone was somewhere between doubting and resentful—perhaps because she recognized the advantage that the GLF's intelligence source would give Petora in establishing the pecking order in a new coalition. "That's some pretty specific intelligence."

Petora flashed a superior smirk. "General Garvin isn't the only one with inside information." She turned to Garvin himself. "The GLF has an agent in Task Force Yama."

"Which is?" Garvin asked.

"An all-prowler assault wing operating independently out of Battle Group X-Ray." As Petora spoke, Garvin looked a bit more fascinated with each word. "Their mission is to cripple the alien invasion fleet by using space assault teams to board key vessels and detonate nukes within the hulls."

"That's a *very* desperate plan." Castilla thought for a moment, then turned to Garvin and added, "And just the kind of thing Preston would dream up with his back to the wall."

Garvin nodded. "You would know better than me."

Petora was flabbergasted at the exchange. Could *Preston Cole* be the UNSC officer that Castilla had seduced and married? The familiarity in her voice when she said his name certainly supported the possibility.

Castilla noticed Petora gawking at her and returned the smirk. "The rumors are true," she said. "Yes, I was once married to Vice Admiral Cole—though he was only a captain at the time."

What Petora wanted to ask was whether Cole's child, who would be more than twenty by now, was a crewmember aboard the *Bellicose*. But insurrectionists did not share information about their children with people they'd just met, and Petora would not win anyone's confidence if it seemed like she was prying. So she swallowed her pride and tried to look impressed.

"How lucky for us." Petora was careful to put some enthusiasm in her voice. Castilla's past with Cole would give her a lot of influence over how the GLF's intelligence was viewed, and that meant Petora needed her as an ally. "It would be great if you could help interpret our agent's field reports."

"I'll be happy to offer my opinion," Castilla replied, almost warmly. "What else has the spy told you?"

"Communications are limited," Petora said. "But we do know that Admiral Cole has turned mission planning over to the task force commanders. They hope to engage the Covenant fleet at Biko—"

"Biko?" It was a barrel-chested man with a long red beard—Erland Booth of the Biko Independence Army—who blurted the question. "That can't happen!"

"I doubt anyone here has a say in the matter, Commandant." Garvin turned to Petora and raised a querying brow. "*Do* they?"

"Not anyone the GLF knows, General. Our agent isn't that high up." In truth, the spy's identity was known only to Arlo Casille, a thirty-year-old Ministry of Protection clerk who was running half of the GLF out of his cramped little office, right under the CMA's nose. But she didn't want to weaken her position by admitting there were some secrets that Arlo didn't trust her with. She shot a sympathetic look in Booth's direction, then added, "Perhaps Biko won't suffer much. If the UNSC plan works, the battle should be in orbit."

"That's a big *if*," Booth grunted.

"Not as big as you may think. The Spartans have already boarded and destroyed two vessels themselves." Petora did not mention that, at Netherop, the Spartans had succeeded despite a deliberate attempt to get them killed. Until she knew that Garvin and the other envoys supported the GLF tactic of using the aliens to eliminate the Spartans, some things were better left unsaid. "And in this operation, they'll be using three teams supported by the 21st ODST Space Assault Battalion."

"The Black Daggers." Garvin seemed more impressed by the ODSTs than by the Spartans. "They're a dangerous outfit. They captured our resupply depot at Bomogin before anyone realized they were coming."

"Which is why our agent thinks the attack may work." Petora turned back to Booth. "Whether that would save Biko or get it annihilated is anyone's guess."

"And not a question we should be asking," said Reza Linberk.

Booth's face grew as red as his beard. "Why the hell not?"

"Because we have no control over the situation," Linberk replied. Venezia was only nine light-years from Gao, so Petora had worked with Linberk on a few joint missions. The woman was a cunning foe and a dangerous ally, someone who was so utterly cold-hearted that she would betray even her closest comrade to complete an assignment. "What we need to be discussing is how the Insurrection can benefit from the situation."

"Benefit?" Nanci Ander was aghast. "From an alien invasion?"

"Exactly," Linberk said. "If we coordinate our reaction, there are any number of ways to turn this to our advantage."

"I am in complete favor of this," said Nemesio Breit. The vice counselor of the People's Occupation on Reach, he was a tall man with a gaunt build and—as someone who lived on a planet with a major UNSC base—an infinite hatred of colonial authority. "We need to prepare now, so we're ready to finish the Unified Earth Government after the Covenant has crippled it."

"What makes you think we'll be around as well?" Castilla asked. "As far as we know, the aliens aren't playing favorites here."

"Not so far," Garvin agreed. "According to my sources, they glassed the Galodew Emancipation base on Redstow VI. The entire cadre was wiped out."

"What do you mean, glassed?" asked Ander.

"Orbital plasma bombardment," Petora said. "So hot it fuses a planet's surface silica. The ground literally turns into glass."

The color drained from Ander's face. "Oh my God. Is that what happened to Harvest?"

If Ander had not heard what had become of her world after the evacuation, Petora didn't want to be the one to tell her. Instead, she looked to Garvin. "What have you heard from your FLEETCOM spy?"

"Glassed, yes." Garvin turned to Ander. "I'm so sorry, Nanci."

Ander slumped back in her chair, her lips trembling.

"Okay, then—we have to throw in with the UNSC," Booth said. His face had gone as pale as Ander's. "It sucks, but what choice do we have? Let the Covenant glass *everything*?"

"We could educate them," Petora said. "The aliens probably don't understand how many humans hate the UNSC. If we can enlighten them, they may see us as an ally instead of an enemy."

"In time to save Biko?" Booth asked.

"Would you rather rely on the UNSC?" Petora asked. "Your Independence Army has tried to overthrow their chancellor six times."

"Seven," Booth replied. "And last time, we held Mandelam for two months."

"So you're getting stronger," Petora said. "And now the UNSC is busy fighting aliens, and not us."

"I like how you think," Booth said, his smile widening. "It really is the perfect opportunity, isn't it?"

"And one you must seize," Garvin added.

"I'll take it up with the Chamber." A note of resentment crept into Booth's tone. "But keep in mind: nobody tells the Biko Independence Army what to do."

"He wasn't," Petora said. "The BIA literally has no choice, Commandant. Biko has always been a thorn in the UNSC's side."

"So?"

"So even if the UNSC could save it, why would they?" Petora shook her head. "Biko takes more resources for them to hold than it's worth to them."

"I agree," Garvin added. "If the aliens attack, Biko is on its own. The chancellor will resist with the planetary forces available to her, but it won't be enough."

"You have only one hope," Petora said. "Take control of the planetary government *before* the Covenant arrives—and try to make them see that you're not their enemy."

Booth dropped his eyes and nodded. "Okay, but we're going to need help."

"I'm sure we can arrange support," Garvin said. His eyes were bright with excitement. No doubt this was exactly the outcome he had hoped for when he called the meeting—the birth of an insurrectionist coalition. "What will you need?"

"Troops and transport," Booth said. "We can assemble on Seoba, then take the orbital facilities before the Chancellor's Guards—that's the planetary militia—know what hit them."

"Where's Seoba?" Garvin asked.

"Third moon," Booth said. "There's an old ice quarry there we can use as a mustering zone. The Chamber's been eyeing it as a staging area for our next try."

"Good." Garvin looked around the table, then asked, "Who's in?"

Petora was the first to raise a hand . . . then Linberk spoke.

"Aren't we moving rather fast on this?" It was more of a complaint than a question. "Maybe we should consider another option."

"Like what?" Petora asked. "Leaving Biko to get glassed?"

"Like doing what the commandant first suggested," Linberk said. "Offering our help to the UNSC instead of continuing to harass them."

Castilla shook her head. "Our support wouldn't convince the UNSC to defend Biko," she said. "The Insurrection has, at best, several dozen outdated frigates and a few hundred corvettes. Putting them at the UNSC's disposal wouldn't affect their strategic thinking at all."

"But it *would* give them one less problem to worry about," Linberk said. "If the aliens are as powerful as we're hearing, that might be enough to negotiate independence for all of our worlds. You scratch my back, I'll scratch yours."

"And get us all glassed, *chica*." Petora was being deliberately dismissive. The suggestion would be a tempting one to her fellow envoys—a quick way to achieve what the insurrectionists had been pursuing for decades—and she didn't want it undermining the idea she was about to offer. "Why would the UNSC defend us if we're independent? They're going to have enough problems defending their own worlds."

"Señora Zoyas is right," Garvin said. He gave Petora an approving nod. "We'd be doing the UNSC a favor by giving their fleets that much less to defend."

"Then we make defending our worlds a condition," Linberk said. "If the UNSC can't stop the Covenant *now*, we're signing our own death warrants by continuing to harass them."

Petora clucked her tongue. "Don't be so dramatic, my friend. You make it hard to think clearly."

Booth scowled. "You have a better idea?"

"One that has a greater chance of saving our worlds, yes." She shifted her gaze to the rest of the table. "We should offer the aliens a separate peace—one that will deliver us independence, no matter who wins."

"Nice in theory." The doubt in Linberk's voice was exaggerated, no doubt a reprisal for Petora's putdown earlier. "But why should the Covenant accept? Can we even communicate with them?"

"Probably," Garvin said. "My source in FLEETCOM says they sent a message at Harvest . . . in English: '*Your destruction is the will of the gods, and we are their instrument.*' "

"Oh, *that* makes them sound like they're open to an alliance," Linberk said, unable to hide her sarcasm. "And the way they're rolling over the UNSC, they can't be worried about an attack from us."

"If they even know who *we* are," Ander added. "They probably think all humans are the same. That seems more likely."

"They won't when they see what we can offer them," Petora said. "Fear is not the only way to bring an enemy to the bargaining table. Need often works as well."

"And what do we have that they need?" Linberk asked.

"Intelligence, of course." Garvin's voice was enthusiastic. "It's what every invading force needs."

Petora smiled. "Exactly," she said. "The Covenant will spare our worlds not because they're afraid of us, but because they need us."

"Need us for what, exactly?" Breit asked. "To tell them where to find Earth?"

His proposal was received in silence.

Breit looked around the table. "Come on," he said. "This is how we *win*. We tell the aliens where to find Earth, then *poof*—our colonial masters are out of the picture!"

"And afterward?" Castilla asked. "We just hope the aliens understand that we're the good humans and leave us alone?"

"We *are* the good humans!"

"All the same, I'm not sure we should start with destroying humanity's birthplace," Garvin said. "Let's offer something smaller and see if they can be trusted."

"Easy for you to say," Noti said. "While you're dancing around with the Covenant, we're being slaughtered by the Spartans on Jericho VII."

"Then we start by using the Covenant to get *rid* of the Spartans, okay?" Petora said. "That's what we offer the aliens first—intelligence on the prowler ambush at Biko."

"Works for me," Booth said. "But only if saving Biko is part of the deal."

Garvin smiled. "I like it." He turned to Castilla. "Lyrenne?"

"Yeah. Yeah, it's worth a try," she said. "The intelligence is valuable enough that the aliens will want to keep it coming, so it's the perfect chance for us to see if they can actually be trusted."

"Does it matter whether they can be trusted?" asked Noti. "Every Spartan they kill means a thousand of our brothers and sisters will still be alive to keep fighting when the aliens are gone."

"And what if they're not gone?" Ander said. "If they just turn around and glass us too, we're cutting our own throats by helping them get rid of the Spartans."

"Which is all the more reason to see if they can be trusted *now*," Garvin said. He turned to Petora. "How many Spartans does the UNSC have?"

"Our agent says there are three teams with Task Force Yama." Petora spread her hands. "But in the entire UNSC? There could be three platoons, or three divisions. He doesn't say."

"Not three divisions, no way," Garvin said. "If there were that many, my guy in FLEETCOM would have warned me about that."

"So, maybe a battalion, then?" Castilla suggested. "If there are Spartans on Jericho VII, they're probably on other worlds too."

Garvin thought for a moment, then said, "I imagine a battalion at the most. I can't see them keeping it secret if the program's any larger than those numbers."

"A battalion would only be about a thousand Spartans—if that many," said Breit. "What happens when we run out? We're gonna need to keep feeding the aliens valuable intelligence, and Earth's location—"

"Is the *last* thing we reveal." Garvin's voice was firm. "We hold that back until we know they can be trusted."

"Agreed," Petora said. "That information will be worth more to us when we know which side is likely to win. If the Covenant gets the upper hand, we can use Earth's location to buy their goodwill. If the UNSC is winning, we'll have the leverage to strike a deal for our independence. Either way, we win."

Garvin remained silent for a moment, his gaze sliding slowly from Petora to the other envoys, pausing on each for a confirming nod. When he finally received one from Castilla, he smiled and drew himself up straight.

"Then it looks like we have a plan, folks," he said. "And the UNSC be damned."

CHAPTER 7

1426 hours, March 18, 2526 (military calendar)

UNSC *Razor*-class Prowler *Ghost Song*

Insertion Approach, Moon Seoba, Biko Planetary System, Kolaqoa System

The drop bay of a *Razor*-class prowler could hold a full forty-member ODST platoon in vacuum-rated armor and thruster packs, but just barely. With an ONI special ops advisor and a Spartan in Mjolnir power armor attached to the unit, the bay was packed so tight that John-117 stood with his back pressed against the rear bulkhead. When he looked forward, all he saw between him and the jump hatch was a black pond of helmet-tops.

That was the first problem with Colonel Crowther's assault plan. It would take a minimum of four seconds to deploy forty-two soldiers, so even a standard drop-and-go would leave the platoon strewn across thirty kilometers of space—a real problem when they couldn't break comm silence to locate each other and assemble. And slingshot maneuvers were out of the question. Any attempt to simultaneously launch that many people through a jump hatch would end with personnel ricocheting off each other like billiard balls.

The second problem with Crowther's plan was that the Spartans were still bringing up the rear. That meant they would be dismounting last and unable to provide support if the platoon came under fire as it was forming up. It was a poor use of their speed and power, but even Avery Johnson had been unable to convince the colonel to change his mind. Crowther was obviously impressed with the Spartans' abilities, but with their comparative lack of experience in the field, he didn't trust their judgment. His most-seasoned Black Daggers had hundreds of engagements under their belts, and when his platoons entered combat, those were the people he wanted in front.

He was wrong, of course.

But John didn't see how he could prove that. Today's exercise was supposed to be a rehearsal for dismount-under-fire, but there wouldn't be any fire, and the enemy hadn't even arrived yet. Task Force Yama was simply slipping into an abandoned ice quarry on the moon Seoba and taking cover until the aliens arrived in the Biko planetary system. Crowther had decided to use the opportunity to practice a full-scale landing. The drill would probably expose a few logistical problems, but it wasn't going to convince anyone that the colonel was making a mistake.

John was still considering his options—just brooding, really—when the husky voice of the *Ghost Song*'s female communications officer came over the prowler's internal communications net.

"First Platoon Alpha Company, stand by for Top Urgent burst from Dagger Actual."

Dagger Actual was the comm designation for Colonel Crowther, and a burst transmission was an encrypted, prerecorded message compressed into a millisecond-long signal. The idea was to minimize the chance of interception by an unintended party, but even burst transmissions could be detected by an alert enemy about a third of the time. There was no way Crowther would be taking that kind of risk just to throw a curve into the drill. Something was wrong.

A moment later, Crowther's voice sounded inside John's helmet. *"All personnel: Operation: ICE DANCE is no longer a drill. Repeat, no drill. Post-slip comm intercepts indicate the Biko Independence Army is preparing a coup against the colonial chancellor. Under normal circumstances, we would share our intelligence with the chancellor and place ourselves at her disposal.*

"Circumstances are now anything but *normal. Our mission against the Covenant still takes precedence. Captain Ascot and I agree that our original plan still offers the best chance of success, so Task Force Yama will occupy the Seoba ice quarry as planned.*

"Unfortunately, we're not the only ones to recognize an abandoned quarry's value as a staging area. An insurrectionist force has already occupied Seoba and appears to be using our *quarry as a mustering area."*

John smiled inside his helmet. The 21st was going into battle under perilous conditions . . . and perilous conditions were what Spartans did best. Once Crowther saw how they performed under pressure, he'd be falling over himself to move them to the front of the attack.

Crowther's message continued—the entire Uniform Code of Military Justice could have been compressed and transmitted in a single microburst—and John paid close attention, looking for opportunities for the Spartans to shine.

"The key to this operation will be isolating local forces before they can report they're under attack. To that end, the Vanishing Point *will be jamming insurrectionist communications on Seoba. But we don't know what kind of anti-jamming or delayed transmission technology they may have, so if you happen across anything that looks like a portable comm station . . . take it out.*

"When the insurrectionist commanders lose contact with their force on Seoba, they'll probably assume the chancellor's militia discovered their base and took it out. With any luck, that will force them to abandon their coup and fade back into hiding. But it could also push them into an early

attack. Either way, they won't have any reason to return to Seoba—and if they do, our prowlers will make sure that none of their vessels get anywhere near us.

"To maintain operational security, we'll identify ourselves to any insurrectionist captives and survivors as Chancellor's Guards Battalion Five. Your accents won't sound right, but do it anyway. Our primary concern is keeping our nature hidden from the aliens, so once the prisoners are no longer in our hands, we want them confused about our identity. And the more confused, the better."

Crowther's voice deepened. *"I cannot emphasize this enough: humanity itself may depend on our success today. We must capture Seoba, and we must do it without revealing our presence to anyone offmoon. Do not hesitate to act with extreme prejudice against anyone who opens fire on you. I mean it—do not think twice. You must not fail."*

The message ended.

And John began to think about how far he could push his orders without actually violating them.

After training with the Black Daggers for the last week, he had no doubts about their ability to eliminate a force of Biko Independence Army irregulars. But improvised operations had a way of exploding in an attacker's face—especially since UNSC commanders tended to underestimate insurrectionist capabilities—and something was bound to go wrong. When that happened, John would be ready to move his Spartans out front, where they would be able to use their speed and power to disrupt any enemy counterattack before it developed.

If the Spartans could do that, they would save a lot of Black Dagger lives—and Crowther would be forced to trust their judgment under fire. He might even be grateful for the lesson.

The drop bay's rear access hatch hissed open, and John looked over to see Ghost Flight Leader stepping into the drop bay. A square-faced officer with a bushy black mustache hanging over a heavy-lipped mouth, Hector Nyeto wore a half-headset over curly hair and a rumpled gray service uniform with a lieutenant commander's gold oak leaves on the collar tabs.

"Listen up, people." Nyeto's voice came over the First Platoon comm net. "Ghost Flight is dropping Alpha Company at the docks as planned, but there's a hitch. The insurrectionists have a comm center at the top of the mass driver. The prowlers will hit it hard on the way in, but you know how that goes. The bad guys could have it transmitting again in thirty minutes. Alpha Company's job is to prevent that."

No one looked toward him—the drop bay was packed too tight for turning around—but the voice of the First Platoon lieutenant, Nelly Hamm, replied over the same comm net.

"Thanks, Commander. How does that affect First Platoon's objectives?"

Nyeto spread his hands in a gesture that only John and Avery Johnson—standing adjacent to Nyeto's far shoulder on the opposite side of the access hatch—could see.

"Your guess is as good as mine," he said. "Colonel Crowther's message wasn't specific. Maybe your captain will fill you in once you've hit the ice."

"Sure," Hamm said. The company captain was with Third Platoon aboard Ghost Flight's number three prowler, *Ghost Wind*. "If our own comms aren't being jammed."

"You worry too much, Lieutenant," Nyeto said. "It's just rebels down there. They don't have jamming equipment."

Nyeto crooked a finger at John, then backed out through the access hatch. John glanced over at Johnson, who was outfitted in the same Black Dagger space assault armor as everyone but John, and cocked his helmet in inquiry. Though Johnson was not technically above John in the chain of command, it had been made clear to him by both Captain Ascot and Dr. Halsey that John should give the sergeant's advice a lot of weight—especially when navigating the vagaries of protocol inherent in the Spartans' attachment to the 21st.

Johnson merely spread his hands and gave a sharp nod toward the hatch. Whatever Nyeto wanted, it was never wise to keep the commander of a prowler flight waiting.

John ducked through the access hatch and found the lieutenant commander standing in the passageway. He came to attention, banging his helmet against the overhead, and saluted.

"You wanted to speak with me, sir?"

Nyeto returned the salute with a casual hand flip and waited for the hatch to close, then motioned John to remove his helmet. "This shouldn't go over any comms."

It would have been simpler to deactivate his communications system, but John felt certain that a lieutenant commander would realize that. He checked the chronometer on his HUD again, then broke the airtight seal on his skinsuit and removed his helmet.

"I hope we can make this fast, Commander. It will take a couple of minutes for me to reseal, and Lieutenant Hamm will vac the drop bay five minutes before—"

"She'll vac it when I tell her to." Nyeto grinned up at John. "So don't worry, okay?"

"I'm infantry," John replied. "I worry or I die."

"Yeah, but not when it comes to getting left behind," Nyeto said. "At least aboard my boats. I see how valuable you Spartans are."

"Very kind of you to say so," John said. "It still wouldn't be good if I were the reason the dismount was delayed."

Nyeto waved a dismissive hand. "Don't worry about Crowther. He can't cause you any serious trouble—not with Mike Stanforth backing you."

"You say 'don't worry' a lot," John observed.

"Worry interferes with clear thought." Nyeto's grin broadened, and he added, "But then again, you're infantry. Maybe clear thought isn't an advantage."

"Ha-ha, sir," John said. "Very funny. Can we get to the point?"

Nyeto gave a hearty laugh. "And not worried about me *at all*, I see." He took a second to collect himself; then the mirth drained from his face, and he craned his neck back so he could look John square in the eye. "Actually, I wanted to apologize—to you and the other Spartans."

"Apologize for what, sir?"

"For the snafu at Netherop," Nyeto said. "The open transmission. That was one of my people, so it's on me."

"I see," John said. He had complained to Captain Ascot, of course, but that had been primarily to mollify Daisy-023 and some of the other Spartans who had been angered by the mistake. He had not really expected to hear anything more about the matter, as such things were usually handled far above a petty officer's pay grade. "Thank you, then. I'll pass the word on to the rest of the squad."

"I'd appreciate that," Nyeto said. "But I hope you won't let Spartan-023 anywhere near my crewman. He's actually a pretty good sensor operator, and I can't afford to lose him."

John recalled what Daisy had wanted to rip off, and it was his turn to be embarrassed. "You heard the playback of our mission?"

"Yes. The crewman did too," Nyeto said. "But just that part. Dr. Halsey wanted to be sure we appreciated the gravity of the situation."

John wasn't happy about having TEAMCOM downloads being shared, but he knew that Halsey was just trying to protect her Spartans. She could be a little extreme about that.

"Dr. Halsey expects perfection."

"That she does." Nyeto chuckled. "By the time she let us go, my petty officer was so sick about it that he was volunteering to find Spartan-023 and introduce himself."

"That would be a mistake," John said. "Tell him I'll pass his apologies along. No reason it has to go any further than that . . . as long as it doesn't happen again."

"It won't," Nyeto said. "I was yelling at him louder than Halsey did. I thought he'd gotten you all killed, but I guess I'd forgotten who you guys are."

John frowned. "What do you mean?"

"You know . . . how *good* you are," Nyeto said. "I guess that's what happens when you start training at five."

"Five?" John blurted. Actually, they hadn't even been conscripted until they were six . . . but Nyeto's information was closer to the mark than it should have been. "Where did you hear that?"

Nyeto's gaze slid away. "I can't remember," he said. "Just around."

"Well, that information is wrong." It seemed pretty clear that Nyeto was lying, and John realized that his own kneejerk reaction had only convinced the commander that the rumblings he'd heard were true. "And even if it wasn't, it's classified."

Nyeto gave a wry smile. "They must have been talking about somebody else, then," he said. "I had a buddy in the ODSTs who used to train against these eight-year-old kids on Reach. They kept kicking his company's ass in jungle maneuvers. It was probably them."

"Who is this buddy?"

"Nobody important," Nyeto said. "The thing is, that was seven years ago, so these kids would only be about . . . fifteen right now, I guess?"

"Seriously, sir—who is this buddy?" In any military organization, no program was immune to rumors, and the more classified it was, the juicier the stories would be. But the intel that Nyeto's friend had disclosed was far too accurate to be the result of casual speculation. It was coming from someone on the inside, someone who was working with the Spartans themselves. "He clearly can't be trusted with classified material."

"Don't worry," Nyeto said. "If I didn't know how to keep a secret, I wouldn't be a prowler commander."

"And as a prowler commander, may I respectfully say that you know your friend has been breaking *all* kinds of security protocols," John said. "He has no idea what he might be placing at risk . . . and neither do you. If you don't report him, I have to report *you*. I have no choice. Sir."

"You serious?" A sly look came to Nyeto's eye. "Those eight-year-olds *were* you, weren't they?"

"I didn't say that."

"You didn't have to," Nyeto retorted. "Huh. How about that. So . . . how long has the SPARTAN program been going on? How many of you are there, anyway?"

"I can't talk about that. And you're not doing yourself any favors by asking."

Nyeto suddenly looked disappointed. "Sorry, John. I didn't mean to make you uncomfortable." He shrugged and looked up the passageway. "You do what you have to. I'll be okay."

John began to feel guilty . . . and confused. He hadn't violated any regulations. In fact, John had done everything by the book, but his denials only seemed to confirm the rumors Nyeto had already heard. It would have been better to keep quiet and report the conversation later.

But then ONI would start sniffing around, and Nyeto would be even *more* certain that his friend was telling the truth. John glanced back toward the drop bay and wished Avery Johnson was at his side. The sergeant had a knack for dealing with unofficial situations like this, a talent developed over two decades that allowed him to safely navigate the murky backwaters of special forces service. It was one of the skills John knew his superiors wanted him to pick up from the sergeant—and a skill that John realized he sorely needed to develop.

He looked back to Nyeto. "Maybe we should forget this conversation ever happened, sir. I'll chalk it up to mere scuttlebutt, and you might want to tell your friend he talks too much."

"No need," Nyeto said. "He died during Operation: TREBUCHET. My wing inserted his company."

"I'm very sorry to hear that," John said. A lot of ODSTs had died during Operation: TREBUCHET, but he could at least confirm the basics of Nyeto's story and see what Sergeant Johnson made of it. He looked toward the access hatch, then started to raise his helmet toward his head. "If that's all, sir, I should probably seal up."

"Of course," Nyeto said. "And, just so you know, nobody in the prowler wing supports what Crowther is doing."

John paused with his helmet at chest height. "Doing, sir?"

"To your Spartans," Nyeto said. "It's stupid to make you fight from the back. Everybody knows you tanks should be leading the charge."

"I agree—it *is* an odd tactic," John said. He was starting to think that he'd been too suspicious of Nyeto. "But the colonel hasn't fought with us before. He doesn't know our capabilities."

Nyeto snorted in disgust. "The colonel is trying to protect his reputation. He doesn't want his Black Daggers being shown up by a bunch of teenagers."

"No . . . *really*?" John kept his helmet at chest height. "I can't believe that, sir. He wouldn't allow personal pride to affect his tactical planning. Not with an ODST command."

"Oh, maybe not on purpose . . . but so what? Your Spartans are still fighting from the back. The operation is still going to suffer."

John exhaled. "Yeah. What am I supposed to do about it?"

Before Nyeto could answer, the hatch slid open, and Avery Johnson stepped into the passageway. His reflective faceplate turned first in Nyeto's direction, then in John's.

"Everything all right out here?" Even through the external speaker of his assault armor, his voice sounded gravelly and familiar. "Lieutenant Hamm wants to vac the bay in two."

"That will be fine, Sergeant. We're done here." As Nyeto spoke, his gaze remained fixed on John. “Just do what you do best, son. It’ll work out in the end.”

“I will, sir.” John raised his hand in a salute. “And thank you.”

“Anytime, John.”

Nyeto returned the salute and started up the passage.

Johnson watched him go, then turned to John and spoke over his external speaker. “What was that about?”

“Tell you later, Sarge.” John slipped his helmet on, then turned back toward the drop bay. “The bay vacs in two, remember?”

CHAPTER 8

1433 hours, March 18, 2526 (military calendar)
UNSC *Razor*-class Prowler *Ghost Song*
Insertion Run, Mass Driver Launching Docks, Seoba Ice Quarry

John felt his weight sink as the *Ghost Song* pulled up, sweeping across Seoba toward the drop zone. The bulkhead alert lamps flashed one last time, flooding the crowded bay with steady green GO light, and the prowler decelerated hard. John could see nothing outside, but he knew they were entering the First Platoon dismount area. They would be a hundred meters above a kilometer-wide ice bench, with the vast quarry pit behind them and a ring of frozen slopes ahead. It was hardly an ideal drop zone, but they were infantry. They got out where they were told.

The jump hatch split down the center. Looking over the mass of ODST helmets ahead of him, John saw four troopers at the front of the platoon dive through the exit portal. Before he could blink, they began to trail plumes of crimson mist. Then a jet of vapor erupted from a thruster pack, and the entire four-trooper team vanished in a cloud of blood and flame.

The next team did not even hesitate. They stepped forward and spouted geysers of blood and tissue; then ricochets started to bounce off the overhead, and troopers began to drop everywhere in the bay.

John heard his own voice inside his helmet. "Damn it!"

Then he realized that this was the moment he had told himself to be ready for. It was a terrible moment, a tragic one, and he needed to fix it. He started forward, using his forearms to plow aside anyone in his way. The motion tracker on his HUD showed Avery Johnson following close behind.

Lieutenant Hamm's voice came over the First Platoon comm channel. "Abort—emplacements! Abort!"

The *Ghost Song* began to glide forward. A trooper bounced off John's thruster pack and went down with a hole twice the size of a thumb punched through the front of his helmet. John used his foot to roll him over and saw a star-shaped exit hole on the opposite side.

"John!" Johnson said over TEAMCOM. Although TEAMCOM was a Spartan-only channel, Dr. Halsey had given the sergeant access to facilitate his role as a Spartan-ODST liaison. "What the hell?"

"Look at the holes." John maneuvered his boot to flip the trooper back over so Johnson could see the entry hole. "The same size. That means armor-piercing rounds—big ones. Probably depleted uranium."

"Probably from Vulcans," Johnson agreed. He was referring to the M41 light anti-aircraft gun, a cumbersome weapon that had to be either vehicle- or turret-mounted in order to fire accurately. "They were waiting for us."

"I'll buy they were ready," John said. "But *waiting*? That would mean they knew—"

"I know what it means."

The *Ghost Song* accelerated hard, climbing away from the Vulcan fire and leaving John's stomach behind. He pushed forward another few steps and came to the jump hatch, where an injured trooper lay across the threshold, more outside the drop bay than inside it. Lieutenant Hamm and another ODST were holding the unconscious soldier by the arms, struggling against the prowler's thrust to pull him back into the drop bay—and losing the fight.

John placed a boot in the guide track to keep the hatch from closing, then lifted the man inside and passed him to Hamm. Blood was frothing out of armor punctures in the soldier's chest, abdomen, and hip. By dropping a casualty into the lieutenant's lap, John hoped to buy a few moments to check the situation below. It worked. Hamm immediately hit the wounded man's thruster pack quick-release and got busy saving his life.

John turned back to the portal. Two hundred meters below, a torrent of munitions strikes was spraying icy shards off the moon's frozen surface. Seoba's gravity was barely an eighth-g, so there was only a trace atmosphere, and the shards sublimated instantly into vapor and began to drift across the battlefield in banks of crystalline mist. In the milky twilight, John could see more than a dozen black-armored corpses scattered across the four drop zones beneath Ghost Flight's prowlers. A like number of survivors were maneuvering through veils of glimmering fog, taking heavy fire from three sides as they tried to reach a row of ice-coated preparation docks.

It wasn't easy to trace the enemy fire back to its sources, but a few heartbeats later, John spotted a series of bunkers dug into the steep slopes that ringed the dockyard. The emplacements had been carefully faced with layers of ice, camouflaged so perfectly that their locations were betrayed only by muzzle flashes blinking through their embrasures.

John was almost relieved. "They were ready, but not waiting," he said, speaking to Johnson over TEAMCOM. "It took hours to build and camouflage those bunkers."

Johnson came and stood next to him in the portal. "So?"

"So, we left slipspace less than thirty minutes ago," John said. "They didn't have time to build all that just for us. It's general preparedness. Has to be."

"That's one possibility."

"You think they were tipped off *before* we slipped?"

"I think it'd be foolish to rule that out."

John thought for a moment, then said, "No way. That early, the tip would have to come from command level. Nobody else knew the target."

"So you've never seen someone with brass on the collar let a secret slip?" Johnson asked. "Or put other loyalties before duty?"

As a matter of fact, John *hadn't* seen a senior officer make either mistake, but he took the sergeant's point. Colonel Crowther was doing a pretty good job of putting his own ego before the mission, so it wasn't hard to imagine him—or some other brass hat—doing something that comprised mission security.

John exhaled in frustration. "Are you always such a pessimist, Sarge?"

"Yeah. I'm infantry."

"Okay," John said. "Fair enough."

The *Ghost Song* was a kilometer above the battlefield now, and John could see the frost-crusted tube of a century-old magnetic mass driver rising up from the docks, climbing the face of a two-thousand-meter ice mountain. The end was located just below the summit, pointing at the pink-swaddled immensity of Biko. John knew from the mission briefing that the mass driver had once launched thousand-ton payloads of steel-encapsulated ice toward the planet. As the ice-capsules entered the exosphere, they were intercepted by the purchaser, then guided to a rendezvous in the stratosphere, attached to a dirigible, and floated gently to their final destination.

But, like the quarry itself, the mass driver had gone out of service in 2424, after Biko had finally developed a climate humid enough to supply its own rain.

On the summit of the ice mountain, just above the mass driver's muzzle, sat the comm center Nyeto had mentioned earlier. It was surrounded by strike craters, but largely intact, with the relay antenna lying on its side and still half-attached to its base.

If the insurrectionists had a half-decent comm technician supervising repairs, they'd need no more than a half hour to erect a new antenna and restore their communications.

On the opposite side of the jump hatch, Lieutenant Hamm stuck the last patch over the last hole in the casualty's armor, then passed the injured man off to a pair of subordinates. As she stood, she faced John and hooked a thumb toward the casualty.

"Smooth move, Spartan." She was speaking over the First Platoon channel. "Don't ever pull something like that again."

"Of course not, ma'am," John said. "I should have passed him to a corpsman."

"Damn right," Hamm said. "And you're not supposed to be up here in the first place. You're out of position."

"Yes, ma'am." As the platoon's designated fire-support soldier, John was carrying a variety of heavy weapons. He removed the largest—a man-portable SPNKR rocket launcher—from the magnetic holder on the back of his Mjolnir. "Very sorry about that, ma'am."

Hamm's faceplate followed the SPNKR as John brought it over his shoulder. "Spartan-117, what the hell do you think you're doing?"

"Volunteering, ma'am." John armed the SPNKR's first tube. "We need to take out those bunkers."

Avery Johnson placed a restraining hand on his forearm, but John shook it off and linked the SPNKR's targeting sight to his heads-up display. The conversation with Nyeto remained fresh in his mind, and he had no intention of letting Crowther's jealousy screw up the assault—at least, not any more than it already *had* been.

Johnson grabbed John's arm again. "John, you can't fire that thing in here. You'll crisp half the platoon."

John glanced down at Johnson. "I *know* the safety parameters of an MAV/AV Bore 102mm M41 rocket launcher, Sergeant." He put the firing rest on his shoulder and focused his HUD targeting reticle on the nearest bunker. The prowler was still climbing, and the distance had increased to a kilometer and a half. "Besides, we're out of range."

Hamm's voice grew sharp. "Spartan-117—"

But John was already stepping out of the prowler. In Seoba's weak gravity, it would have taken him nearly a minute to simply fall the eleven hundred meters back into the SPNKR's effective range. He hit his thrusters and accelerated downward. That would cut his descent time to more like ten seconds. Still, if he gave the enemy gunners that long to track him on a straight line, he would arrive full of holes. Being careful to keep his HUD's targeting reticle locked on the bunker, he began to make random changes of vector.

Avery Johnson's voice sounded over TEAMCOM. "Blue Team, dismount! Come heavy!"

John continued to drop, and he began to see Vulcan muzzles flashing through the bunker embrasures. The weapons were using vacuum-suitable tracers, so he could see that the insurrectionists' fire was lagging well behind his maneuvers—though by less and less as the range decreased. Finally, after he had descended a full kilometer, John reversed thrust.

He decelerated hard, but had built a lot of velocity and was still dropping fast. By the time he fired the rocket launcher, the range had fallen to 350 meters.

The missile streaked away in blinding brilliance, shrinking into a silver dot as John rolled into an evasive corkscrew. He felt a round glance off his thigh armor. The gunner was still firing as his bunker erupted into a spray of steam and ice.

John followed a second line of tracers back to another bunker and spotted the flash of an additional Vulcan. He designated it as a target and fired the SPNKR's second barrel.

The round streaked away, then Seoba's milky surface was coming up fast. John managed to get his legs under him as he landed, but lost his footing on the slick terrain and went sliding. He had managed to land in Alpha Company's drop zone and was still on the ice bench between the quarry pit and the launching docks, gliding along on his back, watching arm-length geysers rise behind him as Vulcan rounds stitched the white ground.

Tossing the empty SPNKR aside, he rolled onto his hip and slapped off, launching himself three meters high in the weak gravity. John snatched the MA5B off its holder, then pumped an HE grenade into the underslung launcher and swung it toward the bunker from which his attacker was firing—then, before he could fire, saw the entire front wall erupt in a spray of bodies and ice blocks.

Kelly-087's voice came over TEAMCOM. "Thanks for the invite, Sergeant Johnson. Blue Leader likes to hog the fun."

"Not this time," John said. He touched down almost gently, then turned to see masses of ice and what was left of their insurrectionist attackers fanning down the slopes below four more wrecked bunkers. "Let's form up in the docks. Switch comms back to Alpha."

A series of green LEDs acknowledged the order, and John raced across the ice toward the launching docks, using his thrusters and sometimes his feet to dodge enemy fire. The low gravity and poor traction made it difficult to change directions abruptly, and a few times he found himself falling to a knee or flying ten meters on a single course. Falling was not much of a problem, but there were still hundreds of insurrectionists hiding in hollows or behind ice blocks on the surrounding slopes, and they were decent marksmen. Whenever he continued on a straight line for more than a second or two, he began to feel small-arms fire dinging his Mjolnir armor.

John returned fire as he moved, of course, and took out a few attackers. But the battalion intelligence squad had either lost its reconnaissance drones or failed to establish a Mjolnir linkup, and the TACMAP on his HUD remained blank. So he devoted most of his attention to reconnoitering, looking for anything large enough to be an enemy hangar, or trying to guess how long it would be before the insurrectionists got their comm center working again.

Unfortunately, the largest part of the battlefield lay more or less behind him, in the sheer-walled vastness of the quarry pit itself. Easily ten kilometers in diameter, the pit was the shape of an octopus, with a large central cavity surrounded by long curving canyons that extended farther than John could see. The walls were pocked by caves with oddly shaped mouths, many of them large enough to hold a transport vessel of considerable size. The bottom of the quarry could not be seen from his angle, but a blanket of fog was rising into view, with prowlers dipping in and out as they swirled down to drop their platoons or lay fire on enemy positions.

In all likelihood, the insurrectionist transports were hidden somewhere in the bottom of the vast quarry, and it would fall to Crowther to be sure the enemy vessels were disabled before they could launch and sound the alarm. It was not a task John felt good about entrusting to someone else—least of all the colonel—but he had no choice. A convoy of tracked Civets was climbing a service road toward the top of the mass driver, their cargo boxes loaded with soldiers in pressure-sealed armor, heavy weapons, and equipment to repair the damaged comm center.

The Ghost Flight prowlers came swooping over the battlefield, their belly turrets spewing streams of 30mm rounds and their drop bays trailing dark-armored ODSTs. The incoming fire faded to almost nothing as the enemy took cover, and John hit his thrusters and leap-soared the last hundred meters to the fog-swaddled docks.

There was a total of ten separate structures, each about two meters high and as wide and long as a Pelican dropship without the wings. A set of ice-caked rails ran the length of their decks, serving as guide tracks for a huge gantry crane that stood about halfway to the bottom end of the mass driver. A half dozen ODSTs had already taken shelter in the sunken capsuling bays between docks and were standing on their toes, holding their assault weapons over their heads so they could return fire.

John dropped into an unoccupied bay near the center of the row and saw a flight of M28 Shrieker missiles flash from the prowlers toward the Civet convoy. The mountainside erupted into geysers and hid the Seoban sky behind a boiling curtain of steam; then a pair of yellow streaks lanced back through the fog toward the attacking prowlers. An orange ball blossomed inside the cloud and began a slow descent behind the mountain.

"That's it for us," Nyeto said, speaking over Alpha Channel. "We're bingo ammo and down one bird. You're on your own, Alpha."

"Affirmative," answered the raspy voice of Captain Zelos Cuvier, the Alpha Company commander. "Thanks for the ride, Ghost Man. We have it from here."

John was not so sure. With enemy fire picking up again—and raining down from three sides—he didn't need a TACMAP to tell him Alpha Company was more or less surrounded. And when he stuck his head up to check on the comm center, he could just make out a ghostly line of Civets still climbing through the fog toward the mountaintop. There seemed to be only about half as many as before, but that was at least seven vehicles—plenty to carry the repair crew and a heavy weapons platoon to protect them.

John's motion tracker showed five friendlies entering the capsuling bay behind him—the rest of Blue Team, plus Avery Johnson and Lieutenant Hamm. He crouched down behind the cover of an ice-crusted steel half-capsule that had been hanging alongside the dock for the last century, then went to meet them.

Lieutenant Hamm was first in line. Not bothering to crouch—her helmet was still half a meter beneath the top of the dock—she stepped forward and jammed a gloved finger against John's breastplate.

"You disobeyed my order."

"Sorry, ma'am," John said. "By the time I realized what you were saying, I was already two steps out of the drop bay."

"Because you stepped off without authorization."

"Spartans are trained to take the initiative." As John said this, Fred and Kelly remained behind Hamm, looming over her and turning their helmets back and forth in astonishment. Linda just kept her faceplate turned toward the Civet convoy and showed no sign she was listening. "Naturally, I assumed ODSTs were too."

"Cute." Hamm grabbed John by the top of his armored chest plate, then pulled him down in an effort to equalize their height. "If I allow you to stay in my platoon, you're going to learn to follow orders. And until you do, your life is going to be one long shitshine after another. Is that clear, Spartan?"

"Yes, ma'am." John had never heard the term *shitshine* before, but he suspected it involved polishing hardware with a nonapproved agent. He glanced over his shoulder toward the magnetic catapult. "How about a suggestion?"

"How about a sitrep instead?" Johnson said, sounding almost mad. "That should have been the first thing you communicated when you rejoined your platoon leader. Or do they *not* teach battle protocol in Spartan school?"

"They do."

John did not point out that Hamm had given him no chance to communicate *anything* before reading him the riot act, because he was pretty sure Johnson realized that already—the sergeant was a master at convincing officers that what he wanted them to do was their own idea. John pointed up the fog-shrouded slope toward the top of the mass driver, then began his situation report.

"Ma'am, there's a convoy of seven tracked Civets climbing toward the disabled comm center at the top of the mountain. They have repair equipment, a security force of at least platoon strength, and heavy weapons—including at least one vehicle-mounted multiple rocket launcher."

"The one that got the *Ghost Star*?" Hamm's helmet tipped back as she searched for the convoy; then she finally seemed to see them. "Well, crap in a helmet. They're halfway up now."

"Yes, ma'am," John said. "We need to stop them."

"No kidding." Hamm turned away and dropped her chin in the posture of someone carrying on a conversation inside her helmet, then finally returned her attention to her companions. "Ascot says no strafing runs. The prowlers are out of Shriekers, and with those rocket launchers on the Civets, she doesn't want to risk losing another boat."

"So . . ." Johnson sighed. "The hard way."

Hamm shrugged her armored shoulders. "You know what they say—infantry is the queen of the battlefield."

Just about every soldier who had been through infantry school in the last five hundred years understood the reference. In the game of chess, the queen was the most versatile piece on the board; and in a war, infantry was the most versatile force on the battlefield. Hamm studied the mountainside, trying to assess whether her platoon stood any chance of surviving an uphill assault on a convoy equipped with heavy weapons—all while being attacked from both flanks.

The answer was, of course, no way in hell.

Her faceplate shifted toward John and the rest of Blue Team. He felt pretty sure that she was pondering their capabilities, wondering whether the four of them could accomplish what would be impossible for an ODST platoon with ten times the personnel.

John knew they could, and he was about to volunteer when a squall of ice chips and fog began to roll over their heads. A trio of inbound friendlies appeared on his motion tracker, on foot about twenty-five meters away and coming from the direction of the gantry crane.

"Cover fire!" John ordered.

He and the rest of Blue Team rose to their full height and began to loose three-shot bursts at the slope beyond the trio, targeting the closest muzzle flashes first. The enemy fire trailed off as casualties mounted, but the survivors did not seem to realize how quickly they were being picked off and continued to attack from fixed positions.

Definitely irregulars, *not* well-trained.

The lead friendly took a round in the shoulder and went down face-first, sliding across the ice before pushing himself to a knee again. His companions came up on either side and slipped a hand beneath his arms, then continued forward in a straight line. Within a couple of steps, they were close enough to the capsuling bay that they were blocking Blue Team's firing lanes.

"Forty-mike-mike," John ordered. "High arc."

All four members of Blue Team pointed their MA5Bs skyward and began firing 40mm grenades from the underslung launchers. In the weak gravity, the orbs arced so high they vanished into Seoba's dark sky. A moment later, they returned to view, a dark rain falling slowly toward the enemy positions.

The insurrectionists stopped firing and craned their necks, all trying to guess whether they would be in a blast radius of a slowly incoming grenade. About half leapt up and scrambled for better cover—and were promptly cut down by the platoon of ODSTs that had taken positions on the gantry crane.

The trio of friendlies reached the dock and jumped down into the capsuling berth, the injured man falling on his rear as soon as his boots hit the ice. One of his companions knelt next to him and opened his thigh pouch, then extracted a patching kit and set to work repairing the hole in his armor. Any actual first aid would have to wait until the casualty reached a pressurized environment, but space assault armor was tough stuff. Even armor-piercing ammunition surrendered most of its kinetic energy penetrating it, so there was a good chance the wound was not serious.

The second companion made a beeline for Hamm. There was no rank insignia on his armor—it was never smart to help snipers identify high-value targets—but the name stenciled on his breast was CUVIER.

The company captain.

Cuvier stopped halfway between John and Hamm. Nobody saluted, but Hamm stood slightly more erect. Had one of John's Spartan snipers been an enemy watching through a scope, the subtle shift of posture would have been enough to get the captain's helmet blown off.

"Good work, Lieutenant," Cuvier said over the First Platoon channel. "I like your initiative."

"Sir?" Hamm asked.

"Sending in the Spartans," Cuvier said. "That was brilliant. You saved a lot of ODSTs. Maybe the whole operation."

Hamm's faceplate shifted in John's direction, but before she could set the record straight, Avery Johnson spoke up.

"It was quick thinking, sir. But don't blame Lieutenant Hamm for jumping the gun. That's all on me."

"Jumping the gun, Sergeant?"

"Failing to confirm the deployment order. Once things started moving, I just got excited and—"

Cuvier waved him off. "There wasn't time." He turned back to Hamm. "By the time he explained the plan, it would have been too late to make it work. I know that."

"Thank you, Captain." Hamm's tone was strained. "I appreciate your understanding."

"But let's keep this between us." Cuvier's faceplate pivoted toward Johnson, then to Fred, Kelly, and Linda, and finally came to a rest on John. "The colonel isn't a big fan of spontaneity in combat operations, and I don't want him blaming Lieutenant Hamm for doing her job. Clear?"

After everyone had acknowledged the order, Cuvier craned his neck to look up the mountainside toward the convoy of Civets.

"I was monitoring your conversation with Captain Ascot," he said. "So, tell me, what do you need from me to stop that repair company without prowler support?"

Hamm looked toward John and his team. "Just your blessing, sir."

"You have it," Cuvier said, also turning toward the Spartans. "Tell me what you have in mind."

"We need to beat those Civets to the comm center," Hamm said, "and right now, the Spartans are the fastest thing we have. I suggest we send them up the mass driver."

Cuvier continued to study the mountainside, no doubt inspecting—as John was—the ice-crusted tube running up the slope. A full three meters in diameter, it was easily large enough to hold the Spartans and any munitions they would need to demolish the comm center and attack the convoy. But over the course of a century without maintenance, several support towers had collapsed, and the curtains of ice hanging beneath some of the induction coils suggested that a half dozen seam welds had opened.

Most worrisome was a miniature glacier flowing out of the loading breech. Easily twenty meters wide and ten meters thick, it spilled from beneath the buckled hatch and spread out in a mound the size of a small house. Judging by how far it had pushed the hatch up, the bottom half of the tube was packed with ice that had accumulated over a hundred years of sublimation cycles.

Cuvier nodded in approval. "Excellent plan, Lieutenant. The enemy will never see them coming."

"Because they'll never get there!" Johnson objected. "You can see from here the tube is full of ice."

"Half full," John said.

After Blue Team's success in taking out the bunkers, he was feeling good about his chances of proving just how crucial his Spartans were to the success of Operation: SILENT STORM. If they could reach the top of the mountain in time to demolish the comm center and take out the convoy, even Colonel Crowther would be forced to admit that the Spartans should be leading the way into battle—instead of bringing up the rear.

John turned to Cuvier. "Blue Team is in," he said. "We'll need some flamethrowers and thermite paste to handle blockages."

"And C-7," Fred added. The foaming explosive was especially suitable for use in a vacuum. "Lots and lots of C-7."

CHAPTER 9

Ninth Age of Reclamation
34th Cycle, 16 Units (Covenant Battle Calendar)
Fleet of Inexorable Obedience, Assault Carrier *Pious Rampage*
Low Polar Orbit, Planet E'gini, Illa System

It seemed a cruel way to set the unworthy on the Path of Oblivion, this rain of fire that devoured all it touched, that burned bone and boiled stone and turned dirt to glass. Yet so glorious was the bombardment, so magnificent the white lances blossoming upon the nomadic villages below, and so sublime the scarlet rings dilating across the smudges of green pasture, that Nizat 'Kvarosee could not turn from the sight. He was Master of the Fleet of Inexorable Obedience, and this terrible beauty was his doing.

The annihilation of the contemptibles was his gift to the gods of the Covenant, the tithe he offered to be deemed worthy of one day joining the ancient Forerunners in divine transcendence. To turn his back on the splendor of his weapons was to abandon the Great Journey itself, to declare himself a traitor to his people and his faith.

And that he would never do, no matter the growing darkness within.

To a Sangheili warrior, one's word was all, and when Nizat had become Master of the Fleet of Inexorable Obedience, he had sworn to execute the will of the Prophets as if it were his own.

The strike ended, leaving nothing in its wake but a white glowing circle the size of his palm. He nodded approvingly and turned to the frail figure floating in the antigravity chair next to him. With his serpentine neck and the fur-covered wattle dangling beneath his chin, the San'Shyuum would appear repulsively weak to most Sangheili; yet Nizat was careful to address him in a tone just shy of veneration.

"That was the last village on this meridian, Your Grace. I will give the order to move on to the next."

The San'Shyuum—the Minor Minister of Artifact Survey—waved a tri-fingered hand.

"Yes, yes, Fleetmaster. As you wish." The Minor Minister—whom Nizat often simply called "Survey" in his own mind—tipped his chair forward to peer out of the blister. "How much longer, do you think?"

"Not overlong," Nizat said. "E'gini is thinly populated. There are barely more than a hundred thousand settlements on the entire world."

"A hundred thousand?" Survey exhaled heavily. "And how many do you think we have destroyed?"

Nizat checked the datatab integrated into the forearm of his shipboard armor. "That makes forty-seven thousand, nine-hundred and twelve."

The San'Shyuum's head sank forward. "So few? At this rate, we'll be here another full cycle."

Nizat tried to hide his revulsion. Like most San'Shyuum who traveled with Covenant battle fleets, the Minor Minister was a ceremonial magistrate rather than a military commander—and Survey, in particular, seemed ill-suited to the rigors of attending a planet-cleansing operation.

"If the Minor Minister is growing weary, he should feel free to return to his compartments. There is no need to remain here."

Survey's head whipped up. "*No need*, Fleetmaster? Perhaps you believe that all the Hierarchs require of us is to *kill* humans?"

"Not at all, Your Grace," Nizat said. "The eradication must be consecrated, I know. But I was not aware you had to observe the entire operation personally."

"You are being ridiculous," Survey retorted. "That would be impossible, even for a San'Shyuum."

"Then I am—" Nizat stopped himself. He'd almost said he was afraid he didn't understand, but that would have been wrong. He was not afraid, and one did not lie to a San'Shyuum . . . not even to one as unimpressive as Survey. "Forgive me. I do not understand."

"It is a matter of bearing witness." Survey's gaze grew distant, and he held his long neck a little more erect. "The Hierarchs must know that the humans are paying for their transgressions, and I must be able to report how they are suffering."

"Ah . . . now I understand."

And indeed, that was the truth. Nizat's orders had said nothing about making humans suffer, only to kill them as quickly as possible, and to survey their worlds and capture those that contained Forerunner relics, and to render uninhabitable those that did not.

But the San'Shyuum were a political species who fought for status the way Sangheili did for honor, and it was clear that Survey intended to win favor among the Hierarchs by describing in detail how the humans were dying in anguish beneath the plasma beams of the Fleet of Inexorable Obedience. It was nothing to Nizat, and in fact the reports were only likely to enhance his reputation with the Prophets who were his superiors and Survey's, so there was no reason to make the Minor Minister's life any harder than it had to be.

"But if I may, Your Grace, the destruction of one village is usually the same as another. Nothing of interest is likely to occur while you are attending to other matters—and if it does, I will, of course, send for you at once."

Survey considered the proposal for only a moment before inclining his elongated head. "As you wish, Fleetmaster. But two cycles is a long time to waste on a mudhole such as this. Is there nothing you can do to complete your work more quickly?"

Nizat hesitated, for he had pondered the subject earlier and concluded that it was feasible. Unfortunately, the method was not as certain as plasma bombardment to sterilize the world—and if it succeeded, it would prove immeasurably crueler. It was not something he was eager to try, but he had been directly asked by a Minor Minister, and it would be blasphemy to lie.

"Did you not hear my question, Fleetmaster?"

"I did," Nizat replied. "I hesitate because the technique has never been tried before. But this world is so primitive that it could work here."

"I hope you do not expect me to guess."

"Not at all," Nizat said. "But there are risks."

"Are we not at war? There are always risks—even when fighting the humans."

"Then your guidance will be most appreciated," Nizat said. "E'gini is unique in two ways that serve our purpose. First, there is a shield volcano on the equator so enormous that we can see it venting ash and steam even from orbit."

"And a plasma bombardment might trigger an eruption," Survey said. "But would that be enough?"

"On any other world, no," Nizat said. "But there is only one spaceport on the entire planet, and it has already been glassed."

"So there can be no evacuation if the volcano erupts."

"It would require a rescue fleet of at least a thousand large transports," Nizat said. "And what is the likelihood of *that* while the Fleet of Inexorable Obedience is nearby?"

"No more than zero," Survey replied. "But even an erupting shield volcano would blanket only a small part of the planet. It wouldn't kill everything."

"Not quickly. But if there is enough ash in the sky?" Nizat waited until he saw Survey's eyes widen, then added, "It would be a slow and anguishing death, Your Grace."

The Minor Minister's head bobbed. "Perfect."

"But uncertain," Nizat said. He did not enjoy the prospect of inflicting said slow and anguishing death on so many—even if Survey did. "There may not be enough ash to cool the planet, and humans are nothing if not resourceful."

"It matters not." Survey gave his fingers a dismissive flutter. "Even if they survive, where can they go? When we return—"

The San'Shyuum was interrupted by the warning rattle of mandibles in the Fleetmaster's Planning Compartment, and Nizat turned to find his steward leading a warrior in indigo assault armor toward the observation blister. His blood ran cold, for the armor was the uniform of the Silent Shadow, a premier hunter-killer force that the Hierarchs often dispatched when they wished to remove a high-ranking commander from his post. Unlike most warriors who came before the fleetmaster, the Shadow had not removed his helmet, for his sect forbade him to show his face to a superior he might one day be ordered to kill.

Happily, this Shadow had left the hilt of his plasma sword in its holster, and he was using both hands to carry a plate-size disk about the thickness of his arm. For an instant, Nizat thought it might be some kind of strange Forerunner artifact—the recovery of such relics *was* one of the Covenant's objectives in attacking the humans, after all. But as the warrior drew closer, Nizat saw the obvious control buttons and a lens of primitive silicate, and he realized the thing had to be a human device.

Nizat looked to his steward, then pointed to the device and demanded, "Why do you allow that abomination into my presence?"

The steward, a young major named Tam 'Lakosee, stopped three paces away. Like all Sangheili warriors, he was an imposing figure with an arrow-shaped head, beady eyes, and a mouth with four mandibles lined by short, curved fangs. Dressed in a sleeveless tabard rather than armor, he had a heavily muscled frame, long sinewy arms that ended in four-fingered hands, and huge legs supported by long, powerful tarses that resulted in a springy digitigrade gait.

He touched his fingers to his brow. "Fleetmaster, all will grow clear in a moment. Until then, I beg your indulgence."

"You have it—for now."

"I will be quick." 'Lakosee gestured at the Silent Shadow beside him. "First Blade Tel 'Szatulai recovered the abomination on the world that humans call Amasa, in their Grenadi sector."

Amasa, known to the Fleet of Inexorable Obedience as Alay'oso, was the tenth target in line to be attacked under Nizat's current invasion plan, so he knew that 'Szatulai's unit would have been there to take the measure of its defenses. Even more importantly, the patrol would have been scouting for any hint that the world had once been occupied by the holy Forerunners, who had held dominion over the galaxy before their ascent to divinity.

Nizat clacked his mandibles horizontally to indicate that he knew of the world, and 'Lakosee continued his explanation.

"The device was left in front of 'Szatulai's reconnaissance squad—deliberately."

"Deliberately?" Survey echoed. He floated his chair close to 'Szatulai and leaned forward so that his wattled face was within a finger's length of the warrior's red visor. "A first blade of the Silent Shadow allowed himself to be seen? On a world not yet under attack?"

'Szatulai regarded Survey and did not reply. For five long breaths,

Nizat wondered whether the warrior was too much of a coward to speak directly to a San'Shyuum . . . or such a fool that he believed he needed his fleetmaster's permission to reply to a Minor Minister.

Then 'Szatulai spoke, and Nizat realized he was neither.

"That is so, Your Grace." There was just enough loathing in the first blade's tone to indicate that he did not appreciate having his field performance disparaged by a member of the audience. "I made a mistake."

Red circles broke out around Survey's eyes, and the San'Shyuum turned to Nizat, the curl of his prehensile lips making clear that he expected such insubordination to be dealt with harshly. But Nizat had developed a sudden fondness for this Shadow, and anyway, first blades were too valuable to sacrifice to the petulance of a Minor Minister.

Nizat flipped a hand in indifference. "It is nothing to worry about, Your Grace. The infidels are not feebleminded. They already know that we are going to attack Alay'oso."

"That is not my concern," Survey hissed.

"I am glad we are in agreement." Nizat turned to 'Szatulai. "You have ensured that this device is not a trap?"

The first blade's helmet swung upward and to the right, a sign of confirmation. "We captured the courier and forced her to demonstrate its use before she died. It brought harm to none of us."

"Well done," Nizat said. "Then tell me, why is this device worthy of my attention?"

"Because it contains a message from a faction of humans who wish to help us."

"A trick," Survey said. "Why would any human help destroy their own species?"

"I will let the message explain. It is . . . complicated." 'Szatulai placed the disk on Nizat's writing stand, then asked, "Do you understand the human language, Fleetmaster?"

"The one they call English and a few others," Nizat said. "There are so many."

"English is a common tongue, much as Sangheili is ours," 'Szatulai said. "It is used for the message."

"What about me?" Survey asked.

"You did not honor my decree that the Vicars of the Fleet learn the language of our enemy?" Nizat did not hide his surprise, for he had always found the Minor Minister more ambitious than determined, and 'Szatulai's example had emboldened him to let his disapproval show. "Truly?"

The wattle beneath Survey's chin reddened. "My other duties have demanded my attention."

"Of course. 'Lakosee will bring a translation disk for you." Nizat used a hand gesture to signal the steward to take his time returning, for he wanted an opportunity to digest the message on his own before enduring the Minor Minister's advice. He turned back to 'Szatulai. "Let us begin."

"Before I am ready?" Survey was indignant.

"I am certain we will listen to it more than once."

Nizat had barely spoken the words before 'Szatulai touched a button. The hologram of a human head appeared above the glass lens. Like nearly all human heads, it was quite unattractive, with a gaunt face, oddly placed skin folds, and a tiny oval mouth set beneath a nose too skinny for its length.

The head probably belonged to a male, but Nizat could not be sure. There was no hair on the chin, lips, or cheeks, which was usually a female trait. Yet the hair atop the head was worn so short that it was almost not there, and Nizat had been told that it was rare for a female to go bald on the crown of her head.

But it hardly mattered. Humans seemed as uncertain of their own sexual stations as the Unggoy. Nizat had even heard that it was common for human males to manage the family keep and for females to fight as foot soldiers. It was little wonder that the Hierarchs had judged the species unworthy of the Great Journey. With such confusion about their places even in their own society, they would have brought only chaos to the Covenant.

After it had coalesced, the face in the hologram spoke.

"Greetings." Its voice was deep and gravelly, a trait that Nizat associated with size—and therefore maleness. *"I am General Harper Garvin of the United Rebel Front, and I have a proposal for the leadership of the Covenant.*

"The United Nations Space Command, upon whom you are currently making war, is a vast colonial empire that oppresses hundreds of worlds—"

Nizat signaled 'Szatulai to stop the message, then asked, "What is this word, *colonial*?"

"It means those worlds are ruled by a military authority," 'Szatulai explained. As a commander of the Silent Shadow, he had spent many cycles on human worlds and no doubt understood their customs far better than did Nizat. "Sometimes it is called the Colonial Military Authority, and sometimes it is called the United Nations Space Command. I am uncertain of the difference, but it matters not. The vessels of both forces are as the flesh of a captive *keifra* before our knives."

"And humans do not wish to be ruled by their own military?"

'Szatulai's helmet tipped forward and to the left, signaling negation. "It is very strange, Fleetmaster," he said. "But many humans view this colonial rule as enslavement."

"I agree," said Survey. 'Lakosee still had not returned with the translation disk, so the Minor Minister was responding only to the short exchange between Nizat and 'Szatulai. "It should be their prophets who rule their worlds."

'Szatulai's visor swung toward the Minor Minister and remained fixed there for a time; then he finally deigned to speak. "The infidels follow too many faiths to be ruled by any of them," he said. "And a vast number of humans follow no faith at all."

"Which is undoubtedly why the Hierarchs consider their species unworthy of the Great Journey," Survey said. "You would do well to keep that in your thoughts, First Blade."

"As I do, Your Grace," 'Szatulai said. "My faith stands as the pillar of my obedience."

Which could mean, Nizat reflected, that it was only 'Szatulai's faith in the Great Journey that kept him from snapping the Minor Minister's snaky little neck. On occasion, Nizat had pondered the same murderous blasphemy himself—but it was better to avoid dwelling on that now. He signaled 'Szatulai to resume, and the first blade touched the device again.

"—yearning to breathe free," the head—Garvin—continued. *"And on many of those worlds, desperate groups of resistance fighters have organized themselves into insurrectionist armies who are determined to throw off the yoke of imperialism."*

Nizat decided not to inquire about the meaning of *imperialism*. No doubt it had something to do with being oppressed, and what did he care about the oppression of humans? They would *all* be free soon enough, right after he killed them.

The thought had barely passed from his mind before it became a pang of guilt that he felt like a dagger through one of his hearts. He put the pain aside and returned his focus to the hologram.

". . . suggest an alliance with the Covenant," Garvin was saying. *"And to prove our value in such a bargain, we offer you this intelligence as a gift: recently, you lost a vessel at Netherop under mysterious circumstances. That vessel was destroyed by the same unit that did the same to your ship at Chi Ceti IV a few months ago."*

Nizat's interest was already spiking as the hologram changed from an image of General Garvin to a human-shaped figure in bulky armor. The engagement at the world the humans called Chi Ceti IV had been the subject of much speculation among his staff officers. A dispatch sent during a lull in the battle had expressed the confidence of the *Unrelenting*'s shipmaster that, after a fierce initial engagement, the *Unrelenting* would emerge victorious and seek repairs at Zhoist, a supply world and staging area just beyond human space that had once been home to ten ancient Forerunner cities.

But the *Unrelenting* had never arrived, and at Netherop, the *Radiant Arrow* had simply vanished. If the human traitors were willing to tell Nizat what had befallen the two Covenant vessels, he was certainly willing to listen. He might even allow them to believe that it would save their own worlds . . . at least for a time.

The armored figure in the hologram spun slowly around, allowing Nizat and his companions an opportunity to inspect it from all angles, and then Garvin's voice continued.

"This is an elite special operations soldier known as a Spartan. Everything concerning Spartans—their origin, capabilities, number—is classified ultra-secret, so there's a lot we don't know about them. What we do *know, however, is that they are what happened to your vessels at Netherop and Chi Ceti IV.*

"And they're going to do the same thing to you at Biko—to the entire Covenant fleet."

The image changed back to Garvin's face.

"If you care to learn more, we'll be waiting in the abandoned ice quarry on Biko's third moon, Seoba. Send someone who can strike a deal. We have a little project we'd like your help with."

The image contracted into nothingness. Nizat absentmindedly began to spread and close his mandibles.

After a moment, he said, "I am uncertain that I understand."

"Understand *what*?" Survey said. "I should have made you wait for the translation disk."

Nizat glowered at him, then said, "That was not your decision to make."

Survey smacked his lips in outrage, but Nizat ignored him and turned back to 'Szatulai.

"Does this traitor—this General Garvin—does he truly expect us to perform a *service* for him?"

"I believe he hopes to strike a bargain," 'Szatulai said. "He warned us about these Spartans, and now he hopes we will feel obligated to provide something in return."

"Other than our favor?" Nizat asked.

'Szatulai turned his palms down, a gesture of bewilderment. "It is the way humans are," he said. "They have no understanding of the natural order of dominion."

"No, it is something else," Survey said. "You are underestimating him . . . the one you call General Garvin."

'Szatulai's helmet tipped sideways in a gesture of irritation, and Nizat feared the Minor Minister had finally grown too bold in his arrogance. How could he presume to know what the humans were thinking, when he did not even understand their words?

"Your Grace," Nizat said, "First Blade 'Szatulai has spent many cycles hiding on human worlds, learning their ways and studying their weaknesses. He understands how their minds work."

"And *I* understand the art of intrigue," Survey countered. "This General Garvin is using a classic ploy, saying he wants one thing when he is seeking another."

Nizat was doubtful. "What he wants is survival for his faction, and he is willing to betray the rest of his species to win it. That is what cowards do."

"And yet he made a point of showing you that armored soldier," Survey said. "Was that one of the Spartans the first blade mentioned?"

"It was." Nizat did not see where Survey's questions were leading, but the Minor Minister was right about this much: no one understood the art of intrigue better than the San'Shyuum. "You find that significant, Your Grace?"

"In a negotiation, everything is significant," Survey said. "First Blade 'Szatulai said this General Garvin 'warned' you about the Spartans. Am I to take it they are a danger to us?"

"So he claims." Nizat would have to revisit his evaluation of the Minor Minister; clearly, the San'Shyuum was shrewder than he seemed. "General Garvin says that the Spartans destroyed our ships at Chelav and Neska—the worlds they call Chi Ceti IV and Netherop."

Survey's eyes bulged. "*Did* they?"

Nizat thought for a moment, considering whether *two* of his vessels could have been destroyed by some more conventional method, perhaps by being surprised and vanquished so quickly there had been no time to dispatch an action report. He decided not. If the humans had ships *that* capable, they would not be holding them back from battle.

Finally Nizat said, "It seems the most likely explanation."

"Humans against ships?" Survey remained aghast. "How is that possible?"

"By sneaking aboard and planting a bomb," 'Szatulai said. "That is how the Silent Shadow would do it."

"Perilous, but possible," Nizat said. "But would it work against a fleet?"

'Szatulai thought for a moment, then said, "The Silent Shadow would never attempt such a thing. It would be impossible to infiltrate an entire fleet undetected. Too much can go wrong."

"Fleet?" Survey asked. "What is this talk of *fleets*?"

"General Garvin says the Spartans will be waiting for us at the human world Biko,"

"I do not know this Biko," Survey asked.

"We call it Borodan," Nizat said. "But the name is less important than what General Garvin claims the Spartans will do: attack the Fleet of Inexorable Obedience."

"Ah." Survey calmed and settled back in his chair, steepling his hands before his chin wattles. "Now I see."

Nizat glanced at 'Szatulai, but the first blade showed no sign that he understood either, and together they waited for the Minor Minister to enlighten them.

At last, Survey lowered his hands. "General Garvin is trying to motivate you. He wants you to kill the Spartans, so he claims they are a danger to the fleet."

"That is a sound motivation," Nizat said.

"If he is telling the truth, yes," said 'Szatulai. "But boarding an entire fleet? They would have to be mad."

"They have succeeded twice before," Nizat said. "Perhaps they were testing a new device—a personal cloak or a shield-lance—and now they are ready to deploy it on a larger scale."

'Szatulai offered a small bow. "I had not thought of that."

"It is only a possibility," Nizat said. "But one we must consider. You will assemble a *kai'd* of the fleet's best warriors to hunt down these Spartans, then go to the third moon—this Seoba—and learn how General Garvin and his traitors can help."

"And after I speak with them?"

Knowing that his answer would depend more on doctrine than strategy, Nizat turned to the Minor Minister.

"Do you remember what I showed you on the *kelguid*?" Nizat was referring to a holographic star chart, developed from technology reverse-engineered from the Forerunner equivalent. "The importance of establishing a forward operating base, so we can press our attack with speed?"

Survey nodded. "Of course," he said. "You are thinking that Borodan is the place?"

"Yes, provided we can capture it without a prolonged fight," Nizat said. "And if General Garvin wants to meet our representative there for the reason I believe, then perhaps *he* can make that possible."

"Indeed," Survey said. He turned to 'Szatulai. "For now, the fate of General Garvin and his traitors is yours to decide. Spare them for as long as it serves our cause."

"As you command," 'Szatulai said. "And when it does not?"

"They are human," Survey said. "You know what to do with them."

CHAPTER 10

1456 hours, March 18, 2526 (military calendar)
Launching Docks, Seoba Ice Quarry
Moon Seoba, Biko Planetary System, Kolaqoa System

The battle in the ice quarry had settled into an eerie ballet of light and ghosts, with muzzle flashes winking in every direction and wispy figures dodging through the fog. Heavy-weapon strikes blossomed near and far, and the comm channels delivered a shrill score of casualties screaming into John's helmet. Vacuum-suitable tracer rounds blazed past, sparking off the century-old mass driver and leaving thumb-size dimples in the giant acceleration tube through which Blue Team would climb five kilometers to the mountaintop. If all went well, they would reach the summit ten minutes ahead of the insurrectionist convoy and demolish the comm center before it could be repaired.

And then they would rain hell down on the enemy from above.

John led his three companions across the last dozen meters to the bottom of the decrepit mass driver, then dropped to a knee next to an ice-encrusted support pier. The massive bulk of an old gantry crane stood just fifteen meters away, blocking most of the fire from the enemy positions on the slopes ringing the dockyards. But there was a narrow angle of exposure straight up the mountain, running adjacent to the acceleration tube. There didn't seem to be any fire coming down the slot, but he signaled Linda-058 to watch it anyway. She was Blue Team's best marksman, and even with an MA5B assault rifle instead of her usual Series 99 sniper rifle, she was a deadly shot.

Kelly-087 knelt next to John beneath the acceleration tube and eyed the far side of the basin, while Fred-104 kept watch to their rear. Once everyone was in position, John rose to inspect the loading breech the team would use to enter the mass driver.

About twelve meters long by two meters wide, the opening was covered by a sliding hatch forced ten centimeters upward due to the ice flow spilling out of the acceleration tube. The lip was buried too deep in the ice to budge, so John used a length of thermite-carbon cord to burn a Spartan-size rectangle free. After pulling it away, he peered inside and found the acceleration tube about two-thirds full of ice. Above the ice there was a dark, semicircular cavity large enough to crawl through . . . maybe.

"We need a bigger flamethrower," Fred said over TEAMCOM. He was standing next to John, sweeping his lamp beam over the glassy surface inside the accelerator tube. In his left hand, he held the nozzle of a compact, vacuum-suitable version of the M7057 flamethrower, an M705 Incendiary Jet Tool fed by a tank-pack full of self-oxidizing fuel. "And more time."

"Did I ask for your input, Fred?"

"It must have slipped your mind," Fred said, completely undaunted by John's irritation. They had been training together since they were six, and they both knew that Fred had a duty to speak up when he saw a problem. "Too much can go wrong with this plan. Hamm is up to something."

John looked into the ice-filled accelerator tube again. The cavity was tighter than he had expected. They would have to crawl on their bellies, dragging the flamethrower's tank-packs behind them. It was going to take a while—but he didn't see how Hamm could have known that.

"You think?"

"She's an officer," Fred said. "And ODST on top of it. She didn't come up with this idea because she's trying to make Spartans look good."

Avery Johnson joined them on TEAMCOM. "Maybe she just wants to get the job done the best way she can think of."

John turned and saw a figure in black space assault armor—presumably Johnson—leap-soaring through the huge arch beneath the gantry crane. Beyond him, barely visible through the fog, the rest of Alpha Company was scattered along the edge of the dockyard, a ragged line of phantoms preparing to launch a feint that would keep the insurrectionists too busy fighting to wonder what might be happening inside the mass driver. The longer it took Blue Team to reach the top of the tube, the longer those troops would have to maintain the charade—and the more of them would likely end up dead.

Johnson came to rest next to the loading breech, then said, "What's the holdup? Alpha Company is ready to jump off."

"We were considering the optimal deployment of the I-JeT," John said, using the M705's nickname. "It's a little tighter in there than we expected."

Not quite tall enough to peer into the loading breech from a standing position, Johnson tapped his thrusters and rose a half meter off the surface.

"Doesn't look that tight to me."

"It would if you were wearing our armor," Fred said. He had turned away from the breech and was again watching the area to their rear. "No offense, Sarge, but you need to think on our scale."

Johnson glanced over at Fred and John. With fission reactors and detachable thruster packs mounted on the back plates of their armor, their torsos were more than eighty centimeters thick.

"Fair enough." He shut off his thrusters and dropped back to the surface. "I can probably talk the captain into sending First Platoon up the pipe and having you take their place on the feint. You'd make a better diversion anyway."

"Negative," John said. If Fred was right about Hamm being up to something sneaky, switching places would be the perfect way to spoil her plan—but being a diversion was the last thing John wanted. It would only reinforce Crowther's conviction that the Spartans didn't belong in the lead. "We'll make it work, Sergeant."

Fred and Johnson both turned to stare at him through their faceplates, and Kelly rose from where she had been kneeling. She glanced into the loading breech for about a second, then faced John.

"You know we're with you," she said. "But how are you going to do that? It's a five-kilometer belly-crawl, and we can only squirm so fast."

"We won't have to crawl for long," John said. "We're at the bottom of the accelerator. The ice won't get any thicker than it is here—and it will start thinning out in a hundred meters, when the tube starts up the slope."

"But we'll still have to squirm through an ice-packed tunnel for a hundred meters, using the I-JeT to melt through thick spots." Kelly turned to Johnson. "That's going to take time—maybe a lot of it. Can Alpha Company take the heat that much longer, Sergeant?"

"Not my call." Johnson kept his faceplate fixed on John. "And not the issue. If you can't beat that Civet convoy to the top of the mountain—"

"We'll beat it." John secured his assault rifle to the magnetic mount on the back of his Mjolnir. "Trust me."

Johnson was not convinced. "You'd better be sure. If you let that comm center go active, the only thing you're proving is that Crowther is right."

"About *what*?" Linda asked.

"That we're not ready," Fred said. "Haven't you noticed? He's spread us through the battalion like we're a bunch of newbies in need of blooding."

"I thought he was just trying to beef up his Black Dagger platoons," Linda replied.

"By using us as *support*?" Kelly snorted. "No way. He doesn't trust us."

"Something like that," John said. It would have been insubordinate to undermine the authority of a superior officer, so he didn't repeat Nyeto's theory about Crowther trying to protect the reputation of his Black Daggers. "But Sergeant Johnson has a point. We *have* to make this work—and that means no crawling."

John pushed himself up until his waist was at the edge of the opening he had cut into the breech-hatch and leaned forward. As soon as he turned his head to look up the acceleration tube, the Mjolnir's onboard computer anticipated what he wanted and activated his helmet lamp. The ice looked fairly smooth, the height of the cavity between its surface and the interior of the tube fairly even. He scrambled the rest of the way in and lay on his back, with his feet pointed uphill so that they would be the first to hit if he collided with something, then pulled himself forward until he was actually inside the tube.

His faceplate was just centimeters from the top, and his shoulders were pressed tight to the sides. John couldn't see his feet—he was resting on the fission reactor that sat behind his shoulder blades, and the thruster pack mounted beneath it would be the first thing to hit anything sticking above the surface of the ice.

No good.

"John," Fred said. The motion tracker on John's HUD showed Fred standing at the loading breech, no doubt looking up the tube at the top of John's helmet. "What the hell are you doing?"

"Not sure yet."

John pushed himself back into the opening, then sat up, swung his legs around, and lay on his belly with his arms at his sides. Now he felt steady and he could see where he was going but if he hit anything, it would be with his head instead of his feet. Even worse, his hands would be pinned to his sides as soon as he entered the tube—a very bad way to join battle. He raised himself up, took his assault rifle off its mount, and placed it on the ice in front of him. He then realized he wouldn't be able to reach his equipment pouches either, and grabbed a coil of thermite-carbon cord.

He lay on his belly again, this time with his arms stretched in front of him, holding his assault rifle in one hand and the coil in the other.

"Yeah," he said. "This'll work."

"How?" Kelly asked. "All you can do is wriggle your butt and curl your toes. It'll take a year to crawl to the top that way."

"I didn't say anything about crawling," John said. "We're going to slide."

"Uphill?" Fred paused an instant, then pulled the I-JeT tank-pack off the magnetic mounts on his back and stepped over to the loading breech. "Ah. I'd have thought of that sooner or later."

"Thought of *what*?" Johnson asked.

"Come on, Sarge," Kelly said. She removed the SPNKR rocket launcher and extra barrels from the weapon mounts on the back of her armor. "You want to hang with Spartans, you gotta pay attention."

Johnson faced her for a moment, then finally seemed to realize how Blue Team intended to ascend the tube. He turned to John.

"Uhh . . . just take it easy. No need to play human cannonball." He looked at Fred. "And maintain your spacing. The last thing you need is a thruster jet igniting that tank-pack."

"Thanks for the reminder, Sarge," Fred said. "I've only had a thousand hours of demolitions training, so it probably wouldn't occur to me to avoid exposing combustible gas to open flame."

"We all get careless, son." Johnson's tone was wary, as though he could not quite decide whether to take Fred earnestly or berate him for being sarcastic. "You'd be smart to remember that, if you want to make it to my age."

"I'll remember, Staff Sergeant," Fred said. "Getting old and preachy is certainly better than the alternative."

"Damn right," Johnson said. He started back toward the gantry crane. "Get it done, Blue Team."

As soon as Johnson was gone, John began to issue orders.

"Linda, you're our observer and sniper cover. I know that MA5B you're stuck with is no Series 99, but do the best you can for as long as you can."

Inside John's helmet, Linda's status light winked green.

"Fred, you follow me, pushing the I-JeT in front," John continued. "If we hit a tight spot, I may need you to pass the nozzle up. Kelly, you bring up the rear with your SPNKR, extra barrels, and plenty of thermite-carbon cord in front. I don't want to engage from inside the tube—"

"Because that would be crazy," Kelly said.

"Right," John said. "But the choice may not be ours."

Fred and Kelly's status lights blinked green. John activated his exterior lamp and cringed at the cramped gullet ahead. Barely a meter high in the center, its frost-coated walls curved down to an icy bed studded with fist-size bumps. At the end of the beam, where the light dimmed into darkness, he could see a curtain of ice dangling halfway down into the passageway.

It was going to be a rough ride.

"See you at the top, everyone."

John had barely spoken before the Mjolnir's onboard computer sensed his intention and began to pulse his thruster jets. He accelerated slowly but steadily, his shoulders scraping along the walls and his helmet banging against the ceiling as he bounced over one bump after another.

The ice curtain grew more distinct as he drew close, and he fired a couple of rifle rounds to test its strength. The curtain shattered, and a sparkling cloud of frost crystals filled the tube.

"Blue Two beginning run," Fred said over TEAMCOM. "I have Blue Leader on motion tracker, maintaining twenty-meter separation."

"Affirmative." John passed through the cloud of frost crystals, and another ice curtain appeared in the dimness at the end of his lamp beam. "How's your visibility?"

"Zero," Fred replied. "You're leaving a fog bank in your wake."

"I was afraid of that." Between his thruster jets and the friction of his scraping armor, John was creating a lot of heat in the passage. In Seoba's trace atmosphere, that would turn ice directly into vapor. "I'll alert you to any obstacles I encounter."

Fred's status light winked green.

"Be advised, you're also having an effect outside the accelerator tube," Linda said. "As you advance, I see little ice plumes rising off the exterior."

Probably knocked loose by his shoulders and helmet banging against the walls. John bit back a curse, then asked, "How noticeable?"

"Very," Linda replied. "If you see the tube, you see the plumes. But it's hard to know what the enemy can see. Alpha Company has initiated the diversionary attack, and the whole mountainside is blanketed in fog."

"Acknowledged," John said. "Keep us updated."

"Then we're continuing as planned?" Kelly asked.

"Give me a second."

Anyone inside the accelerator tube was as good as dead if the enemy brought their heavy weapons to bear. But Blue Team was still the company's only hope of demolishing the insurrectionist comm center, and

John was probably halfway across the flat part of the run already. Once the tube started its uphill climb, in fifty meters, there would be a lot less ice inside. That would give him the room he needed to stop banging the walls. Besides, it would take John longer to turn back now.

He really had only one option left—go forward, and go faster.

"Blue Leader?" Kelly asked. "I'm ready to—"

"Negative," John said. "I'm already committed, but there's no reason to risk anyone else. You and Fred extract—"

"Fat chance," Kelly said. "Blue Three beginning run."

"Kelly—"

"Too late," Fred said. "Keep moving."

John instructed the onboard computer to pulse his thruster jets longer and more frequently. He shot forward and crashed through a second curtain of ice, his Mjolnir bouncing along so ferociously that he feared the system might activate the armor's protective lockdown system. He knew that outside in the dockyards, the rest of Alpha Company was arrayed along the basin perimeter, launching volley after volley of rockets and grenades. Where a reasonably safe opportunity existed, fire teams would be leapfrogging up the mountain, trying to make the attack appear sincere.

It was all just for show. Alpha Company would continue the barrage as long as they still had rockets and grenades, but with the enemy holding the high ground on three sides, the terrain was simply too unfavorable for the attack to have a realistic chance of stopping the Civets from reaching the damaged comm center.

If the insurrectionist commander was inexperienced and poorly trained, it would probably take ten minutes to realize the attack was a feint, and about ten more to guess the enemy's plan and bring some heavy weapons to bear on the accelerator tube. By then, Blue Team would already be on the mountain and planting charges around the comm center.

But if the insurrectionist commander was a good one—or if someone had reported the ice plumes rising off the lower part of the accelerator tube—then the rebels would already know what the Spartans were doing. The heavy weapons units would be moving into attack position, and John, Fred, and Kelly would be dead in about sixty seconds.

A bad way to end a friendship.

John crashed through a third ice curtain and saw the next one appear in the dimness ahead. Given their regular spacing, he assumed they formed beneath the electromagnetic rings that had once been used to pull ice capsules through the accelerator tube, but this one did not seem quite as pale or translucent as the others. In fact, as he continued to accelerate toward it, he realized that the dark parabola at its base was not the same kind of opening that he had seen at the bottom of the others.

It was a seam, where the ice bed met the frost-covered floor of the accelerator tube. And the only way that could happen was if the tube was running up an incline.

John tried to slow down and adjust his vector, but by the time the onboard computer responded and flipped the thruster nozzles around, he was already entering the transition. He managed to raise his arms and chin quickly enough to keep his weapons and head from striking first, then slammed his chest into the slope and ricocheted into the ceiling.

Linda's voice came over TEAMCOM. "John, I hope that was you."

"Yeah." John hit the tube floor again and bounced back toward the ceiling. "Blue Two, watch—"

"No kid-ding!"

"Be more careful," Linda said. "You're launching ice clouds ten meters high."

"Yes, ma'am."

John had finally decelerated enough to bring himself under control and was continuing up the passage. As he had hoped, this part of the accelerator tube had far less ice. There was a full meter between his back and the overhead, and about the same distance between his chest and the small ribbon of ice running along the floor. His thruster nozzles were angled slightly downward to help keep Seoba's weak gravity from pulling him down, but every ten meters or so, he still had to drop a leg and kick off to keep from sinking to the belly of the tube.

"Any hostiles moving into attack position?" he asked.

"None that I see," Linda said. "But I don't see much. The mountainside is all fog."

"The barrage still going on?"

"Slowing down," Linda said. "I think they're running out of grenades."

"Okay. Tell us more when you have it."

"Affirmative," Linda said. "I am moving up-slope now."

"No high-risk maneuvers," John said. "That's an order."

"How funny, coming from you," Linda said. "But acknowledged. I will do my very best to avoid getting killed."

The tube ahead suddenly filled with fog and crystals. He slowed at once and let himself drop to the floor, then used his thrusters to hold his position. He checked his chronometer and saw he had been in the tube for eight minutes—enough time to put him roughly two-thirds of the way up the mountain, at about the same elevation as the Civet convoy.

Recalling the heavy weapons mounted in the cargo beds of some of the vehicles, he shut off his lamp and continued to stare into the ice fog. It took only a few seconds to spot dozens of ivory-colored rays shining through the line of bullet holes that had been punched through the wall of the accelerator tube.

John looked to the opposite wall and saw a like number of rays beaming through a similar line of holes where the rounds had exited the tube. So, *not* small arms—probably a vehicle-mounted anti-aircraft gun similar to the ones that had shredded the Black Daggers during the initial deployment.

The motion tracker showed Fred approaching, with Kelly about twenty meters behind him. John switched his helmet lamp on again, then shined it down the passage so his location would be obvious even in the fog.

"Hold up," he said. "We have a Vulcan chewing up the tube just ahead."

Fred decelerated and dropped to a knee next to John, then watched as a new line of ivory-colored rays began to illuminate the fog near the belly of the tube.

"Good news is, they don't know where we are," Fred said.

"Bad news is, we've got to go through there," Kelly said, dropping in on John's other side. "Time to break out the SPNKR?"

John thought for a moment, then made a slicing sign with his hand. "Negative. That's what they're waiting for."

"How can you tell?" Fred asked.

"That's denial fire," John said. "They don't know where we are—they're just trying to keep us from advancing beyond there."

"And doing a fine job," Kelly said. "This new Mjolnir is good stuff, but even a titanium-alloy outer shell can't stop a twelve-seven depleted uranium round—much less a dozen of them."

"Which is why they're expecting us to attack the Vulcan," John said. "And the instant we open a firing hole for ourselves, they'll know exactly where we are—and hit us with the missile launcher that took out the *Ghost Star*."

"Okay, so how do we get past the Vulcan without taking it out?" Fred asked.

"That's the easy part," Kelly said. "Look at that fire pattern. They've got an amateur behind the triggers."

John looked forward again and saw that the third line of bullet holes was being drilled along the top of the tube.

"Exactly." He took his coil of thermite-carbon cord and outlined a ten-by-twenty-centimeter rectangle low on the tube wall. "He's predictable. When he goes back the other way—"

"We follow him," Fred said. He pointed at the thermite rectangle. "Is that what I think it is?"

"It is if you think that's where you're leaving the I-JeT."

"The convincer." Fred leaned the tank-pack against the rectangle and laid the nozzle atop it. "How much of a delay do you want for the thermite?"

John looked up the accelerator tube. They were still four or five minutes from the top, but he doubted the insurrectionists would wait that long before deciding their trick hadn't worked and start trying something else.

"Give it thirty seconds," John said. "That should give us enough time to clear."

"If you say so," Fred warily replied.

Fred prepared the fuse and clipped it to the thermite cord. John waited until a new line of holes began to appear in the wall, this time about two-thirds of the way down, then pushed off and hit his thrusters. He shot up the passage just a meter above the bullets zipping silently past, with Kelly and Fred close behind him.

Once they were safely past the danger zone, Fred said, "Thirty seconds from . . . now."

They continued up the tube in staggered formation, occasionally dropping a leg to kick off the floor and keep themselves aloft. Thirty seconds passed, and John glanced back down the tube. The ice fog was so thick he couldn't even see the flare of the thermite burn.

Nothing happened.

He wasn't sure what he had expected. They were already two

hundred meters from the decoy site, but it seemed like the flash of a missile strike should have been visible through even that much fog. Maybe the insurrectionists had missed the thermite burn and didn't realize a firing port had suddenly opened in the wall of the accelerator tube. Or maybe John had been completely wrong about their plan. That was one of the hazards of spending time with Dr. Halsey—you started to overthink things.

John gave up wondering and focused on getting to the top of the accelerator tube. The end was perhaps fifteen hundred meters ahead, a bright speck the size of a pinhead. Had it not been glowing pink with light reflected from Biko's atmosphere, it would have been indiscernible.

Then the speck vanished behind a veil of swirling ice crystals.

It took John a moment to realize what he was seeing—that the frost had suddenly leapt off the walls and was now obscuring the view ahead. There had been no boom or shockwave, because Seoba's atmosphere was too thin to carry sound or kinetic energy. But the accelerator tube itself had just shuddered beneath a tremendous impact, and when John glanced back to where they had left the I-JeT and its tank-pack, he saw a bright ball of orange flame floating in the fog.

So he had been right about the insurrectionist plan after all. They were just a little slow.

Linda's alarmed voice came over TEAMCOM. "Status Blue?"

"All fine," John said. "The detonation was part of the plan. Just a decoy."

"Glad to hear it." Linda's tone remained wary. "But continue with caution. Something strange is happening up there on the mountain."

"Strange how?"

"It is hard to see through this fog," Linda said. "But there are many explosions on the mountain near your decoy detonation. From my position, it looks like the whole slope is catching fire."

"Acknowledged," John said. "What is *your* position?"

"Under the accelerator tube, seven hundred meters above the dockyards." Linda paused, then added, "I am trying to move higher, but progress is slow. The path requires a lot of sweeping."

By *sweeping*, John knew, Linda meant sniffing out and killing enemy soldiers. As a sniper working alone, she would not want to risk leaving a mobile foe behind her.

"Understood," John said. "Hold position until we figure out what's going on here."

Once Linda had acknowledged the order, John and his companions damped their thrusters and dropped to the belly of the accelerator tube.

"Thoughts?" John asked.

"We started something with that I-JeT detonation," Kelly said. "Something the innies weren't expecting."

Innies was an ironic term for the insurrectionists, given that they wanted *out* of the Unified Earth Government, which had taken full military control over the previous Colonial Authority as the primary organizing body for humanity's growing interstellar footprint. For much of the 25th century, the Colonial Military Authority had been the policing arm that managed the stability of Earth's exosolar colonies, but when corruption began to surface two decades before the Covenant arrived, the UEG took a firm hold of the reins and the UNSC initiated full-scale efforts to stem the Insurrection. It was the innies whom John and his fellow Spartans had been created to destroy, and the one positive aspect he saw in the alien invasion was that it might persuade the insurrectionists to forsake their rebellion to stand with the rest of humanity against the Covenant.

Unfortunately, events on Seoba suggested the insurrectionists were not yet thinking along the same lines.

When Fred remained silent, John asked, "Fred? Anything to add?"

"You're not going to like it."

"Try me."

Fred sighed into his helmet mic, then said, "You remember when I said Lieutenant Hamm was up to something?"

"How could I forget?"

"I hate to brag, but . . ."

"Really?" John was already beginning to fume. If Fred was right—and he usually was—Hamm had sent Blue Team up the accelerator tube knowing they would be spotted and attacked while in an extremely vulnerable position. "*We* were the diversion?"

"Only one way to find out." Fred knelt against the side of the tube and pressed a rectangle of thermite cord to the wall, then glanced back at Kelly. "You might want to be ready with that SPNKR, in case I'm wrong."

"You're not wrong, but why not?" Kelly knelt behind him and pressed the SPNKR barrels to the rectangle he had outlined. "I'd really like to blow something up right now."

"As long as it's not Lieutenant Hamm," John said. "I want her for myself."

Avery Johnson's voice sounded over TEAMCOM. "You know I can hear you, right?"

"Affirmative," John said.

John gave Fred a thumbs-up, then looked away as Fred ignited the thermite cord. The interior of the tube flashed white, and a ten-by-twenty-centimeter chunk of steel fluttered out of the wall.

Kelly peered through the hole, then shifted position so she would be firing down the mountain, then finally lowered the SPNKR.

"Damn Daggers." She secured the firing safeties again and backed away from the firing port. "Always in the way."

John stooped down and peered out at the mountain. The ice-fog was as thick as a smoke screen, but a couple of hundred meters below he saw plumes of burning fuel boiling out of half a dozen crippled Civets, their shadowy hulks surrounded by flashing coronets as the ammunition inside cooked off. About halfway between the convoy's wreckage and the Spartans' position inside the tube, a ghostly line of dark-armored ODSTs was leapfrogging down the slope, pouring rockets and small-arms fire into the convoy wreckage.

John looked toward the mountaintop. The comm center was not visible from his position, but he could see a rising prowler silhouetted against Biko's swirling pink disk.

"I don't believe it," he said. "It was a prowler drop. Hamm lied about the availability."

"I told you," Fred said. "She's an officer."

"*And* ODST," Kelly said. She secured the SPNKR on her Mjolnir's weapon mount, then grabbed her assault rifle and turned up the tube. "If we hurry, maybe we can still blow the comm center while they're busy finishing off the convoy."

"Oh, boy," John said. "The consolation prize."

As they ascended the last kilometer to the end of the tube, John ran through all of the different comm channels assigned to Alpha Company and finally understood why Hamm's deception had slipped past him so completely. The rest of the company was operating on their assigned channels, but First Platoon had switched to the logistics channel. He was beginning to think that the lieutenant might be more of an enemy than the insurrectionists—maybe even the Covenant—but he wasn't sure what to do about the situation. Running a formal complaint up the chain of command would only lead to Crowther, who was—if anything—an even greater problem.

Maybe Staff Sergeant Johnson would have a suggestion.

Unless, of course, he was in on it too.

A few minutes later, Blue Team emerged from the acceleration tube to find that they would not even be the ones to destroy the comm center. A team of First Platoon Black Daggers was already inside planting charges—supervised by Lieutenant Hamm herself.

When Hamm saw John, Fred, and Kelly approaching, she stepped away from the building and came over to meet them. John did not salute, and she did not seem surprised.

"Where's Blue Four?" Hamm demanded. "She didn't get—"

"She's fine, ma'am," John said. "We use Linda on long cover."

"Glad to hear it." Hamm's helmet tipped up and down as she looked Blue Team over, taking them in from head to foot. "And it looks like you three came out unscathed. Well done."

"Well done?" John didn't even try to keep his bitterness out of his voice. "You played me. We were decoys."

Hamm braced her hands on a pair of ammo pouches and leaned back, turning her faceplate up to look at him.

"I needed to get that missile launcher looking in another direction, so Nyeto could do a prowler drop without losing another bat." *Bat* being the nickname for a prowler. She reached out and flicked a gloved finger against the abdomen of John's outer shell. "In these tank suits, I figured you Spartans had a better chance of surviving than anyone else."

John was a bit taken aback. He hadn't really expected her to have a solid reason for the assignment—but having a solid reason was no excuse for deliberately deceiving him.

"That makes sense," he said. "But you still lied to me—and that put my people at unnecessary risk."

"That's right, soldier." Hamm rose on her toes, pushing her faceplate a few centimeters closer to John's, then thumped his Mjolnir with her finger again. "I guess that's what happens when you don't obey orders. It's one shitshine after another."

CHAPTER 11

0816 hours, March 19, 2526 (military calendar)
Assembly Chamber 4L430, Abandoned Habitat, Seoba Ice Quarry
Moon Seoba, Biko Planetary System, Kolaqoa System

With portable stand-lights flanking a folding conference table and a UNSC flag hung on rough polycrete-coated walls, the subsurface assembly chamber looked more like the venue of an impromptu court-martial than of an after-action debriefing. John-117 advanced to the front of the room and presented himself to the task force commander, then selected a seat on the respondent's side of the table, as far as possible from Nelly Hamm. Like all ODST personnel present, she wore plain grays—a fire-retardant working uniform with a four-pocket shirt and cargo pants. On her collar tips, she now sported the double bars of a Marine Corps captain—a field promotion that could only mean Alpha Company's previous captain had been killed during yesterday's assault on the quarry dockyards.

John hated to see that, and not only because Hamm had it in for him. Captain Zelos Cuvier had impressed him as an intelligent, commonsense commander who cared more about getting the job done than protecting his turf. The Spartans had only been integrating with the regular military for a few months, but John had already come to understand how rare that was.

Once John was seated, Captain Ascot folded her hands on the table and leaned forward, her gaze drifting between John and Captain Hamm. Situated between Dr. Halsey and Colonel Crowther, Ascot wore naval utilities in star-pattern camouflage—a not-so-subtle reminder that *she* was the task force commander, which meant this was an ONI operation first, UNSC second.

John hoped it also meant she had a soft spot for Spartans.

"I'll begin by reminding everyone here that this informal debriefing is *not* a disciplinary action," she said. "Our purpose is not to assess blame, but merely to determine what went wrong with Ghost Flight's drop on the dockyards yesterday."

"Who says anything went wrong?" Halsey asked. "The dockyards were captured in less than an hour."

"And Alpha Company took *fifty-two* KIAs," Crowther said. "Including Captain Cuvier and his staff. That's a thirty-two percent casualty rate. The rest of the battalion took six percent, without losing any captains."

"Taking out the comm center was a mission-critical assignment," Avery Johnson said. He was seated at the end of the table, adjacent to Crowther. "To do it, Alpha Company had to drop blind into a kill zone against an enemy who was expecting us. We're lucky we didn't lose *seventy*-two percent."

"The enemy was *expecting* us?" Halsey said. "How do we know that?"

"The bunkers," John said. "That's not something you can put together on the fly. It takes hours to dig in and camouflage like that."

"Doesn't mean they were expecting us," Nyeto said. "Just that they were ready when we showed up."

"You weren't in the drop bay when the jump hatches opened, when those Vulcans started firing," Hamm said. "It sure *felt* like they were expecting us."

"And yet you dismounted anyway," Crowther said. "Explain that."

"Not my idea." Hamm looked down the table toward John. "Spartan-117 acted on his own."

Crowther let his gaze slide toward John. "And how did *that* happen from the back of the drop bay?"

"I wasn't in the back." John was pretty sure Crowther already knew the answers to his questions, but if a colonel asked, you answered. "When First Platoon started taking casualties, I moved forward to assist."

"With the casualties?"

"With *stopping* them," John said. "As the designated fire-support soldier, I carried the platoon's heavy weapons. Upon reaching the jump hatch, I observed Vulcan fire coming from six camouflaged bunkers. It was clear that Alpha Company would not be able to complete its dismount until those positions were eliminated."

"So, naturally, you reported your observation to the platoon commander." Crowther's tone was sarcastic. "Because, even after leaving your assigned position, *that* would have been the proper way to handle a battlefield intelligence report."

"Captain Hamm was tending to a casualty," John said.

"I'd like to clarify that," Hamm said. "I was tending a casualty because Spartan-117 had dumped one into my lap. I believe he was trying to keep me busy."

"Don't be silly," Halsey said. "You can't possibly know someone else's motivations."

"We can find out," Ascot said. She looked to John. "Spartan, why *did* you hand a casualty to your platoon leader?"

"Because I wanted to assess the situation," John said. "And to do that, I needed to keep Captain Hamm busy for a minute."

Nyeto sighed and pressed his palms to his brow.

Ascot looked to him. "Is something wrong, Commander Nyeto?"

"You call this a debriefing?" Nyeto flung a hand toward John. "This kid saved our asses at the dismount, and you're hanging him out to dry? Are you crazy?"

"That's not our intent here," Crowther said. "We're trying to determine why Alpha Company's casualties were so high."

"Your casualties were high because you ordered a hot dismount without recon," Nyeto shot back. "What the hell did you expect?"

"What I *didn't* expect was a petty officer to start freelancing." Crowther was speaking between clenched teeth now, and he turned his glare directly on John. "His team was carrying most of the heavy weaponry, so when they went, the rest of the company had to follow—and the Black Daggers don't have titanium-alloy power armor."

The anger drained from Nyeto's face, and even John began to see how he might have forced Alpha Company's hand by ignoring his platoon commander's abort order.

"I was just trying to support the boots on the ground, sir," John said. "I didn't expect the rest of Alpha Company to follow."

"What did you *think* we'd do?" Hamm demanded. "Leave you alone down there?"

"That's what you *were* doing," John said. "Alpha Company already had a dozen troopers down there, being chewed apart by the Vulcans."

"And Ghost Flight was getting ready to come around for a missile run," Ascot said. "Until *you* decided to do something else, Petty Officer."

John did not know how to respond. He had been trained to take the initiative and operate independently, but he was beginning to think that those qualities weren't valued in the 21st. Worse, it seemed to him that officers like Hamm and Crowther actually considered them liabilities.

Hoping to find some hint of support—or at least an indication of how he should respond—John looked toward Avery Johnson. But the staff sergeant was deep in thought, his gaze fixed on Nyeto, his brow lowered in contemplation.

When John made no attempt to defend himself, Nyeto stepped in. "Look, maybe he got excited—"

"Oh, it wasn't excitement," Hamm said. "He knew exactly what he was doing."

"And he got the job done," Nyeto said. "Maybe not the way you would have done it, but cut the kid some slack, okay? I'll bet you took a few shortcuts when you were that young."

Hamm's eyes narrowed. "I'm twenty-two," she said. "Just three years older than Spartan-117."

Nyeto smirked and started to correct her, then suddenly looked away. Everyone fell silent and watched Nyeto with expectant expressions, and John knew better than to hope the slip had gone unnoticed.

Crowther asked, "You were going to say something, Commander?"

"No, it was nothing," Nyeto said. "I just thought a captain in your outfit would be a little older."

"Captain Hamm graduated first in her class at Luna OCS *and* in ODST school," Crowther replied. "She's been a Black Dagger for three years. And *she's* the one who salvaged the mess at the dockyards yesterday. Does her promotion meet with your approval now?"

"Sure thing." Nyeto caught Hamm's eye. "I didn't mean any offense. You just look, uh, mature for twenty-two."

Hamm gave him a frosty glare. "No offense taken." Her voice grew ten degrees cooler as she added, "Sir."

"Glad to hear it." Nyeto looked back toward Crowther. "Now maybe we can talk about what *really* went wrong with yesterday's dismount."

"I'm dying to hear your thoughts," Crowther replied. "But since you've broached the subject of age . . . your reaction a few moments ago has made me curious. Is there something about Spartan-117 that we should know?"

Nyeto shrugged. "I don't really know what you mean."

"Commander . . . how old is he really?"

"I don't see what John's age has to do with this debriefing," Halsey said. "Perhaps we should stick to the subject at hand."

"John-117's judgment is at issue in this discussion," Ascot said. "And his age certainly has a bearing on that. If he's not actually nineteen, I'd like to know his true age—and why the DOB in his personnel jacket would have been falsified."

"All I can tell you is that the true age of any Spartan is compartmentalized, and classified Top Secret Level One," Halsey said. "But, I assure you, a few years at the Luna OCS doesn't compare to John-117's training. His tactical judgment is beyond reproach."

Ascot did not quite roll her eyes. "I need more than the assurances of a proud mother, Dr. Halsey." She turned to Nyeto. "And I won't be kept in the dark by a specious top-secret designation. Commander Nyeto, have you been read-in on the Spartans' ages by a proper authority?"

"Not exactly."

"But you *do* know John-117's real age?"

Nyeto sighed and shot a glance toward John. "Sorry, son."

Halsey's jaw fell. "John, you didn't tell—"

"Of course not, ma'am," John said. "He had a friend who trained against us on Reach. Commander Nyeto worked out our age from there."

Ascot's glare remained fixed on Nyeto. "Is that so?"

"It was just scuttlebutt," Nyeto said. "I didn't realize he was breaching security, or I would have shut him down."

"We'll worry about your friend's security violations later," Ascot said. "Just give me the math."

Nyeto looked at the tabletop and sighed. "I had a buddy who used to get his unit's butt rightly kicked when training against a bunch of eight-year-old 'kidmandos' on Reach," he said. "He was bellyaching about it seven years ago, so when you add it up . . . the kidmandos would be about fifteen now."

Halsey leaned forward, placing her upper body between Ascot and Nyeto, then asked, "And what makes you think these *kidmandos*—as you call them—are my Spartans?"

It was a clever move, John realized, designed to make Nyeto feel shielded from Ascot and reinforce the out she was giving him. From what he had said so far, there was no way he could be certain the children his friend described had grown up to become Spartans.

But, apparently, Nyeto was not comfortable deceiving his superior. He merely nodded at John, then said, "Spartan-117 has a lot of skills, but lying isn't one of them. I had him pegged as one of those kidmandos the first time he denied it."

"So figuring this out was just an accident?" Avery Johnson asked. He was staring down the length of the table, watching Nyeto with unblinking attention. "Just one of those things that comes up in a conversation?"

"Yeah." Nyeto met Johnson's gaze evenly. "How'd *you* find out?"

"Who says I did?" Avery flashed a tight smile that left John wondering what he was missing between the two men. "I'm not even sure I believe *you*."

Nyeto shrugged. "Fine with me," he said. "I didn't want to tell anyone their age anyway."

"But you *did*." Halsey looked around the table, then added, "And it's an unfortunate disclosure that can't leave this room."

"I can see why you wouldn't want it to," Crowther said. "But deploying child soldiers is a violation of about six articles of the Uniform Code of Military Justice. When the Judge Advocate General hears about this, you're going to confinement for a very long time, Doctor."

"The Spartans are the UNSC's best hope of stopping the aliens," Halsey said. "Do you really think my superiors will *let* the Judge Advocate General hear about this?"

"Is that a threat, Dr. Halsey?"

"All right, that's enough." Ascot shot them each a warning scowl, then turned her gaze on John. She spent several moments studying his two-meter bulk—no doubt trying to reconcile his size and physical development with that of a fifteen-year-old boy. Finally, she exhaled and seemed to conclude there might be some aspects of the SPARTAN program she was better off not knowing. "I'll discuss the legal aspects with Admiral Stanforth personally. But outside this room, no one breathes a word about the Spartans' age. Clear?"

Crowther's face reddened, but he said, "Very well—as long as I'm allowed to take it into consideration when making assignments. I won't be a party to sending children into combat."

"They're *not* children," Halsey retorted. "That should be rather obvious from looking at them."

"Nevertheless . . . Colonel Crowther will have autonomy over his personnel assignments." Ascot paused, then added, "I'm not quite sure what you've involved us in, Dr. Halsey. But until I am, we'll be playing this by the book."

"And losing the war."

Halsey's voice was bitter, and John shared her sentiment. The Spartans were being excluded from the operation—not because John had made a mistake, but because their true age gave Crowther an excuse to sideline them. He just hoped Halsey was wrong about the consequences. Humanity's destruction seemed a high price to pay for one man's vanity.

Ascot's reply was surprisingly calm. "I hope you're wrong, Dr. Halsey, but it's my decision to make."

"Then you should reconsider."

"I won't."

Halsey sighed. "Of course not."

John's stomach sank, and he sneaked a glance toward Johnson, half expecting to find a gleam in the sergeant's eye that suggested he had already figured a way around Ascot's decision. Instead, all John saw were arched brows and soft eyes, a battle-hardened soldier watching him as if John had just taken a Vulcan round to the gut, as if all that remained was the bleeding out.

It was a look of pity.

John snapped his gaze away. That was the last thing he wanted from Avery Johnson. Hector Nyeto seemed to be the only soldier in the room who respected him and his Spartans, who could see beyond their age and enhancements to what they really *were.*

But Hector Nyeto did not command Task Force Yama. Halima Ascot did, and if she wanted the Spartans to stand down, then that's what would happen. They were soldiers—even if only three people in the room actually realized it—and soldiers obeyed orders.

Just when John was starting to think the long silence meant the meeting was drawing to a close, Dr. Halsey gave another disgruntled sigh and looked past Ascot to address Crowther.

"Now that you've secured your scapegoat, Colonel," she said, "perhaps we should examine the underlying reason for Alpha Company's high casualty rate?"

"By all means, Doctor." Crowther's tone was surprisingly open. "The initial situation certainly wasn't John's fault."

"The initial situation was a mess." Avery Johnson's tone was reasonable, but firm. "Alpha Company was *going* to take casualties dropping into that. There's no way around it."

"Precisely." Halsey nodded toward Nyeto. "As the lieutenant commander pointed out earlier, whether or not the insurrectionists were expecting us, they were certainly *ready.*"

"I'm not sure I see the distinction," Ascot said.

"*Expecting* means they knew *we* specifically were coming," Nyeto said. "Somebody would have had to tell them before we entered slipspace."

"That's hardly impossible," Johnson said. "The innies have spies everywhere."

"Which is why we take extraordinary precautions with movement orders," Ascot said. "The number of people who knew we were headed to Biko was substantial. But the number who knew we intended to stage out of the Seoba ice quarry? I can count that number on my hands."

"*I* didn't even know myself until we were in-system," Nyeto said. "And the orders came with a comm-lockdown directive. No way anyone on Seoba knew we were coming."

It seemed to John the discussion was focusing on the wrong thing. Even if the insurrectionists *had* known that Task Force Yama intended to stage out of the ice quarry, it didn't make any sense for them to be there when the prowlers arrived. Alpha Company might have had a 32 percent casualty rate, but between KIAs and captures, the insurrectionists had suffered a 100 percent rate. If they had known a task force full of crack space-assault troops was headed their way, why would they have stuck around to take that kind of punishment?

Simple answer: They wouldn't have.

But John kept his thoughts to himself. He was keenly aware that most of the people at the table now saw him as nothing more than a supersized version of the "kidmando" from back on Reach, and he didn't want to say anything that might contribute to that impression—at least, not until it grew clear they couldn't figure out the situation themselves.

"What about intercepts?" Hamm asked. "Anything there to suggest they knew we were coming?"

Ascot shook her head. "They were keeping their comm traffic light," she said. "We intercepted a few unattributed comm clicks and some encrypted line-of-sight messages, mostly from a few supply transports they were using as recon boats. It's obvious they were mapping Guards positions, but there was no alert from the quarry about us. Just a couple of standard acknowledgments and a directive about the next surveillance target."

"So when *did* they realize an attack was coming?" Halsey asked.

"If they were good, when we started to jam their outgoing communications," Ascot said. "Their operators nearly broke through before Commander Nyeto downed the antenna, so I'd say they were decent. They probably sounded the alert right after we started jamming."

"Perhaps you could put that in chronological terms," Halsey suggested. "For those of us who *aren't* intimately familiar with the timing of an insertion run."

Ascot smiled. "Of course. The jamming would have started on final approach, about five minutes out."

Halsey looked surprised. "That little?"

"The sooner the jamming starts, the longer you need to hold it before taking out the comm facilities," Ascot said. "Five minutes is about the maximum you can count on."

"More to the point, it's plenty of time for a unit to reach its gunnery positions," Crowther said. "But only if those positions are preassigned and the personnel have been well drilled."

"Of course, five minutes *isn't* enough time to build those bunkers," Hamm added. "Or even to move the Vulcans into position. Those defenses were prepared long before the innies knew we were coming. Probably even before *we* knew we were coming."

Silence filled the room, and John tried to be patient and avoid looking bored. They were thinking from the top down—like the officers and intelligence operators they were—and he had studied enough planning histories to know that their approach usually produced good results . . . sooner or later.

"What about *after* the jamming started?" Halsey asked. "How soon did they start firing on you?"

"Right after we launched against the comm center," Nyeto said.

"And it was fast. Our second missile hadn't even hit before they opened up with those Vulcans."

Ascot frowned. "They didn't fire on you during approach?"

"That's what I just said," Nyeto said. "Not until we launched."

"Then why did you miss?"

Nyeto flushed and dropped his chin. "We didn't *miss*, exactly," he said. "We just didn't score a direct hit."

"And that's a miss," Crowther said. What he didn't say—though his tone made it clear—was that Nyeto's miss had cost the lives of a lot of Alpha Company soldiers. "Why was there no second run?"

"There *was* a second run, when we came back to finish the drop." Nyeto was starting to sound testy. "That's when we lost the *Ghost Star*."

Another pause settled over the table, and John began to wonder how long it would take them to reach the obvious conclusion.

The insurrectionists had been expecting *someone*—just not the UNSC.

"John?"

John blinked and looked down the table to see Avery Johnson leaning back in his chair, tugging at his mustache and appearing expectant.

"Sorry, Sergeant," he said. "I didn't realize I had missed something."

"Relax, son. You didn't miss anything."

John was really beginning to hate that—being called *son*—but nothing good would come of complaining about it. They would probably just dismiss him as a moody teenager. He swallowed his irritation and sat a little straighter in his chair.

"What can I do for you, Sergeant?"

"Why don't you tell us what *you* think," Johnson said. "You were in the thick of things, same as me. Did it seem like they were expecting us?"

"Not *us*," John said. He wasn't sure what to make of the prodding. Was Johnson still feeling sorry for him—or trying to give him a chance to win Ascot's confidence? "They had to realize they couldn't win. If they had known we were coming, they would have been long gone when we arrived."

Only Johnson's eyes did not light with realization. He was infantry—he understood what happened when someone started a fight they couldn't win. They got killed.

"But you know that as well as I do, Sergeant."

Johnson shrugged. "Never hurts to confirm your range."

It was an old sniper saying, a reminder to check your assumptions before taking the shot.

"You seem certain of your assessment, John." Crowther sounded more intrigued than challenging. "But maybe the enemy thought they *could* win?"

John shook his head. "Sorry, sir, but no. If they had built the bunkers to defend against *us*, they would've had to know we were coming before we entered slipspace. And if they had *that* kind of intelligence, they would have known we were coming heavy and they were going to die. So why stay?"

"I'm afraid I have to agree with John on this, sir," Hamm said reluctantly. She did not quite sound like she was in physical pain, but close. "They had nothing to gain by staying."

Crowther nodded, but kept his attention fixed on John. "Go on, son."

John let out a breath, then continued, "What if they were waiting for someone else?"

Crowther nodded more vigorously. "That makes sense," he said. "The rebels we captured yesterday are from all over—Eridanus Secundus, Jericho VII, Venezia, even Reach. Maybe they were waiting for more reinforcements."

"Yeah," Nyeto said. "Like maybe from Gao."

"Gao?" Ascot asked. "Isn't that where you're from?"

"That's right," Nyeto said. "Place is filthy with insurrectionists."

"So what are they doing on Seoba?" Halsey's question had a rhetorical ring to it. "Not the Gaos in particular—*all* of them?"

"This is bad." Johnson was no longer leaning back in his chair. In fact, he looked like he was about ready to spring out of it. "It's the coup attempt. The insurrectionists are unifying their command."

The officers exchanged uneasy glances, and Nyeto seemed more shaken than anyone, with a queasy expression and beads of sweat forming on his brow.

"But they've *got* to know the aliens are glassing Etalan." As Nyeto spoke, a terrible thought—an unbelievable possibility—was forming in John's mind. "Why take Biko when it's next—"

"Wait," John said. "I know who the innies were expecting."

All eyes turned toward him, and Crowther said, "How long are you going to keep us in suspense, son?"

John frowned. "I wish . . ." *. . . you'd all stop calling me* son. He caught himself, then said, "Never mind. They were expecting the Covenant."

"They were going to ambush—" Crowther stopped in midsentence, and his brow rose in astonishment. "*No.* They were going to *meet* the aliens?"

"That's my guess." John was beginning to think he might have a chance of winning over Crowther after all. "It explains why they're mounting a coup attempt at such a bad time. Surrendering Biko to the Covenant is the only way to save it—and overthrowing the chancellor is the only way to surrender it."

"What if it isn't *surrendering*?" Ascot asked. "What if it's an *offer*?"

"An offer?" said Crowther.

"Exactly," Ascot said. "We're here because we know that if the aliens bypass Biko, they're leaving an operating base in their rear. We can also assume their logistics lines are getting pretty long, so they could use a staging base of their own. What if the insurrectionists are trying to strike a deal to give it to them?"

John went cold inside. "Who would do that?" he asked. "Who would form an alliance against their own species?"

"Maybe the insurrectionists don't see it that way," Johnson said. "Maybe they see it as saving themselves from *us*."

"That's crazy," Hamm said. "The Covenant will butcher them, same as the rest of us."

"Agreed," John said. "But would *they* know that?"

Crowther shook his head, then pointed a finger at John. "You're right, son," he said. "They wouldn't."

Son. John gritted his teeth and said nothing.

"And an alliance *would* save them . . . for a while," Ascot added. "If the aliens are as smart as we think, they'll know a good intelligence source when they see one. They'll milk it for as long as they can."

A chill seemed to settle over the room, and their collective eyes dropped to the table as they considered what came next, contemplating the inescapable danger and coming to the same terrible conclusion.

At last John said what everyone was thinking.

"If we're right about this, the alien delegation must be coming soon." He paused to swallow, then continued, "And we need to ambush it. We need to make the Covenant think the insurrectionists set them up."

The nodding in agreement started at the other end of the table with Hamm, then Johnson, and down the far side of the table, Crowther, Ascot, and Halsey, and finally Nyeto, who said: "You know what that will mean for Biko, right? They'll glass it in retaliation."

"They'll glass it anyway, when they're ready," Ascot said. "And until they are, the rebels will be helping them glass one loyal world after another."

"It's a simple equation," Halsey said. "One world now, or a hundred later."

"Then we go with John's suggestion," Ascot said. "We ambush the Covenant delegation."

"With one proviso," Crowther said. "We can't abandon the original operation. We divide our force and still board the fleet."

"Of course," Ascot said, rising. "That goes without saying."

When Crowther smiled and started to get up, John saw his chance and also stood.

"Colonel Crowther," he said. "You're going to—"

John stopped as a chorus of high-pitched alarms began to chirp from the tacpads everyone wore on their wrists. He glanced at his own and felt his throat go dry.

Vanishing Point REPORTS:

COVENANT FLOTILLA INBOUND

FIVE VESSELS CORVETTE CLASS EQUIVALENT

ETA 22 MINUTES

"Damn," Avery Johnson said. "That's some delegation."

"And not one I want catching us on the surface." Ascot started around the table, already speaking into her tacpad microphone. "Load all prowlers and scramble, seventeen-minute maximum."

Nyeto and Johnson turned to follow her out the door, but Crowther remained where he was, regarding John with a cocked brow.

"You had something to say, John?"

John glanced at Halsey, then swallowed hard and nodded.

"Yes, sir. You're going to need all the Black Daggers you can get for the boarding action, and the alien ambush would be the perfect assignment for the Spartans."

"It's quite true, Colonel," Halsey said. "This is exactly the sort of thing I created them for."

Crowther shot her an uncomfortable frown, then started around the opposite end of the table toward John.

"I appreciate the offer, son," he said. "But you're fifteen."

John's heart sank, and he had to let his chin drop as he watched Crowther approach. "I understand, sir."

Crowther stopped a step away, looking for a moment as though he wanted to reach up to lay a hand on John's shoulder, then seemed to realize how awkward that would be and simply motioned him to follow.

"Besides, I have another assignment for the Spartans."

"Of course, sir." John knew better than to hope it would be important. Crowther probably wanted them to carry his bags or something. "Whatever you need."

"I knew I could count on you." They reached the assembly chamber door, and Crowther turned to face John. "When we took the quarry yesterday, we captured more than three hundred insurrectionists."

"You want my Spartans to babysit prisoners, sir?"

Crowther allowed himself a small grin. "I was going to say *guard*," he replied. "But look at it however you like—as long as you get them all loaded aboard an internment transport. We can't have any falling into Covenant hands. The last thing we want is someone telling the enemy what really happened here. Is that clear?"

"Yes, sir," John said. "I think we can handle it."

"I'm sure you can, son," Crowther said. "I'll ask Captain Ascot to assign a prisoner transport."

"Very good." John raised his hand to salute, then said, "Colonel Crowther . . . with all due respect, sir, I'd like to make a request."

"What is it?"

"Please stop calling me *son*," John said. "I've been a soldier for so long I can't even remember what my father looked like, but I'm pretty sure you aren't him."

Crowther's eyes went wide—then he nodded. "Very well, Spartan—consider it done." He raised a hand and returned John's salute. "I think you've earned that much."

CHAPTER 12

Ninth Age of Reclamation
34th Cycle, 41 Units (Covenant Battle Calendar)
Bloodstar Flotilla, Intrusion Corvette *Sacred Whisper*
Orbital Approach, Third Moon, Planet Borodan, Kyril System

They looked like *mulegs* leaping from the head of a bald human, those dark specks rising from the surface of the pale moon the humans called Seoba. Silhouetted against the pink disk of the planet Borodan, they rose in singles and pairs and arced away, so tiny and swift that it was easy to think they were a trick of the eye. But after watching five of them vanish into nothingness in as many units, Tel 'Szatulai knew what he was seeing.

Enemy vessels, departing the site of his rendezvous with the human traitors.

'Szatulai remained in the forward observation blister, noting how his mandibles had begun to clench and the way his two hearts now pounded in counterpoint. Such responses were unworthy of a First Blade of the Silent Shadow, and he could not even say whether they rose from fear or anger. He would meditate on this failure later, riding the spine of the ship in his contemplation sphere. But for now, it was enough to perceive the reactions and give them their space. That would quell the power of his control-hungry emotions and leave him free to focus.

Which he now felt prepared to do.

Without looking away from the observation blister, 'Szatulai rattled his mandibles to draw the crew's attention, then spoke in a gentle tone. "Summon the shipmaster."

The bridge of the *Sacred Whisper* quieted. 'Szatulai heard his order repeated four times as it was passed back to the shipmaster; then a set of footsteps began to click up the deck toward his position. The gait was easy and confident, and 'Szatulai was troubled by that. Given the failure of the sensor readers to report the five—now *six*—vessel launches that he had watched with his own eyes, the shipmaster should have been ashamed of his crew's performance and fearful of the consequences.

Perhaps the fault lay with 'Szatulai himself. A common—though incorrect—belief held that a member of the Silent Shadow would not kill a fellow Sangheili who had looked into his eyes. Thinking that the crew of his new flagship would perform better if they felt secure in his presence, 'Szatulai had chosen to play to their superstition by not wearing his helmet aboard the *Sacred Whisper.* And now here was the shipmaster himself, approaching in complacence despite the shortcomings of his crew.

'Szatulai hoped it had not been a mistake to put everyone on board at ease. He would meditate on that as well.

The shipmaster paused at the threshold of the observation blister and started a polite mandible-rattle to draw attention to his presence—then let out a hiss of surprise as a seventh speck rose and arced away from Seoba.

"What is that?"

'Szatulai turned to face the shipmaster. "What does it look like, 'Budyasee?"

"An enemy vessel." A stocky, block-faced Sangheili with blunt-ended mandibles, Hulon 'Budyasee was half-again 'Szatulai's sixty years and almost twice his girth. "But there has been no report from the readers."

"It is good that you perceive the problem," 'Szatulai said. "I am not sure your second is ready to assume command."

'Budyasee's eyes bulged, and he turned back toward the bridge. "Summon 'Gusonee and 'Terib—"

'Szatulai silenced 'Budyasee with a touch. "Will we learn more by bringing the readers to us, or by going to their station?"

"Going to their station," 'Budyasee replied. "If the problem is in their equipment, I will see it there."

"Then let us proceed wisely," 'Szatulai said. "I am not some San'Shyuum minister who must be served before our cause."

'Budyasee's mandibles parted in shock, though the way his head canted suggested he was not quite sure whether 'Szatulai had meant to slur their San'Shyuum leaders or honor them. After a breath, he managed to close his mandibles and turn toward the rear of the bridge.

"As you prefer, Blademaster."

The shipmaster led the way through a maze of control consoles and equipment stands to the back of the bridge, where a tactical hologram of Seoba's side of the Borodan planetary system floated above a projection pad surrounded by ten data-collection lecterns. At each lectern stood a reader, his eyes focused on a crystal display screen filled with a melange of alphanumeric codes and vector symbols that they used to plot images on the hologram.

Behind the readers were the two obedientaries who oversaw the plotting operation. Normally they would be standing opposite one another, each supervising a team of five readers, but 'Budyasee's aborted summons had brought them together to discuss what kind of trouble they might have fallen into.

'Budyasee went straight to the obedientaries and began questioning them about unreported vessels fleeing Seoba. 'Szatulai circled the tactical hologram, occasionally peering over a reader's shoulder at his display screen, but mostly pondering the thousands of images the hologram *did* contain.

Borodan itself was surrounded by a shell of orbital traffic—thousands of satellites, hundreds of vessels both military and civilian, dozens of manufacturing stations, and a handful of shipyards. A steady stream of cargo drones moved between the manufacturing stations and the two metal-heavy moons currently on the *Whisper*'s side of the planet, and several passenger ships were climbing out of its gravity well in preparation for transition to slipspace. But, aside from a shell of reconnaissance boats in ultra-high picket orbits and a few dozen large military vessels waiting in rapid-response geosynchronous orbits, 'Szatulai saw no sign that the humans were preparing for battle. And he saw *nothing* moving toward Seoba.

That was to be expected—or at least hoped for. Even the Covenant's best masking systems were only about 80 percent effective, so there was always the possibility of detection. But 'Szatulai's small flotilla of intrusion corvettes had emerged from slipspace well beyond detection range and engaged active camouflage long before approaching the picket orbits, so he saw no reason to believe the situation at Borodan was anything but what it appeared: a world aware that an attack by a superior force might be imminent, but choosing to believe it would not come.

Only the steady stream of vessels rising from Seoba—from the designated rendezvous site—gave him pause. It looked to 'Szatulai as if they *might* be reacting to the approach of his flotilla—but they were not turning to engage. And neither were any of the military vessels in the rapid-response orbits above Borodan. It made no sense. Had the humans known about his flotilla, they would be sending a force to meet it.

He needed to know more—*something*—about the vessels fleeing Seoba. It was the only way to solve this riddle.

When he looked over the reader's shoulder at the seventh data-collection lectern, 'Szatulai finally found the display screen that showed Seoba. He could see several data codes creeping along the edge of the screen, where the moon's bulk did not block the planet's face, but there were no codes near Seoba itself. Indeed, the moon appeared empty, which was exactly what had been reported by the information harvesters in the *Sacred Whisper*'s eavesdropping cadre.

"Why is there no data for this moon?" 'Szatulai asked.

The reader dropped his gaze in a gesture of submission, then replied, "There *is* data, Blademaster . . . a great deal."

"Then why does your screen show nothing moving on the moon or away from it?"

"Because there is nothing to show," the reader replied. "It has been deserted for a hundred human years, just as the harvesters reported."

'Szatulai heard 'Budyasee hurrying over with the two obedientaries, and without looking away from the lectern, he raised a hand to stop them. Their presence would be intimidating, and in eagerness to please his superiors, the young reader would grow reluctant to speak unpleasant truths.

"Tell me about this data that shows nothing," 'Szatulai said. "Tell me how you know it is nothing."

"As you command." The reader touched the screen in two places. The moon grew indigo blue, though there was a notch on the horizon where it paled to merely deep blue. "The color shows the ambient temperature on the moon's surface. The closer to black, the colder."

'Szatulai touched a finger to the notch. "And why is it paler there?"

"That is the ice quarry where we are bound," the reader explained. "The paler hue indicates that it is a few units warmer."

'Szatulai sensed a knot of anger forming between his hearts. He took an instant to acknowledge it and rob it of power, then pointed at the tactical holograph in front of them.

"And why did you not think to plot this?"

"It would have been misleading." The reader's voice scratched with fear. "The readings suggest the month-old impact of a small comet or asteroid more than they do a vessel, and I found no wave radiation or magnetic readings that supported the possibility of even a small vessel. Ask Utu 'Gusonee to confirm—"

'Szatulai raised a hand. "You have nothing to fear. I only wish to know your reasoning, yes?"

The reader relaxed and pointed his mandibles up to the right, indicating he understood.

"You know why we are traveling to the ice quarry?" 'Szatulai asked. Their exact destination and the purpose of their trip were supposed to remain unknown to the crew, but in the confines of a bridge, it was often difficult not to overhear and still perform one's duties. "Be truthful."

"I have heard it is to rendezvous with a human spy."

Close enough. "And yet you did not consider the possibility that the heat signature was made by the spy's vessel?"

The reader dropped his mandibles to the left, indicating he had not. "I should not have had that knowledge," he said. "And even knowing it, the signature does not support such a conclusion. If there is a vessel waiting for us in the quarry, it must be hidden beneath thirty . . ."

Realizing his mistake, the reader let the statement trail off.

"My error, Blademaster." The reader's nostrils quivered with fear. "There could be a vessel waiting inside a deep cave system. That would explain the low temperature variation and lack of support readings."

"One vessel or many?"

"Many, if the cave system was large enough."

'Szatulai pointed at the screen again. "What if I were to tell you that at least seven vessels have launched from that moon even as we approach?"

"That is impossible," the reader said. "The thermal blossom would have been difficult to miss. And, if they were human spacecraft, there would have been magnetic fluctuations and electromagnetic emissions."

"What if I were to tell you that I witnessed those launches with my own eyes?" 'Szatulai allowed his voice to sharpen. "And that there is *nothing* wrong with my eyes?"

The reader's mandibles fluttered; then he spoke in a dry voice: "I would conclude that the impossible has occurred."

"How wise you are, for one so young." 'Szatulai looked over and motioned 'Budyasee to approach with the two obedientaries. "Now, let us imagine how the impossible would occur."

"A cloaking field," suggested one of the obedientaries, 'Gusonee. "I know that Mudoat Path Works is attempting to develop an energy barrier for its frigates that conceals as well as protects. Perhaps the humans have an emplaced version—"

"The humans have *no* manner of energy barrier," 'Szatulai interrupted. "And even if they did, a cloaking field does not explain why their vessels are invisible to our readers *after* they . . ."

Leaving the word *launch* unspoken, 'Szatulai turned to the reader.

"If it were the *Sacred Whisper* rising from the quarry, how bright would the thermal blossom be?"

"Not very bright," the reader replied. "Our repulsor engines produce only a small amount of heat, so there would be only a red flare that lasted but a moment before vanishing."

"Brighter than what you are seeing now?"

"Far brighter, Blademaster. If the humans are launching anything, it is but a shadow compared to the *Sacred Whisper*."

'Szatulai was thunderstruck by the sudden realization, and immediately pummeled by a wave of nausea, swift and powerful. It spread through his body like a fever. He found himself warm and almost trembling, his knees and hands and the nostrils beneath his eyes prickling with shock. It was unthinkable that human stealth craft could be superior to those in his flotilla . . . and yet, here it was. The simplest explanation.

The only explanation.

'Szatulai turned to 'Budyasee. "We need to take down one of those shadow vessels. Open fire."

"At this range? We would be lucky to hit the moon, much less a target we cannot even detect."

"You can identify the ice quarry, can you not?" 'Szatulai felt his hearts hammering and knew his astonishment was turning to anger, but he did not know how many shadow vessels remained to launch, and time was short. "Target *that*."

"If we open fire," 'Budyasee said, "we won't be able to keep our rendezvous with the human traitors. The attack will reveal our presence—"

"The humans already *know* of our presence," 'Szatulai said. "There *are* no traitors on that moon to welcome us. Perhaps these Spartans they spoke of are not even real. The entire rendezvous is a trap."

'Budyasee's nostrils flared wide. So did those of the obedentaries and the reader. No one moved or spoke.

"I gave an order," 'Szatulai said. He allowed his hand to drift toward the energy sword clipped to the waist of his armor. "So if you continue in this defiance . . ."

"Caution is not defiance." As 'Budyasee spoke, he refused to let his gaze drop to 'Szatulai's sword hand—an act of will that spoke to his courage. He knew that what he said next might cost him his life, yet he would utter it nevertheless—as was his duty. "We are a lightly armed intrusion force, not a battle fleet. If we allow the humans to engage, we *will* be destroyed."

"Then the *kai'd* will have to work fast." 'Szatulai moved his hand away from his sword hilt and turned toward the gravity lift at the rear of the bridge. "Do not question me on this again, Shipmaster. Those shadow vessels are a danger to the fleet. And I *will* have one to examine."

CHAPTER 13

0847 hours, March 19, 2526 (military calendar)
Subsurface Maintenance Grotto 6M430, Seoba Ice Quarry
Moon Seoba, Biko Planetary System, Kolaqoa System

Over the years, John-117 had been paraded before enough admirals and generals to know one when he saw one, and the tall prisoner with the gray shirt and starched collar was definitely a general. The man's spine was so straight it looked like a Series 99 sniper barrel, and he was surrounded by a half dozen even taller insurrectionists who kept shifting around, trying to shield him from their Mjolnir-armored babysitters. Concealing their leader had been simple enough when the Spartans arrived to find three hundred captives packed into the center of a cold and murky maintenance grotto. But now that the prisoners were being marched up a brightly lit loading ramp into the troop hold of a *Banta*-class transport that had belonged to the United Rebel Front only hours earlier, their efforts to hide the suspected general were obvious.

The Covenant ETA was ten minutes—barely enough time to get the transport loaded and away. The plan was to have one of Hector Nyeto's backup flight crews deliver the insurrectionist prisoners to Biko in one of their own transports, where they would be remanded to the colonial authority for judicial disposition. But John knew his superiors would want a general held back for ONI interrogation.

He stepped to the bottom corner of the loading ramp and spoke through his helmet's external speakers.

"Prisoners, halt!"

The embarking column shuffled to an uneasy standstill with the imprecision of irregular soldiers everywhere, and the companions of the suspected general left him unshielded for a full second and a half. John took advantage of their sloppiness to store the image of a slender-faced man with salt-and-pepper hair and eyes the color of gun steel. Before the request had actually formed in John's mind, the Mjolnir's onboard computer displayed the subject's identity on the HUD.

FMR MAJOR-GENERAL HARPER GARVIN

UNSC MARINE CORPS DESERTER

SUSPECTED TERRORIST

UNITED REBEL FRONT HIGH COMMAND

TARGET PRIORITY C-NK-2A

The target priority flashed red, telling John that ONI wanted Garvin captured, but not killed—which suggested it was more important to interrogate him than to remove him from the battlefield. It was a common designation for those second- or third-in-command of an insurrectionist organization. The "2A" meant that the general's capture did not take priority over an ongoing mission. So, Garvin was an important figure in the United Rebel Front—but not the *most* important. The "2A" designation also meant the operative's safety was not a consideration in executing a capture attempt. Welcome to special ops.

After the target priority stopped flashing, the general's file began to scroll down the HUD, listing attributed operations and possible sightings. John wasn't interested, so the onboard computer advanced the file until it reached Garvin's most recent post in the UNSC. The general had deserted after receiving a two-year billet teaching logistics at the Corbulo Academy of Military Science on Circinius IV. The assignment had been a humble one for a major general, and there was speculation that he had joined the Insurrection to retaliate. The theory sounded a bit far-fetched to John—but then again, generals didn't get to be generals by having small egos.

"Spartan Leader, what's the holdup?" The leader of Gold Team, Joshua-029, was using SQUADCOM, a channel open to all twelve Spartans on Task Force Yama. "I thought we wanted to get these prisoners out of here before the aliens arrived?"

"Spotted one we need to hold for ONI," John said. He switched back to his external speaker and pointed at Garvin. "You there. Present yourself for inspection."

The cluster of bodies surrounding Garvin milled about and tried to look confused. Meanwhile, the Spartans flanking the column stepped back and checked their spacing, ready to respond if the order drew any resistance from the prisoners.

"Even on Seoba, this armor weighs"—John paused until the onboard computer displayed the number on his HUD—"fifty-six kilograms. If I have to wade through the column to retrieve you, there will be a *lot* of broken toes."

The cluster rippled, then a thin, olive-skinned woman emerged and began pushing her way toward John. She had a broad mouth, bright blue eyes, and a mocking smirk. John gave her a quick appraisal, checking for the possibility of a bomb or other undetected weapon, then motioned her to stop at the bottom of the loading ramp.

"What are you doing?"

"Presenting myself as ordered." The woman craned her neck to look up at his faceplate. "But I got to warn you, I'm not into robots."

A chorus of nervous chuckles.

"I'm not a robot," John said.

"Sorry, big boy," the woman said. "You want me to believe that, you got to lose the armor."

More laughter.

Kelly-087's voice sounded over SQUADCOM. "John, that's not *real* flirting. She's trying to—"

"Distract me. Affirmative." He looked back toward the cluster of prisoners shielding Garvin. Of course, the general had vanished into their midst. Deciding to use the "robot" image to his advantage, John said, "All teams, stand ready."

The Spartans brought their assault rifles up. John lashed out; before the woman could react, her tunic lapels were knotted inside his gauntlet.

"John, do you need assistance?" This from Kurt-051, the leader of Green Team. "I don't see the threat."

Rather than waste one of the eight minutes remaining before the Covenant arrived, John ignored him and spoke through his external helmet speaker.

"The UNSC Military Code of Conduct authorizes the summary execution of any prisoner interfering with a guard while on the field of combat. As you are engaged in an ongoing effort to conceal the presence of General Harper Garvin from the imprisoning authority—"

"Let her go, soldier." Garvin emerged from the back of the transport and, pushing past a crowd of insurrectionists who were trying to block his way, started down the ramp. His gaze dropped to the woman in front of John. "Thanks for trying, Petora. But we never stood a chance against those things."

John waited until Garvin had presented himself at the bottom of the ramp, then released the woman. "The prisoners will resume loading."

When the insurrectionists were slow to obey, Garvin looked over his shoulder. "Don't give them an excuse, people." Once the embarkation column had started up the ramp again, he turned back to John. "How did you identify me, soldier?"

Seizing the initiative was a classic counterinterrogation technique, one that John's instructors on Reach had hammered home when he was ten years old. Rather than go with the standard response of ordering the prisoner to shut up—which would tell Garvin only a little less about the SPARTAN training program than an honest answer—John checked the general's personnel file on his HUD and selected something misleading.

"In 2508, you lectured on quelling planetary insurrections at Luna OCS." John had not even been born in that year, so the misinformation would cause Garvin nothing but trouble if he tried to use it later. "It was memorable."

Garvin's brow rose. "You were a student there?"

"You ask a lot of questions, General." John checked the chronometer on his HUD; the ETA was now seven minutes. "Let's just say I was disappointed you turned traitor."

The major general's lips tightened and his gaze slid away. "As you like, soldier. I'm in your—"

The last few words of the sentence were swallowed by the deafening rumble of an artillery strike; then the air was filled with ice flakes fluttering down from the darkness above.

Another rumble shook the grotto, and ice blocks began to tumble down from the ceiling and bounce off heads and shoulders. Several prisoners were struck and fell to the ground, clearly injured.

Ascot's voice came over the Task Force Yama command channel.

"Launch-launch-launch! Emergency protocol. The aliens have opened fire. Repeat: Emergency protocol. Launch—"

The transmission ended in a crash of static, and a constant growl filled the grotto as distant strikes began to shudder through the surrounding ice. As the static faded, a cacophony of chatter filled the void left by Ascot's absence, but Nyeto's voice stood out.

"*Starry Night* was hit on launch and downed." That would be Ascot's prowler. "Intact. She dropped in the quarry—"

Crowther's calm voice cut in: "Thank you, Commander. That's enough for now. Will advise if we need more information."

"Will advise?" Nyeto sounded livid. "They could be *alive*! They could need—"

"We'll do what we can, Commander," Crowther said. "Please proceed as planned and use Protocol Echo for all communications."

Protocol Echo was an instruction to regard a communication mode as nonsecure. In this case, Crowther seemed to be reminding Nyeto—and everyone else on the channel—that the extent of Covenant eavesdropping capabilities was unknown, so it was safer to assume that even encrypted comm channels were compromised. John thought the precaution was probably overkill, but the colonel had a point. There was no sense in taking unnecessary chances.

The discussion on the command channel continued in a guarded manner, with references to direction and location relayed in terms relative to the ice caves where the prowler wing had been berthing when the scramble order came.

John listened with one ear, in case the Spartans were given a new assignment, but stayed focused on the prisoners. The insurrectionists were holding their arms over their heads to protect themselves from falling ice blocks, and many were eyeing their injured comrades with worried looks.

"Grab your wounded and load up," John ordered over his helmet's external speaker. "Anyone not aboard the transport in one minute dies here."

The prisoners broke into action, grabbing their hurt companions and ascending the loading ramp into the *Banta*'s troop hold. The internal hatches had been secured from the other side and the emergency escape pods could only be armed from the flight deck, so there was little chance of any rebels mounting another escape attempt from inside the vessel. They would be going nowhere but Biko, where they would face the consequences of their planned coup.

Garvin dodged an ice block as it bounced off John's armor, then cast a concerned look into the darkness above.

"What's happening?"

"The aliens opened fire," John said. On the command channel, Crowther was asking for a response from the *Starry Night* and receiving none, which could indicate anything from the prowler's destruction to a disabled antenna. "Guess they weren't interested in making friends with you after all."

Garvin's eyes widened. "So *that*'s what you're doing here," he said. "How did you know?"

"Dumb question." John knew a nonanswer would leave Garvin's imagination running wild and make him an easier target for the interrogation team later. "How do you think ONI knew where to find Colonel Watts?"

Garvin's face went pale.

Now Crowther was asking about availability, trying to find a Black Dagger unit in position to reach the downed prowler. He wasn't receiving any positive responses. Most of the 21st had departed before the alien barrage started, and the final company had launched aboard the four prowlers of Ascot's own Night Flight. The survivors were eager to assist, but they would be forced to turn back into a plasma barrage that was growing more intense by the moment.

"Negative," Crowther said over the command channel. "The last thing we need is more bats down."

From what John was hearing, the only unit still in position to check on the *Starry Night*'s status was his own squad of Spartans.

Responding to the crash site would mean leaving the prisoners locked inside the *Banta*'s troop hold without guards, but a breakout would be impossible—all Nyeto's flight crew had to do was depressurize everything between the troop hold and the flight deck. The biggest drawback was that Garvin wasn't wearing a pressure suit, so John couldn't take him along on the rescue attempt. Instead, the general would have to remain with the other prisoners and go to Biko. With any luck, ONI would be able to extract the general before the colonial authority executed him—but even if that didn't happen, the thought of a prowler falling into Covenant hands was a far more troubling possibility.

John pointed Garvin up the loading ramp. "Go join your people."

"What?" Garvin looked confused for a second, then narrowed his eyes. "Wait. You can't let us launch into an alien—"

"Now." John grabbed a fistful of shirt and tossed him up the ramp into the troop hold. "Enjoy Biko, General."

He commed Nyeto's flight crew. "Sierra-117 to *Banta* transport," he said. Sierra was a comm code for Spartan. "Change of plans. You're on your own."

"No way." The pilot seemed almost panicked. "You can't send us up without an onboard escort."

"I can and I am." John was puzzled by the alarm in the woman's voice—she had already been informed that the hold hatches were secured from the outside, and any military pilot who had been through even a basic ship security course would realize that all she had to do to secure the bridge was depressurize the main cabin. "Just follow flight deck isolation protocols. You'll be fine."

"But Commander Nyeto wanted you—"

"Not going to happen," John said. "We're the only unit available to go after Captain Ascot and the *Starry Night*. Have a good trip."

John closed the channel, then motioned for his eleven Spartans to follow him toward the airlock. He didn't contact Crowther because that would only be putting the colonel in a bad spot, forcing him to choose between abandoning a downed prowler and violating military law by sending fifteen-year-olds into harm's way. Given the colonel's tendency to cover his own ass first, it seemed pretty clear he would abandon the prowler.

"Okay, I'll ask." It was Joshua-029, speaking over SQUADCOM. "What are we doing?"

"Going after the *Starry Night*."

"Funny," Kurt-051 said, "I didn't hear Colonel Crowther authorize that."

"He didn't need to," John said. "We're all that's left."

"Maybe so," Kelly said. "But we're still going to need a ride out of here when we're done."

She had a point, but John wasn't sure how to handle things. If he asked Crowther for permission to respond to the *Starry Night*, the prowler's crew would be abandoned and any survivors left to their fates. But Kurt and Joshua were right to be concerned. This kind of rescue operation required coordination, and undertaking it without informing the rest of the task force would expose his people to a lot of unnecessary risk. It would have been nice to have Avery Johnson here to consult, but he'd disappeared right after the debriefing.

Maybe he didn't like working with fifteen-year-olds either.

"Let's see what we see," John said. "The first thing he'll want is a sitrep."

They proceeded to the maintenance grotto's access vestibule, an oversize airlock that opened into the bottom of the vast quarry pit. The crew chamber was more than large enough to hold twelve Spartans, so John led the squad inside and sealed the inner hatch. Crowther was going to be pissed, but lives were at stake—and so was any high-risk intel aboard the prowler. If the Covenant captured Task Force Yama's mission plan, it'd be the end of SILENT STORM. If they captured Earth's coordinates, it would mean the end of the human species. The priorities were clear—John had to go after Halima Ascot and the *Starry Night*.

CHAPTER 14

0859 hours, March 19, 2526 (military calendar)
Exterior Maintenance Yard, Seoba Ice Quarry
Moon Seoba, Biko Planetary System, Kolaqoa System

John stepped out of the airlock into sublimation fog so thick he could barely see the end of his assault rifle. The clouds overhead were flashing bright with the constant arrival of plasma bolts, and it felt like walking into the heart of a thunderstorm. He led his squad of Spartans thirty meters forward, far enough from the quarry walls to escape the unending cascade of ice tumbling down from above, then stopped.

John opened the command channel. "Sierra-117 requesting waypoint to target location."

If the rest of the task force was following standard rescue protocol—and John felt sure they would be—one of the surviving prowlers would be on station above Seoba, monitoring the surface situation via signal intercepts and tactical drones. They would know the locations of all twelve members of his squad from their Identification Friend-or-Foe codes. Most importantly, they would be able to guide the Spartans toward the *Starry Night*'s crash site.

Able, but possibly unwilling.

Crowther's voice came over the channel. "What do you think you're doing, so—er, Blue Leader?"

The colonel's tone wasn't entirely hostile, which John decided to take as a tacit authorization of his plan.

"We're checking *Starry Night*'s status, sir. We seem to be the only unit available."

John thought Avery Johnson would be proud of his tact. He was answering Crowther in a way that gave him plenty of cover—the Spartans were undertaking the assignment without asking for permission, so the colonel could easily deflect blame if something went wrong. Besides, there wasn't any choice—the Spartans really *were* the only unit available.

John signaled his team leaders—Kurt-051 and Joshua-029—to deploy in a search line. That would create a hundred-meter-wide rank of Mjolnir-armored Spartans, with the four members of Green Team spaced every ten meters on the left flank and the four members of Gold Team spaced every ten meters on the right flank. Blue Team and its four members would remain in the center, gathered more tightly so he would have a ready reaction force.

When Crowther still hadn't replied, John signaled the squad to advance at a trot, heading more or less away from the dockyards where Alpha Company had suffered so many casualties.

Over the command channel, he said, "We'll take a look and report."

"Affirmative." Crowther sounded relieved. "But take action only if immediately warranted. Biko is responding to the plasma barrage in force. Commander Nyeto assures me the alien flotilla will be destroyed or in retreat within the hour."

"More or less," Nyeto added. "But don't worry, Spartan. We've got your backs down there."

"Acknowledged." John hoped he sounded more impressed than he was. He liked Nyeto and truly appreciated his support—but in his experience so far, when the lieutenant commander told him not to worry, it was time to start thinking the opposite. Besides that, John knew humanity's track record all too well: even if the local naval forces outnumbered the flotilla three-to-one, the alien ships were resilient and dangerous enough to nullify the advantage of superior numbers. "I'll keep that in mind."

A waypoint appeared on John's HUD, pointing about thirty degrees to the right of dead center. The distance was imprecise, four to eight kilometers.

"That's a big help," Fred remarked over SQUADCOM. "If we leave the quarry, we'll know we've gone too far."

"Adjust course," John ordered.

He checked the Covenant ETA and cringed inwardly. Two minutes, and the sublimation fog was thicker than ever. His motion tracker showed Blue Team in a diamond formation with five-meter spacing between its members, but he had no visuals on anyone. All he saw in any direction was a featureless white veil so thick that it blurred the gauntlets at the ends of his own arms, strobing silver from the constant flashing of the plasma barrage overhead.

"Advance at a full run," John announced. The Spartans were now using SQUADCOM to communicate among themselves, so they were the only ones who would be able to hear the exchanges—along with Avery Johnson, if he was in range. "Keep your eyes on your feet. That's all you can see anyway, and if the *Starry Night* disintegrated on the way down, the first thing we'll find will be debris on the quarry floor."

"Didn't Commander Nycto say she went down intact?" asked Kelly.

"That's what he said," John replied. "Doesn't mean he saw what happened once she dropped into the quarry."

The *Banta*'s temporary crew announced their departure over the command channel. A moment later, the vessel passed low over the Spartans' heads, opening small tunnels of visibility as it burned through the swirling fog. John caught glimpses of the surrounding terrain—his squad stretched across the quarry floor and, in the distance, stacked terraces of ice rising two kilometers high. Then the transport lifted its nose and left the quarry atop a trio of spear-shaped efflux columns.

The alien plasma barrage trailed off, plunging the area into a gauzy twilight as the enemy vessels changed targets. Moments later, they resumed fire, and a flashing cone of silver flame chased the *Banta* over Seoba's horizon. John traced the individual trajectories back to five different points.

So, five inbound vessels.

One minute remaining.

The waypoint remained steady in the center of his HUD, the arrow pointing straight into the white haze ahead. The distance now read five to seven kilometers. No way they were going to find the *Starry Night* before the Covenant reached Seoba's surface. Had the squad been wearing their thruster packs, John would have given the order to use their maneuvering jets to augment their speed. But when they had donned their Mjolnir, they'd been preparing to babysit prisoners, not go into combat. The quartermaster hadn't thought to issue them any packs.

In all fairness, John hadn't thought to ask.

Fortunately, Seoba was a big place. Even after the Covenant arrived, even with five vessels, it wouldn't be easy for them to find the Spartans—or the *Starry Night*'s crash site. Plenty of time.

The enemy plasma bolts began to rain down inside the quarry again. The sublimation fog settled back in, and the Spartans resumed running through a ground cloud. A minute passed, and the fog swirled as something big and twinkly passed overhead. Another couple of minutes, and three more big twinkly things passed by, lower this time, and crossing back and forth over the quarry. The maximum distance to the target had fallen to five kilometers, and still they saw no sign of debris.

John tried to tell himself that was good news. Once they started to find debris, they would know for certain that the *Starry Night* had disintegrated before impact. Until then, there was still hope for a controlled crash.

By the time the maximum distance had diminished to two kilometers, the fog had dropped to shoulder-height, and John could see why the distance readings were so uncertain. The *Starry Night* had crashed about halfway up the quarry wall, demolishing a two-hundred-meter section of terrace, which in turn had created an icy avalanche that stretched all the way to the quarry floor. The prowler sat partway down the debris fan, perhaps seven hundred meters from the bottom.

At least, *part* of it did. All John could see of the vessel was the aft section, primarily the thrust nozzles and tail. Everything forward of the wing crescent was either buried in blue ice or missing entirely—and there was an awkward bend in the fuselage that made it difficult to tell which.

"Okay, that's bad," Fred said over SQUADCOM. "Maybe even *really* bad."

"Not entirely," John said. "At least it didn't vaporize. There could still be someone—"

"Not the crash," Fred replied. "Look."

He pointed back along the length of the quarry, toward a distant silhouette just sliding into view over the rim of the pit. Shaped like a pair of teardrops connected by a thin middle fuselage, it was covered in randomly placed rows of glistening blue lights. John hoped it might be just another of the vessels that had been passing back and forth over the quarry since the Covenant arrived, but no such luck. Once its stern was clear of the quarry wall, it dropped into the pit and began to descend toward the downed prowler.

"Crap," Kelly said. "Are they trying to recover it?"

"They're sure not here to offer assistance," Fred answered.

Fred's conclusion was confirmed an instant later when the vessel began to spray plasma bolts in the Spartans' direction. Its primary cannon was more of a ship-to-ship weapon than antipersonnel, so the strikes tended to land where the Spartans had been rather than where they were. Still, the curtain of sublimation fog quickly rose again, and once more the squad found itself chasing waypoints through a flashing cloud of grayness.

John did not have to remind anyone to dodge and change speeds. They knew as well as he did that the fission reactors powering their Mjolnir armor would be putting off enough heat to light them up like signal flares on even the crudest form of infrared sensor. Giving the alien gunners a steady vector would be a sure way to get vaporized.

"This is no longer a rescue mission," John declared over SQUADCOM. He was pretty sure everyone knew what needed to be done, but it was always good procedure to spell things out. "Our first objective is to deny equipment recovery to the enemy. We can't let the Covenant capture *any* of the *Starry Night*'s data."

"Affirmative." Joshua's tone was enthusiastic, almost cheerful. "What's the plan?"

"Open to ideas," John said. "But let me check in with the bat patrol."

His HUD showed the distance to the target as thirteen hundred meters, so he estimated they were still about thirty seconds from the base of the avalanche run-out, and probably three or four times that from the prowler itself. The fog had risen back above his head, and he couldn't see how far away the alien ship was—but he doubted it would take the Covenant vessel more than a minute to reach the crash site.

John opened the command channel. "This is Blue Leader," he said. "We have a situation."

Crowther was on the channel instantly. "Go ahead."

"We've sighted the *Starry Night*," he said. "It's damaged, but appears largely intact."

"Good news."

"Negative," John said. "The aliens have spotted it too. One of their vessels is moving to recover."

Crowther was silent for a moment, then said, "John, you can't let that happen."

"I figured that."

"I mean it," Crowther said. "The data on that prowler . . . the NAV computer alone could give away everything from the locations of our smallest outposts to the force deployment of the entire UNSC. You need to confirm the destruction of *all* onboard data devices. Clear?"

"Yessir," John said. "So . . . wouldn't it be ideal to have some sort of self-destruct capability aboard?"

It was Nyeto who answered. "You bet. There's a one-megaton Fury tactical nuke in the engineering compartment. It's programmed to detonate automatically if it determines there's been a catastrophic event. Trouble is, if there's somebody alive onboard, it won't make that determination until there hasn't been any shipboard motion for two hours."

"So, there are definitely survivors?"

"*Definitely* might be overstating it," Nyeto said. "I'd commit to *likely*. There might be other reasons it didn't switch to automatic."

"Only one way to find out." John checked his distance to target—one kilometer. "Go up there and look."

"Up there?" Crowther asked. "Explain, soldier."

"The prowler is on an avalanche slide," John said. "About seven hundred meters above us. It's going to be tough to reach it first."

Somebody sighed heavily; then Crowther said, "Commander Nyeto, isn't there some way to remotely activate the self-destruct?"

"Sure," Nyeto said. "The flight commander can do it. But the *Starry Night* is Ascot's boat, and she *is* the flight commander."

Another sigh. "And if the flight commander is unavailable?"

"Then it's the wing commander," Nyeto replied. "But same problem, since that's Ascot too. The last backup is the captain of the *Vanishing Point*."

A third sigh. The *Vanishing Point* was holding station two planetary orbits out. Even at the speed of light, it would take nearly an hour for a request to be sent and the return signal to arrive.

Crowther said, "John, I hate to—"

"We'll find a way, sir."

On SQUADCOM, someone warned, *"Incoming!"* Finger-size lances of bright white fire began to shoot through the fog.

"Anything you can do to keep the other vessels off our backs would be appreciated," said John. "One is about all we can handle."

"That could be tough," Nyeto said. "Prowlers aren't designed for ship-to-ship—"

"We'll *find* a way," Crowther said, cutting Nyeto off. "Stand by for instruction on manually activating the self-destruct—"

"No time," John said. A small vehicle had appeared on the edge of his motion tracker, and it was coming his way fast. "But no worries. If it's a nuke, a Spartan can detonate it."

A stream of plasma bolts came flying out of the fog, a couple glancing off the titanium shell of John's Mjolnir at chest height. He threw himself to his belly, dropping below the plane of fire, and rolled left. His motion detector showed the unseen vehicle changing course to follow. The plasma fire continued to fly past overhead, a hint that the driver was as blind in the fog as John and fighting by instruments only. John pumped a grenade into his assault rifle's underslung launcher and rolled twice in the other direction, then came up on his knees, ready to fire.

The vehicle was barely visible but swerving in his direction, not emerging from the fog so much as manifesting inside it like some kind of ghost. It was almost on him now, wide in the front and narrow in the back, with nothing beneath it but a shimmering cushion of emptiness. In its cockpit, hunched behind the vehicle's winged chassis rode a huge Brute in deep-red armor. John extended the MA5B with one arm and fired the launcher. The grenade caught the Brute in the side of the helmet and detonated in a white ball.

A clatter sounded inside John's helmet as his Mjolnir was pelted with bits of metal and bone. The vehicle weaved past with the lower half of the Brute's body wobbling in the seat, leaking red mist into the fog.

John checked his HUD and saw four more vehicles dipping in and out of view on his motion tracker. Only half of his squad was in range, so he doubled the number of enemies, estimating there would be fewer than ten vehicles left.

"Green and Gold Teams, take out the rest of those hoverbikes. . . ."

A line of LEDs winked green inside his helmet.

"Everyone else . . . with me." John continued toward the waypoint on his HUD, still sprinting. After a seven-kilometer sprint and a close encounter with another hoverbike, he was finally starting to breathe hard. "And load your grenade launchers."

There was another line of green flashes, but Kelly said, "John, even if we had the range, you know these forty-mike-mikes aren't going to scratch a prowler's armor."

"They won't need to." John checked the distance to target and found the range between one and eight hundred meters—which he interpreted to mean it was a hundred meters to the base of the avalanche, and another seven hundred meters up-slope to the prowler. "We'll bring it to us."

Kelly was silent for a moment, then finally said, "Or *on* us."

By then, they had closed to within forty meters of the avalanche, and John was starting to see faint pyramid shapes hanging in the graying fog ahead—the corners of ice blocks protruding from the avalanche run. He took a flying leap and, in Seoba's weak gravity, was able launch himself ten meters off the quarry floor.

The fog blanket was only three meters thick, so he had a clear view of the slope above for a full second. He almost wished he hadn't. The alien vessel had floated to a halt about thirty meters from the impact site and was hovering over the adjacent terrace, dropping a patrol of EVA-equipped soldiers—Elites, Brutes, and Jackals—down a blue column of light that looked like some sort of anti-gravity elevator. The lead elements of the company were already circling the *Starry Night* and looking for a way inside.

As John started to drop, a plasma bolt thicker than his waist flashed past at an angle and vanished into the fog. An instant later, a geyser of mist and ice shot twenty meters up and blossomed into a cone.

Grace-093 cried out over SQUADCOM, then abruptly went silent, and Joshua ordered, "Daisy, take—"

"Got her."

By then, John was starting his downward arc. He glanced up and glimpsed a second Covenant vessel gliding over the quarry rim, the blue dot of a fresh plasma attack already pulsing in the muzzle of its bow cannon.

"Green and Gold, be ready for more vehicles." John shifted to the command channel. "Commander Nyeto, how about that support? We've got a second bandit firing on us and more on the way."

"Setting them up now," Nyeto said. "No worries."

"Please stop *saying* that, sir." John sank back into the fog. Another bolt flashed past overhead, and SQUADCOM crackled with static as somebody went offline. "And hurry. We're taking casualties down here."

John dodged to the bottom of the avalanche and took a knee in the ice, then pointed his grenade launcher up the slope and switched back to SQUADCOM.

"Mass grenade fire," he said. "Maximum range, directly below the *Starry Night*."

"John, wait!" Fred exclaimed. "That could bring the whole slope—"

"On one," John said. "Two, one—"

He launched his grenade, and a row of LEDs winked green as the other Spartans acknowledged their own launches.

The volley was still in flight when the slope vanished in a silver blink. It took a moment to register that the flash had been a plasma strike landing a couple of meters away. John felt a gentle shudder in his boot soles, then suddenly there was a wall of ice rising up before him, full of tumbling slabs and churning snow. He turned away and leapt for the sky, trying to gain enough height to land on top and surf it out, but it was no good.

Avalanches could move all at once, the bottom sliding out from beneath the top, and when that happened, *nobody* was fast enough to dive out of the way . . . not even a Spartan.

John felt the wall hit his feet and roll up his legs and swallow his hips and torso, and it had him, hurling him forward and down, then around and back up inside a mass of icy debris, and he lost all sense of direction, knew only that he was tumbling head over heels and then he wasn't, he was just there, hanging in the dark, with no idea of what was up and what was down, SQUADCOM filled with curses and questions and none of it making any sense at all.

CHAPTER 15

0909 hours, March 19, 2526 (military calendar)
Quarry Floor, Seoba Ice Quarry
Moon Seoba, Biko Planetary System, Kolaqoa System

Status reports began to scroll down John's HUD as the Mjolnir's onboard computer, sensing his desperation to know how badly the avalanche had decimated the squad, began to query its counterparts in the other Mjolnir units. Naomi-010 and Solomon-069 were listed as incapacitated. Four more Spartans, including John himself, were listed as immobile—probably because they were trapped beneath tons of snow and ice. But no one was KIA yet, and that left half the squad available for immediate action.

"Son of a . . ." Fred said. The avalanche was not deep enough to block comm waves, so Fred's voice was as clear as if John had been standing next to him—rather than buried somewhere beneath him. "It *worked*."

By *worked*, John assumed that Fred meant the avalanche had carried the *Starry Night* to the quarry floor. "Then don't stand there talking about it," he said. "You're in command now. Board it and blow it."

"What about survivors?" Fred asked.

"Rescue if possible." John switched to the command channel so he could report to Crowther and Nyeto. "Squad elements boarding the target now. Where's our support?"

"On the way," Nyeto said. "No worries. They don't even know we're here."

No worries, still? John had to fight to keep from yelling. "Sir—I *want* them to know you're there. You need to get them off—"

"We'll be there soon." Crowther didn't sound quite as confident as John would have liked. "Just hang on."

"I *have* a plan," Nyeto added. "The best way to be sure the Covenant doesn't come back on you is to eliminate them on the first pass."

John bit his tongue, battling the temptation to ask how long that would take. His Spartans were being used as bait—again—and the only thing he could do about it was soldier up, get unburied, and try to keep them alive.

"Affirmative."

John activated his headlamp and saw nothing but blue ahead of him. He was hanging in tightly compressed ice and snow like a beetle in amber, with the limbs on one side of his body pulled back behind him and those on the other curled beneath. His helmet was cocked at an angle that made his neck feel like the neural splice at the base of his skull was a putty blade pressed against his spine, and he didn't have the vaguest idea which way was up.

The onboard computer displayed an arrow on his HUD, pointing toward his left shoulder. When John did not react, the words WHAT ARE YOU WAITING FOR, SOLDIER? appeared beneath the arrow. Either the onboard computer was developing a sense of humor, or it had used John's neural interface to access his memories of Chief Mendez—the SPARTAN-II program's primary training instructor on Reach.

John began to twist his left hand back and forth, trying to create a little space. Most victims buried beneath the incredible weight of an avalanche couldn't even do that much . . . but most victims weren't wearing fission-powered Mjolnir armor. John quickly created a space around his hand, then around his forearm, and he began to dig, scraping the ice down toward his elbow and pushing it down under his arm. Before long, he had his entire arm free. He cleared the space around his helmet and worked his other arm loose, always pushing the ice downward, and soon his entire upper body was mobile.

After a minute of that, it was another minute of just crawling, continually pulling himself up, then pushing packed ice and snow downward. His assault rifle had gotten lost at some point during the spin-cycle, but he didn't bother digging around for it. It was probably packed so full of ice that it would be good for nothing but a club. Besides, he still had his M6D sidearm, and with its 12.7mm semi-armor-piercing high-explosive ammunition, it would be easier to clear and *almost* as effective as the assault rifle. In fact, in the hands of someone who knew how to operate it, the M6D had remarkable stopping power, and it was one of the most effective conventional infantry weapons the UNSC had at its disposal.

But the sidearm didn't have an underslung M301. The grenade launcher he was going to miss—especially since, as he climbed, Green and Gold Teams began to chatter over SQUADCOM, coordinating attacks on what was beginning to sound like an endless stream of vehicles.

When John finally broke through to the surface, he found the downed prowler almost on top of him. The surface of the run-out drift was above the fog blanket covering the quarry floor, so he could see that the *Starry Night* lay a dozen meters away. She was resting upside-down with her stern buried and her forward fuselage rising from the run-out drift at a thirty-degree angle. All that remained of the bow were the soot stains it had left on the fuselage's crumpled neck when it exploded.

Fred and the other Spartans were nowhere to be seen, but ten aliens were clambering up one of the *Starry Night*'s wings onto her belly. Judging by their sizes and helmet shapes, there were a couple of Elites leading four Jackals and a like number of Brutes. All were wearing armor so deeply red that it was almost black, and all appeared to be armed with stubby weapons suitable for close assault.

John stayed in his hole and checked the motion tracker on his HUD. It showed three nearby Spartans where he saw nothing but run-out drift—they were probably still attempting to dig their way to the surface.

John couldn't see what was happening on the quarry floor behind him, but from the SQUADCOM chatter, it sounded like the hoverbikes were being supported by at least three more Covenant ships. He didn't bother opening the command channel to ask for support again. Nyeto was clearly using the Spartans to bait his trap—and complaining about it would only give Crowther another excuse to throw their immaturity in their faces, to treat the Spartans like they had no business on a battlefield in the first place.

The aliens were all standing on the *Starry Night*'s upturned belly now, checking their weapons and generally looking like they were preparing to board. The Covenant vessel that had dropped them off was leaving its position near the original crash site and starting to float toward the prowler's new resting place.

"Fred, you aboard the *Starry Night*?"

"Affirmative," came the reply. "And you'll never guess who—"

"Hold on," John said. A pair of Jackals started up the *Night*'s fuselage toward the crumpled neck, no doubt intending to enter the vessel through the opening at the end. "What's the self-destruct status?"

"Arming manually now," Linda-058 said. "It's a Fury, so the codes are taking a while."

"Take your time," John said. "Fred, what's your strength?"

"Three Spartans, four ODST survivors, and Sergeant Johnson,"

Fred reported. "Uh, make that half a Johnson. He's had his bell rung pretty hard."

"My bell iss just fine, if shomeone would stop ringing it." Slurred speech and hearing impairment—Johnson definitely had a concussion. "And I can shtill ring yours any—"

"Better take his grenades away," John said. "But let him keep the firearms. You've got ten hostiles boarding now from the forward breach, with more on the way."

"Boarding *now*?" Linda echoed. "And you tell me to take my time?"

"Didn't want to pressure you," John said. "Let me know when it's armed."

"Soon," Linda said. "What timer delay do you want?"

"Two seconds longer than you need to get clear," John said. "This is going to be close."

"Give us thirty seconds," Fred said. "We'll leave via escape pod."

John approved. Because Seoba had only a trace atmosphere, the shockwave of a Fury one-megaton thermonuclear device would barely be noticeable from a half kilometer away, and both Spartan Mjolnir and ODST space-assault armor was already shielded from EMP. So they would need to worry only about the heat blast, which could be avoided by simply hiding behind something . . . the farther away, the better, of course.

"Okay," John said. "Let the first two aliens board uncontested—they're scouts."

"Understood," Fred replied.

"We'll catch the others in a crossfire as soon as the last one goes in."

"Affirmative," Fred said.

"What about me?" Johnson asked. "What's my ashignment?"

"Guard the escape pod," Fred said. "We can't have the aliens stealing it."

"Nothing gets past me," Johnson said. "Hey, where's the pod?"

"On the ceiling," said Malcolm-059. He was supposed to be on the quarry floor fighting the vehicles with the rest of Green Team, but John wasn't going to worry about it. The squad was well into the Plan J—*just do something*—part of the battle. "We're upside-down, remember?"

"Oh, right," Johnson said. *"Cool."*

Which was a very un-Johnson thing to say. Clearly, the sergeant's bell was still ringing.

The two Jackal scouts disappeared into the *Starry Night.* When nothing blew up, the two Elites started up the fuselage with the four Brutes in their wake. The last two Jackals stayed behind, crouching on the prowler's upturned belly to act as a rear guard.

John was about to advise Fred of the situation when a series of flashes strobed down from above, illuminating the avalanche path and run-out drift and everything else in flickering orange light. He glanced back up to see a pair of giant fireballs blossoming above the quarry, and another Covenant vessel turning to flee with three prowlers on its tail, still firing missiles into its energy shields.

Nyeto had sprung his trap, and now his jubilant voice filled the command channel. "*Two* down! The others are turning tail. No worries now, John!"

"If you say so, Commander."

John looked back along the run-out drift and was not at all surprised to see that Nyeto's attack had only made the situation on the surface much worse. The Elites were waving the last of their patrol down the *Starry Night*'s neck, and the alien vessel was moving into position above the prowler, as though it was preparing to drop some sort of recovery device.

"But stay off the channel for the time being, sir. We're busy down here." John switched to SQUADCOM, then said, "Fred, new situation out here. They're all boarding *now.* Do whatever you can to repel them."

"Understood."

Almost instantly, a pillar of flame erupted from the prowler's neck, launching one Brute like a cannonball and leaving another hanging halfway out of the opening, smoke and red mist rolling out of his breached armor. The two Elites went prone and reached over the end of the fuselage, trying to grab hold of their companion's body and pull it free.

John clambered out of his hole and started across the run-out drift, his boots sinking to his ankles with each step. The Covenant ship was hovering in place now, its stern a hundred meters directly above the prowler. The leaves of a huge iris hatch were retracting into the hull, revealing an interior bathed in cool blue light.

John *really* wished he still had his grenade launcher—but since he didn't, he raised his M6D sidearm and opened fire on the Elite who seemed to be in charge. The first round deflected, creating a golden shimmer around its personal energy shield. Both Elites rolled off the *Starry Night* and started in his direction, activating a pair of what appeared to be blades of energy, blood-red and longer than their arms.

John stepped to the right—it was impossible to spring in the soft surface of the run-out drift—and positioned himself so his foes would be stacked one behind the other. He continued to fire at the same Elite. After the next shot, the shield fell and the M6 rounds began to stagger the alien and dimple his armor.

John charged, still firing and hitting more often than he missed. Finally, two rounds penetrated, and the alien almost seemed to deflate, his legs folding beneath him and the blade of his energy sword retracting into nothingness, his purple blood misting out through the holes in his chest armor. John drove forward, using his free hand to grab the dying Elite by the throat and shove him back toward his companion.

But the other Elite was already leaning around to slash head-high with his blazing red blade . . . a feint designed to make his opponent duck, so the death strike could be delivered from above. John stepped inside the attack, spinning the mortally wounded Elite around to push the advancing one off-balance and keep the energy blade at bay. Then he shoved the M6D against his attacker's faceplate and fired.

But this one had an energy shield as well. The rounds deflected in a gold flash that caused absolutely no damage to the armor, and then John's pistol was empty.

No matter. With the enemy off-balance and half-blinded by a muzzle flash, John shifted his hand from the throat of the dead Elite to the wrist of the remaining one. He dropped the pistol in his other hand and grabbed his attacker under the armpit, then hoisted him overhead and folded him onto his own energy sword.

The blade pushed through shield and armor as though neither existed. It winked out . . . then John found himself stumbling forward as a round punched into his armor from behind.

He dived into a forward somersault and started to hear a shrill chirp—the Mjolnir's pressure-loss alarm. It felt like somebody had punched him hard in the shoulder blade, but there was no real pain or numbness, just a dull ache that was already fading. So no wound, just a hole in his armor that would slowly suffocate him as his suit lost pressure. At least the operative word was *slowly.*

Unless he got hit again.

John somersaulted twice and came down on his back, so that his head was toward the *Starry Night*, then rolled sideways twice. He stopped on his stomach, digging down into the ice to make himself a smaller target. His HUD showed his suit at 98 percent pressure, so he had time, and his motion tracker showed two Spartans coming up behind him.

"Watch out for the—"

"Got 'em," Anton-044 said over SQUADCOM. "You're still alive, aren't you?"

"For now," John said. "I've got a pressure leak."

"I've got a patching kit," Joshua-029 said. "Just hang on."

John lifted his head and, atop the *Starry Night*, saw two Jackals crouching behind a pair of circular energy shields mounted on their arms. The shields were shimmering gold from top to bottom as rounds deflected in all directions, but neither alien appeared all that eager to return fire. They just remained behind cover and kept glancing up at the open hatch above their heads, as though they expected help to drop down from their vessel at any moment.

Or expected to be drawn up into the safety of its hangar.

Recalling that the aliens had descended to the surface inside a blue beam of barely perceptible light, he realized they might be expecting to return the same way—and take the *Starry Night* with them. The hatch at the bottom of the Covenant vessel was certainly large enough.

"Linda, how's that Fury—"

"Armed," she reported. "I'll initiate the timer as soon as we can drag Sergeant Johnson into the escape pod."

"Do what you have to," John said. "Just initiate *now*. The Covenant's about to engage some kind of a lift system."

"A left system?" Johnson said. "What kind of—"

The question ended in a clunk; then Johnson began to protest and curse in the thick voice of a concussion casualty.

John ignored him. "All personnel, take cover!" he said. "Fury-class tactical nuke detonation thirty seconds! Repeat, tactical nuke thirty seconds!"

Joshua and Anton stopped firing. The two Jackals cautiously peered out from behind their shields and raised their weapons—then went tumbling as the *Starry Night* blew her escape hatch. A half-second later, the escape pod launched and went arcing out over the quarry pit. A second after that, two streams of small point-defense plasma bolts erupted from the alien vessel's stern—but the gun crews had clearly been caught by surprise, and the likelihood of a target lock seemed remote.

John was already up and bounding down the run-out drift with Joshua and Anton when Crowther's voice came over the command channel.

"What the hell was that?"

"Fred and Linda with *Starry Night* survivors," John reported. "Be advised, self-destruct detonation in twenty-five seconds."

"Thanks for the warning." Nyeto's tone was complaining. "See if you can cut it a little closer next time."

"Affirmative," John said. "And we appreciate all the fire support."

"Hey, I got them out of—"

"Can the chatter," Crowther said. "John, we'll be down to recover your squad as soon as the EMP clears. Good work."

Crowther closed the channel without giving Nyeto a chance to offer further comment. John didn't know quite what to make of the exchange with the two commanders, but he'd figure that out later—assuming he cleared the half-kilometer safety range before the Fury detonated.

He glanced back up the slope toward the *Starry Night.* The prowler was sitting in a column of pale blue light, cloaked in a sparkling veil of ice crystals and trembling almost imperceptibly as it was drawn free of the snow and ice.

Then John and his companions reached the bottom of the run-out drift, dropped into the blanket of sublimation fog, and started across the quarry floor at a sprint. He didn't want to distract the squad by asking for a count-off, but his motion tracker showed five Spartans fleeing in the same direction. Counting the two with him and the two that had ridden the escape pod away with Fred, that was all but one of the squad right there. With luck, he wouldn't lose any.

The gray silhouette of a wrecked Covenant hoverbike emerged from the fog ahead, and a moment later his onboard computer displayed a yellow five-second countdown on the HUD. Four, three . . . John and his companions leaped over the vehicle and crouched down behind it.

The count on his HUD reached one. His helmet speakers crackled with static, and the quarry grew as bright as a muzzle flash. The vehicle rocked ever so slightly, and the fog cleared, carried away on the shadow of a shockwave that Seoba's trace atmosphere could support.

John rose, then looked back toward a billowing wall of steam where the run-out drift had been a moment before. He was happy to see the blocky shapes of several Spartans—first three, then four, then all five that he had seen on his HUD earlier—emerging from the cloud, stumbling and weaving, but still on their feet. Their Mjolnir was shielded from the EMP released by nuclear weapons, and the lack of atmosphere had protected them from any shockwave effects. But if they had been close enough to the detonation, their armor could have taken some heat damage—and if the shielding had been breached, the Spartans themselves might even have suffered some radiation poisoning. But there was no use imagining the worst—he wouldn't know the full effects until they returned to the *Vanishing Point*'s infirmary and got checked out.

The final Spartan staggered out of the fog and hurried after the others.

Tumbling down the quarry's terraced walls behind them, leaving equipment and bodies strewn in its wake, was the forward half of the ruined Covenant vessel. The *Starry Night* had not gone out alone.

The static in John's helmet speakers gave way to the high-pitched chirping of a pressure alert; then his HUD flickered back to life, displaying the urgent message that his suit pressure had fallen below 80 percent. He turned to Joshua and hooked a thumb toward his shoulder blade.

"Patch me up," he said over SQUADCOM. "I need to check on my squad."

CHAPTER 16

0630 hours, March 20, 2526 (military calendar)
UNSC *Point Blank*–class Stealth Cruiser *Vanishing Point*
High Parabolic Orbit, Planet Biko, Kolaqoa System

Two-hundred-and-three. That was the number of gray duraplas interment capsules arrayed before the hangar doors in the *Vanishing Point*'s command hangar. Hector Nyeto was at parade rest with a hundred fellow officers. They were standing at a right angle to the calf-high cylinders, listening to the chaplain drone on about the honor of service and sacrifice. Across from them stood the other half of the honor company, a hundred-and-one enlisted personnel in blue dress uniforms, including Sergeant Avery Johnson, John-117, and the other five Spartans who were not currently in the infirmary.

Fifty-four of the gray duraplas cylinders were empty. That was the number of humans who had died aboard the *Starry Night* and been atomized by the prowler's one-megaton self-destruct charge. Another one hundred-and-twenty-seven capsules contained the ashes of the ODST casualties from the initial assault on Seoba, men and women who would never again take up arms against the Insurrection. And twenty-two of the cylinders held the ashes of the *Ghost Star*'s crew—insurrectionist agents whom Hector had personally recruited into a still-growing network of sleeper cells.

A network that would one day destroy the UNSC from within.

Unfortunately, not one of the interment capsules contained a Spartan, despite Hector's best efforts to get them killed. At Netherop, one of his sensor operators had "accidentally" transmitted over an open channel. And only yesterday, Hector had intentionally stalled while responding to John-117's call for support. The Spartans had not only survived both assassination attempts, they had won the battles and even managed to capture some Covenant equipment.

Hector might have been relieved to be on the same side as the bioengineered freaks, had they been created to defend humanity from the alien invaders. But they hadn't. The Spartans had been specifically meant to decimate the Insurrection by launching surgical strikes against its leadership, and they were proving far too effective. He had seen a couple of ONI reports describing how Spartan teams on Jericho VII and Mamore were chewing through the leadership of the local rebel fronts. And just six months earlier, Blue Team had dealt a crushing blow to the United Rebel Front by capturing its leader—his own friend and mentor—Colonel Robert Watts.

Given the damage the Spartans had inflicted in just half a year, Hector was almost grateful to the Covenant for attacking and dividing their attention. He just hoped the reprieve would buy the Insurrection enough time to get organized and massacre them—because if that didn't happen, it would be the Insurrection facing annihilation.

The chaplain's droning finally came to an end, and she turned to Hector with sorrow-filled eyes and an expectant smile. Hector cursed himself for letting his mind wander. Halima Ascot had died when the *Starry Night* went down, and he was the senior surviving flight commander. That meant he was now the de facto commander of Task Force

Yama—and expected to assume all of the ceremonial duties that Ascot had performed with such effortless grace.

"Take your time, Commander Nyeto," the chaplain said. "I think a moment of silence is appropriate before committing so many of our brothers and sisters to the stars."

"Thank you, Major Ojombo," Hector said, genuinely grateful for the hint about the Committal. "I'll just miss them so damn much."

And he would. Despite his hatred of the UNSC, many of the people represented by those capsules had considered Hector a friend. Most had trusted him with their lives at one time or another, and betraying them had not been easy. There was even a part of him that pitied John-117 and his Spartans for what Halsey and her ONI masters had done to them—not a big part, but it was there.

Hector looked across the enlisted formation to Avery Johnson, who was the senior sergeant present. "Call the formation to attention, Staff Sergeant."

Johnson snapped his gaze to dead-center. "Honor company, atten-*hut*!"

Both sides of the formation shifted from parade rest to attention, bringing their feet together and their arms to their sides.

"Raise the pressure barrier, Staff Sergeant."

Johnson called the order for the hangar crew. A transparent AlON barrier rose out of the deck to separate the burial detail from the interment capsules. Nyeto brought his hand up in salute, and the entire formation followed his lead.

"Open the outer hatch, Staff Sergeant."

Johnson gave the order. The hatch retracted into the overhead, and the decompression wave lifted the interment capsules and carried them out through the portal and into the void. The *Vanishing Point* was at the apogee of its parabolic orbit, so the extra momentum would be enough for the cylinders to break orbit and continue into deep space.

Hector held his salute and recited the Committal he had prepared.

"From stardust we came, and to stardust we return. Our fallen brothers and sisters are not gone from our hearts, for they have left us only to scout ahead, and we know that when our time comes to follow, they will be waiting to show us the way. May they rest in peace, for they have fought valiantly and died nobly. No commander could ask for more."

Hector finished his salute with a snap, then added, "Farewell."

He waited for the formation to follow his lead, then turned back to Johnson. "Close the outer hatch, Staff Sergeant."

Johnson called the order, and the outer hatch came down.

"Dismiss the honor company, Staff Sergeant."

Johnson's gaze returned to dead-center. "Company, dismissed."

And, in typical military fashion, that was the end of it. No long eulogies, no post-service gatherings. The AlON pressure barrier simply sank back into the deck, and the personnel in attendance departed to return to their duty stations and get on with the next thing. Only Avery Johnson, the Spartans, Colonel Crowther, and a handful of senior officers lingered, no doubt waiting for the new commander of Task Force Yama to give them some idea what the next thing was going to be.

Hector was not surprised to see John-117 studying him with a gaze that was both obvious and intense, and he could almost see the wheels turning as the young Spartan contemplated the amount of time it had taken to answer his call for support. Clearly, Hector had some work to do if he wanted to recapture the kid's trust. Giving Crowther and the other officers no chance to corner him, he put an approving smile on his face, then crossed to John and clapped a hand on the Spartan's huge arm.

"You and the Spartans did a great job yesterday, Petty Officer. There were heavy casualties, but you saved everyone who *could* be saved." Hector cast a meaningful glance at Johnson, who still looked just a bit glassy-eyed from his concussion, then turned back to John. "And you kept the enemy from capturing one of our prowlers."

"They did more than *that*," Dr. Halsey said, stepping to Hector's side. Halsey was dressed in a white lab smock that was probably as close to dress whites as a civilian scientist working for ONI could come. "They eliminated an alien ship. Their *third*."

"And recovered that thing out of the flight deck's cinders," Hector added with enthusiasm. Halsey was always bragging on about her Spartans like a proud mother—and getting on her good side would probably go a long way toward keeping John's trust. "That was a lucky break for us. Maybe you'll figure out something important."

The smile Halsey gave him was more calculated than flattered. "Maybe, Commander. I *am* making progress."

"Impressive, without question," Hector said. "And between my prowlers and your Spartans, just yesterday we downed three enemy vessels. It's too bad that the recovery teams weren't able to capture any live aliens, but if you can figure out anything at all from the Covenant equipment they brought back, I'd say that makes the Battle of Seoba the UNSC's best showing against the Covenant thus far."

"I'm glad you feel that way, sir," John said. "And now that you're in command of the task force, I hope that means you'll reconsider Captain Ascot's decision to sideline us."

Hector did not need to fake his smile. "Don't worry," he said. "You and your Spartans are going to be seeing all the action you can handle. Trust me on that."

"That decision isn't yours to make," Crowther said, pushing in between Hector and John. "The Spartans report to me."

"And *you* report to me now." Hector turned to face Crowther. "We can talk chain of command later, but the Covenant fleet will be arriving to attack Biko at any time—and when it does, we need John and the Spartans leading our ambush. They have as many ship-kills as the rest of the task force combined."

"They're still fifteen," Crowther said.

"I'm sure Admiral Cole was well aware of their age when he

assigned them to Task Force Yama." Hector was growing impatient with Crowther's stubbornness. It almost seemed that the colonel really *did* view the Spartans as a threat to his Black Daggers, as Hector had suggested to John in a calculated attempt to manipulate him. "I'm sorry, Marmon, but you've seen what the Spartans can do. I'm going to have to overrule you on this one."

"To send kids into battle?" Crowther's tone grew sharp. "That would be a mistake, Commander Nyeto. A big one."

"Are you threatening me, Colonel?"

"Take it as you like." Crowther's eyes hardened. "But I'm serious about this. You *won't* be sending underage soldiers into battle with my Black Daggers—and if you try to, you'll find yourself explaining your actions to a court of inquiry."

Hector's pulse began to pound in his ears—but the threat was one he couldn't afford to ignore. A court of inquiry was an investigative proceeding to determine whether the facts of a situation warranted further action—and the last thing Hector wanted was a team of JAG officers sniffing around his prowlers. He had worked hard to recruit high-quality agents for his sleeper crews, and they all had airtight cover legends. But he couldn't risk trained investigators digging into him and his people. Too much could go wrong.

"Very well, Colonel. We'll run this Biko ambush by the book." Hector turned to leave. "But your Black Daggers had better be up to the job—or we won't even have time for a court of inquiry."

The hangar began to empty in a tense and astonished silence, Nyeto and the Prowler Corps leaving by the port exit and the Black Daggers by the starboard. Avery Johnson found himself thinking that maybe he should have listened to the medics and stayed in his bunk. The only reasonable explanation for what he had just witnessed was that his concussion was a lot worse than the docs thought. There was no way the task force's two senior officers would have argued like that in front of their subordinates. He had to be hallucinating.

Avery was still pondering this possibility when he saw Dr. Halsey grab John by the arm, then redirect him and the rest of the Spartans toward the starboard exit being used by the Black Daggers. At least *that* made sense. John was a hell of a soldier, but when it came to military politics, he was still just a kid. The Spartan was letting his frustration with Crowther blind him to Nyeto's manipulations, and Halsey was guarding John like a mother hen, keeping him clear of the quagmire of a contested chain of command.

As Avery turned to follow, Colonel Crowther fell in at his side. "I'm sorry you had to see that, Sergeant."

"I've seen worse, sir." Avery was only being half-truthful; he *had* seen shouting matches between commanding officers before—just not one where they openly threatened each other with career-ending charges. "But with all due respect, I wouldn't make a habit of it. This isn't a pissing match you're going to win."

Crowther looked amused. "Is that so?"

"I'm afraid it is," Avery said. Crowther hadn't been at Avery's initial meeting with Halsey and the two vice admirals, so he probably didn't realize that it was ONI's Section Three sending young Spartans into battle—and colonels who butted heads with Section Three didn't stay colonels for very long. "Look . . . I understand your reservations about sending underage soldiers into battle. I mean, who in their right mind wouldn't? But those Spartans *aren't* children, believe me—and *that* decision was made way above your pay grade."

"I'm aware of that, Sergeant."

Crowther locked gazes, then glanced at the deck and stopped walking. Avery took the hint and did the same.

Crowther waited until the hangar was finally clear, then continued, "I can't say I approve of the process, but there's no denying the outcome. Those Spartans are magnificent soldiers. If they hadn't saved our butts on Seoba, SILENT STORM would be over."

Avery frowned. "And you still want to keep them sidelined?"

"Not exactly," Crowther said. "They're ready for battle. They convinced me of that by saving you and preventing the *Starry Night*'s capture."

"Then I'm not following you, sir." Avery frowned. "Maybe it's the concussion."

Crowther chuckled. "It's not the concussion, Sergeant. It's Nyeto."

"Okay. Now I'm really confused."

"Because you weren't aboard the *Ghost Song* when John called for support," Crowther said. "Commander Nyeto left him and the rest of the Spartans exposed . . . all just so he could spend eight full minutes maneuvering for the perfect attack on the enemy squadron."

"Hold on. You think Nyeto was deliberately *stalling*?"

"I think he would have taken out the other two corvettes, had he attacked right away," Crowther said. "And until I understand why he *didn't*, I don't want those Spartans anywhere near him. I don't even want him to know where they *are*."

Avery nodded slowly. "Yeah. I can understand that."

He wasn't as surprised as he might have been. Avery had his own reservations about Nyeto—the lieutenant commander's efforts to befriend John already rubbed him the wrong way. And at the briefing where Nyeto had revealed the Spartan's age, Nyeto had clearly been trying to drive a wedge between John and his commanders—and now Avery knew why. Nyeto was trying to set himself up as John's only ally in the command structure.

After a moment, Avery said, "So what are we going to do about it?"

Crowther smiled. "How much have you studied Sun Tzu, Sergeant?"

Avery replied with what seemed appropriate for their current circumstances: " 'Great results can be achieved with small forces.' "

"Very impressive," Crowther said. "May I take it that you remember what the general had to say about supply trains?"

" 'An army without its baggage train is lost,' " Avery said. " 'Without provisions it is lost; without bases of supply it is lost.' "

"Then I think you know what you're going to do, Sergeant."

"Me?"

"You and the Spartans," Crowther said. "I assume you know where you're going?"

Avery thought for a moment, then said, "I think so." When large forces launched the kind of rapid-penetration attacks that the Covenant was using, they had little choice but to leave their supply trains at the site of their last victory. "At least, I know where to start looking."

"And that is?"

"The planet they just glassed," Avery said. "Etalan."

Crowther grinned. "I'd say you're over your concussion," he said. "In fact, I'd say you're thinking pretty damn clearly, Sergeant."

CHAPTER 17

1534 hours, March 20, 2526 (military calendar)
UNSC *Point Blank*–class Stealth Cruiser *Vanishing Point*
Libration Point Three, Biko/Seoba, Kolaqoa System

The Covenant fleet appeared on the bulkhead monitor in a single instant—a hundred specks of blue-shifted light emerging from slipspace in the span of a heartbeat. They drifted toward Biko's rosy crescent in a slow-swirling swarm, each blue speck sprouting dozens more as the alien ships launched their starfighter complements. But instead of streaking off to screen their fleet and harry the human defenses, the specks stayed close, swirling around their motherships in escort patterns so tight they melded into glowing, button-size smudges.

It was hardly the planetary assault doctrine John had been taught in his fleet tactics course back on Reach. Then again, the unspoken assumption had been that the Spartans were training for battles involving one human force confronting another, and that the attacker's objective would be something more logical than the utter destruction of an entire planet. Certainly no thought had been given to situations that involved an enemy fleet whose energy-shielded vessels could bombard a populated world with plasma beams the size of skyscrapers.

"That's an odd formation," said Fred.

He was standing next to John in one of the *Vanishing Point*'s smaller maintenance hangars. Their Mjolnir armor was in the support module for maintenance and repair, so they were currently wearing black utilities with no identifying insignia or badges. Kelly and Linda were on either side of them, also attired in black utilities. There were four more Spartans in a back corner of the hangar, familiarizing themselves with some of the Covenant weapons recovered on Seoba. The other four members of the squad were still in the infirmary with injuries ranging from decompression sickness to a ruptured spleen. Meanwhile, Dr. Halsey was locked in her lab with some kind of Covenant holoprojector, recovered from the wreckage of the vessel that the *Starry Night* had downed when she self-destructed.

When no one responded, Fred added, "You'd think their commanders have never been to fleet warfare school."

"Different weapons, different tactics," John replied.

"True, but you fight to your weapon's advantage," Kelly said. "If I were the Covenant, I'd stand off behind a fighter screen. I'd use those badass plasma cannons to attack the orbital defenses and make the Biko fleet come to me."

"That would be the smart thing to do," Linda agreed. "But it would also be predictable."

A flotilla of white slivers began to gather on Biko's daylight side as the planet's small space navy positioned itself to give battle. There were about fifty vessels, but John knew most of those would be patrol frigates designed to disable smuggling boats—not go nose-to-nose with energy-shielded capital ships. There was no way they could hope to stop the invasion fleet. But if they bided their time and employed wolf-pack tactics, the Bikon sailors might be able to take a few enemy ships with them.

UNSC doctrine dictated launching a fighter assault to disrupt such a formation before it could swarm a capital ship. Yet the alien fighters remained with their motherships, maintaining a tight-but-brittle defensive shell that could crack under the assault of even a couple of frigates, and the Covenant fleet seemed to be actually accelerating toward Biko's defenders. The alien tactic didn't make sense.

"What's their hurry?" Fred asked, clearly coming to the same conclusion. "The Covenant will blow through that screen like a missile through a shower curtain, but they're going to lose more than a few ships doing it."

"Then they must believe they'll lose even more by taking their time," Linda said. "They lost over half of their intrusion flotilla at Seoba. Perhaps our prowlers have earned their respect?"

Kelly shook her head. "Those were just scout corvettes. Nyeto was knocking them down with just a few lucky missile salvos." She pointed at the monitor. "But that fleet is filled with cruisers and assault carriers. Their shields could absorb a half-dozen salvos and not even flicker."

"Right," John said. "If they're worried, it's not about prowlers."

"Could it be about *us*?" Kelly asked. "Or, actually, about the Black Daggers?"

The correction was due to the Spartans' still-uncertain standing. As the senior flight commander in Task Force Yama, Hector Nyeto was now in charge of Operation: SILENT STORM, and he wanted the Spartans returned to active status. But Crowther continued to resist, and not even Dr. Halsey had been able to convince him to change his mind. John and the rest of the Spartans were frustrated and angry at being sidelined, but what could they do? Orders were orders, and after the stunt John had pulled during the Seoba insertion, it was clear that he was not going to change Crowther's mind by disobeying them now. The upshot was that the Black Daggers would be attempting to board the alien fleet on their own, and the Spartans would be watching from the *Vanishing Point*.

After a moment, John nodded to Kelly. "I think maybe you're right. Being worried about a boarding attempt would explain why they're keeping their fighters in close escort."

"It would explain a lot of things," Linda said. "Might have been one of the reasons why the Covenant was trying so hard to capture that prowler yesterday. If they know about the boarding at Netherop, they would want to know how we got close enough without being detected."

"Makes sense," Fred said. "Except for the part about knowing there were prowlers at Seoba. The innies never got a message off, and it's pretty clear they weren't expecting us to show up."

"It doesn't matter," John said. "Maybe the aliens just spotted a prowler visually and wanted to find out why they couldn't see it on their sensors, or maybe they had a reconnaissance boat watching the rendezvous point before we arrived. What *does* matter is that they knew what they were seeing—and they were willing to take big risks to capture one."

"Damn." Kelly's gaze went back to the smudges of light on the monitor. "They're guarding against boarding actions, and they're trying to capture prowlers. They know the plan."

"Either that, or . . ." Fred hesitated, then sighed and said, "Okay, they know the plan. How?"

"Maybe they figured it out after Netherop," Linda suggested. "If the captain managed to report that he was being boarded, they might have guessed we would try it on a larger scale."

"Possible," John said. "But that's a big leap—especially on their own."

"You think someone helped them figure it out?" Kelly asked.

"That's a simpler explanation," John said. "But simplest is that someone told them. General Garvin had to have some pretty decent intelligence to lure the Covenant to a rendezvous. And he must have been able to promise them even more, if he thought he could strike a deal with them."

"Only one problem with that theory," Fred said. "Garvin is an innie. How would he *get* that kind of high-level intelligence?"

"I don't know," John said. On the monitor, the two sides were already exchanging fire, the aliens hurling salvos of plasma bolts and the humans countering with missile barrages. And *still* the Covenant capital ships were holding their fighters close, cocooning themselves inside a picket web so tightly woven that a firefly couldn't slip past. "But I'm going to find out."

They continued to watch the monitor as the two fleets tore into each other and the first evacuation ships began to rise out of Biko's pink clouds and head for orbital transfer stations. The Covenant made no attempt to interfere, perhaps because the number of refugees likely to escape was such a small percentage of the planet's population. Even the largest passenger liners carried no more than thirty thousand people, and Biko's total population ran into the tens of millions.

John heard a pair of boots thumping across the deck toward them, then turned to see Avery Johnson approaching in blue light-duty utilities. Other than a brow still lowered in post-concussion pain, he looked healthy and alert enough, and his gait was steady.

"Sergeant Johnson," John said, "aren't you supposed to be resting?"

"Depends on who you ask," Johnson said. "And I was getting bored."

"Join the club," Fred said. "How are you feeling?"

"Like I have the worst hangover in history and can't remember how I got it." Johnson slipped between Fred and John, then looked around and scowled at the four of them. "So were you all just gonna spend your day lounging around this hangar bellyaching?"

"Just watching the battle from a safe distance," John said. "And it's starting to look like that's *all* we're going to do on this mission."

Johnson leaned close. "And what if it wasn't?"

John and Fred exchanged frowns; then John asked, "Are you talking outside the chain of command?"

"Not exactly," Johnson said. "It's authorized—just quietly."

"I don't like it," Kelly said. "Crowther let us slide on going after the *Starry Night* without authorization—"

"He did more than let it slide." Johnson leaned behind John to address Kelly. "He knows you saved our butts with your initiative."

"Whatever," Kelly said. "If he finds out we're going behind his back to do something for Nyeto—"

"It isn't Nyeto," Johnson said. "Crowther wants you to volunteer."

"For what?" John asked.

"Does it matter?"

John glanced up at the bulkhead monitor. The two fleets were close enough now that they had entered evasive maneuvers, filling the darkness with little commas of light as they swerved and bobbed and tried to make themselves unpredictable targets. The Covenant vessels still looked like blue smudges, though they had begun to grow larger and more diffuse as their shells of escort fighters struggled to stay in formation around their motherships. Clearly, even in the middle of a fleet action, the alien commanders were still concerned about being boarded.

John turned to the sergeant. "Yeah," he said. "It might."

Johnson looked confused. "I thought Spartans *always* volunteered."

"Nasty rumor," Fred said. "Who knows how those things get started?"

Johnson ignored him and looked at the monitor. "Okay, what am I missing?"

Before answering, John turned his palm up, a signal that the Spartans used to ask each other for permission. Aside from Dr. Halsey, Avery Johnson was probably the one person aboard whom the Spartans *could* trust. But John's next decision would affect the entire squad, and the one training weakness that this mission had exposed in him was his lack of political savvy. John knew *someone* was playing games with the Spartans—he just didn't know who or why.

When he received nods from the other three members of Blue Team, John caught Johnson's eye and looked back to the monitor.

"Look at the Covenant fleet," he said. "You see how hazy their ships are?"

"Sure," Johnson said. "Their fighters are hanging too close for us to attempt any boarding actions. That's why Crowther sent me down here."

"What's he want?" Kelly asked.

"To send us to Etalan," Johnson said. "To hit their logistics convoy."

For a moment, everyone was silent. Finally Fred said, "Sarge, maybe you should listen to your doctor."

Johnson scowled. "What is it with you people?"

"You're talking crazy," Linda said. "The only place the colonel wants to send us is back to Reach."

Johnson's eyes lit with understanding. "You're worried about the argument at the service?"

"Among other things," John said.

"That was just a cover," Johnson said. "Crowther wanted to hold you back for this mission."

"So he threatened to relieve Nyeto of command?" Kelly asked. "Wouldn't it have been simpler to explain what he was thinking?"

"Not really." Johnson's gaze dropped. "There are other issues."

"We have a few of our own," John said. "The Spartans aren't volunteering for anything until you level with us."

Johnson thought for a moment, then shrugged. "I guess you deserve to know," he said. "Colonel Crowther didn't like how long it took Nyeto to respond to your support call on Seoba."

"Neither did we," John said. "But he took out two corvettes."

"The colonel thinks he could have downed the rest by moving quicker." Johnson paused, then added, "And there's something else that he just learned. The prisoner transport never made it to Biko."

"Not surprising at *all*," Kelly said. "The Covenant was firing on everything that left Seoba, and *Bantas* aren't exactly stealth craft."

"It wasn't hit—not even a little bit," Johnson said. "The *Black Widow* has her on a combat camera moving to break orbit."

John began to have a queasy feeling in his stomach. "And the pilots were from Nyeto's Ghost Flight."

"You see the problem here," Johnson said. "It doesn't mean they were innie spies, or that Nyeto knew about it if they were. But we need to be careful."

"You think?" Fred shook his head in frustration and turned to John. "Now it all makes sense. Maybe Colonel Crowther is right. Nyeto really took his time supporting us on Seoba."

"He was using us as bait." As exasperated as John had been with the slow response during the search for the *Starry Night*, Nyeto had been nothing but supportive of the Spartans before and since, and it was hard to believe the commander might really be an insurrectionist spy. "And it worked. He destroyed almost half of the alien flotilla and sent the other two vessels running."

"John, he's been trying to get us killed since the capture attempt at Netherop," Kelly said. "That sensor operator's open comm was no accident."

John dropped his chin and said nothing.

He was no JAG investigator, but the evidence against Nyeto seemed pretty flimsy. There were a lot of coincidences that could be explained in a dozen different ways, and it certainly seemed possible that everything being attributed to the commander had actually been done by the missing flight crew on their own. Even the way Nyeto had been forced to reveal the Spartans' true age could be attributed to simple curiosity and poor social skills.

So there was the possibility that Nyeto was not the traitor that circumstances suggested.

But were the lives of John's entire squad worth that bet?

After a moment, Johnson asked, "You want it to be Crowther, don't you?"

"That would be a lot easier, yes," John said. "And who's to say sending us to Etalan isn't a setup as well?"

"Hadn't thought of that," Johnson admitted. "Get the Spartans out there alone and eliminate the 21st's competition. That's possible, I guess."

Kelly snorted, Fred shook his head, and Linda rolled her eyes.

A small smile came to Johnson's face at Blue Team's collective reaction; then he continued: "But there's only one way to find out. You have to take the mission."

"Yeah, I guess so," John said. "That's what Spartans are for, right?"

CHAPTER 18

Ninth Age of Reclamation
34th Cycle, 64 Units (Covenant Battle Calendar)
Bloodstar Flotilla, Captured *Banta*-class Transport *Emmeline*
Libration Point Four, Third moon/Planet Borodan, Kyril System

Perhaps Tel 'Szatulai *would* kill the entire ship's complement later, after his passions had cooled and he could be certain their deaths came at the will of the Prophets and not his own.

Until then—until his jaws stopped grinding and the knot between his hearts loosened—he would stay his hand and learn what had brought the humans to him, why they had risked their vessel and their lives to trail after the *Sacred Whisper* in a transport as clumsy, poorly armed, and strangely designated as the *Emmeline*.

'Szatulai's two young Jiralhanae escorts were also on edge, shifting back and forth in their new Bloodstar armor as the pressure in the transport's spacious airlock slowly equalized. The pair were the most assured and cunning of the special pack that 'Szatulai had assembled to help destroy the hated Spartans, and both were emerging as strong leaders. To prevent them from becoming rivals—a development that would quickly lead to a death match in the brutish Jiralhanae culture—he was taking every opportunity to give them tasks that forced them to look upon each other as brothers-in-arms. Today, he had told them to leave their weapons aboard the *Sacred Whisper* and accompany him aboard the human vessel, an order that seemed to unsettle both escorts even more than it puzzled them. Finally, Orsun—always the more circumspect of the two—could bear the mystery no longer.

"This is madness, Blademaster." His voice was booming and certain, even through the transceiver in 'Szatulai's helmet. "A ship this size can hold five hundred humans. Even Castor and I cannot defend you from so many without weapons."

"You Jiralhanae." 'Szatulai sissed into his transceiver. "Always being humorous."

Orsun was silent for a moment, then said, "I was not being humorous, Blademaster."

'Szatulai turned around and looked up at the Jiralhanae's unhelmeted head. With its leathery muzzle and long tusks, it was a ferocious-looking visage, one that could still draw a modicum of fear even from him, who had been assigned to kill twenty-seven of the Brutes over the years.

"Are you not?" 'Szatulai tried to sound astonished. "So, then, you are trying to insult me?"

"Never!" Orsun said. "I am only wondering how to defend you without weapons."

"I am a First Blade of the Silent Shadow," 'Szatulai said. "I need no defending."

"Ah." Orsun sounded more confused than ever. "As you wish, then."

They stood in silence for a moment; then Castor asked, "Blademaster . . . if we are not here to defend you, then why did you command our presence?"

"To make a point," 'Szatulai said. "How would it look if I were to board a human ship alone?"

"No stranger than boarding one without weapons," Castor said. "But I am honored to accompany you."

"As long as it doesn't get you killed?" 'Szatulai asked.

"That matters not." Castor's tone was earnest. "I have set my boots on the Sacred Path, and I will walk where it leads."

"As will I," Orsun said. "But I would be much the happier if the Sacred Path does not lead to our deaths."

'Szatulai sissed again, this time in genuine amusement. "Not today." A clunk sounded inside the inner hatch, and he turned to face forward again. "Once we board, stand to your full height, and do not accommodate for their fears—they are not allies."

"You wish us to appear intimidating?" Orsun asked.

"Imposing," 'Szatulai said. "Disdainful and unconcerned. Do not speak to the humans. You may kill one or two, if necessary, but say absolutely nothing to them."

"As you command, Blademaster." Castor sounded bewildered but obedient. "It will be done."

The hatch retracted, revealing a pale-blue passageway containing twelve wide-eyed humans holding projectile guns with long barrels. Their attire was at best nonmilitary, consisting of threadbare pants and shirts with torn-off sleeves. But 'Szatulai had studied human culture deeply enough to realize that such a sartorial choice was a type of uniform in its own right, a statement proclaiming the wearer to be fiercely independent and unconcerned with the opinions of others. From previous encounters with such types, he knew it meant they would likely be courageous, but undisciplined, poorly trained, and more likely to initiate a battle out of fear or misunderstanding.

Their apparent leader, a square-bodied man with hair to his shoulders and all over his face, spoke in the human language known as English.

"Welcome aboard." He used his rifle barrel to wave 'Szatulai and his companions out of the airlock. "General Garvin is waiting for you in the forward briefing compartment."

'Szatulai remained in the airlock, his helmet tipped forward to make it clear he was looking at the man's weapon. The leader followed 'Szatulai's gaze and swallowed hard, then flicked something on the body of the gun, lowered it, and turned to his companions.

"Weapons down."

Only half of the man's team obeyed instantly, confirming a lack of discipline that would make this visit more hazardous than 'Szatulai had expected. He had originally debated insisting that the humans come to him aboard the *Sacred Whisper*, then decided against it. The demand might be interpreted as anxiety, but more importantly, he did not dare to sully the ground of the Covenant's vessels with the footprints of vermin—that had happened enough as of late.

When 'Szatulai continued to wait inside the airlock, the leader glared at the holdouts and growled, "*Now*, people."

The rest of the man's team lowered their weapons and stepped back. The leader used his free hand to gesture toward the front of the vessel, and 'Szatulai led Castor and Orsun out of the airlock. The passageway was large by human standards, but tiny by those of the Jiralhanae. The warriors had to walk single-file behind 'Szatulai, each filling the space so completely that his armored shoulders scraped both bulkheads and his head kept thumping against the overhead.

At the first two junctions, a handful of slack-jawed humans stood watching as the trio passed, murmuring among themselves and shrinking back from the huge Jiralhanae. 'Szatulai paid these spectators no attention until the third junction, when one raised a device he recognized as a "datapad" and began to record his approach. He could not tolerate such an affront, of course. He was not some harmless oddity being paraded down the passageway for these lowly traitors' entertainment.

Rather than snatching the item out of the man's hand—which his fellow humans might regard as merely rude—'Szatulai waited until he was passing the datapad, then pointed at it. He had barely lowered his hand before Orsun's fist lashed out to shatter the datapad and send its holder, limp and bloodied, flying into the two humans standing behind him.

A startled outcry arose from the man's companions. The one leading 'Szatulai forward abruptly stopped and turned, his weapon automatically rising. 'Szatulai grabbed the barrel and held it down, then wagged his head back and forth, successfully mimicking a human gesture of warning. Clearly frightened, the man then lowered his weapon again and spoke into a device on his wrist. After that, there were no more gatherings at the junctions, and the procession soon entered a large compartment containing several rows of cushioned chairs, all facing a blank display screen at the far end of the room. Eleven humans were gathered in a large foyer area at the back of the compartment, where a large table had been overturned and an urn of brown liquid spilled on the floor.

The humans were watching each other far more carefully than they were 'Szatulai and his Jiralhanae escorts. Several held smaller projectile weapons, not quite pointing them at a heavyset man with a large amount of reddish hair on his face, who was standing alone in the aisle between the cushioned chairs. The man's brow was dripping with perspiration (a curious physiological trait, 'Szatulai thought) and his eyes were bulging, and in his arms he held an oblong device about the size of a Jiralhanae's head. At one end of the device, a green panel shined bright.

That was the trouble with traitors. They lacked discipline.

'Szatulai moved deeper into the compartment, forcing the humans to fall back so that Castor and Orsun would have space, then turned toward a slender man with intelligent eyes and a firm jaw, whom he recognized from the renegades' holographic message as General Garvin.

"Oh no, you don't!" It was the heavyset man with the oblong device who said this. "You talk to me. I'm the one with the nuke."

'Szatulai glanced toward him only briefly, then turned back to Garvin.

"Sorry about that." Garvin gestured toward the device in the man's hands. "It's a Havok Mark 2521 Medium Fusion Destructive Device thermonuclear warhead, liberated from Task Force Yama. We thought you might like to know how the Spartans intend to destroy your fleet, so we brought it along. Unfortunately, the moment you boarded, Commandant Booth here snatched it up. He claims it's armed."

"I was a munitions maintenance chief aboard the *Roman Blue*, so you had better believe it's armed." Booth directed his next words toward 'Szatulai. "Either you call off the attack on Biko, or I let it detonate."

'Szatulai turned his helmet toward this "Commandant Booth" again and said nothing. Could the man actually believe that a minor Sangheili flotilla commander had the authority to call off a planetary assault? Surely the humans would never entrust their weapons of mass destruction to such a fool. Booth's threat had to be a ruse—some negotiating trick through which the humans hoped to manipulate him.

When 'Szatulai did not reply, Booth grew impatient. "We had a deal. You were going to spare Biko—"

"Shut up, Erland," said a small woman with olive skin. She was holding a sidearm with a barrel as long as her forearm, the muzzle pointed at Booth's foot. Her knuckles were white from squeezing the grip, and her finger was on the trigger. "There was never a deal—only our offer."

Booth scowled in her direction. "Well, there's a deal now, Petora." He looked back to 'Szatulai. "Call off the attack, or we all die together."

'Szatulai realized that Booth was actually a *deranged* fool. That much was clear from how the woman looked warily at him, and from his apparent belief that a Sangheili warrior could be intimidated by the mere threat of death. In 'Szatulai's experience, most beings believed of others what they knew to be true of themselves—so would a man who feared death be willing to forfeit his own life?

Perhaps, if he valued his world more than his own safety and was insane enough to believe he could save it with one bomb. But would he do so instantly? 'Szatulai thought not. He would create a delay, give himself an escape in case something unexpected happened—or in case he changed his mind.

'Szatulai started toward Booth.

"Stay back," Booth said. "I'm not giving this up until the attack stops."

'Szatulai extended a hand, palm up, and continued forward.

Booth's gaze dropped to the extended hand. "What? What's this about?"

'Szatulai lashed out with his other arm, sweeping the Havok from Booth's grasp into his own upturned palm. When a countdown appeared on the green panel and his existence did not end in a single instant of searing brightness, he knew he had been right about Booth's character. He brought the warhead up and then used it to crater the man's skull, leaving the body to crumple to the deck. 'Szatulai turned toward the door . . . and found the olive-skinned woman—Petora—standing in front of him.

"Allow me." Petora holstered her sidearm and took the warhead from his hands, then examined the green panel. "Fifty seconds. Anyone know how to disarm this thing?"

General Garvin immediately came to her side and began to study the panel. 'Szatulai's grasp of human chirography was not strong enough to identify the numbers as they flickered past, but he counted twenty breaths before Garvin began to peck at the touchpad. General Garvin was obviously a disciplined and well-trained warrior—perhaps even one who had taken the Death Vow and considered his life already sacrificed to the cause he served—and 'Szatulai would have to treat him with more caution than the rest of these traitors.

If they all survived the next few seconds, of course.

Garvin finally stopped pecking, and the countdown ceased before the green panel went dark. The general cleared his throat—was that a sign of human anxiety?—then took the warhead from Petora and held it out to 'Szatulai.

"Please accept this as a token of our goodwill."

'Szatulai studied the weapon for a moment, pondering the possibility that the gift was simply a trap designed to sneak powerful munitions—or possibly a spy device—aboard a Covenant ship. But aside from Garvin himself, the personnel aboard the human ship did not seem disciplined enough to execute such a deception—and even if he was mistaken, it seemed an overly elaborate ruse to destroy a single Covenant vessel.

'Szatulai motioned Orsun to come forward and accept the warhead. To be on the safe side, he would suggest having the device studied in isolation on a smaller ship. But the potential intelligence value was too great to forgo. If the Engineers could learn how to prevent the devices from detonating, then the threat to the Covenant fleets would be greatly reduced.

Once Orsun had taken the warhead, Garvin said, "What happened on Seoba wasn't our doing. The Spartan task force showed up the day before our meeting with you and took us by surprise." He looked at the floor, then added, "We think it was just an unfortunate coincidence. They were intending to stage their operation out of the same ice quarry that we chose for the rendezvous."

Knowing that his black, elongated faceplate would make him appear all the more enigmatic and menacing, 'Szatulai kept his helmet tipped toward Garvin and remained silent. The only thing about the coincidence at Seoba that did *not* seem plausible was that Garvin had not foreseen it. There were three moons orbiting the planet the humans called Biko, but two were being actively mined for heavy metals. Only Seoba was deserted, and its abandoned ice quarry was an ideal staging area for an attack on the world itself.

And that thought made 'Szatulai remember Garvin's first message: *We have a little project we'd like your help with.*

Now 'Szatulai understood why there had been so many traitors on the moon. Garvin hoped to overthrow this planet's rulers and take their place—and he wanted the Covenant's help.

After a few more awkward moments, Garvin said, "We have another gift."

He slowly began to reach toward his shirt pocket. 'Szatulai knew the general feared the movement would be interpreted as a hostile act, but there was no need. Now that he understood what the traitors wanted, he no longer was concerned about their intentions. When Garvin removed his fingers from the pocket, they were holding a small flat object about the size of his palm, what the humans called a "data card."

"We've been trying to procure a suit of the Mjolnir power armor that the Spartans wear. Unfortunately, we haven't been successful—not yet." He held the card out to 'Szatulai. "But this data crystal contains schematics for their armor. If you haven't captured a datapad, we can supply one."

'Szatulai had captured many datapads during his infiltration assignments and knew how to use them all. He motioned Castor to come forward and accept the data crystal, then tipped his helmet forward and continued to study Garvin.

By now, Garvin had realized that 'Szatulai was not going to speak to him.

"We have nothing more to offer at this time," Garvin said. "But our spies are well-placed in Task Force Yama, and they've been able to plant a number of listening devices in key locations. If you can help us take control of Biko, we can help *you* anticipate the Spartans' next moves."

'Szatulai would be happy to accept the offer. On his terms, at least. He had listened in dismay as his Bloodstars fell to the Spartans in the battle of the ice quarry, and his efforts to capture one of their "prowlers" had brought only disaster and the mockery of the Fleet of Inexorable Obedience's San'Shyuum magistrate, the Minor Minister of Artifact Survey. 'Szatulai cared little enough about the opinion of the Minor Minister, but he despised any shame the order of the Silent Shadow might incur due to those failures. If 'Szatulai could leverage General Garvin to actually capture these Spartan abominations, he would more than make amends for the loss of so many warriors and vessels on Seoba.

Of course, any perceived alliance on Garvin's part would be utterly false. The planet would be cleansed soon enough, as the others before it. These Spartans, however, could not be allowed to continue, even if it required stringing along a disorganized clan of human rebels for a time. In 'Szatulai's estimation, the Spartans were the only real threat humanity had displayed so far, and he would use every tool at his disposal to eradicate them before they became a danger to the Hierarchs' plans.

'Szatulai extended a hand and turned it palm up. Garvin stared at the hand in perplexity for a moment, then finally seemed to take it as a gesture of acceptance.

"If that's a *yes*, I'm going to need a way to contact you."

'Szatulai pointed to the small woman called Petora and motioned for her to follow him. She seemed someone intelligent enough to understand the principles of operating a supraluminal communicator . . . and the consequences of allowing it to fall into Spartan hands.

CHAPTER 19

0546 hours, March 26, 2526 (military calendar)
UNSC *Point Blank*–class Stealth Cruiser *Vanishing Point*
Assault Approach, Planet Etalan, Igdras System

An invasion fleet needed five things to press its advance: munitions, medicine, food, fuel, and spare parts. Fuel was rarely a problem because most vessels carried enough aboard to power their fusion reactors for years at a time. But eliminate any of the other four necessities and, sooner or later, a fleet was just so much scrap metal.

During the slipspace journey from Biko to Etalan, John-117 and Avery Johnson had decided to attack the Covenant munitions supply first and its food supply second, since those were the two quickest ways to bring the alien offensive to a standstill. The trouble was, after observing the enemy logistics fleet for several days, it was still hard to tell the munitions carriers from the hospital ships or equipment freighters. The *Vanishing Point*'s intelligence analysts were fairly certain that the vessels with transparent domes were agricultural ships, but there were three low-orbiting behemoths that remained a complete mystery to everyone. The trio kept skimming the atmosphere and sinking into orbital decay, then having to activate their engines and boost themselves out of trouble.

And time seemed to have run out. The alien logistics fleet was syncing orbits and bringing their fusion reactors to full power, probably because the Covenant assault fleet had secured the battlefield and was ready for replenishment. There was no way to confirm that supposition—the *Vanishing Point* and its two-prowler escort had been out of touch since slipping away from Task Force Yama six days earlier. But only a fool would think that Colonel Crowther and his Black Daggers could have tipped the battle in favor of the Biko Guards' tiny armada and stopped the aliens from glassing the planet.

"This can still work," Johnson said. He was standing with Blue Team in the *Vanishing Point*'s aft fighter hangar, watching a trio of green "friend" dots lead a swarm of red "foe" triangles across the display screen hanging high on the bulkhead. "Let's take out the agricultural ships."

"What we *think* are the agricultural ships," Fred said. Like John and the rest of Blue Team, he was standing in full Mjolnir, holding an armed Mark 2521 Havok in the crook of one arm. "They could be petting zoos, for all we know."

"Yeah, but at least we'd be eliminating *all* their petting zoos," Johnson said. He wore black space assault armor and had his own Havok at his feet, next to an M99 Stanchion Gauss rifle. On his armor's mag-mounts, he carried an M41 SPNKR rocket launcher. Technically, the SPNKR was a surface-to-surface weapon, but it could be devastating in space assaults, where its range and accuracy were not degraded by gravity and atmospheric drag. "So whatever they need petting zoos for, they'd be stuck until they could bring more forward."

"I think we can do better than that, Sergeant Johnson." Dr. Halsey's voice came from the hangar hatch behind them. She crossed in front of

Task Force Yama's five captured Banshee fighters, then stopped in front of the team and continued in a low voice, "In fact, I'm quite sure we can eliminate the munitions carriers as planned."

"You've identified them?" John asked.

"Do you really think I'd be allowing you to sacrifice my Banshees if I hadn't? The value of those craft to my research is inestimable, and we have no idea when we'll capture more." Halsey turned to the bulkhead display screen and spread her fingers, expanding the tactical map until it showed fifteen red designators, all spread along a line on the near side of Etalan—the alien logistics fleet syncing orbits in preparation for departure. She pointed to a trio of crimson diamonds still preparing to transfer out of a low orbit. "Those big air-skimmers are the munitions carriers."

"No offense," Avery Johnson said, "but how can you be sure?"

His faceplate was turning between Halsey and the tactical map, where twenty green dots were diving into Etalan's gravity well, blowing through the mass of red triangles and squares that had come up to meet them. Each green dot represented an S-14 Baselard Space Striker assault fighter with a two-person crew, while the red symbols represented two different kinds of alien fighters—triangles for exo-atmosphere Banshee fighters, and squares for a much larger and deadlier craft nicknamed the Seraph.

Fortunately, there were a lot of Banshee triangles and only a few Seraph squares in the swarm, and John was hopeful that the Baselard squadron would be able to penetrate the enemy fighter screen. The four Baselards in the center of the formation were crewed by Havok-carrying Spartans. If they could get near enough to the four logistics vessels identified on the tactical map by the red octagons, all eight of those Spartans would go EV and use the empty fighters as decoys while they sneaked their Havoks aboard the target vessels by infiltrating through a hangar, an airlock, or even a plasma-cannon port.

It was a risky mission, but to John that seemed par for course lately. The Spartans had been created to serve primarily as a high-impact force against enemy surface formations, so any space operation that involved them going EV was fraught with perils they were not equipped to handle. During an EVA mission, a Spartan could easily be lost to a stray plasma strike or a chance collision, and just like that, a soldier with eight years of expensive elite training, protected by a suit of armor that cost as much as a UNSC starship, would be gone.

But if one thing had become clear after fighting the Covenant for just a few short months, it was that humanity needed to fight the aliens however it could, even if that meant assuming exceptional risk for an operation with this kind of potential to rock the Covenant back on its heels. The intelligence analysts felt about seventy-percent confident that the vessels represented by red octagons were equipment freighters carrying the spare parts and raw materials needed to keep the enemy battle fleet operational.

If those ships could be destroyed, the Covenant fleet would be forced to avoid fighting until replacements were brought forward—a process that would delay their invasion timetable by at least a month. And in this war, a month's respite might well mean the difference between humanity's survival and its destruction.

But Spartans were too valuable and rare to risk lightly. Kurt-051 and Joshua-029, who were leading Green and Gold Teams in the attack, had firm instructions to abort their mission if it appeared the Spartans' Baselards would not reach their targets. And, of course, there was a flexible but robust retrieval plan with five different contingencies for recovering each Spartan whether or not the attacks succeeded—or were even attempted. Despite this, John knew his fellow Spartans well enough to know that the last thing on their mind were mission aborting contingencies. They would do whatever it took to complete the objective.

After a moment, Halsey seemed to decide it would be easier to answer Johnson than argue with him. "I'm sure because I understand how the Covenant's plasma weapons function," she said. "Do I really need to explain the engineering to you, Sergeant?"

"How about the short version?" There was a suspicious undertone in Johnson's voice, as though Nyeto's was not the only command he viewed as being infiltrated by insurrectionist spies. "It's not like I'm trying to build one myself."

"Good, because humans don't have the magnetic stabilization technology," Halsey said. "But the theory is simple enough. A quantity of liquefied carrier gas is passed through an electric arc, where it's stripped of electrons and transformed into a thermal plasma. Then it's confined inside a magnetic capsule and launched at a target."

"So the air-skimmers collect the gas?" Kelly asked.

"And cool and compress it into a liquefied form, yes," Halsey said. "That's why they've been dipping into Etalan's atmosphere."

John frowned inside his helmet. There was no way Dr. Halsey was a spy, but her story didn't add up. "And it took you four days to figure that out?"

Halsey flashed him a tight smile. "Hardly," she said. "I figured it out about five minutes after we arrived."

"And you waited until *now* to tell us?" Johnson said, raising his voice. "Are you crazy? We could have planned—"

"No plan is adequate if the enemy knows your intentions," Halsey interrupted. "And it's impossible to be certain what kind of comm technology the insurrectionist spies we're currently hosting have at their fingertips."

"Are you telling us that there are still spies aboard the *Vanishing Point*?" Linda asked. Like Avery Johnson, she had a SPNKR on her magmount and an M99 Stanchion Gauss rifle resting on the deck at her feet. "Then why are they still alive?"

"I don't know who they are," Halsey said. "Or even *if* they're aboard. All I know for certain is that this ship has more bugs than the kitchen in my first apartment."

"And you haven't had them removed?" John asked.

"No, and I'm not going to," Halsey said. "They're vital to my operational strategy."

"*What* strategy?" Johnson asked. He turned to John and spoke over TEAMCOM. "Did she tell you about any operational strategies?"

Halsey turned and tapped the bud in her ear. "I can hear you, Sergeant Johnson."

"Still a fair question," Johnson said. "And how long have you known that Lieutenant Commander Nyeto has spies in his command?"

"I've known that Nyeto *is* a spy since the after-action briefing on Seoba, when he exposed John's age," Halsey said. "There's only one way he could have developed that information, so I swept my office and lab for eavesdropping devices."

"And you found some?" John asked.

"Oh, many," Halsey said. "Some quite sophisticated. I almost missed the data miner in my lab systems."

"*That* makes me feel better." Fred raised his arm and twisted the armor-encased limb back and forth. "Any chance our Mjolnir systems are compromised?"

"None."

"How do you know?" John asked.

Halsey appeared puzzled by the question. "Because you're still alive, John. Hector Nyeto has been trying to destroy the SPARTAN-II program since the moment he learned of it. I should have seen what he was doing sooner."

"We should have seen it too." Kelly tipped her helmet toward the others, suggesting that the entire team should have been more suspicious of the man, then said, "Are you *sure* our systems are clean? The last thing we need is a rogue subroutine putting our armor into lockdown in the middle of a battle."

"I'm sure," Halsey said. "Nyeto isn't the only one who knows how to use surveillance devices. The maintenance module hasn't been breached."

"So let's say ninety percent confidence," John said over TEAMCOM. "Have your onboard computers run a diagnostics check on your suit systems, then run one on the computer itself. If anything looks funny—"

"I can *hear* you," Halsey reminded him. "And I wouldn't let you go out if there was any chance your systems had been compromised."

"Yes, you would," Johnson said. "The Spartans may be your creations, Dr. Halsey, but they're soldiers. You're not doing anyone a favor by trying to sugarcoat that."

Halsey thought for a moment, then nodded. She turned to John and said, "We'd better put that confidence rating at eighty percent, then. One of Nyeto's people could have been in the maintenance module before I realized there was a problem."

"Fair enough," Johnson said. "Now, about your operational strategy . . ."

"What about it?"

Johnson merely cocked his helmet to the side, a gesture of frustration that he had picked up from the Spartans.

Halsey sighed. "I suppose you're right."

She glanced up at the bulkhead display, where the tactical map showed the various chases between the alien fighters and the *Vanishing Point*'s Baselard strikers continuing unabated. The Baselard squadron diving down Etalan's gravity well was shooting through the enemy fighter swarms and well on its way toward the logistics fleet's orbit, and John knew it wouldn't be long before the two Spartan teams in the center of the formation had to fake the destruction of their craft and go extra-vehicular. Rather than missiles, the Spartans' Baselards were carrying pods full of chain-linked debris that would help camouflage their Mjolnir armor from pursuers—and, with a little luck, cause a few high-velocity collisions.

A separate trio of Baselard decoys was closing on the *Vanishing Point* from a slightly lower orbit, with another swarm of enemy fighters on their tails. These Baselards were part of a second mission that would target the munitions carriers. The plan called for Blue Team to infiltrate the munitions ships by flying a captured Banshee straight into one of their hangars. Once inside, the Spartans and Johnson would crash their Banshees in an area where it would be difficult to jettison the fighters, then activate the thirty-second timers on their Havoks, leave them inside the cockpits, and extract by going EV for a prowler pickup.

As a precaution against losing all twelve of Task Force Yama's Spartans in the same attack, Blue Team's mission would only be a "go" if it appeared that Green and Gold Teams' mission was proceeding as planned. So far, that seemed to be the case, and the three decoys would be leading their pursuers past the *Vanishing Point*'s bow in nine minutes. Given that it would take Johnson and Blue Team five minutes to fire up their captured Banshees and another two minutes to depressurize the hangar, there wasn't a lot of time left for Dr. Halsey to explain the subtleties of one of her intricate strategies.

"You'll need to trust me on the details of my strategy for now," she said. "But one of the devices we captured from the downed vessel on Seoba was a holographic slipspace chart."

John almost gasped. "And you can *read* it?"

"A little better every day," Dr. Halsey said. "In fact, I believe I'm well on the way to discovering the Covenant's primary supply depot for this area of space."

"Well on the way, huh?" Johnson asked. "What's that mean, exactly?"

"That I've identified several possibilities," Halsey said. "If we succeed here and force the invasion fleet to resupply, I'll be able to narrow that number down to one."

"And then we can slip in and nuke it," John said. The implications were huge. Even an unsuccessful attack on the Covenant supply depot would force the aliens to divert resources to defending it. And actually destroying it? That would not only shake their confidence, but it would erode their ability to carry on offensive operations in this part of human-occupied space. "I like it."

"I thought you might." Halsey pointed at the trio of air-skimmers. "But first you have to eliminate *those.* It's the only way to force the Covenant's hand."

CHAPTER 20

0559 hours, March 26, 2526 (military calendar)
UNSC *Point Blank*-class Stealth Cruiser *Vanishing Point*
Assault Approach, Planet Etalan, Igdras System

Not one of the captured Banshee fighters looked combat-worthy. Their hulls had been carefully riddled with cannon holes, their canards and tail stabilizers had been shot half off, and their identifying symbols had been obscured by soot or gouging. Impact stars and stress cracks had been painted across the integrated antennas in the canopies—a precaution to explain their comm silence to any Covenant pilots visually checking on the craft. John was pretty sure that if Dr. Halsey had known the Banshee equivalent of a flat tire, she would have added that too, as a way to cover for any deficiencies in Blue Team's piloting skills.

Fortunately, the Spartans had spent most of their spare time in Dr. Halsey's projects hangar learning how to operate all manner of captured Covenant equipment, and they were decent pilots. Even more fortunately, all of the Banshees were in at least fair working order and capable of holding their own in a dogfight, and John had every reason to believe they would hold together long enough to get him and the rest of Blue Team into the middle of the alien logistics fleet.

Once the hangar hatch had snicked closed behind Dr. Halsey, John made a twirling motion with his finger, signaling the team to take their Havoks and load up. He stepped into the middle Banshee, lying prone on the pilot's cushion and securing his own Havok to a temporary mag-mount on the back of his Mjolnir armor.

John pulled the opaque canopy down and sealed the cockpit, then brought the fighter's impulse drive online and activated the instrument console. He couldn't read any of the symbols that appeared in the holographic readout panels, but after a few lessons from Dr. Halsey, he and the four other Banshee pilots—the other members of Blue Team and Avery Johnson—had learned through trial and error what panels they needed to watch closely.

Once the drive's panel had assumed a warm amber glow and the symbols remained more or less steady, he pulled the stability harness up over his flanks and hips, then placed his hands on the control grips to either side of the viewscreen. A blue luminescence arose inside the spheres, and more symbols began to swirl through the holographic readout panels. He slid his palms toward the front of the control grips.

The Banshee rose off the deck and hovered in place. Through the wide-angle viewscreen, John could see that the four other Banshees were also floating about a meter off the deck. In front of them, a remotely piloted S-14 Baselard was powered up and trembling on its struts, its single thrust nozzle glowing pale orange with thermal buildup.

The throaty voice of the Baselard's remote pilot, who would be controlling the S-14 from an observation bubble high in the *Vanishing Point*'s stern, came over the internal comm channel.

"Hangar depressurized," she said. "Blue Team ready?"

A row of LEDs—including one for Avery Johnson—winked green inside John's helmet.

"Affirmative," John said. "Blue Team ready."

The hangar lights darkened; then the exterior doors retracted to reveal the pallid face of the planet Etalan. The entire world was suffocating in its own ash, with slate-gray bands of ground showing between pearl-colored ribbons of airborne smoke. In a clear swath, John could see a hundred giant, charcoal-colored plumes billowing up from an orange lake of lava as wide across as his palm.

"Ten seconds," the remote pilot announced.

John could not quite understand what he was seeing on the planet below. From what he had been told about the Covenant's method of orbital bombardment, the aliens could glass no more than a few square kilometers of ground at a time, leveling man-made structures and incinerating plant life with plasma beams so hot they melted the silica in the ground itself. But what he saw on Etalan was on a whole new level. It was as though the Covenant had punched through the planet's crust into its mantle, creating a volcanic geyser that was going to burn away the last traces of humanity by flooding the entire world with molten stone. And if the aliens had *that* kind of power, if they were capable of cruelty on such a massive scale, Task Force Yama *had* to slow their invasion.

Whatever the cost.

"Five seconds," the remote pilot announced. "You should be able to see the decoy flight crossing from right to left, and on course to pass above the eruption."

She had barely finished speaking before slivers of plasma began to lance past the launching portal, followed an instant later by the wedge-shaped silhouettes of three S-14 Baselards. A breath later, the cruciform shadows of an alien Banshee squadron appeared on their tails, closing slowly, but filling the intervening distance with white fire.

The *Vanishing Point* cold-launched a salvo of twenty pre-targeted M42 Archer missiles, using compressed air to push them out of their firing tubes with engines quiet. In the hangar, the remotely piloted Baselard retracted its struts and shot out of the launching portal. It was accelerating so hard that, in a heartbeat, its thrust nozzle shrank from a two-meter circle of blinding brilliance into a white dot the size of a thumbnail.

It attacked the Banshee squadron at once, firing both of its M42 Archer missiles and opening up at extreme range with its twin rotary cannons. An eyeblink later, the *Vanishing Point*'s Archer salvo ignited engines and flew after the Banshees as well. The astonished aliens broke formation and scattered, leaving the three Baselards free to roll out and escape.

"Blue Team, launch," John ordered.

He pushed the control grips forward, and the captured Banshee blasted from the hangar at such speed that only the stability harness kept him from sliding toward the back of the cockpit. Johnson and the rest of Blue Team followed in the remaining Banshees, and they all fell in behind the remotely piloted Baselard. Behind them, John knew, the *Vanishing Point* would be vacating its waste holds, dumping depleted fuel pellets, empty shell casings, irreparable equipment, damaged parts, and any other kind of metallic refuse that a long-range sensor probe might interpret as shards of destroyed space fighters.

John began to tap the undersides of the control grips, pouring plasma bolts into the tail of the remotely piloted Baselard. His companions did likewise, and the space fighter quickly self-destructed in a giant fireball designed to draw the aliens' attention—and help the *Vanishing Point* withdraw undetected.

Elite voices began to sound inside the cockpit, no doubt other Banshee pilots asking for identification from Blue Team. John ignored them and led his flight straight toward the reassembling squadron.

Since they had no way of convincingly communicating with the aliens, the team's best chance of slipping into the enemy formation was to ignore any attempt to contact them and hope the Covenant would assume their comm equipment had been damaged. And if that didn't work? The *Vanishing Point* and her two escort prowlers were staying close in case Blue Team needed a distraction.

When no one in Blue Team responded to the hails, a trio of enemy Banshees broke away from the squadron and came out to intercept the new arrivals. John kept his fingers away from the weapon controls. He had no idea what the alien protocol might be for such situations, and he didn't want to find himself automatically responding to a challenge rush or signal burst. He wished he had thought to suggest the same thing to the others, but it was too late now.

To prevent the possibility of the Covenant noticing strange transmissions coming from the "damaged" Banshees, Blue Team would be maintaining complete comm silence until it grew apparent that the enemy wasn't buying their act.

The intercepting Banshees swelled quickly from tiny specks silhouetted against thumb-size thrust halos into drooping crosses being pushed along on thirty-meter efflux tails, then dropped their noses and flashed past beneath Blue Team. On his own craft's tracking panel, John saw the enemy fighters swing up behind his flight and match velocities. Two of them hung back, ready to open fire on the formation from behind, while the third crept slowly forward, passing within twenty meters of each "damaged" Banshee—no doubt so the pilot could inspect them. Finally it reached the front of the formation and hung alongside John at about the same distance.

The enemy pilot remained alongside for nearly a minute. When Elite chatter started to sound over John's comm system, it began to seem likely that the alien had been awaiting some signal and was requesting instructions from his commander. John tried the standard wing waggle, but that drew no response. He slid his hands toward the back of the controls.

The Banshee responded by dropping its tail and lifting its nose, and John quickly returned his hands to the original position. More comm chatter filled the cockpit, and the alien inspector finally moved ahead of the flight. He rocked his own craft in a manner similar to what John had done, then led the entire flight back into the main squadron.

Once all the Banshees were together, the unit commander quickly aligned them above the logistics fleet and began to sync orbits. Because of the squadron's much higher orbit, the process would involve a lengthy series of thruster burns timed to drop it into position either just ahead of or behind the logistics fleet. John relaxed a bit. They had planned this attack to the last detail that could be foreseen, and that was what made it possible to handle the little things they had no way of predicting.

Below him, he could see the tiny wedges of twelve Baselards juking and jinking as they tried to drop into orbit ahead of the logistics fleet. He suspected that the eight missing craft had been destroyed as they passed through the fighter screen, but the fact that the squadron had not aborted its run suggested that the Baselards carrying Green and Gold Teams were still intact. Which was a good thing. With so many enemy Banshees in formation behind them, Blue Team had just passed its own mission's no-abort point.

Planning.

It was as much of an asset to the Spartans as their Mjolnir armor. A pair of Baselards burst into orange flashes and vanished. John watched for hints that it had been one of his Spartan teams going EV, but saw no signs either way—no tiny specks silhouetted against the pearly clouds below, no Covenant fighters circling back to attack unseen targets, no flickers of small-arms fire. Either the attack was working as planned, or the *Vanishing Point* had just lost two more fighter crews.

The thought made John queasy, and he found himself feeling a bit guilty about all of the lives being sacrificed to deliver his Spartans to their targets safely. At least the cause was worthy. Assuming Dr. Halsey was right about finding the Covenant supply depot, succeeding today would not only slow the enemy invasion, it would give Task Force Yama the opportunity to serve the Covenant a pushback they would never forget.

Another pair of Baselards exploded, and John now felt confident that both Green and Gold Teams had gone EV to attack their targets. When their Havoks detonated, Blue Team would take advantage of the inevitable confusion to slip away from their escorts and head for the three air-skimmers. After that, it would be a simple matter of flying into the closest hangar and crashing their Banshees, then setting a timer switch and shooting their way out before their own Havoks detonated.

The Banshee squadron escorting Blue Team dropped into orbit ten kilometers behind a huge, pear-shaped materials freighter, and John started to worry about timing. If the Green and Gold Team bombs didn't detonate before—

John's viewscreen flashed silver as the freighter suddenly vanished in the white wink of a nuclear detonation. His comm system erupted first into static, then into unintelligible chatter as the aliens reacted to the vessel's destruction. John checked his Banshee's tactical readout and saw the logistics fleet stretched out along its orbit, a gently arcing line of alien symbols shaped vaguely like commas, asterisks, and wavy equal signs.

Another white wink appeared in the distance, this time so far away it was little more than a flare atop the rim of Etalan's gray horizon. The chatter coming over the cockpit comm system was now a full-blown cacophony, and swarms of fighter-dots began to appear beneath the remaining symbols on the tactical readout.

John didn't know whether the detonations were the work of Green Team or Gold, but it was clear that one of them had succeeded and its members were on their way to the extraction point. They had definitely inflicted some damage on the Covenant's logistics fleet, but it was going to take far more than a two-vessel loss to make Halsey's strategy work.

The other two materials freighters suddenly vanished into balls of blazing light, and John knew that his second team of Spartans had completed its mission. One detonation was so close that his Banshee's instruments flared gold as the pulse of gamma rays overwhelmed its radiation shielding. The comms fell silent, and a second later the cockpit sank into darkness as the readout panels and control grips flickered out. Etalan's gray horizon began to tip and slide past the canopy as the Banshee started a slow tumble, dead in space.

"What junk," Fred remarked over TEAMCOM. "They call *that* radiation shielding?"

John was about to chastise him for breaking comm silence, then noticed all of the other Banshees drifting dead in space around him and realized that comm silence was no longer needed. The pulse had taken out the entire squadron's instruments and controls, so the Covenant pilots no longer *had* the capability of noticing a TEAMCOM transmission. And with logistics vessels vanishing one after another, the comm officers in the rest of the fleet were going to be too busy and confused to track down a few stray signals that probably sounded like blast static anyway.

But there was a drawback, of course. A big one.

Blue Team's Banshees were just as dead in space as those of the Covenant. If the Spartans stayed with their craft, they would be out of the battle and eventually taken prisoner by the Covenant's recovery teams. Which meant that Blue Team had to go EV, because the only mission outcome worse than dying and triggering their Mjolnir's automatic self-destruct mechanism was *not* dying and allowing the enemy to capture it.

"We still need to take out their munitions train," John said over TEAMCOM. He didn't need to remind them of what Dr. Halsey had said—that taking out the munitions carriers was the key to her strategy to find the enemy supply depot. “Anybody have a visual on those air-skimmers?”

“Maybe,” Fred said. “What do they look like?”

“Big and fat,” Avery Johnson said. “Like an overstuffed cigar with a huge megaphone on the front.”

“How do you know that?” Linda asked.

“’Cause I’m looking at two of ’em right now,” Johnson said. “The first one is going to pass underneath us in about . . . hell, I don’t know. Soon.”

“EV range?” John asked.

“Are you crazy?” Johnson replied. “Making an impromptu EV attack . . . under *these* circumstances?”

“We have to go EV anyway,” Fred said. “These Banshees are toast.”

“And there is no way a prowler can retrieve us from this orbit,” Linda added. “Not when it will soon be filled with Covenant search-and-rescue craft.”

“So we might as well do something useful while we’re out there floating around,” Kelly said. “Are the air-skimmers in range?”

“For you nutjobs, probably,” Johnson said. “I’ve spun away from them now, but my rangefinder had the leader at fifty-two kilometers. I’d guess that puts their orbit about ten kilometers below ours.”

Ten kilometers was nothing at orbital velocities, but the timing could be difficult. If Blue Team failed to transfer to the lower orbit in time to intercept the targets, they would have to drop into an even lower orbit and try to catch up—or remain in a higher orbit and wait for the air-skimmers to pass underneath them again. Either maneuver would take time to execute, and there was no telling how soon the alien fleet would break orbit and flee into slipspace.

It was now or never.

“Prep for EV,” John said. Since they were already wearing sealed armor, all the process entailed was switching their air supply to their rebreather systems—a task the onboard computer performed for John automatically. "I'll take the first skimmer. Kelly has the second, Fred the third. Linda and Sarge, you know what to do."

There was a reason Linda and Johnson were armed with M99 mass-driver sniper rifles instead of the MA5Cs that everyone else carried. The M99s used magnetic accelerator technology to fire undersize ammunition at velocities so high that the rounds created shockwaves as they passed through their targets. The rounds might not be able to pierce a Covenant fighter's energy shield, but they could penetrate thirty centimeters of titanium armor, and in the vacuum of space, their range was limited only by the accuracy of the person firing. They had been included in the team's load-out to discourage any harassment by Banshees and other unshielded craft during extraction, but they could serve the same role on an attack insertion.

Three status LEDs flashed green inside John's helmet, but one blinked amber.

"Go ahead, Linda."

"The air-skimmers have already deployed their fighters, so there won't be much hangar traffic," she said. The original plan had called for John, Fred, and Kelly to simply park their Banshees in a hangar, then leave their Havoks in the cockpit and exit on foot. Now that their Banshees had been disabled, that wouldn't be possible. "How will you bypass the energy shields?"

John hadn't actually worked out that part yet, but Avery Johnson had. "Won't have to," he said. "The skimmers are still retracting their collection cones."

"So?" Linda said.

John realized what Johnson was thinking. "So it's pretty hard to skim gas with your energy shields up." He checked to make sure the magclamp holding the Havok to his back armor was secure, then reached for the canopy's manual release. "If we can intercept before they secure the collection cones, we won't need to board."

"Piece of cake," Fred said. "We just intercept an alien vessel traveling twenty-five thousand kilometers an hour, slip through its fighter screen, land on the hull long enough to stick a thermonuclear device on it, and get clear before the device detonates."

"Technically, you don't need to get clear," Linda said. "But I would miss your wisecracks, so do your best."

"Everybody gets clear, got it?" John released his stability harness. "Jump-off in three, two—"

He pulled the manual release. The canopy popped open, and the decompression lifted him out of the slowly spinning Banshee. The maneuvering jets on his thruster pack began to fire intermittently as his onboard computer worked to stabilize his tumble. He pulled his MA5C assault rifle off its magnetic mounts and worked to orient himself, trying to keep his gaze fixed on Etalan's gray surface and locate the fat cigar shapes Johnson had described.

At first, all John saw were disabled Banshees drifting past. He had no doubt the Elites inside were surprised to see Spartans going EV in the middle of their formation. But so far none of them seemed to be popping their own canopies to offer battle—which was hardly surprising. Most pilots were not equipped for zero-g small-arms combat.

Once his tumble had stabilized, John located a trio of purple, finger-length tubes drifting across Etalan's gray face. They had bulging centers, visibly contracting cones at the front end, and swarms of fighter-specks swirling around their entire length. He designated the lead vessel as his target. The Mjolnir's onboard computer placed a waypoint on his HUD that pointed at a spot just above the planet's horizon, then initiated a thruster burn.

"Blue Leader on intercept vector target one. ETA . . ."

John paused while the computer put the figure on his HUD, then was momentarily taken aback at what he saw—apparently, it was going to require a constant thrust maneuver to catch the air-skimmer. He just hoped the computer was leaving some propellant in reserve so he would be able to accelerate away after attaching the Havok.

The waypoint rose a little higher, and the ETA adjusted upward.

"Five minutes twenty," John read.

"I'll be on your six," Avery Johnson reported. "A thousand meters back."

"Negative," John said. He only had two snipers available right now, and he wanted them covering his people . . . not him. "Go with Fred or Kelly."

"Blue Two and Three have closer intercept angles," Linda said. "I'll be able to cover them both for most of the way."

"*Most* isn't good enough," John said. He wasn't going to risk losing Fred or Kelly so *he* would be covered. Not when Sam had died because he had stepped in front of a plasma bolt meant for John. No chance. "I want Blue Two and Three covered separately."

"John, you need to get over the hero complex," Johnson said. "Blue Four's disposition makes the best use—"

"Sergeant, I'm in command of Blue Team," John said. "Let's do it my way."

"I almost wish we could," Johnson shot back. "But I'm committed to this vector."

"You're *what*?"

"You can yell at *me* . . . but later, okay?" Linda said. "I had to make a snap decision, and that's what I decided."

TEAMCOM filled with static and space flared white as a Havok detonated behind them.

"Oh, yeah," Johnson said. "Fire in the hole. I left my Havok in the Banshee."

John did not need to ask Staff Sergeant Johnson's reasoning. The last thing Blue Team wanted was to leave witnesses who could describe their infiltration techniques—and the detonation would help cover their target approaches. If a sharp sensor operator happened to defeat their armor's ablative coating and notice a few contacts moving away from the detonation, there was a good chance it would be attributed to explosion debris and not investigated further.

John let out a sigh. He was starting to remind himself of Crowther, focusing on how much control he had rather than on getting the job done.

"Good thinking, Sarge."

"Imagine that." Johnson's tone was about half amused and half irritated. "The old guy has a few tricks up his sleeve."

By now, the lead air-skimmer was just a dozen kilometers behind John and about five below, in a position where he could keep an eye on it without having to wrench his helmet around. It had swelled to the length of his arm, and to him it looked more like a pregnant cigar than an overstuffed one. Its hull was lined with bands of blue lights that occasionally seemed to writhe or wink as an escort fighter passed over. The fighter craft themselves were still just specks, too small to identify . . . and an indication of just how massive the munitions carrier actually was.

The cone at its bow had contracted to about half its previous diameter. Now it seemed to be slowly sliding back into the vessel itself. Even more alarming, the stern was trailing a faint blue glow—a sign that it was firing up its reactors and preparing to break orbit.

The ETA on John's HUD gave him almost three minutes to interception. He watched the cone carefully, trying to figure out how soon it would be fully retracted—since that would probably be when the huge vessel reactivated its energy shields.

The construction of the cone seemed as strange as everything else about the aliens. From what John could see, it consisted of eight flexible poles that occasionally sparked and crackled with energy as they were drawn into the air-skimmer's bow. The gossamer panels between them seemed to wrinkle like cloth one moment and flicker like light the next, and from John's angle, he could not see whether they were vanishing into the bow with the poles or just fading into nothingness.

The cone was down to a quarter of its original length when fighter specks began to bleed away over the air-skimmer's sides. At first, John feared they were returning to the hangar in preparation for breaking orbit. But when a quarter of them remained on station above the vessel, he realized something else was happening.

The mystery was solved a few moments later when a pair of bell-shaped silhouettes appeared above Etalan's ashen clouds—the *Vanishing Point*'s escort prowlers approaching in a low retrograde orbit. The two *Razors* were engaged in recovery operations, plucking Green and Gold Teams out of low orbit after their attacks. But, of course, the Covenant would not know that. The aliens would assume the two craft were preparing for a strike on their munitions train. John hadn't actually planned on having the recovery operations serve as the diversion for Blue Team's attack, but he was grateful for any help he could get.

Lances of light began to streak back and forth as the two sides opened fire on each other. The human attacks appeared to be coming out of nowhere, though John knew that was just an illusion. Each prowler was being escorted by some of the *Vanishing Point*'s Baselards, but the UNSC fighter craft were too small to be visible at such an extreme distance.

When the ETA on John's HUD reached two minutes and thirty-seven seconds, the onboard computer chimed a warning. He shut off his primary thruster and used the maneuvering jets to swing him around so he was descending toward the interception point backward. Two seconds later, he reignited the primary thruster and fired it hard, decelerating in preparation for syncing orbits with his target.

No stealth system was perfect, and even the ablative baffles affixed to his thruster pack could not conceal the sudden heat blossom of a triamino hydrazine blast pointed directly at an alert enemy. In the next heartbeat, a handful of fighter flecks rose from the small swarm keeping station above the air-skimmer and streamed toward John.

There were only eight of them. But when a soldier's only anti-spacecraft weapon was a MA5C assault rifle—and evasive action was impossible because he was on an intercept vector that could not be varied—that was eight fighters too many.

"Sergeant, are you seeing this?"

"Damn right," Johnson said. "You want me to do something about it? Or would you rather handle it on your own?"

The pointed questions were obviously a reminder of John's attempt to overrule Linda's decision to have Johnson cover him, but the wily sergeant was not the kind to rub in a mistake for no reason. He was trying to teach John a lesson he wouldn't forget—and John wouldn't have minded so much, if all hell weren't about to break loose on him.

"Just give them something to worry about," John said. He could not help thinking that either Fred or Kelly might be facing the same situation right now—*without* backup—but there was nothing to be done about it except trust Linda's judgment. "Can you tell what kind of fighters they are?"

"Banshees," Johnson said. "The Seraphs went after the prowlers."

"That's something, I guess." Banshee fighters were smaller, lightly armed, and far less resilient than Seraphs—primarily because Seraphs had energy shielding. "*All* of them?"

"All the ones I can see through this scope," Johnson replied. "Shooting past you. No sudden moves, Blue Leader."

"No problem."

Sudden moves could be catastrophic during an active thruster maneuver, since they could throw off the traveler's center of gravity and send him spiraling out of control as his thruster nozzle pointed in different directions. If that were to happen, his onboard computer would take control and bring his tumble back under control within a few seconds—but by then, John would be off-vector and completely unable to intercept the target.

He continued to watch between his feet as the Banshees approached. They were coming straight at him now. Their efflux glow made them look like eight pinhead-size halos rising up beneath his feet. His own thruster exhaust was dark but hot, and it created distortion waves that made the halos seem to jump and bounce as they approached.

One of the halos veered off, either hit by M99 fire or reacting to it; then it curved away and descended toward the air-skimmer. It didn't seem possible that Johnson had actually hit the craft at a range that was probably in excess of fifty kilometers, but he saw no other explanation for the Banshee's sudden departure.

"Did you get it?"

"All the way from here? I'm good, but not—" Johnson broke off as the Banshees opened fire, hiding their halos behind a blinding spray of plasma bolts. "John, abort!"

"Negative." Covenant plasma bolts began to flash past him on all sides—but not closely. He was still a small target, and the enemy was still a long way off. "Keep firing."

The plasma barrage continued to intensify, and John lost all sight of the enemy behind what had become a column of white fire boiling up around him. He checked his ETA and realized he would never survive the two minutes it would take to sync orbits, much less the time it would take to execute a proximity maneuver and actually land on the air-skimmer's hull. Eventually the range would drop to the point where the Banshee plasma cannons grew accurate. Of course, Johnson's aim with his M99 would grow more accurate too—but there were still seven Banshees and only one Johnson.

Hoping to obscure some of the enemy targeting sensors, John

emptied the MA5C's underslung grenade launcher. The plasma barrage abated for a moment, then quickly reintensified as the Banshees reacquired the heat signature from his thruster pack.

In response, John shut down the thruster pack, and the waypoint on his HUD began to drift as the onboard computer struggled to calculate a new syncing vector. But John didn't actually need to sync orbits; he just needed to intercept the air-skimmer for about a second. He fired a maneuvering jet, spinning himself around so his primary thruster was no longer pointed toward the approaching Banshees, and the fountain of oncoming plasma fire quickly grew more diffuse as they lost their targeting data.

John breathed a little easier, then felt a maneuvering jet fire as his onboard computer put him on a new interception course. The ETA on his HUD lost forty seconds, and he found himself with less than a minute before impact.

"John, I've lost you," Johnson said. "Are you—"

"Keep firing!" John slid the Havok's control panel open and checked his new ETA—fifty seconds—then entered a time delay of thirty seconds. He set the trigger to automatic but didn't initiate the countdown. "And set an avoidance vector. In about forty seconds, you're not going to want to be within five kilometers of that skimmer."

"John?" Johnson's tone was worried. "John, what the hell are you doing?"

John kept his gaze on his ETA readout. He couldn't afford to blow the timing. Thirty-six seconds.

"Son, listen to me," Johnson said. "Don't be a goddamn hero."

John *really* wished the staff sergeant would shut up so he could concentrate.

The ETA readout reached thirty-one seconds. He initiated the Havok countdown and felt a thrill of satisfaction as it flashed thirty in the same instant as his ETA readout.

Below him, the air-skimmer had swelled to the size of a Mongoose ATV. The gossamer scoop in front had retracted so far into the vessel's bow that it looked more like a cup than a cone, and the bloated hull was undulating like a soft-sided bag filled with liquid. A kilometer or two above the hull, John could see the teardrop shapes of the remaining escort fighters sweeping up in an ever-widening search pattern. Clearly they had been warned to expect his approach. If they could see him from their position, he might look like a small insect falling into the open maw of an enormous fish—except, by the time the fish reached him, he'd be long past it and there would be a surprise there instead.

John detached the Havok from its magmount and let it float free. The device was on the same interception vector he was, so even if the enemy fighters took *him* out, the Havok was likely to destroy the target.

John checked the ETA on his HUD. In fact, he could almost guarantee it would.

"Damn it, answer me, John!"

"I'm here, Sergeant." John activated his primary thruster and shot past the air-skimmer, barely seven kilometers above its dorsal hull. "But, Sarge, with all due respect . . . you really need to stop treating me like a kid."

Whatever Johnson replied, it was lost to blast static.

Space flashed white everywhere but in front of John, and his HUD showed the Mjolnir armor's shell temperature climbing *way* above the danger level.

Priorities, though. As long as his HUD was still functioning, he was still alive.

CHAPTER 21

Ninth Age of Reclamation, First Annual, Second Month
34th Cycle, 208 Units (Covenant Battle Calendar)
Fleet of Inexorable Obedience, Assault Carrier *Pious Rampage*
Middle Equatorial Orbit, Planet Borodan, Kyril System

Nizat 'Kvarosee had not expected the planet's atmosphere to combust when he ordered mass plasma strikes on the capital city, but the result—a blanket of flame that had spread across an entire world—caused him no horror or remorse. The human defenders had stalled his advance with their stubborn resistance, harrying the Fleet of Inexorable Obedience for five of Borodan's days, destroying five of his cruisers and all of the orbital shipbuilding stations that he had hoped to capture for the use of his own flotilla. Even more infuriating, they had used the battle to hold his attention while a smaller force slipped away to decimate the supply convoy he had left at the site of his last victory, the world E'gini, which humans called Etalan. Was it any wonder that when Nizat looked down on the terror and suffering that his word was laying on the world below, he felt nothing but satisfaction? The humans had brought his advance to an ignominious halt, and they had shamed him in the eyes of the Prophets. Now he could not kill them fast enough.

It did not escape Nizat that his path on the Great Journey seemed to be darkening with every step, but there were some things that even a Sangheili fleetmaster could not change. His path had been chosen for him by the Hierarchs themselves, and he could not turn from it without renouncing the possibility of his own divine transcendence.

"This time you have outdone yourself."

The Minor Minister of Artifact Survey was floating next to Nizat, his serpentine neck fully extended as he watched the mangled torus of a human shipbuilding station drift past in low equatorial orbit. The station's much-perforated hull was still white with heat dissipation, and its rotation was a lopsided gyre that would soon send it spiraling into the flame clouds below.

"I shall inform the Hierarchs of your efficiency when next I visit High Charity."

High Charity was the moon-size space station that served as the Covenant's sacred capital city. Nizat doubted that Survey would be returning there anytime soon—or that the San'Shyuum would ever mention Nizat to the Hierarchs in terms that were not vaguely derogatory and self-aggrandizing—but he clacked his mandibles in acknowledgment.

"I am honored by the thought, Your Grace."

Survey flicked a tri-digit hand. "Think nothing of it," he said. "But I wonder how wise it is to *continue* the cleansing of this planet with our supply of carrier gas running so low. How many survivors can there be, when the air itself is aflame?"

"The firestorm looks more fearsome than it is," Nizat explained. "If we do not keep feeding it more plasma, it will burn itself out. And the flames alone are not hot enough to fuse the ground. Without the bombardment, there will still be fertile soil and foundations that can be used to rebuild."

"Forgive me if I am wrong," said a voice behind them, "but I believe the Minor Minister is concerned about a human counterattack."

Nizat turned to see Tel 'Szatulai gliding into the observation blister as quietly as a breath—at least, he *assumed* it was 'Szatulai. As always, the first blade was encased in the indigo armor of the Silent Shadow, complete with closed helmet and a total absence of identifying emblems. A few steps behind him, Nizat's abashed steward, Tam 'Lakosee, was scurrying to catch up.

Nizat sent 'Lakosee off with a motion, then fixed his gaze on 'Szatulai and took a moment to swallow his anger. He was furious with the first blade for allowing part of the human prowler force to slip away earlier and devastate his logistics train at E'gini. Only the agricultural ships and a couple of medical vessels had survived, and they had been stranded there for five of the humans' days, waiting to break orbit until a properly protected convoy could be organized.

But Nizat also recognized how 'Szatulai's intelligence sources had saved him—and perhaps prevented the destruction of the entire Fleet of Inexorable Obedience. Had the first blade's spies not warned them about the human boarding strategy, Nizat's shipmasters would have sent their fighters forward to strike the enemy fleet instead of holding them in close escort, and the human prowlers would have been able to deploy their boarding parties practically unopposed.

Nizat allowed his eyes to narrow, then finally asked, "Are the Minor Minister's concerns warranted? Should I be expecting a counterattack?"

"Why would you trust his answer?" As Survey spoke, he made a point of keeping his antigravity chair turned toward the front of the blister. "The blademaster's guidance has proven nothing but incorrect."

'Szatulai stopped next to the San'Shyuum's chair and tipped his helmet sideways, as though he was glaring down on the top of the Minor Minister's head. It was a gesture that made Nizat wonder if a member of the Silent Shadow had ever been ordered to execute a San'Shyuum—and whether 'Szatulai would accept such an order from Nizat.

It was a dangerous thought to entertain—even as a fantasy. The Silent Shadow lived by a code known only to them, but Nizat suspected that it would include eliminating anyone who posed a danger to any member of the Covenant's San'Shyuum leadership caste.

After ridding himself of such a blasphemous impulse, Nizat turned to face Survey head-on. "Without the intelligence supplied by First Blade 'Szatulai, we might have lost fifty ships instead of five."

"But his assignment is to kill these so-called Spartans," Survey said, now apparently oblivious to the threat of a counterattack he had mentioned just a dozen breaths earlier. "*If* they actually exist. I am beginning to suspect they are phantasms created to frighten us."

"They are real," 'Szatulai said.

"Then you have killed one?" Survey's tone suggested he already knew the answer. "You have provided a body for the Minister of Infidels to contemplate?"

"No," said 'Szatulai. "But we have learned their names—at least, the names of twelve assigned to what they designate as Task Force Yama."

Nizat had not heard this before—perhaps it was the news 'Szatulai had come to report. "How?"

"From the Blacksuits we captured aboard the *Purifying Flame*," 'Szatulai said. "Castor and Orsun have been making progress."

Survey whirled his chair around. "You are allowing *Jiralhanae* to interrogate the prisoners? Are you that stupid?"

'Szatulai tipped his helmet toward the Minor Minister and did not speak.

"How many have they killed?"

'Szatulai ignored Survey and turned to Nizat. "The Blacksuits call themselves 'Black Daggers.' They are part of a military force that the humans refer to as Orbital Drop Shock Troopers, though this battalion specializes in space assault. They have been so well trained in resisting interrogation that even the mind melters failed."

"But your battle chiefs succeeded?" Nizat asked.

"The Jiralhanae have a game called 'tossers,'" 'Szatulai said. "And humans do not like the sight of their companions' limbs being torn off. There are some who will reveal anything after helping a disabled companion eat, drink, and eliminate for a day."

"That is a start," Nizat said. "But if that is all you have learned thus far, you may run out of prisoners before they reveal something useful."

"We *have* run out."

"And you expect the fleetmaster to sacrifice *more* ships in an attempt to capture new prisoners?" Survey glanced up at Nizat, an invitation in his bulbous eyes that made the fleetmaster want to gouge them out with his thumbs. "You will have enough to answer for in High Charity as it is."

A strange sound, perhaps some kind of amusement, came from inside 'Szatulai's helmet. "There is no need to sacrifice ships on purpose. We will no doubt lose some to battle . . . and there will be ample opportunity to take more prisoners."

"That sounds . . . unfortunate," Nizat said.

"It has been a mistake to judge the humans by their vessels," 'Szatulai said. "If they cannot fight us on our terms, then they are determined to fight us on theirs."

"They sound like followers of the Silent Shadow." Survey's tone suggested he was not offering a compliment. He shot Nizat a sideways glance. "That may make it difficult for the fleetmaster to explain his failures to the Hierarchs."

"If the task were simple, I would not have assigned it to the Silent Shadow," Nizat said. Clearly, Survey was trying to draw him into some kind of blame-passing—and Nizat had no intention of participating. "We are fighting a war out here, not maneuvering for a seat on the High Council."

Survey rocked back in his antigravity chair and stared at Nizat with a trembling throat wattle. "I see. . . ." he said. "This is not going to end well—not for *you*."

"Nevertheless, I *will* hear the blademaster's report," Nizat said. "Uninterrupted."

Survey's eyes narrowed. "As you request."

Nizat turned back to 'Szatulai. "Tell me the rest."

"All we learned from the prisoners, I have already spoken of." 'Szatulai glanced toward Survey. "But the human traitors have confirmed what we guessed—the attacks on the Fleet of Inexorable Obedience here were meant to distract us while the Spartans destroyed our logistics train at E'gini."

"Did I not say that?" Survey asked.

"We *all* said that—after the fact." Nizat looked back to 'Szatulai. "Why did the traitors not warn us beforehand?"

"They claim their spy was misled—that he was told the Spartans were holding here in the Kolaqoa system," 'Szatulai said. "They claim he didn't know the truth until after Task Force Yama rendezvoused with the Spartan detachment."

"And you do not believe this story?" Nizat asked.

"The traitors are using us to rid themselves of the Spartans," 'Szatulai replied. "Everything I have seen tells me that is so."

"And yet?"

"And yet . . . this is the second time that believing the traitors' story has brought catastrophe," 'Szatulai said. "The humans may be even more cunning than we believe."

"Or they know their task force has a spy," Survey said. "And they have been using that human to lead us into traps."

'Szatulai paused, then said, "It seems possible."

"It seems certain," Survey insisted. "Where is Task Force Yama now?"

"Unknown," 'Szatulai said. "The spy reported the rendezvous, but the traitors have not heard from him since."

A ripple ran up Survey's long neck, and he turned to Nizat. "Stop the cleansing right away. We need to conserve our plasma."

Nizat understood Survey's sudden fear—that the humans were about to attack the Fleet of Inexorable Obedience while it was low on munitions—but what the San'Shyuum knew about fleet warfare would fit into the bottom of his throat wattle.

"Doing that would reveal our dependence on the bladder ships," Nizat said. "The humans would know we are low on carrier gas and be more likely to attack in force. It is better to make them believe our supplies remain ample."

"Until the cleansing stops because you have run out completely," Survey replied.

"That will not happen," Nizat said. "I have called a new logistics flotilla forward. It is already at E'gini, gathering the vessels that survived the Spartan attack. They will join us here in fifty units."

"What?" 'Szatulai was aghast.

Nizat tipped his head to the side. "Fifty units," he repeated. "The humans will never know we are low on carrier gas."

"Because they are not *in* the Kolaqoa system," 'Szatulai said. "The new logistics flotilla stopped at E'gini?"

"Did I not say just that?" Nizat asked. The Silent Shadow did not frighten easily, so he was troubled by what he heard in 'Szatulai's voice. "What is your fear?"

'Szatulai looked down and hesitated, a clear indication that he was not eager to reply. Yet the Silent Shadow prided themselves on their integrity and courage, and their code of honor demanded the same conduct whether they were standing on the battlefield or in the presence of a superior. He raised his helmet again.

"I beg your forgiveness, Fleetmaster, but I did not think this important until now." As 'Szatulai spoke, he was careful to avoid looking in Survey's direction—though, of course, that only caused the San'Shyuum to tip his chair forward and pay closer attention. "I sent a demolitions band to find and destroy the wrecks we lost on Seoba. Unfortunately, they were not the first group to arrive."

Nizat felt a hollow forming between his hearts. "What did the humans obtain?"

"From what we can tell, only a palmful of things," 'Szatulai said. "But after hearing about the logistics flotilla that you called to E'gini, the one that concerns me most is the *kelguid* from the bridge of the *Worthy Silence*."

Nizat hissed in a breath. A knowledgeable reader would be able to use a *kelguid*—the interactive star map that Covenant navigators used to plot journeys through slipspace—to lay bare the Fleet of Inexorable Obedience's supply network and identify its critical support nodes.

"You are certain they have it?"

"The floor mounts had been neatly cut," 'Szatulai said. "They have it."

"That does not mean they can operate it," Nizat said. "A *kelguid* is a complicated device, far beyond their technological capabilities."

"We did not believe they would be able to pilot Banshees either," 'Szatulai said. "We were not even aware that they had captured any."

"What are you fools saying?!" Survey nearly shouted. "They are preparing to attack High Charity?!"

"Not High Charity," 'Szatulai said. "Zhoist. That would make the most sense to the humans."

"You have a poor record of predicting what the humans will do," Survey said. "We have no choice but to return to High Charity at once. They will need the Fleet of Inexorable Obedience there to aid in its defense."

"And leave Zhoist on its own?" Nizat splayed his mandibles, then clacked them closed again. "High Charity has a home fleet a dozen times our size. Zhoist has only a rapid-response flotilla that would be hard-pressed to stop a human attack."

"Have you learned nothing from your defeats?!" Survey was livid, his voice warbling with rage. "Every time you think the humans are doing one thing, they do another! We must go to High Charity's defense, if only because *you* think the humans will go to Zhoist!"

"Your Grace," 'Szatulai said, "why would the humans attack High Charity? If they know of it at all, they also know they will find nothing there but death."

"What does death matter to a doomed species?!" Survey's voice was pitched high in panic, although Nizat felt certain that had less to do with High Charity's safety than with Survey missing a chance to present himself to the Hierarchs as the savior of the sacred city. "The humans will go to High Charity because they are soon to perish, and they thirst for vengeance!"

'Szatulai raised his helmet toward the overhead, and Nizat thought perhaps he would find out after all whether a member of the Silent Shadow would dare kill a San'Shyuum. A part of him hoped that was true, and that he would not be wandering too far off his own dark path if he offered to conceal the blasphemy.

But when 'Szatulai lowered his gaze again, his gloved hands remained at his sides, and he addressed Nizat over the top of the San'Shyuum's head.

"The humans do not thirst for vengeance, because they refuse to believe they are doomed," he said. "They will go to Zhoist because attacking our supply chain buys them time—time to study us and learn our weaknesses, time to develop weapons that are the equal of our own."

"Weapons equal to the *Covenant*'s?" Survey warbled in incredulity. "Impossible."

'Szatulai turned to the San'Shyuum. "It would be foolish to underestimate them, Minor Minister," he said. "Our human spies acquired the schematics of the power armor that helps make the Spartans so ferocious. It is impressive, even by our standards."

"You have examined these schematics yourself?" Survey demanded. "That could be considered blasphemy. You will turn them over to me at once."

"At the first opportunity, Your Grace." 'Szatulai spoke in a nonchalant tone that suggested the first opportunity would not be coming soon, then turned back to Nizat. "As I said, Fleetmaster, we must meet them at Zhoist."

Nizat raised his head to indicate agreement, then thought better of it and dropped his gaze to the San'Shyuum. "It is a pity the humans are not as wise as Your Grace," he said. "But I trust 'Szatulai's judgment in this. The humans are not intelligent enough to know that their days are truly numbered."

CHAPTER 22

0626 hours, March 31, 2526 (military calendar)
UNSC *Point Blank*-class Stealth Cruiser *Vanishing Point*
Deep Space, Rendezvous Point Sierra-Yama, Polona Sector

To Catherine Halsey, the holographic image above the captured starholo resembled a half-eaten dinner of spaghetti and meatballs that had just entered zero-g and floated up off the plate. In this case, the plate was a silver disk sitting atop the cylindrical, waist-high equipment cabinet Task Force Yama had recovered from the Covenant frigate that the Spartans had downed on Seoba.

The "meatballs" represented gravity wells of various sizes, and the "spaghetti" represented the curvature of space-time around them. Sometimes, the spaghetti would bend so tightly they touched themselves somewhere along the strand, creating connection points that could be used as transit nodes by a slipspace-capable vessel.

With a little luck and a lot of hard work, Catherine hoped to use the starholo to trace the Covenant's slipspace routes back to the primary supply depot serving their invasion fleet. She had already identified more than twenty transit nodes that opened near gravity wells she believed to be Harvest, Netherop, and Etalan—all planets that the Covenant had attacked and glassed. But only four nodes were also near other nodes that created a slipspace route into Covenant space—or, looking at it another way, *out* of human-controlled space.

Since it had taken five days for a new supply convoy to arrive after her Spartans destroyed the one at Etalan, she assumed the Covenant supply-depot had to be located somewhere between half and three-quarters of that distance at their slipspace travel rates, which seemed to be several times faster than human rates. Even if the message calling the replacement fleet forward had traveled faster than their vessels could, it would still need some time to traverse such vast distances.

Unfortunately, there were no gravity wells within that range on her short list of likely routes into Covenant space. Clearly, she was making an incorrect assumption somewhere along the line.

Without looking away from the starholo, she said, "Déjà, how certain are you about the size of the logistics base required to support the Covenant fleet? I don't see any worlds in range."

There was a pause and an unusual *clitch*-sound, and then the limited artificial intelligence created to assist Catherine with the SPARTAN-II program answered. "The calculations are correct, Dr. Halsey. The amount of resources required to support and maintain the enemy fleet are immense. The only feasible way to marshal them is from a depot supplied by a habitable planet—and because of the logistics involved in moving such vast amounts of cargo, efficiency dictates that it be a single habitable planet. Gathering supplies from two locations even in the same star system would create inefficiencies that would inevitably result in significant shipping delays."

"Then where *is* this planet?"

Catherine waved a hand into the starholo and felt a cold tingle. Startled by the sensation, she quickly realized that sticking her hand into an alien projection field might not be healthy, and removed it. There was so much she didn't know about Covenant technology, and that grew more apparent every time she used the starholo. Capturing it intact had been the kind of lucky break that could change the course of the war—and, unfortunately, the kind that was unlikely to come along twice. She had to make the most of the opportunity and figure out how to find the depot planet.

She turned toward Déjà's projection pad. The AI presented herself as Greek goddess with flowing brown hair and brown, almond-shaped eyes.

"Habitable worlds create gravity wells," Catherine continued, "and there aren't any—not within four days of the most likely transit nodes."

"But there is a habitable world within five days of Transit Node Bhadra." Déjà made the *clitching* sound again, then paused for a decisecond before continuing, "Perhaps it's not my calculations that are mistaken, but *your* assumption."

"Are you suggesting the Covenant has instantaneous interstellar communications?"

Déjà spread her hands and *clitched.* "I am suggesting the Covenant has a great deal of . . . *clitch* . . . technology that we don't . . . *clitch* . . . understand."

Catherine already understood the cause of Déjà's erratic pauses. She had tracked it down to a sophisticated data miner, which had been slipped into her quarantined lab computer by Hector Nyeto or one of his operatives. She was putting up with it not only because it had already succeeded in stealing her most closely guarded data, but because Catherine didn't want Nyeto to realize she was onto him until she had decided his usefulness was at an end.

She turned back to the starholo and began to study the likely routes into Covenant space, looking for others with a world in the five-day range. Two had planet-sized wells within six days of Etalan, but the gravity well at Transit Node Bhadra was the only one at five days.

"Very well, Déjà," Catherine said. "Your theory is the only one that fits the facts. We'll assume that the Covenant *does* have instantaneous interstellar communications—and visit Transit Node Bhadra first."

"A superb choice, Dr. Halsey." Déjà drained back into her projection pad, saying, "And now I think I should take my leave. Your gentleman caller has arrived."

"About time."

Catherine deactivated the starholo, then went to a mirror and ran her fingers through her black hair. Despite being the mother of a one-year-old daughter named Miranda—a daughter who occupied her every non-working thought, who deserved to grow up on a planet that had not been glassed by the Covenant—she still presented a striking figure and didn't think she would have much trouble convincing her caller to accompany her to her private compartments. She went to the door, then thumbed the control pad and put on a big smile.

"Colonel Crowther, what a delight."

The colonel stood on the threshold in a rumpled work uniform. His weathered face looked confused and tired. "Your message said you wanted to see me as soon as the rendezvous was complete? For a . . . *personal* matter?"

"That's right," Catherine said. Knowing that she was almost certainly being watched by Hector Nyeto or one of his subordinate spies, she grabbed Crowther by the elbow and drew him into the lab. Then she hooked her arm through his and started across the deck toward her private compartments. "I just couldn't wait another hour for us to be alone."

Crowther looked confused, but tried to play along. "I see."

"I *hope* so," Catherine said. They reached the entrance to her private compartments. She placed her thumb on the biometric reader and stared into the retina-scanner, and the door slid aside. "It's not easy for me, you know."

“I should imagine not.” Crowther was being a good sport, but Catherine could see that he was a bit flustered by how tightly she was pressing her flank against his. After all, she’d had no secure way to warn him about her intentions. “You’re still a young woman. I can’t understand what you see in a man my age.”

“*Experience.*” Catherine pulled him through the door into her little galley area. “You really know how to handle yourself in a clench.”

“Well, I *am* infantry.” Crowther stood just inside the threshold, surveying the compartment as though looking for snipers. “You’re quite apt yourself.”

Halsey flashed him a warm smile. “Why, thank you, Marmon.”

She thumbed the control pad and waited until the door had snicked closed, then released Crowther’s arm and pointed him to a stool at the breakfast counter.

“It’s safe to talk in here,” she said. “I sweep for eavesdropping devices three times a day. It’s been clean so far.”

Crowther took the stool and continued to study the compartment in silence.

“I can offer you water.” Catherine was starting to wonder if she had picked the right man for this job. “Warm or cold?”

“Cold would be nice.” Crowther smiled and almost looked relieved. “I *am* feeling a bit flushed.”

Catherine returned his smile. “Sorry for the show, Colonel,” she said. “But we need to talk about how we’re going to handle Hector Nyeto before he tries to kill my Spartans again.”

CHAPTER 23

0458 hours, April 14, 2526 (military calendar)
UNSC *Point Blank*–class Stealth Cruiser *Vanishing Point*
Covenant Space, Slipspace Transit Node Bhadra, Muruga Sector

Nobody knew what the Covenant called sectors in their part of the galaxy, or what terms they used for slipspace transit nodes, or how they described the vast emptiness that separated one star system from another. But Halima Ascot had named Task Force Yama for the Hindu god of death, so in her honor, Dr. Halsey had chosen Hindu names for the alien territory that Task Force Yama was invading. The transit node, where one slipspace route ended and another began, she had named Bhadra, after the goddess of the hunt. And their current sector she had named Muruga, after the god of war.

They were good references, and John hoped they would prove prophetic.

It had been just under four weeks since Halima Ascot's death at the Seoba ice quarry, but it felt like months. After observing the arrival of the alien relief convoy at Etalan, Dr. Halsey had used their captured starholo to retrace the convoy's route into enemy space and identify the likely location of the enemy supply depot. Even with the improved slipspace efficiencies due to Dr. Halsey's understanding of the alien starholo, it had taken the task force two weeks to arrive at Slipspace Transit Node Bhadra—a pocket of star-flecked space more than two hundred light-years beyond humanity's farthest known exploration. And now the task force was preparing to launch an attack that would show the Covenant just how mistaken it had been to declare war on humanity.

John would have been confident of success, had it not been for one man: Hector Nyeto.

He was still the task force commander, thanks to Dr. Halsey and Colonel Crowther, who claimed they were using him to mislead the enemy. Maybe that was the truth, or maybe Nyeto was playing *them*. Either way, John didn't like it.

He knew from his own interactions just how gutsy and deceptive the commander could be, and Dr. Halsey had made an interesting discovery by researching Nyeto's personnel records. Early in his career, he had apparently spent a lot of time on missions with the infamous traitor Robert Watts, whom Blue Team had captured on their very first mission. It wasn't much of a stretch to think that one of them had radicalized the other, and that Nyeto was aware of the part the Spartans had played in his old friend's apprehension.

And right now, Nyeto was standing across the hangar, waiting at the foot of the *Ghost Song*'s boarding ramp while John received some last-minute guidance from Crowther and Johnson. It was hard to concentrate, because John was about 90 percent certain that Nyeto was going to sabotage the mission in an effort to get all of Task Force Yama's Spartans killed—and never mind who else died, or how much it set back humanity's fight against the aliens.

"Smile." Avery Johnson's voice was low enough to avoid carrying across the fifty meters of deck that separated Nyeto's *Ghost Song* from the *Black Widow*, which John would soon be boarding. "Wave."

"Why do I have to smile?" John raised his hand and waved. "I'm wearing a helmet."

"Body therapy," Johnson said. Like John, he was wearing his assault armor, but his helmet and weapons had already been stowed aboard the *Ghost Song.* "You're so damn mad that even your armor looks tense. Smiling will relax you."

John attempted to do so inside his helmet. Meanwhile, Nyeto raised his hand back to John and smiled as well.

"I can't believe I'm doing this," John said. "Can't I just kill him now?"

"And alienate every prowler crew in the task force?" Crowther shook his head. "I wish you could, especially given how many Black Daggers his treason cost us at Seoba and Biko. But Nyeto is a very popular commander. You kill him, you have to kill his people."

"So you're saying it's a bad idea?"

Crowther chuckled. Apparently, he had grown accustomed to John's dry sense of humor over the past week of clandestine planning sessions. More importantly, it had become apparent that Avery Johnson had not been exaggerating when he told John that Crowther had experienced a change of heart about the Spartans and no longer seemed to consider their age a detriment.

The colonel had hardly apologized about his earlier treatment of John and his squad—far from it. But he *had* been careful to consult John about every aspect of the upcoming mission, and had even designed much of it to take advantage of Spartan capabilities.

And John too had done some reevaluating. He had come to recognize that the colonel's original reticence had been warranted, that the Spartans' relative lack of field experience was a weakness that needed correcting before they could be expected to survive as many special ops missions as had Crowther's oldest Black Daggers. John was actually feeling guilty for the motivations he had recently attributed to the colonel.

It had been a strange week, for certain.

Crowther said, "I'm saying we can't fly those prowlers ourselves." He pointed up the ramp behind John toward the boarding vestibule of the *Black Widow*, which would be serving as Sierra Force's command vessel on this mission. "Let's talk in private for a minute. There's something I need to do, and I don't want a lot of eyes on us."

"Of course, sir." John led Crowther and Avery up the ramp into the small vestibule, then turned and said, "Before we begin, I'd like to apologize for how I reacted to your reservations about our age and experience."

Crowther waved him off. "Never apologize for making yourself clear, John. I don't." He reached into his shirt pocket. "I have something for you, but first I want to make something clear. After what you did at Seoba and Etalan, you deserve these—and you deserve the full ceremony, on the bridge of the largest ship in the fleet. But . . . that's not what you're getting. There are going to be some very experienced Black Daggers in your group wondering why you're in command and they aren't, so we need to act now. This will remind them it's because *I* said so."

He extended his hand and displayed a metal armor insignia with three chevrons capped by a rocker. The UNSC eagle was perched atop the rocker, and above each of the eagle's upraised wingtips was a star.

John wasn't sure he understood. "Sir . . . that's the rank insignia of a master chief petty officer."

Crowther smiled. "I'm aware of that, John." He used a thumb to tap the down-turned dagger that sat between the chevrons and the rocker. "I couldn't find anything without a space assault rating, but what the heck . . . we're all special ops."

John still did not take the insignia. “That’s a four rank jump, sir.”

“And I’m going to catch ten kinds of hell for it from FLEETCOM,” Crowther said. “Maybe even from Admiral Cole. But he’s the one who told me to do whatever’s needed . . . and *this* is needed.”

“Colonel, I . . . I can’t accept that.”

“Not your choice,” Avery Johnson said. “Colonel Crowther and I talked this over at length. We decided it’s the best thing for the mission.”

“Exactly,” Crowther said. “Consider yourself under orders.”

Crowther reached up and affixed the insignia high on John’s chest plate, over the left collarbone where ODSTs wore their rank when under armor. “You’re now going to be leading two companies of my Black Daggers in Sierra Force. That means two captains and a fistful of lieutenants who outrank you, and a bunch of gunnery sergeants who think they do. All of them are older than you, most nearly twice your age . . . and a handful three times.”

He jammed a finger against the insignia, then continued, “*That’s* the only reason they’re going to listen to you. A four-rank bump is unheard-of, so you better believe they’ll know I’m standing behind you. Are we clear on that, Master Chief?”

“Yes, sir,” John said. “I understand.”

“Good. I was starting to think it was a mistake to put you in charge.”

“It isn’t. Sierra Force will get the job done.” John paused, then said, “But I worry about the risks that you and Sergeant Johnson are taking with Dagger Force. I wish there was another way.”

“There’s always another way,” Crowther said. “But not always more time or resources. Especially now. We’re at war. And we work with what we have.”

John nodded. “All the same, I wish I could trade places with you and Sergeant Johnson today.”

Crowther chuckled. “So do I.” He let his gaze drift to the insignia on John's armor, then grew more serious. "John, there's something that goes with that rank that you still don't have—and you need to get it straight, and *fast.*"

John's stomach tightened. "I'm listening, sir."

"You should know that you earned a lot of respect at Seoba, and not just from me."

"Thank you, sir."

Crowther motioned that he wasn't finished. "And you're a good leader. Your Spartans would follow you into a fusion reactor if you asked them to."

"I'd do the same for them."

"I know you would," Crowther said. "And that's the problem. Sometimes a good commander can't be a hero. You have to be willing to send your people into that reactor alone, if that's what it takes. And I honestly haven't seen that ability in you—not once."

John glanced toward Johnson, wondering if it was Crowther's words or Johnson's he was hearing. Both of them had been on him about "leading from the front" since the day his squad was attached to the 21st.

"I've lost Spartans in battle before," John said. "I just try not to make it a habit."

"And I'm not encouraging you to," Crowther said. "But that armor doesn't make you invincible. If you're always the first one in, and the one who takes the biggest chances, sooner or later, you're going to get hit. What happens to the unit then?"

"Fred takes over."

Crowther rolled his eyes. "And command continuity suffers. Even if Fred is as good as you are, it will take your people a couple of seconds to adjust."

"And a lot can happen in two seconds," Johnson added. "A unit can get wiped out."

John didn't reply. He knew they were right. But he just didn't like the idea of ordering his friends to take risks in his place. It seemed cowardly.

But so did getting his squad wiped out because he was afraid to let somebody else take point. Johnson was right about that much—you could lose your entire unit in two seconds of combat.

"The commander of an elite unit has to trust his people as much as he trusts himself," Crowther said. "You don't have that yet—and I'm not sure if it's something that you'll ever be comfortable with. But you're still young—an understatement, to be sure—and that level of trust is something you need to think about if you're going to live up to that insignia on your collar."

"Thank you, sir. I will."

Crowther studied him for a moment, then finally nodded. "You do that, Master Chief."

He gave a curt nod to Johnson, then left the boarding vestibule and crossed the hangar to the *Ghost Song*, which would be serving as Dagger Force's command vessel. John was tempted to offer a salute, but he knew Nyeto would be trying to see what was happening inside the vestibule, and he didn't want an unnecessary show of respect to tip their hand.

Johnson stepped in front of John. "I guess this is good-bye, then, Master Chief." He was making a good show of smiling, but his eyes were stoic, and John knew he believed they would not be meeting again. "You just remember what the colonel said. Do what you have to."

The sergeant extended his hand.

"I will." John took the offered hand in his gauntlet and shook. "Thanks for showing me how much I *didn't* learn on Reach. I needed the lessons."

Johnson's eyes crinkled at the corners. "Anytime."

He tried to withdraw his hand, but John held tight. "I'm going to hold you to that, Sergeant Johnson."

Johnson grew more somber. "Then make it through this," he said. "Listen to Crowther—and *trust* your people."

The sergeant withdrew his hand and left the vestibule, then walked across the deck to board the *Ghost Song.*

John returned to the hatch and watched for a second, trying to digest what had just happened. He was flattered by the promotion, of course, and proud that he had earned Crowther's respect to such an extent. But he was also keenly aware of the heavy responsibility that had just been laid on his shoulders. A four-rank bump was so unheard-of that it was bound to draw as much scrutiny from inferior ranks as it did from his equals and superiors. From that moment forward, John knew, he would have to prove in everything he did that he was worthy of such an honor.

Linda-058 stepped into the vestibule behind him. When he turned around, her helmet tipped slightly, and he knew she was looking at the rank insignia affixed over his collar.

"Nice bling," she said over TEAMCOM.

"Crowther's idea," John replied. "He says I need the cred."

"Can't hurt," Linda said. "Just don't let it go to your head."

"Thanks. I'll try not to."

"All prowlers have checked in clean."

"Anybody find anything?" John asked. Sierra Force had four prowlers divided into two half-strength flights, and he had put Spartans aboard all of them, with orders to sweep for eavesdropping devices and keep a subtle eye on the crews. Aboard the *Widow*, that duty had fallen to Linda, while Fred and Kelly were in the drop bay, watching Third Platoon, Delta Company. "Or take any guff?"

"Negative on the guff," Linda reported. "But I found a bug in the *Widow*'s wardroom, and Kurt found one in the *Quiet Man*'s."

John thought for a moment, then said, "I guess that's a good thing. It means Nyeto isn't counting on our flight commanders for updates."

"It doesn't mean they're going to trust *you* when things start getting . . . weird."

John tapped his new rank insignia. "That's why I have the bling."

As they spoke, a crewman was raising the ramp and securing exterior hatches for immediate launch. The *Vanishing Point* and its escort complement would be staying behind at Transit Node Bhadra. But the rest of the task force, or what remained of it after losing half its strength—over four hundred troopers and seven prowlers at the battles at Seoba and Biko—was clustered in two nearby formations, awaiting the two command prowlers.

Led by Nyeto—at least temporarily—Dagger Force was the larger of Yama's two strike forces, with three prowler flights carrying three half-strength space assault companies that numbered only two hundred and forty-three troopers between them. The mission plan called for it to depart first and approach the night side of the Covenant supply world, a planet they were designating "Naraka." This attack was designed to draw out the defensive flotilla stationed at Libration Point Three. Sierra Force would follow a few minutes later and approach from the same side of the planet. Their primary objective was to infiltrate the remaining defenses and storm the orbital facilities that ringed Naraka.

That was the plan, anyway. John didn't think the coming battle would actually unfold that way, and neither did Crowther or Johnson. They were expecting Nyeto to try to get the Spartans killed somewhere along the way. But how the traitorous commander would do that—and what would happen when Crowther and Johnson tried to stop him—was anyone's guess.

The launch alarm sounded, and the *Black Widow* rose off her struts and exited the hangar. John barely noticed the acceleration anymore. He started forward toward the flight deck, while Linda remained amidship to keep a quiet eye on the crew. Fred and Kelly were in the drop bay with Third Platoon.

John knew the bay wouldn't be as crowded as it had been when he and Avery Johnson had dropped with First Platoon Alpha back at Seoba, which now seemed so long ago. While Delta Company had suffered less attrition than most of the battalion during the Battle of Biko, it had lost forty-three troopers, and Third Platoon's strength had dropped from forty ODSTs to thirty-two. Still, he hoped that Third Platoon's lieutenant didn't take offense at what he was about to do. Thirty-two ODSTs would be a tall order for a pair of Spartans to neutralize—especially if they were trying to avoid a lot of casualties.

And the odds would be even worse for the Spartans on Sierra Force's other prowlers. In most cases, there would be a single Spartan on the flight deck and one in the drop bay. John had four prowlers and only twelve Spartans. That meant the vessels with a full team were the two flight-leads, the *Black Widow* with John's Blue Team, and the *Quiet Man* with Kurt-051's Green Team. Gold Team was split among the two remaining prowlers, with a pair of Spartans aboard each craft.

John reached the *Widow*'s flight deck and stepped into the compartment without asking permission. It was a terrible breach of shipboard decorum, and Esme Guayte—the naval lieutenant who commanded the flight—shot him a fiery scowl.

John pretended not to notice and remained beside her command chair, studying her through the anonymity of his mirrored faceplate. She was a compact woman with black hair, brown eyes, and a round face. Like the Quiet Flight commander, Lim Jinwoo, Guayte had actually been raised on Earth, and she had attended the Luna OCS Academy in Mare Nubium—which was about 90 percent of the reason John had chosen them for Sierra Force. Of all the flight commanders in Task Force Yama, they seemed least likely to be harboring hidden insurrectionist sympathies. But they were also Nyeto's subordinates, and John would be fooling no one—including himself—if he tried to pretend the orders he was about to relay didn't border on mutiny.

The slipspace formation appeared ahead, a band of dark voids hanging against the veil of stars beyond the forward viewport. There were no running lights or illuminated viewports to help define their shapes more precisely—this deep in alien space, it was not wise to increase the risk of being spotted by a passing patrol.

Nyeto's *Ghost Song* was moving into formation with the most distant cluster of vessels, its thrust nozzles a triangle of barely visible purple disks. Guayte looked away from her command screen long enough to glance up at John, no doubt intending to make a pointed inquiry about what he needed on her flight deck, then noticed the new insignia at the top of his chest plate and raised her brow.

"Where did *that* come from?"

John tipped his helmet down toward her. "Colonel Crowther wanted to see how it looked on a suit of Mjolnir armor, ma'am." He turned his gaze forward again. "I guess he liked it."

Nyeto's voice sounded over the flight-deck speakers. "Dagger Force, bring all weapons and power to battle-ready. Execute slip in five, four . . ."

The stars beyond Dagger Force began to dance and twinkle as long tongues of efflux shot from the thrust nozzles of a dozen vessels; then the prowlers were gone, a field of bright purple disks shrinking to a thumb-size dot in the duration of a blink, the dot vanishing into the blue crackle of a slipspace vortex.

Guayte extended a finger toward the comm selector on the arm of her chair.

"Not yet, ma'am."

Guayte glanced at him in puzzlement and left her finger on the selector. "The timing of this operation is intricate, Master Chief. If Sierra Force doesn't enter slipspace as scheduled—"

"Not yet," John repeated. He pulled a data chip from an equipment pouch and handed it to her. "New orders."

Guayte's eyes narrowed, but she accepted the data chip and slipped it into a reader slot. Colonel Crowther's face appeared on her command screen.

"Lieutenant Guayte, I am sure you will recall the conversation we had about operational security," the image said. *"It pains me to say that was not idle speculation. Operation: SILENT STORM has been compromised, and as of this moment, you will consider Commander Nyeto relieved of command."*

Guayte stopped the message and looked over at John. This was the critical moment, he knew. While Crowther's rank was superior to her own, he was not actually in her chain of command. She would be well within protocol to ignore his instruction and carry on with the orders she had been given by Nyeto.

"You knew about this?" Guayte asked.

"We're the ones he's been trying to kill."

"And that's why there's a Spartan standing on the flight deck of both my prowlers?"

"Yes, ma'am. And it's why we swept them for eavesdropping devices as soon as we boarded," John said. "Would you like to see what we found?"

"That won't be necessary," she said. "How would I know they aren't props you brought along to impress me?"

Guayte started the message again, and Crowther's image continued: *"I have provided an alternate vector through which you should exit slip-space. The transit specifications are embedded at the end of this message. As you know, John-117 has been given command of Sierra Force. I hope and expect you'll honor that, no matter what your feelings are about Commander Nyeto."*

Crowther saluted, and the message ended.

Guayte sat staring at her blank command screen in silence, then turned and eyeballed John's new rank insignia for a time.

Finally, she broke her reverie and said, "Very well, Master Chief. You're in charge." She began to tap the keypad on the arm of her command chair. "Please try not to get us killed."

CHAPTER 24

1458 hours, April 15, 2526 (military calendar)
UNSC *Razor*-class prowler *Ghost Song*
Libration Point Three, Naraka/Rudara, Agni System

The Covenant outpost came into view, a smudge of green light dead ahead of the *Ghost Song*'s hushed flight deck. It was blurred by the dust and detritus that always collected in libration points, those odd pockets in space where the gravity of two orbiting masses—in this case, a planet and its moon—interacted to create zones of equilibrium that could be used to "park" objects in a fixed relative position.

In the Naraka/Rudara system, the aliens had parked picket squadrons at Libration Points Three, Four, and Five. The deployment created an equilateral triangle that was perfect for defending the orbital facilities around the distant, pearl-colored marble of the alien supply world. And it was Dagger Force's job to neutralize those picket squadrons so Sierra Force could stage a clean attack.

Ghost Flight was assigned to hit libration point three, on the opposite side of Naraka from its moon, Rudara—both names picked by Dr. Halsey, as she had not yet determined their Covenant names.

According to the battle plan, that would be the side of the planet from which Sierra Force approached with the Spartans and a hundred and thirty-nine Black Daggers. And it was Avery Johnson's job to make sure that when Lieutenant Commander Hector Nyeto tried to sabotage the mission, he would be exposed for the traitor he was.

The alien outpost grew from a green smudge to a thumb-size dust cloud with dozens of glowing points inside. Half of those lights were probably support stations rather than combat vessels, but still . . . Ghost Flight was outnumbered more than five to one. If they failed to attack with surprise, they stood no chance of neutralizing the picket squadron—or even surviving the effort.

A crisp female voice rose from the navigator's station. "Five minutes, Commander."

Nyeto, seated in his command chair near the back of the compartment, glanced over with a look that suggested Avery had no business being there. Fair enough. With five minutes to go before jump, Avery was standing on the flight deck in full assault armor. It certainly *looked* like he was supposed to depart with First Platoon Alpha.

Avery was actually there to back up Colonel Crowther, who stood next to him in Service Dress B, a formal working uniform with a khaki shirt and tie appropriate to the task at hand. Weapons weren't allowed on the flight deck, so neither of them was openly carrying. But Avery had hardened cargo pouches on his thigh armor that could clearly hold concealed sidearms. Only a fool would not realize something was up.

When Avery made no move to depart, Nyeto frowned and turned to the *Ghost Song*'s sensor operator. "What is detection telling us?" he asked. "Any sign of Sierra Force yet?"

The operator, a senior petty officer, shook his head. "Negative, Commander. I should have had a tau surge from their transition sector by now. Nothing."

Nyeto checked his chronometer, then rubbed his chin and made a point of not looking toward Johnson and Crowther. Prowlers could be difficult to detect even when their location was known, so the mission plan called for him to assault the libration point whether or not he confirmed Sierra Force's arrival. Even from profile, Johnson could see Nyeto's eyes narrowing as he struggled with his decision. Unless he knew the Spartans' location before Ghost Flight attacked, he wouldn't be able to do anything to make the Covenant look in that direction. But with Johnson and Crowther present, he had to realize that any deviation from the plan would only confirm to them what he was really up to.

Finally, Nyeto said, "There's no point in attacking if Sierra Force isn't ready."

Avery tried to remain relaxed. Nyeto was starting to go off-protocol now. Once he pushed too far, Crowther would have clear cause to relieve him of command and take over. Of course, there was a good chance that Nyeto recognized what was happening right in front of him and would stop just short of any clear violation.

That was okay too. The mission would be in less jeopardy.

But the traitor was nothing if not determined, and Nyeto seemed to realize that no matter how today turned out, this would be the last chance he had to eliminate the Spartans. He turned to his communications officer.

"Prepare a burst transmission requesting ready-confirmation."

"And send it where, Commander?"

Burst transmissions were usually targeted, point-to-point communications that could be sent with only a small chance of detection. The drawback, of course, was that the target's location had to be known.

Which it obviously wasn't, which meant Nyeto was about to go too far.

The only question was, how would the crew react when Crowther relieved him of command?

A lot of Nyeto's people came from Outer Colony worlds where insurrectionist sympathies were common, and the commander could not have single-handedly planted and monitored all the eavesdropping devices that had been discovered around the task force. There had to be at least a few loyalists aboard the *Ghost Song* working with Nyeto—and one or two might even be on the flight deck right now.

And that was the reason why Avery was standing next to Crowther with a pair of M6C pistols in his thigh pouches.

Nyeto checked his chronometer again, then said, "The Covenant will know they're under attack in a few minutes anyway." He tapped his fingertips on the arm of his chair three times, as though deep in thought, then sighed and said, "Broadcast it in the open."

"Belay that order," Crowther said.

Johnson felt an almost imperceptible shudder beneath his feet, as though the *Ghost Song* were reacting to Crowther's audacity. The communications officer paused only long enough to glance to Nyeto for a confirming nod, then began to prepare the burst transmission. Nobody seemed to be looking in Avery's direction, so he let his hands drift over his thigh pouches and slipped his fingers under the flip-up covers.

Crowther's gaze moved from the communications officer to Nyeto. "Commander, sending that microburst will accomplish nothing," he said. "There won't *be* a response because Sierra Force already knows exactly what you really are. I'm hereby relieving you of command and charging you with treason against the UNSC."

"Relieving *me* of command?" Nyeto laughed and leaned forward, his left hand dropping out of view down in front of his chair. "That's funny."

In a flash, Avery drew both pistols from his thigh pouches. He aimed one at the back of Nyeto's chair and offered the other to Crowther, but the flight deck's sensor operator was already spinning around, bringing up an M6E sidearm. The muzzle flashed twice, and Crowther went down with a crater in his forehead and blood spurting from his clavicle.

Avery returned fire with both pistols, blasting the sensor operator from his seat and putting two rounds into Nyeto's chair, then realized he was stumbling back, his torso armor hammering into his chest as he took round after round, the attack coming from the navigator and the copilot. Hell, even the communications officer was now firing at him, and she was supposed to be preparing a burst transmission.

Apparently *everyone* on the flight deck was a damn traitor.

Knowing his armor could not keep absorbing bullet impacts forever, Avery backed away through the flight deck hatch, still shooting, then started down the starboard passageway and saw a trio of crewmen coming toward him. All three were armed with M7 submachine guns, but holding their weapons muzzle-down as they raced into combat.

Not infantry-trained, clearly.

Avery charged, emptying his magazines as he ran. There was a very small chance that the three crewmen were a legitimate security detail reacting to an order from their commander, but of course there was no way to sort that out in the middle of a firefight.

One of the trio sprayed a burst into the wall as he went down, but those were the only shots any of them managed to fire.

Avery tucked his pistols into his thigh pockets, then snatched up the two submachine guns that hadn't been discharged and started aft. He didn't like leaving the third weapon behind when it might be used against him later, but the situation had gone south in a hurry. As much as he refused to believe an entire flight crew could go renegade, there was no arguing with what had happened to Crowther. Hell, from what he had observed so far, the *Ghost Song*'s entire complement could be insurrectionist traitors.

He needed immediate reinforcements.

Avery brought up the assault armor's HUD and eye-selected First Platoon Alpha's comm channel.

"Red eagle!" The prearranged code that would tell First Platoon to take the prowler by force. "Red eagle, now!"

Five meters down the passageway, two hatches slid open simultaneously on either side of the corridor. One led into the two-deck engineering hold in the middle of the vessel, the other into a crew cabin. Firing both weapons, Avery put a suppression burst through each portal.

A second later, once he was sure his would-be attackers were ducking ricochets instead of watching the passageway, he stopped firing and raced past, then spun around and found two gun barrels emerging from each opening. One was high and the other low, which was smart. But all four weapons were pointed up the passageway in the direction he had been coming from, which was dumb.

Avery stepped between the hatches and emptied an M7 magazine into each opening, firing low first because he knew the recoil would naturally cause the weapons to rise. The air filled with red mist and smoke, and four bodies tumbled out into the passageway.

"Damn, Sarge!" Captain Hamm's voice sounded inside Avery's helmet, coming over the Alpha Company command channel. "Leave a few for the rest of us!"

"There's plenty to go around." As he spoke, Avery was careful to keep an eye on the motionless crewmen lying at his feet. It was still remotely possible that one or two were alive. "Crowther's dead. Looks like the whole crew is with Nyeto."

"All of Ghost Flight, actually," Hamm said. "And they were expecting this."

Another brilliant observation from an officer. Avery took his eyes off the dead crewmen just long enough to check the passageway behind him. Relieved to see Hamm approaching with a pair of Black Daggers beside her, he smashed the stocks of the empty M7s against the edge of the hatchway and took a replacement from the hands of a petty officer first class who had died with his one remaining eye wide open.

By then, Hamm was stepping to Avery's side, motioning the two Black Daggers to check the compartments beyond the body-clogged hatches. Only then did Avery feel secure enough to take a longer look back down the passageway toward the drop bay.

There were only two more assault troopers in the passageway.

"Where's the rest of the platoon?"

"Vacced," Hamm said. "Your 'red eagle' was a tad late."

Avery's heart sank. "Damn it. Nyeto blew the jump hatch?"

"About twenty seconds before you called," she said. "The decompression caught us by surprise—took about two blinks to empty the bay. Connor grabbed the hatch release, and I held on to his ankles, watching everybody go. It was like seeing a vacuum cleaner suck sardines out of the can."

Avery thought for a moment. Nyeto had told the comm officer to broadcast in the open—and tapped his fingers on the arm of his chair.

"Oh, damn," Avery said. "Nyeto gave his crew a *go* signal. It was nonverbal, but I should have caught it. Warned you. I'm so sorry."

Hamm waved him off. "They're still alive, Sergeant. Our guys were buttoned up," she said. "All we have to do is take the flight deck and go pick them up."

"*After* we hit the L-point," Avery said. "We don't do that, this mission is a bust."

"The *Night Watch* is carrying on," Hamm said. The sole surviving prowler from Watch Flight, the *Night Watch* had been attached to Ghost Flight to replace the *Ghost Star*, which had been lost at Seoba. "She's carrying Third Platoon under Olinda MacDonnell."

"I thought Third Platoon was at half-strength after Seoba."

"They are," Hamm said. "But Olinda is kind of the Black Dagger version of John-117—stubborn as hell and doesn't know when to quit. She'll get the job done, one way or another."

A couple of assault rifle bursts sounded inside the engineering hold; then Hamm's trooper returned and gave a thumbs-up. Hamm looked up the passageway in the direction of the flight deck.

"How many did you get down there, Linberg?"

"Two," Linberg reported. Her voice was a bit quavery. "Not sure whose side they were on, but they had weapons and wouldn't drop them."

"That makes them the enemy," Hamm said, reassuring her. "Johnson, how many have you taken out?"

"Seven in the passageway."

"Seven?"

"Plus the sensor operator on the flight deck," Avery added. He didn't care for the note of surprise in Hamm's voice—it made him think she had a poor opinion of what old sergeants could do. "Maybe Nyeto too."

"Just maybe?"

"Best I could do." Avery pointed to the dimples in his chest armor. "I was taking fire and trying to shoot Nyeto through a chair."

"We'll take it from here, Sergeant." Hamm sounded amused. She turned to the two troopers who had been waiting behind them. "Counting our measly six, that's fourteen. That means Nyeto still has two crewmen running around loose, and someone might have left the flight deck too. Don't let us get surprised."

The troopers answered almost in unison, with young-sounding voices: "Yes, ma'am."

Hamm turned to the trooper who had checked the crew cabin. He had a flat-black second lieutenant's bar on the collar of his armor, which made him First Platoon's new lieutenant, Nolan Connor.

"Let's take this bat, Nolan," she said. "I don't want our people adrift any longer than necessary."

"Yes, ma'am." Connor pulled a coil of thermite-carbon cord from one thigh pouch and a pair of flashbangs from the other. "Which do you want, Sergeant?"

Before answering, Avery glanced around at the weaponry everyone was carrying. All five of the Black Daggers held MA5B assault rifles, which were decent weapons for close-quarters boarding actions. Their selectors were set to three-round burst fire, and the red paint on their magazines meant they were loaded with hollow-point ammunition that was perfect for the current circumstances—highly effective against unarmored personnel, but unlikely to penetrate equipment cabinets, hulls, or viewports. They knew how to take a flight deck.

Avery clamped the M7 to his armor, then reached for the thermite-carbon cord. "Let me have the T-C-C," he said. "I wouldn't want to get in your way when the shooting starts."

They moved forward at a trot, the two young troopers clearing each compartment they passed.

When they finally reached the flight deck, no one was surprised to find it sealed from the inside.

Hamm sent the two young troopers to clear the port side of the prowler, then stood watch while Avery pasted the T-C-C in place.

The hatch was designed to suck tight against its seals in the event of a pressure loss in the main body of the ship, so when Avery ignited the T-C-C, it would fall inward. As it dropped, Connor would toss both flashbangs into the compartment, and Hamm would step inside and shoot the traitors while they were still stunned from the flashbangs.

And, with any luck, they would do all that before Nyeto located Sierra Force and started hitting them with tight-beam transmissions to draw the attention of the Covenant.

Avery was pressing the cord down the last side when a young trooper's voice sounded over the platoon channel.

"Captain, we can't access the emergency airlock."

"Why not?" Hamm asked.

"Unclear. The pressure is equalized. We should be able to open the hatch."

"What do you see inside?"

"Nothing. The viewport is fogged."

Avery didn't like the sound of that. He came to the corner of the hatch and ran the T-C-C across the bottom. The whole reason airlocks had viewports was so that if something was wrong, you could look inside and see the problem. He reached the detonation cap and wrapped the extra cord around it to complete the circle, then looked up to see if Hamm was ready . . . and, on the wall above her head, saw a dark bulb about the size of a pencil eraser.

A security camera.

"Oh, shit," he said.

Hamm's faceplate dropped in his direction as a tremendous *boom* sounded somewhere aft, and she rose off her feet and flew down the passageway, bouncing off the bulkhead and vanishing down the portside passageway. And Avery went tumbling after her, his arms and legs tangled with Connor's, and together they hit the bulkhead and ricocheted down the portside passageway after the captain.

The air was filled with blankets and pillows and clothes, tools and crates and weapons, all of it sailing toward the midpoint of the passageway and disappearing through a jagged hole where the emergency airlock used to be.

Avery saw Hamm being drawn toward the breach, flailing and clawing at the bulkheads; then she jackknifed at the waist and went through the hole. Connor was next, back arching and head going first. Avery's stomach rose as though he were falling, then he felt himself bend at the waist and suddenly he too was out among the stars, his ragged breath roaring in his ears and his heart hammering in his chest.

Vacced.

Avery was not wearing a thruster pack, so he had only his assault armor's integrated maneuvering jets to stop his tumble. He began to fire them carefully, in half-second bursts that slowly brought his spinning under control, then his head-over-heels flipping, and finally the stars stopped whirling past in mad paisley patterns and he found himself adrift in the emptiness.

The comm channels inside his helmet were not quite silent. He could hear Hamm and the others huffing into their helmet mikes, trying to bring their own breathing under control. There was a clatter that sounded like chattering teeth, and a low growl that was probably a young trooper groaning in pain.

Avery used the suit's finger-position maneuvering controls to begin a slow spin, and quickly located a nearby mass of shadow that could only be the *Ghost Song*. Beyond it to the left lay the outpost in Libration Point Three, now a thumb-size smudge of green dotted with flecks of brightly lit installations. Naraka itself lay beyond the libration point, a massive emerald disk swaddled by ribbons of golden cloud, with a heavy band of orbital facilities twinkling high above its equator.

There was no sign of the rest of First Platoon Alpha, which was no doubt dozens of kilometers away by now after being decompression-launched out of the drop bay. Nor did Avery see any sign that the *Ghost Song* had located Sierra Force yet, though he knew that couldn't last. Sooner or later, Nyeto or one of his people would spy a cluster of wedge-shaped silhouettes diving toward Naraka, blotting out distant stars as they moved to attack. After that, it would be a simple matter for the traitors to do their work, to send a message—or even a missile—that would warn the Covenant of the approaching Spartans.

And there was only one way to stop them.

Avery activated his emergency locator beacon, then watched in delight as a dozen bright slivers of light appeared inside the Covenant outpost and came streaking in their direction.

"Johnson!" Hamm snapped over the First Platoon channel. "Are you *trying* to get us captured?"

"No, ma'am." Johnson grinned as all three of Nyeto's prowlers suddenly fired their engines and turned to flee. "I'm trying to get Commander Nyeto killed."

CHAPTER 25

1519 hours, April 15, 2526 (military calendar)
UNSC *Razor*-class prowler *Black Widow*
Insertion Approach, Planet Naraka, Agni System

The harsh beep of a heads-up alarm broke over the *Black Widow*'s flight deck, and John-117's heart climbed into his throat.

With Sierra Force approaching Naraka and Dagger Force already infiltrating the enemy's libration-point outposts, the assault plan was both immutable and at its most vulnerable. His HUD showed eleven minutes before a wave of nuclear detonations was due to take out the Covenant picket squadrons. During the confusion that followed, the four prowlers of Sierra Force would penetrate the alien defenses and insert a platoon of Spartan-led space-assault troopers at four different locations near the orbital fleet-support ring. The platoons would then use EV tactics to board and destroy as many facilities as possible from the inside, using time-fused nuclear devices and tubs of a high-yield explosive called octanitrocubane. Nicknamed "octas," the tubs cost more to produce than a Havok thermonuclear device, but they were worth it because they were shaped charges and their explosive yield did not decrease in a vacuum.

But none of that would matter if Sierra Force wasn't in position when Dagger Force began its attack.

The sensor operator silenced the heads-up alarm, then turned toward the commander's chair at the back of the flight deck.

"Ma'am, that was a space assault distress beacon transmitting in the open." The sensor operator glanced toward John, then added, "The identifier reads Staff Sergeant A. Johnson."

"*Avery* Johnson?" Esme Guayte's voice betrayed her surprise. Dressed in black utilities with her name and lieutenant's rank appropriately displayed, she was a small woman with stocky limbs who nevertheless made the oversize chair seem as though it had been built just for her. She regained her composure, then asked, "Any other signals?"

"Negative."

The communications officer, sitting at her station on the opposite side of the flight deck from the sensor operator, pressed a fingertip to her earphone.

"Actually, ma'am," she said, "I'm picking up some suit chatter on the First Platoon Alpha comm channel. I don't have their encryption up, but if you give me a minute—"

"I'll let you know if I need it." Guayte kept her attention fixed on the sensor operator. "Ensign Jones, what's the enemy reaction?"

"Heavy," Jones reported. "I have nine—make that ten—frigate-size vessels departing the Point Three outpost."

"What vector?"

"Too early to tell," Jones replied. "Could be the emergency beacon, or it could be us."

"Very well," Guayte said. "Keep me informed."

She looked over at John. She was no doubt thinking the same thing he was—if the communications officer was picking up suit-to-suit chatter, it could only mean Avery Johnson wasn't the only soldier floating around out there. Clearly, something had gone very wrong with the effort to take control of Hector Nyeto's prowlers.

Guayte continued to look at John.

Finally he realized what she was waiting for. He couldn't believe what he was about to say, but Avery Johnson understood signals discipline as well as anyone. He would never compromise the mission by activating an emergency beacon the enemy was sure to detect. The only reason he would do something that drastic was that he *wanted* the Covenant to hear it.

John just wished he understood why.

"I think we have to stick to the plan." John was careful to phrase his decision as a suggestion. Crowther might have put him in charge of the mission, but he was enlisted and Guayte was the highest-ranking officer aboard the prowler. If push came to shove, there could be no doubt whom the crew would obey. "We need to stay on mission."

Guayte's lips tightened, but she gave John a crisp nod. "Very well, Master Chief." She turned forward again. "Detection, continue to monitor the signal. Navigation, fix the location for return. We'll try to swing by later and pick them up."

"Ma'am, that assault armor only has ninety minutes of air," the navigator said. "Even if the aliens don't—"

"You heard the Master Chief," Guayte said. "Do your damn job and fix the location."

"Yes, ma'am."

An uneasy silence fell over the flight deck. John might have just condemned Avery Johnson and dozens of Black Daggers to death, but the sergeant would also have been the first to tell him to do it. If Sierra Force failed to destroy the fleet-support facilities at Naraka, the Covenant would be able to resupply and resume their invasion of the Outer Colonies unimpeded—and allowing *that* could mean the end of humanity.

Only a few seconds passed before the sensor operator said, "Ma'am, I've lost the beacon, and I *think* the aliens have too—if they ever had it. They're accelerating on a vector that bypasses Sergeant Johnson's location."

"Will they also bypass Sierra Force?" Guayte asked.

"Could be close," the sensor operator replied. "I'll pass my data to navigation for vector analysis."

"Very well," Guayte said. "Comms, prepare for a Sierra Force burst transmission with a new course and instructions."

John's gut clenched. Even if the Covenant failed to detect the burst transmission itself, a change-of-course order would cause a cascade of messages and thruster burns as four prowlers coordinated to minimize the chances of collision. A top-notch prowler wing like Sierra Force's might be able to pull that off without alerting the aliens to their presence, but it would be a long shot.

"I have that vector analysis," the navigator reported. "It looks like a hundred-kilometer miss, but they could be trying to position themselves to swing around for a tail attack."

"Comms, stand by."

Guayte's gaze grew distant. A hundred kilometers in open space was practically a sideswipe, and John knew she had to be debating the best course of action.

"Ma'am, I think we take the chance," John said. "Between the emergency beacon and the comm chatter, there's something going on with Ghost Flight. The Covenant is probably reacting to that, not us."

Guayte shifted her attention to John. "Even if you're right, at a hundred kilometers, sheer proximity raises our chances of being detected to thirty percent—and that's with human sensors."

"Still has to beat our chances of changing course undetected."

"Assuming you're right about what the aliens are doing."

"Ma'am, I don't know whether the Master Chief is right," the navigator said. "But the alien vector is odd—it intersects our original approach."

"The one we abandoned after Dagger Force entered slipspace?" Guayte asked.

"Yes, ma'am," the navigator said. "It's like they were expecting us to be there."

"Not *us*," John said. He was beginning to think he knew why Johnson had activated his emergency beacon. "Could they be chasing a Ghost Flight prowler?"

"It's possible," the sensor operator said. "But why would a prowler leave—"

"Just keep watching that vector," Guayte ordered.

She had obviously reached the same conclusion John had. Avery Johnson had activated his emergency beacon not to call for help, but to draw the Covenant's attention—and prevent Hector Nyeto from sabotaging Sierra Force's arrival.

But even with an enemy squadron on his prowler's tail, Nyeto had not given up. Now he was trying to lead the aliens into Sierra Force headlong. And he might have succeeded, had John not changed their approach vector just before Sierra Force entered slipspace.

After a moment, Guayte added, "And look for a tau burst. If the Master Chief is right about who the Covenant is chasing, that prowler won't be coming back to help us out."

The sensor operator was quiet for a moment, then said, "Understood. I'll keep you informed."

The flight deck quieted again. A tau burst, John knew, occurred anytime a slipspace vortex opened. Tau particles were extremely short-lived—less than a billionth of a second—so they were impossible to detect unless a sensor dish happened to be pointed directly at the vortex. Even then, it wasn't the tau particle that was actually observed, but the burst of energy that occurred when it encountered its antimatter complement and self-destructed.

John checked his HUD. The first nukes were due to detonate in the libration-point outposts in just over five minutes. Given the apparent trouble that had befallen First Platoon Alpha, he did not expect to see any bright flashes at Libration Point Three. But the *Black Widow* was far enough away from Naraka that any detonations at Libration Points Four and Five should be visible to either side of the planet, in about the same plane as its equator.

"Covenant squadron reaching closest approach in thirty seconds," the navigator said.

"And they've opened fire with their plasma cannons," the sensor operator added.

"On us?" Guayte exclaimed.

"Sorry, ma'am, no. On whoever they're chasing."

"Very well. Carry on." Guayte's voice had dropped back into its normal calm tone. "Comms, prepare burst message reading *'Break Break Engage All Weapons.'* Hold transmission for my order."

"Acknowledged."

John fixed his gaze on the port side of the viewport and quickly spied a handful of blue slivers approaching from the direction of Libration Point Three. Though the distance was minuscule by the standards of space, he never saw a glint or silhouette that suggested the vessel itself. Even the plasma bolts the aliens were firing at the fleeing prowler were barely more than flecks of light. Then, almost before he knew it, the slivers had passed out of sight.

The tension on the flight deck bled away, and a dozen breaths later, the sensor operator reported, "Covenant squadron continuing on vector. No indication they've detected us."

Guayte exhaled hard, then said, "Comms, kill that burst transmission." She turned to John. "Nice call, Master Chief."

John thought of Avery Johnson. "I hope so."

He checked his HUD. In two minutes, the nukes should start detonating and taking out picket squadrons and libration-point outposts. If all went to plan, Sierra Force would drop ten minutes later and start attacking the ring of orbital fleet-support facilities that encircled Naraka. The facilities were connected by a transit tube enclosed within a skeletal frame of support trusses—Dr. Halsey had called it a 'trussing armature' when she saw the reconnaissance vids—and the objective of the attack was to destroy enough of the armature to take down the entire ring. If Sierra Force could destroy at least ten facilities—along with the connecting armature—there was a ninety-two percent chance that the orbit of the entire ring would grow unstable and fall into a rapid, irreversible decay.

At least that was what Dr. Halsey said, and she did not make a habit of being wrong.

"We have tau bursts," the sensor operator reported. "Several. I make it three separate vessels, all entering slipspace in close formation."

John was stunned. During their planning sessions for this mission, Crowther and Johnson had speculated about how deep the conspiracy might go, but nobody had even suggested that it might include *all* three prowlers in Ghost Flight.

Guayte looked over. "Surprised?"

"Yes, ma'am, you could say that," John said. "The Prowler Corps is an ONI division. How could Nyeto crew three entire craft with traitors?"

"Easier than you think," Guayte said. "Commanders approve all crew replacements. Once Nyeto had his flight, he could start slipping in his people every time there was a transfer."

"For the entire crew of three prowlers?" John still couldn't believe it was possible. "That would take years."

"Maybe decades." Guayte turned forward again. "Put yourself in Nyeto's place, John. To the insurrectionists, *we're* the alien invaders, the horde that can't be stopped. They've already been fighting us for thirty years any way they can—just like we're fighting the Covenant now. If that meant spending twenty years in the UNSC just to steal a few prowlers—then that's what he'd do."

A brilliant flash caught the corner of John's left eye. He turned to see white spheres blossoming into existence at the libration points to either side of Naraka's equator, then shrinking back into nothingness, one after another in a beautiful, blinding storm of annihilation.

A few more flashes lit up the port edge of the *Black Widow*'s viewport as a handful of thermonuclear devices detonated at the Libration Point Three outpost, but it was nothing like the eruption of light coming from the other two outposts. And no wonder. With the alien picket squadron out chasing Ghost Flight, the only targets left at Point Three would be a few support stations.

"Sensors, what's the status of the Covenant squadron behind us?"

"Intact," the sensor operator said. "And coming around. Looks like they're responding to the attack."

"Keep an eye on them," Guayte said. She looked over at John. "It'll be a hot insertion."

John shrugged. "Is there any other kind?"

Actually, he had led hostile insertions only a handful of times—most recently when the Spartans attacked the logistics fleet at Etalan—but he was pretty sure that no insertion was ever easy. There would always be someone willing to do whatever it took to keep the UNSC from setting foot on their ground.

"Just get us within EV range of the orbital ring," John added. "We'll handle the rest."

"Deal."

Guayte's gaze was locked forward, where Naraka's mottled green disk was expanding rapidly across the viewport. Already its ring of fleet-support facilities could be seen orbiting above the equator, a ragged band of curled shapes connected to one another by the yellow-green filament of a transit tube.

The shapes ranged in size from almost indiscernible to as large as John's fist, and they were flecked with the twinkling lights and glowing bubbles of active industrial facilities. Beneath a handful of these facilities, spokes of blue light descended into Naraka's yellow cloud cover and vanished from sight.

In front of the orbital ring hung twenty Covenant vessels, each so large that John mistook them for facilities in the ring itself—until he noticed the bright specks swarming around them and realized he was looking at a fighter shell. Even then, it took him a moment to recognize the problem. The ships had no thrust tails. Instead of climbing into higher orbits to expand their defensive cocoon and compensate for the loss of their picket squadrons, they were hanging back in orbit, maintaining a tight anti-infiltration web that would prevent the prowlers from slipping through to attack the orbital facilities.

"Good discipline," Guayte said. "They're not falling for it."

"Imagine that," John said. "Someone leaked our plan."

"Maybe," Guayte said. "But the aliens aren't idiots. After Etalan, they could have guessed what we'd do."

"But not *where* we'd do it." John pointed at the line of slowly growing vessels ahead. "Does that look like a typical garrison force? Or a typical deployment?"

"I'm no expert on Covenant garrison force deployments," Guayte said. "But no. To deploy that tight around the entire ring, they'd have to keep a hundred carrier-size vessels on station. Nobody does that unless they're expecting trouble."

"So we do this the hard way," John said. "Plan D."

"I didn't know there was a Plan D."

"There is now." John explained what he had in mind, then asked, "What do you think? They're expecting us to attack the fleet-support ring from a higher orbit, so we hit it from below."

"If we can *get* below."

John pointed at the faint beam connecting the ring to Naraka. "Those spokes look a lot like the gravity-elevators their ships use. Drop our Sierra units on the surface near the bottom of them, and we'll use the Covenant's own lift-tech to infiltrate the ring. It has to be easier than getting through that defensive line."

Guayte sighed. "Probably so. Even the Covenant can't put a net that tight over an entire planet." She studied her command screen for a moment, then asked, "Detection, what are we seeing over the poles?"

"Standard patrols. Nothing we can't dodge."

"Very well." Guayte turned to John. "Are you sure you want to split up? Massed firepower is—"

"Easier to eliminate with superior massed firepower," John said. "We're never going to punch through that line. We don't have the strength to do that. We have to *slip* through, and splitting up makes that easier. It also gives Sierra Force four chances instead of just one to reach the ring."

"Reaching the ring is only half the battle, Chief," Guayte said. "To bring it down, you still have to destroy ten facilities—and that won't happen if you're short of firepower."

"We won't be," John said. "With all due respect, ma'am, you don't understand Spartan capabilities."

Guayte thought for a moment, then said, "Okay, we'll split up. But even if we can get you in, retrieval is out of the question. If those spokes aren't what you think they are—"

"Just get us in, ma'am," John said. "We'll find our own ride home."

John left the other half of that statement unspoken: *if we're around to need it.* His plan was necessarily short on detail, since he had no intelligence about what they would find on the planet's surface. But it was fair to say that if those spokes weren't some sort of space elevator, getting home would be the least of Sierra Force's problems.

After a moment, Guayte nodded. "Very well, Master Chief. You're in charge." She turned to her command screen and began to type orders. "I just hope you know what you're doing."

"I'm sure you're not the only one, Lieutenant." John came to attention. "With your permission, I'll retire to the drop bay and prepare for insertion."

"I think you'd better." Guayte spoke without looking away from her command screen. "We're not going to bother with establishing orbit. This will be a meteor insertion. I'll burst the other prowlers with your plan, and you'll be boots down in . . . sixteen minutes."

She turned to the communications officer and began to issue instructions for the burst transmission. Taking her change of focus as an informal dismissal, John retreated to the drop bay, where he joined the rest of Blue Team and Third Platoon Delta Company.

Talking as he worked, John explained the new plan and began securing weapons and devices to his armor. He put an MA5B with underslung grenade launcher on his dorsal magnetic mount and, because he wanted a weapon with the power to penetrate the enemy's personal energy shielding, elected to hand-carry an M90 close-assault shotgun. He joined the rest of Blue Team in loading up with explosive devices: a hundred-kiloton octa on each hip and a thirty-megaton Havok on his lower back.

Not being biologically augmented Spartans in Mjolnir power armor, Lieutenant Small Bear carried a one-megaton Fury, and her thirty-one Black Daggers each carried a pair of octas mag-clamped above their thruster packs. John wondered if this was some kind of record for the most nuclear ordnance ever carried by an insertion force comprised entirely of infantry, and he wasn't even considering the other Spartan and Black Dagger teams aboard the remainder of Sierra Force's prowlers with similar kits. It'd definitely make for one helluva fireworks show, hopefully one they would all be enjoying from a safe distance.

A few minutes later, the team was ready, and the *Black Widow* was beginning to shudder as she plunged into Naraka's atmosphere. The Spartans made their way to the jump hatch at the back of the bay.

Anticipating a dismount under fire, John assigned Fred and Kelly to lead the way, followed by twelve ODSTs each.

He and Linda would dismount next. That way the platoon would have Spartan firepower both leading the way and coming up in support, and Colonel Crowther wouldn't chew his butt about leading from the front. Lieutenant Small Bear would bring up the rear of the formation with the remaining ODSTs in case the situation really went south and the platoon needed someone to take charge of fixing the mess.

The illumination in the drop bay dimmed briefly, indicating three minutes to hatch open, then came back to full, indicating a perilous daylight dismount. Couldn't be avoided. With four prowlers hitting targets spread evenly around the planet's equator, only half of Sierra Force's teams were going to be dismounting under cover of darkness. John called for final checks and ran through his own systems list, then turned to exchange visual inspections with Linda.

A crackling roar grew inside the bay as atmospheric friction began to heat the *Black Widow*'s hull. John's HUD showed the temperature inside the compartment climbing rapidly, and the prowler began to buck so hard that even the Spartans had to take a knee to keep from being knocked off their feet.

Guayte's voice came over the Third Platoon comm channel. "Sorry for the rough ride. We're beginning to attract flies, and I want you on the ground before they start biting. Watch the monitors for a view of your landing zone—we should have a visual soon."

She had barely closed the channel before the bulkhead monitors activated, showing nothing but a gauzy yellow haze. John thought for a moment there was some kind of transmission problem; then the haze grew thin and patchy, offering glimpses of a lush volcanic world of fuming calderas and glowing rifts. A paisley pattern of walled fields and serpentine terraces covered most of the ground that wasn't actively steaming or bubbling. A silvery web of luminous roadways converged on a distant city of ivory domes and golden spires, which huddled around the foot of a soaring column of blue light.

As the *Black Widow* continued to bounce and shudder toward the city, crannies and fissures began to define the domes and spires into separate clusters of tall, slender buildings that rose hundreds of meters tall, twisting and arcing in graceful shapes, seemingly centuries old and looking almost like hand-blown glass. The blue light thickened into a pillar the size of a skyscraper, and dark streaks began to appear inside, shooting up the column with a velocity almost faster than the eye could follow.

"Well, that's either a weird alien space elevator—or a weird alien particle cannon," Fred said. "I guess we'll find out which when we step inside."

"Those streaks are too big for a particle cannon," Lieutenant Small Bear said, clearly not accustomed to Fred's humor. "But I'm still not sure we can survive that kind of acceleration."

"Only one way to find out," John said.

"Send Kelly first?" Fred asked.

"Very funny," Kelly said. "And you're coming with me."

The alert lamps on the bulkheads changed from red to amber.

"One minute," John said. "Can the chatter."

The crannies and fissures between the graceful buildings broadened into flyways filled with airborne traffic, and the domes and spires began to loom up higher than the prowler. A series of white circles flared in the bottom of the monitor and quickly shrank into dots as the *Black Widow* fired three Argent V missiles to clear its way to the space elevator. The first missile dropped in behind an oblong flying vehicle with a sleek purple body resting between pair of gray levitation runners, then blossomed into an orange ball that licked at buildings to both sides of the lane. John had no idea whether the vehicle had been military or civilian, and he tried not to think about it. The simple fact was that it had been between the *Black Widow* and her objective, and that unlucky turn of affairs had sealed its fate.

The next two missiles destroyed targets even farther ahead of the prowler, and the flyway quickly began to empty as confused alien pilots swerved down side lanes or dropped toward the street below. The *Black Widow* leveled out at about half the height of the buildings and continued toward the space elevator, now using her pair of 50mm nose-cannons to take out any vehicle not quick enough to clear the lane.

The alert lamps began to blink. Thirty seconds.

John pumped a round into his M90. "Safeties off."

The *Black Widow* began to decelerate hard. A thousand meters ahead, the flyway opened into a bustling transfer yard with pavement that looked a lot like a vast sheet of gray-green glass. Hundreds of haulage sleds with domed driver's compartments, oval cargo beds, and antigravity pads bulging out from their sides sat facing away from each other in double rows, creating a broad center aisle between their rear bumpers.

A small army of alien stevedores—mostly Jackals and Grunts—was unloading the sleds' long cargo beds into the central aisle. From what John could see, it appeared that once the crates were set on the pavement, they floated to the elevator on their own, then disappeared.

The *Black Widow* launched a massive volley of missiles, and suddenly the monitor showed only flame and smoke. The prowler slowed to a near hover and began to swing her nose back and forth, chugging noticeably as she filled the air with cannon fire.

The alert lamps flashed green as the jump hatch opened; then Fred and Kelly were leading the first rows of Black Daggers out onto the surface of the alien planet. John and Linda followed seconds later, dropping two and a half meters through thick black smoke. Naraka's gravity was only about three-quarters of Earth-standard, so the descent was slow and easy, and they landed on a smooth surface that seemed oddly clear of wreckage and rubble.

John felt something scraping across the top of his helmet. Thinking he was taking fire, he dropped to a knee and whirled around—and found himself beneath the *Black Widow*, being carried forward behind a line of similarly kneeling ODSTs. In front of them, the murky shapes of dozens of burning haulage sleds lay rolled on their sides. A few were resting on their tops, their hinged antigravity pads swinging lazily as they slid toward the space elevator.

John glanced down and saw that he was sliding along an emerald-green band of glassy pavement. It appeared level, but it felt like he was on green ice, going down a gentle hill. He slammed the butt of his M90 against it, half expecting to see a web of cracks racing outward from the impact point, and felt . . . nothing. His shotgun just stopped descending and wouldn't go any farther.

"Weird, huh?" Fred said, speaking over TEAMCOM.

John looked over to see the ghostly silhouette of a still-burning haulage sled drifting past in the opposite direction. Fred stepped out from behind it and took a knee next to John, and together they passed beneath the *Black Widow*'s now-silent nose-cannons.

"Get on the gray pavement and you stop moving," Fred continued. "The green bands must be some sort of conveyor zone. They carry you right into the elevator."

John peered into the smoke ahead, trying to make sense of the jumble of shapes and flickering cones of orange, then gave up and switched to his motion tracker. Immediately he spotted Kelly twenty meters ahead, with four ODSTs arrayed to either side of her in a skirmish line. He couldn't tell what lay directly in front of her, but judging from where the space elevator dropped down out of the clouds, she was about a hundred meters short of the entrance.

"Any contact?" John asked.

"After the barrage the *Widow* laid down? We think there are a few wounded Brutes hiding behind some wrecked sleds in front of the elevator plinth, but they haven't shown much interest in coming out to fight. That's why I came back to report."

Before Fred could continue, Small Bear's voice sounded over the platoon channel. "Third Platoon clear."

"Platoon clear," Guayte acknowledged. "*Widow* out."

With the smoke so thick that John could barely see the prowler's wings—much less the blast zone behind its thruster nozzles—he checked his motion tracker again and confirmed that the rest of the platoon was already spreading out in another skirmish line and moving forward.

"Affirmative," John said. "*Widow* out. Thanks for the ride."

"Maybe you shouldn't thank me, Chief," Guayte said. "You could be on your own destroying those ten targets."

John's gut instantly clenched. "The other bats didn't make it?"

"That's what I'm hearing," Guayte said. "The *Widow Maker* and *Quiet Death* got jumped on entry and had to turn back or go down. The *Quiet Man* broke up on final drop. Comms intercepted some chatter that sounded like the Spartans were picking up the surviving Black Daggers and pressing ahead, but it's hard to say how many there are and whether they'll make it to the elevator."

"Acknowledged. Appreciate the update."

John digested the failure and casualty rates with dismay. The four members of Gold Team had been divided equally between the *Widow Maker* and *Quiet Death*, and they were now completely out of the battle. But at least the Spartans aboard the *Quiet Man* seemed to be in one piece so far. That was Green Team, and if anyone could find a way to extract, Kurt-051 could.

He started to wish Guayte a safe flight, but the *Black Widow* was already standing on her tail and climbing for the sky. The thruster wash cleared the smoke long enough to reveal dozens of alien bodies dangling out of shattered pilot bubbles or lying pinned beneath overturned haulage sleds. It was a gruesome sight, and none of them wore armor, carried weapons, or showed any other sign of being in the military. John almost found himself regretting their deaths . . . until he remembered what the Covenant had done to Harvest and Etalan and Biko and probably a dozen other worlds he had not yet heard about. The Covenant had started this bloody war, and John would not allow himself to feel bad about fighting it by their rules.

The conveyor zone carried John and his companions to within a few meters of the skirmish line Kelly had set up. He turned back to Fred and spoke over TEAMCOM.

"You were telling me about some wounded Brutes?"

"We *think*." Fred pointed into the smoke. "There are some haulage sleds ahead that have been pulled together to make a breastwork. We're guessing Brutes, since they're probably the only ones strong enough to drag that stuff around on its side. We could try to go around. . . ."

"But?"

"But who likes getting shot in the back?" Fred said. "We need to take them out."

"And quickly," John said. "If they're holed up, they're waiting for something."

Fred tipped his helmet forward in agreement. "Maybe they've got support coming."

"Or maybe they're waiting for a lockout barrier to power up," Linda added.

"Could be anything," John said.

The one thing nobody mentioned was shutting off power to the elevator. With thousands of tons of cargo in transit to a geostationary orbit tens of thousands of kilometers above the planet's surface, one did not simply shut off the power to a space elevator—not unless they were ready for a high-velocity impact that would make a nuclear detonation seem like a grenade blast in comparison.

"Whatever they're waiting for, let's be gone before it happens." John stepped off the conveyor zone. "Fred and Kelly, flank 'em. Linda, with me."

A trio of status lights winked green, and Fred and Kelly disappeared into the smoke. Linda followed John over to an ODST who was hiding behind a burned-out haulage sled. John handed his M90 to the ODST, then pointed Linda to a nearby sled that was still smoking.

"We'll need two, I think."

"Two should do," Linda said.

She secured her M99 to her Mjolnir, then stepped over to the still-smoking sled and started to push it toward the conveyor zone. John's sled was already adjacent, so he simply squatted next to it and waited for Linda to move hers into position.

He switched to the platoon channel, then said, "Lieutenant Small Bear, Linda and I are going to force the enemy's hand. I'd suggest having the platoon fall in behind us and be ready to move fast."

"You heard him," Small Bear said. "Move it!"

Linda's sled scraped into place next to John's. The smoke ahead was still so thick that they could see barely five meters clearly, and make out shapes at no more than ten. The enemy barricade lay somewhere beyond, but when John looked skyward, he could still see the blue column of the elevator looming. It remained filled with the dark streaks of rising cargo.

John looked over at Linda. "Three . . . two . . ."

She shoved her sled forward, and he lifted, putting all of his strength and the Mjolnir armor's into the effort. The sled came off the glassy pavement and partially flipped, then crashed down on the far side of the conveyor belt. It was more or less even with Linda's, but resting at an angle that left a small gap between the two vehicles.

Close enough. John grabbed his M90 back from the ODST and stepped onto the conveyor zone.

"Let's go," he said over the platoon channel. "And we need someone with a SPNKR up here."

Small Bear barked, "Chavez!"

A few seconds later, an ODST appeared with a rocket launcher and an extra set of barrels. In his black assault armor, he looked like all of the other ODSTs, except he was about a head taller and half an arm's-length wider. John briefly thought about handling the SPNKR himself—then recalled what Johnson had said about trusting his people to do their jobs. He pointed Chavez toward the gap between the two vehicles.

"The enemy has improvised a breastwork ahead of us," he said. "Both barrels, the instant you see it."

"Will do, Master Chief."

Chavez kneeled on pavement and laid the extra barrels next to him, then carefully pushed his weapon into the gap.

John checked his motion tracker and saw that Lieutenant Small Bear and the rest of Third Platoon were lined up behind him in two well-spaced columns, weapons ready. Fred and Kelly reappeared on the tracker, about ten meters ahead and a similar distance off to the side.

"See anything yet?" John asked Chavez.

Yellow flame suddenly filled John's vision as both rockets streaked away.

Instead of immediately pulling out of the gap, Chavez reached for his extra set of barrels—then flew over backward, the SPNKR flying from his hands as he went down with a cluster of white-hot spikes protruding from his chest armor. John stuck his M90 into the break and fired blindly, then pulled his arm back just as another cluster of spikes arrived and ricocheted off the chassis of the adjacent vehicle. He pumped another round into the shotgun's chamber and heard a series of thuds and bangs from his ten o'clock a few meters away—Fred and

Kelly's location, according to his motion tracker—then Kelly's voice sounded over the platoon channel.

"Clear."

John glanced down at Chavez, and his heart sank. It had been a small mistake—and one John had gotten away with himself a few times—but the Brutes had been ready, and now Chavez lay on the glassy pavement, convulsing and kicking.

"Medic!" John yelled.

To make certain there would be no more mistakes, John stuck the shotgun back into the gap.

"Hey!" Fred called. "We *got* 'em!"

"Just checking."

Leaving Chavez for the medic, John stepped through the barricade he and Linda had erected, then saw Fred and Kelly peering over the Brutes' makeshift breastwork. A trio of haulage sleds had been tipped on their sides and dragged into place. The middle vehicle had an enormous hole in the cargo bed where Chavez's rockets had detonated, and through the opening John could see the upper body of a Brute who had been blown apart at the middle. Three more Brutes lay draped over the adjacent sleds, smoke still rising from the grenade craters in their backs.

"Sorry I doubted you," John said. "Now grab as much ammunition as you can and get over here. We've got a ride to catch."

John watched until Fred and Kelly returned to the conveyor zone and began to gather extra SPNKR barrels, then turned back to Chavez. The ODST had been dragged into cover by Small Bear and one of her troopers, and the platoon medic was using a plunger to feed something—probably biofoam—into the medical port on Chavez's assault armor. A four-to-one casualty ratio was nothing to complain about, but it had been John who ordered Chavez to step into that gap, and he could not help feeling sick about it.

He thought of Johnson's words again, and pushed through.

The platoon was carried out of the smoke into an abandoned sorting tunnel, where dozens of pad-tipped poles and odd-looking flashlight guns lay strewn to both sides of the conveyor zone. Fifty meters ahead, the elevator plinth could now be seen clearly. It was a vast gray platform rimmed by a series of vertical pylons roughly fifteen meters tall, each of which were anchored onto the surface, clearly part of a much larger machine buried below. At first blush, the pylons seemed to be channels for the elevator's energy, generating the blue beam from their tips, as well as from some hidden space underneath the platform. Meanwhile, the conveyor was still pushing battle debris into the blue column of the alien space elevator. Once inside, the debris—bodies and chunks of wreckage—would spread evenly across the beam and begin to rise, slowly at first, but steadily gathering velocity. By the time they vanished from sight a hundred meters above, they were traveling too fast for the eye to follow. He briefly wondered how the aliens at the top of the elevator would react.

After a moment, John turned back to Small Bear and nodded toward Chavez. "Will he make it?"

"If we could get him to a Class I combat hospital, maybe. But out here?" She shook her head. "It's the end of the line for him. Mehran is giving him the shot."

The "shot" was a powerful narcotic ODST medics used to relieve the pain and anxiety of a dying trooper—especially when circumstances dictated they had to be abandoned in the field. From Small Bear's remark, John gathered that the medic was giving Chavez a lethal dose. He desperately wanted to say that he would carry the dying trooper, but the mission was just starting, and distracting himself with a casualty would only get more people killed.

And he wasn't about to elevate someone else's risk by ordering them to carry a dying man into battle. Small Bear had made a sound decision, and he would not make anything better by second-guessing her.

"Chavez was a good trooper, and he deserves a big send-off." Small Bear retrieved the Fury tactical nuke from her magmount. "What do you say, Master Chief?"

John turned toward the space elevator and then back to Small Bear. "Lock in forty minutes and leave it here."

CHAPTER 26

Ninth Age of Reclamation
36th Cycle, 176 Units (Covenant Battle Calendar)
Fleet of Inexorable Obedience, Assault Carrier *Pious Rampage*
High Equatorial Orbit, Planet Zhoist, Buta System

Tel 'Szatulai found his hand resting on the hilt of his energy sword . . . again. It was an unconscious action that had arisen with the summons to attend Fleetmaster 'Kvarosee, and the nearer he drew to the *Pious Rampage*'s High Battle Sanctum, the more powerful it became.

And that was a problem. He had been summoned from the *Sacred Whisper* in the middle of a combat vigil, and now he was allowing his resentment to subvert his focus.

With a battle coming.

'Szatulai reached the sanctum and paused at the threshold. The two Sangheili sentries snapped their carbines to present arms, clearing the entrance and indicating he was free to enter. 'Szatulai ignored them and remained where he was, thinking only of controlling his breath and effusing his anger on each exhalation. The Spartans would come to him in their own time; he would not bring them any sooner by crouching in his observation blister, staring out at the emptiness to where he thought they should be.

After a time, a sentry dared to speak. "You are free to enter, Blademaster. They are expecting you."

They. Of course, it would have been the San'Shyuum who sent for him, who believed that the Covenant should be able to command their enemies as they did their acolytes.

Without responding to the sentry, 'Szatulai entered the sanctum. He was immediately confronted by a two-story tactical holograph of the Zhoist planetary system, complete with its moon, its libration-point outposts, and the complex of orbital fleet-support stations known as the Ring of Mighty Abundance. The Fleet of Inexorable Obedience was shown in its shielding circle. Even the positions of the outpost squadrons and fighter patrols were posted. What was lacking, of course, was any hint of where the enemy stealth craft might be.

On the near side of the holograph stood fifteen aides and plotters, all busy conversing with each other and pretending they had not noticed 'Szatulai's arrival. Fleetmaster 'Kvarosee was alone on the far side of the compartment, glaring at the holograph as he paced back and forth. The fleet's San'Shyuum magistrate, the Minor Minister of Artifact Survey, sat in his antigrav chair by the corner behind 'Kvarosee, stroking his chin wattles and swinging his long neck from side to side as he watched the fleetmaster pace.

When Survey noticed 'Szatulai approaching, he floated his chair forward and extended a spindly finger toward 'Kvarosee. "He's been like that since the attack on Outpost Three."

'Szatulai felt his hand dropping toward his energy sword and tried to go around. Survey blocked his way, and 'Szatulai found himself glancing around the compartment, wondering if anyone would be troubled enough by the San'Shyuum's death to report it and risk the Silent Shadow's retaliation.

"Perhaps *you* can make him see what a mistake this was," Survey said.

"Mistake?"

"That." Survey flung a slender hand toward the holograph. "Surely *you* see what the humans are doing?"

"Launching a stealth attack on Zhoist, as I predicted," 'Szatulai said. "What do *you* see?"

"A diversion!" Survey said. "A small force sent to hold us here while they attack High Charity!"

That illogical nonsense again. 'Szatulai sidestepped Survey's chair. When the San'Shyuum tried to block his way once more, the Sangheili pushed the chair aside and continued toward 'Kvarosee. He noticed that his hand had returned to the hilt of his energy sword and did not remove it.

'Kvarosee continued to pace and did not stop until 'Szatulai placed himself squarely in front of the fleetmaster.

"You summoned me, Fleetmaster." 'Szatulai's tone was intentionally flat and hard. "I was in the middle of a combat vigil."

'Kvarosee's gaze finally swung from the holograph, and 'Szatulai was not surprised to see that the fleetmaster's eyes had gone soft with uncertainty. It was clear that Survey had been working on him, filling his head with reasons to return the fleet to High Charity.

"I may have made a critical error in strategy, Blademaster." 'Kvarosee turned and pointed toward the tactical holograph. "The humans have attacked only our outposts."

"So far," 'Szatulai said. It had appalled him to see the doubt in 'Kvarosee's eyes, but now he found himself awed by the fleetmaster's honor. It had been 'Szatulai who argued for a retreat to defend Zhoist, yet 'Kvarosee was blaming only himself. "More attacks will come."

"And how long must we wait?" Survey demanded, floating up behind 'Szatulai. "Until High Charity itself has fallen?"

When 'Szatulai did not reply, 'Kvarosee allowed his mandibles to gape ever so slightly in amusement. He pointed his finger at the holograph again, this time wagging it so 'Szatulai would look.

"The humans are making only minor attacks with a small force," he said. "Three of their vessels have already withdrawn, and there are only a handful engaging now."

'Szatulai looked and saw one apparent engagement, where flights of Banshees and Seraphs were dropping down from the Ring of Mighty Abundance to engage a human craft in a *lower* orbit. He pointed at the fight.

"What is happening there?"

"Nothing to worry about," Survey said. "Another diversion."

"It was a surface raid," 'Kvarosee said, seeming to sense 'Szatulai's alarm. "A handful of stealth craft made comet-strike entries over the poles. Two of them survived long enough to attack sky lifts."

"And?"

"And it was a feint," Survey insisted. "They destroyed some equipment and killed some drudges."

"But the sky lifts were unaffected?"

"Is that not what I just said?" Survey asked.

'Kvarosee shot Survey a look that suggested he wanted to tie the San'Shyuum's long neck into a knot, then turned back to 'Szatulai.

"What troubles you, Blademaster?"

"That I was not told of this sooner." 'Szatulai turned and started toward the exit. "I hope there is still time."

"Time for what?" 'Kvarosee fell in at his side. "Three of their attack craft have been turned away or destroyed already, and the last will not make it out of orbit."

"It doesn't matter," 'Szatulai said. "Their ploy succeeded."

'Kvarosee grabbed 'Szatulai by the shoulder—a liberty he survived only because of the honor he had shown earlier, when he had assumed sole responsibility for his imaginary mistake.

"Explain yourself, Blademaster."

"As you wish, but listen well—I have no time to repeat myself."

'Kvarosee clacked his mandibles for 'Szatulai to continue.

"The humans were not trying to destroy the sky lifts," he said. "They wanted to *use* them."

'Kvarosee's nostrils flared so wide they looked like a second set of eyes. "What?"

"Confirm it with the Planetary Lord, if you wish." 'Szatulai pulled free of the fleetmaster's grasp and headed for the exit again. "But I must go. The humans are already in the sky lifts."

"Then there is no problem," Survey said. "Simply reverse the lifts."

"And *return* them to the surface of a holy world? To defile it further?" 'Kvarosee was clearly aghast. Zhoist was the sacred abode of the Ten Cities of Edification, which had once been a home to the Forerunners themselves. The entire planet was viewed as holy to the Covenant because so much of the knowledge that empowered its starship and weapons technology had been recovered from the ancient guild halls dominating the hallowed cities, and there were still thousands of artisans and engineers hard at work trying to understand the wonders that the Forerunners had left for them to discover—wonders that no infidel could ever be permitted to see. "I cannot believe a Minor Minister would utter such blasphemy."

"I am only suggesting a way to undo your incompetence," Survey replied. "The Hierarchs will punish you less for defilement than for losing an entire fleet station."

"It would be more than defilement," 'Szatulai said. "If we reverse the sky lifts now, the Spartans will escape across Zhoist and bathe in the forbidden light of the Forerunners' divine knowledge, and then who will be to blame?"

"Not I." 'Kvarosee motioned 'Szatulai toward the exit. "Go and kill them while you still can."

CHAPTER 27

1615 hours, April 15, 2526 (military calendar)
Upper Terminus, Unidentified Covenant Space Elevator
Geostationary Orbit, Planet Naraka, Agni System

Through the wall of the antigravity beam, John-117 could see Naraka's horizon falling swiftly away. The distant stars were shifting parallax so fast they seemed to be sinking behind the planet, and above him the elevator terminus was finally coming into view—a tiny yellow oval at the moment.

But John was beginning to think it had been a mistake to assume that a Covenant lift beam would be as fast as a human space elevator.

He had told Small Bear to set a forty-minute delay on the Fury she had left at the bottom, and the countdown on his HUD had just dropped to five minutes.

Normally, that wouldn't worry him, since Third Platoon was tens of thousands of kilometers above ground zero. Normally, that would be more than a safe distance. But John had no idea how the electromagnetic pulse of a one-megaton thermonuclear explosion might affect an alien antigravity beam, or how much of the shockwave would be funneled straight up the narrow column toward the platoon.

The countdown on John's HUD reached 4:45. The terminus above continued to swell larger, and a tiny black dot appeared in the center. The dot was probably the portal where the elevator entered the installation. He kept his eyes fixed on it until the count on his HUD reached 4:30; it was doubling in size every five seconds. The elevator beam was about twenty meters across. . . .

His onboard computer did the calculations, and an ETA of sixty seconds appeared on John's HUD. That gave them a safety margin of three and a half minutes between portal arrival and the detonation of the Fury left with Chavez. Plenty of time. John was relieved.

Then they began to decelerate.

The onboard computer did another set of calculations, and a new ETA appeared on his HUD: 3:05.

Then it helpfully posted the new safety margin in blinking yellow. Twenty-two seconds.

Over the platoon channel, John said, "ETA three minutes. Once we enter the support ring, we're going to have to move fast and *keep* moving fast. Ready your device fuses now, three-minute delay and sixty-minute auto."

The three-minute delay was stingy by design. It did not give an assault team much time to clear an area after activating the fuse, but they would be operating in a heavily populated environment, and a longer delay would give the enemy too much time to find the explosive device—whether a nuke or an octa—and toss it out an airlock.

The sixty-minute automatic was simply a safety protocol to keep the device from falling into enemy hands if it was lost—or the trooper carrying it was killed. If the timer was not disengaged with an override code, the weapon would detonate automatically in an hour.

John and the other Spartans entered the delays on the three devices they were carrying—the octas on their hips and the Havoks mag-clamped on their lower backs—while the Black Daggers worked in pairs to program the octas carried above their thruster packs. By the time everyone reported ready, the ETA had fallen to fifty seconds, and the entry portal overhead had grown so large it filled the sky.

A sky packed with spinning alien bodies and slowly tumbling crates.

"Bad sign," Small Bear said. "There's nobody pulling the cargo out of the elevator."

"We can't wait," John said. "Fred, go left. Kelly, go right. Lieutenant, they could use some support."

Small Bear assigned a fireteam to follow each Spartan; then Fred and Kelly hit their thrusters and led their support teams up the beam ahead of the rest of the platoon.

Their progress could hardly be called swift, since they were working against the decelerating force of the beam itself. But they were able to move ahead of the rest of platoon, then gather in a loose formation beneath the lid of slowly swirling crates and corpses.

Rather than alert the enemy to their presence by poking their heads out to look for trouble, Fred and Kelly simply grabbed the rim of the portal and pulled themselves up. They opened fire with rockets and bullets as soon as they were clear, then vanished into the terminus, their support teams rising out of the elevator beam into a torrent of return fire.

Three troopers fell back into the beam on Fred's side and two on Linda's, missing limbs or heads, their assault armor puckered in front and blown out in back by large explosive rounds.

"Kill zone!" Fred reported. Two more troopers tumbled into the portal. "Wedge-angle crossfire, at least two hundred hostiles at twenty meters, centered three o'clock off my exit bearing!"

"Breakout options?" John asked.

"Transit tube twelve o'clock!"

The ETA on John's HUD showed thirty-two seconds. The Fury left with Chavez would detonate twenty-two seconds after that. What that might mean for anyone still inside the antigravity beam was the last thing he wanted to find out. He pictured the situation Fred had described inside the terminus . . . and realized almost instantly what he had to do.

"Lieutenant," he said, "I need to break out Blue Team to run bombs through that transit tube. Can you give us a rolling screen?"

Small Bear hesitated, a sure sign she understood what John was asking of her, then finally answered in a thin voice: "Sure, Chief. We can do that."

She began to issue the necessary orders.

John swapped his M90 for the MA5B and laid his finger on the trigger guard of the underslung grenade launcher, then switched to TEAMCOM. "Kelly, when we come out of here—"

"I was listening, John." She paused, then added, "I wish there was another way."

"Me too. Let me know if you have one."

"I don't."

The ETA on John's HUD read ten seconds. He and Linda used their thrusters to slip into position with Small Bear and her platoon. Sierra Force had not deployed any comm relay drones for fear of betraying its presence, but he knew from Lieutenant Guayte's parting message that the two prowlers carrying Gold Team and First and Second Platoons Delta had been forced to abort their insertion run. Even more frustrating, there was no way to check with Kurt-051 and see whether Green Team had managed to recover and infiltrate the orbital fleet-support ring. With luck, they'd also made it this far, and there would be four more Spartans and another twenty-five space assault troopers helping Blue Team and Third Platoon destroy orbital facilities.

But John knew better than to count on it. There was just as good a chance that Third Platoon would be the only team to reach orbit at all—and the Covenant would not be shaken by a raid that knocked out just one or two installations. To be sure of taking down the entire orbital ring, Blue Team needed to destroy all ten facilities themselves.

John and Linda reached the top of the lift beam with Third Platoon, then pushed their weapons up through the blanket of drifting bodies and crates.

Small Bear's voice came over the platoon channel. *"Now."*

They blind-fired a volley of grenades and rockets in the general direction of the enemy and hit their thrusters, rising out of the portal into a firestorm. They were in a huge ovoid chamber stacked with crates, ingots, and bodies—all good cover for the enemy.

And these guys were soldiers.

John felt half a dozen spikes and needles glance off his armor and saw an ODST ahead of him separate into three parts. He fired a grenade toward a line of forms wearing the same red-black armor he had seen at Seoba.

Then Small Bear yelled, "Go go go!" and Third Platoon—what remained of it—raced forward, pouring bullets and grenades and rocket fire into a line of Covenant crouched behind a makeshift breastwork of metal ingots.

John fired another grenade over the troopers' heads and started across the deck behind them, angling toward the mouth of the transit tube more than a hundred meters away. A trio of Brutes clambered over a stack of the metal ingots and tried to cut him off, but Fred stepped out from behind a stack of crates and hit them with a pair of SPNKR rockets. John took out the third Brute with a grenade, and he had a clear path all the way to the tube.

He stopped halfway there, dropping to his butt behind a pile of toppled crates to reload his grenade launcher. The safety margin blinking on his HUD had changed to red. Ten seconds until the Fury detonated at the bottom of the space elevator.

John finished the reload, spun to a knee, and stuck his head up to see an approaching Elite literally step through an ODST he had just split down the center with an energy sword. John opened up with his assault rifle. It took half a magazine to knock down the energy shield, but finally the alien's torso armor puckered and began to seep blood. The alien kept coming and did not go down until John sprayed another dozen rounds into his knees.

Linda and Kelly sprinted past and took positions inside the mouth of the transit tube. Third Platoon's rolling screen had fallen to a handful of troopers, and the aliens were pouring out of cover to mount a charge.

Five seconds.

"Disengage!" John called over the platoon channel.

He retreated toward the tube at a run, emptying his grenade launcher as he went. A handful of Third Platoon survivors sprinted past, so heavily laden with spare SPNKR barrels that they were barely keeping ahead of the Jackals and Elites that followed close on their heels. Fred and Kelly slowed the aliens with a couple of long MA5B bursts that left the second rank tripping over the bodies of the first; then Linda went to work with her M99, drilling Brute after Brute between the eyes and sending them tumbling into those behind.

Zero and out of time.

Nothing happened, except that Lieutenant Small Bear appeared ten meters away, a short figure in assault armor vaulting over a stack of ingots. A sword-wielding Elite followed close behind. John raised his assault rifle to cover her, then felt a hand grab his fission reactor.

"Get *in* here!" Kelly said.

She jerked John into the transit tube, and the Elite chasing Small Bear went flying backward as an M99 round blew his torso open.

The lieutenant glanced back, then stumbled over the body of a dead Jackal . . . and was blown flat as the shockwave from the Fury detonation finally arrived, much reduced in power after climbing tens of thousands of kilometers up the elevator column, but still powerful enough to send bodies flying in every direction, knocking the remaining aliens off their feet and hurling them into the stacks of the breastwork.

Miraculously, Small Bear wasn't hit by anything. She looked up, her astonishment at her survival obvious in the way she held her helmet cocked to one side.

John waved her forward, but as she rose, the decompression hit, sucking everything down through the empty elevator portal. Small Bear extended an arm, reaching for help, then went sliding back toward the center of the terminus.

John tried to help, but even a Spartan's arm was not that long.

The transit tube's emergency hatch irised shut, almost closing on John's hand before he could pull it back. His helmet speakers filled with the startled cries and shouts of the wounded and the dying; then Small Bear's voice sounded above the rest, her command status auto-dampening everything else on the channel.

"Carry on, Chief. Make it count."

John banged his fist against the hatch so hard that he dented it, then took a breath and stepped back. An order was an order, and Small Bear had been clear about what she expected.

John turned around to find the rest of Blue Team and six Third Platoon survivors watching him expectantly. Fred sat in the driver's compartment of a half-loaded cargo sled that looked large enough to haul an entire platoon—along with a couple of pieces of field artillery. The sleds were simple vehicles, little more than an egg-shaped driver's compartment attached to the front of a cargo bed long enough to hold two Spartans lying end-to-end. Several more sleds were parked along the sides of the transit tube, most in various stages of being loaded with a variety of materials.

"You heard the lady," he said. "Let's make this count."

He received a chorus of enthusiastic replies and helmet bobs, but they still needed a plan. John looked to Fred.

"You figure out how to drive that thing?"

"Sort of," Fred said. "The controls aren't too different from the Banshees, at least in how you work them."

"Close enough," John said. He turned to the surviving assault troopers and motioned them onto the sled. "If we want to stay ahead of the Covenant and knock out enough installations to take this ring down, we need to move fast. Spartan-104 will show you how to operate this thing. Once you're good, he'll turn it over to you and switch vehicles. Clear?"

The troopers dipped their helmets in quick nods, and a husky male voice said, "So far."

"The rest is easy." John outlined a simple plan, then finished, "When you're out of octas, exfiltrate the best way you can and call for a ride."

The troopers piled their spare SPNKR barrels onto the sled behind Fred, then moved forward to learn how the vehicle was operated. John slipped into the driver's compartment of a second vehicle, which was loaded about three-quarters full with ingots of some kind of silvery-blue metal. Kelly and Linda mounted a third vehicle, also loaded with the metal ingots.

As Fred had indicated, the controls were similar to a Banshee's, but much simpler. There was basically a pair of handle grips to control speed and vector, and no weapon triggers.

John placed his weapons in the driver's compartment beside him, then straddled the driver's bench and placed both hands on the grips. The vehicle immediately whirred to life, its antigravity pads lifting it about a half meter off the floor. He moved the grips forward, and the sled began to accelerate.

Kelly and Linda came up beside him, Kelly driving and Linda kneeling in the cargo bed, using a stack of ingots as a firing rest for her M99. Fred brought up the rear, his voice echoing in John's helmet as he instructed the Black Daggers in driving the alien vehicle.

The transit tube was basically a flattened oval about five meters high and three times that in width, with one "roadbed" running along the "floor" of the tube and another along the "ceiling." Presumably, the aliens used artificial gravity to keep the sleds secured to the appropriate surface, with the floor designated for outbound traffic and the ceiling for empty inbound traffic.

Along the walls ran a two-meter viewing band, through which John could see the criss-crossing beams of the transit tube's trussing armature. Through the armature gaps on the left side, he saw Naraka's cloud-mottled face. If he craned his neck far enough, he could see distant sections of the fleet-support ring. To his delight, the ring had a visible gap about a quarter of its circumference behind him, and he did not see the blue spoke of a space elevator running down to the planet's surface beneath the gap. At least *part* of Green Team had made it that far, and they had destroyed at least one orbital facility. But it was going to take more than a small gap like that to destabilize the entire ring. Blue Team still had a lot of work to do.

Through the right-hand band, John could see the Covenant fleet departing its shielding orbit, repositioning itself to . . . what? Fire plasma cannons against its own support installations? The aliens would no doubt launch swarms of starfighters, but even they would not be of much use against a force that had already infiltrated their facilities. It was an infantry fight now, and in that arena, the Spartans held the advantage.

John felt the sled wobble as Fred jumped aboard and dumped an armload of SPNKR barrels into the cargo bed. A few minutes later, the dark oval of a closed hatch appeared at the end of the transit tube ahead.

Fred grabbed his SPNKR and kneeled in the front of the cargo bed, and the barrier vanished in an orange ball of flame and smoke. John aimed the sled at the center of the ball and, ducking down in the compartment to make himself as small a target as possible, drove straight into the flames.

The sled bounced a couple of times as it struck the edges of the jagged hole, and then they were shooting across the deck of one of the orbiting fleet-support facilities that were linked by the transit tube. This one looked like some kind of huge smelter.

A few needles and plasma bolts rained down from the girders overhead, but the barrage was so light and poorly aimed that it had to be coming from an amateur security team rather than a military unit. John kept the control grips pushed forward and barely bothered dodging, while Fred created confusion and conserved ammunition by flinging ingots at anything they passed.

At the speed they were traveling, the heavy ingots landed with the force of a rocket strike, taking out cargo sleds, cranes, even a crucible filled with molten metal. So far, John's strategy of moving fast was working well—the enemy was obviously scrambling, unable to move effective forces into place quickly enough to defend themselves.

A textbook raiding technique.

Except for losing most of Third Platoon. Casualties that high were *never* textbook.

The cargo sleds reached the far side of the smelter and entered the transit tube. Linda and Kelly pulled up beside Fred and John to maximize firepower if they ran into trouble ahead.

Having paused to find a good place to hide their octa, the Black Daggers had fallen a couple of minutes behind by the time they entered the transit tube, reporting one trooper injured.

John started a new two-and-a-half-minute countdown. The team would have to breach the transit tube before the octa detonated in the smelter—or risk being taken out by their own shockwave.

They reached the next installation at just over two minutes. Again, the hatch was closed, and again Fred hit it with a SPNKR rocket. This time, most of the fireball blew back into the transit tube, and John glimpsed something dark looming on the other side of the destroyed hatch.

"Second rocket!" He began to decelerate. "Barricade!"

Fred fired again, and a gaping hole appeared in the dark mass—but not a hole large enough to drive the cargo sled through.

John stopped the vehicle short and adjacent to the door, then grabbed his weapons and fired a grenade one-handed through the hole.

"Kelly—"

Kelly was already charging through the hole, firing as she moved. Fred followed close behind, the SPNKR clamped to his back and four extra barrels tucked under his arm. In his other hand, he carried his assault rifle. He let off a burst as stepped through the hole, and an instant later, the firefight had ended.

"Clear!" Kelly reported.

Linda stepped through, heavily burdened with her M99, an MA5B, and an extra case of barrels for Fred's SPNKR.

The Black Daggers arrived just as the countdown on John's HUD reached zero. He wasn't sure how much time actually remained until the octa in the last installation detonated, but it had to be less than thirty seconds.

As the assault troopers piled out of their sled, he pointed at the wall of the transit tube. "Hit that with a rocket," John said. "We need a vacuum cushion between us and the detonation."

The troopers ignored him and carried their wounded companion through the breached hatch.

"Already taken care of." It was a husky-voiced trooper bringing up the rear of the line who said this. "You don't have to be a Spartan to know what happens when you set off an octa in a confined space."

He disappeared through the breach after his companions, then stuck his head back through. "Better come along, Chief. There's going to be a hell of a wind in about ten seconds."

Feeling a bit foolish for thinking someone of a Black Dagger's training and experience would need reminding about shockwave hazards, John stepped through the hole and added one to the count of facilities that he could be certain Sierra Force had destroyed.

The aliens had toppled one of their cargo sleds in front of the hatch in an effort to defend their installation, and John helped his fellow Spartans turn the vehicle around so that its rounded nose was pushed into the hatch breach.

When a charge ruptured the transit tube a couple of seconds later, the decompression sucked the sled's nose deeper into the hole, holding the pressure loss inside the installation to a whistling breeze.

By the time they'd finished, a trio of Black Daggers had returned with a pair of replacement cargo sleds and a fresh casualty. Leaving the Daggers to plant their next octa, John and Blue Team climbed into the first sled and took off across what appeared to be a small-arms factory. They exchanged fire with a security detail that was taking cover behind the intermittent bulkheads that separated the transit lane from the work floor, simultaneously tossing crates off the sled to keep everyone else's heads down, and quickly reached the transit tube portal on the far side. The Black Daggers lagged behind in their sled, engaging in a more protracted firefight as they looked for a place to secure their octa. John didn't see where that was, because by then, he and the rest of the Spartans were in the transit tube and speeding away again.

They didn't have time to stop. If what was left of Sierra Force wasn't able to destroy at least eight more facilities, their chances of bringing down the orbital ring fell off sharply. If they managed to destroy a total of nine installations instead of ten, Dr. Halsey's estimates gave them only a seventy-one percent chance of destabilizing the ring. If they managed to destroy only a total of seven facilities, their chances of success fell to just forty-nine percent. John hadn't even bothered to memorize the odds below that—he hadn't brought Sierra Force all this way to take longshots. He was *going* to find a way.

The trip through the next few installations went much the same, with the Covenant security teams trying new tricks to slow the Spartan advance, and the Spartans finding countermeasures to circumvent them. The Black Daggers ran out of luck in the sixth facility, when the husky-voiced trooper—John hated that there had been no time to ask the man's name—spoke over the platoon channel.

"Afraid we can't keep carrying your water, Blue Team." His voice was pained and gurgling. "We'll be going out with our octa this time."

"Acknowledged," John said. "You did the 21st proud."

"'Course we did," the trooper said. "Just make sure you finish—"

The transmission ended in sharp crackle, and John instructed his onboard computer to log the time and conversation so he could recommend the man and his companions for a commendation—assuming he made it back himself.

As Blue Team approached the next installation, John glimpsed a set of efflux tails through the transit tube's lower viewband and stopped the vehicle to investigate. What he saw was both elating and dismaying.

About a quarter of the orbital fleet-support ring was now in ruins, with most of the missing sections directly behind Blue Team and, farther around the circle, a much smaller gap where Green Team had taken out what appeared to be about three facilities. Counting the six installations that Blue Team had destroyed, that made nine—and the orbital ring was already beginning to show signs of destabilization. There were long pieces of transit tube falling out of orbit and entire facilities plunging into Naraka's atmosphere, bright trails of fire behind them.

But the orbits below the section Green Team had destroyed were also filled with Covenant fighters. Many were flitting madly about, firing on tiny specks and unseen targets that might well be Green Team Spartans or their Black Dagger companions. A few craft seemed to be pursuing more deliberate strategies, traveling to specific points along the ring to cut off the advance of potential infiltrators.

And a few kilometers below that, a flight of ten Banshees was passing beneath the viewport where John stood, heading for a point that looked to be a couple of installations ahead of the Spartans' current location. John dropped to his knees and craned his neck around, trying to see the Banshees' destination, and caught a glimpse of a vessel under construction, with a bow so huge that at first he thought he was seeing things.

Fred's voice came over TEAMCOM—the only channel they were using, now that everyone in Third Platoon was gone.

"John?" he said. "Now's kind of a bad time for a nap."

"Very funny," John said. "Come here, wise guy. Give this a look."

Fred came over and kneeled in front of John, then began to crane his neck around. "Okay, what am I . . ." He let the sentence trail off and whistled. "Wow. What are they building there?"

"Who cares?" John said. "Either way, we're going to blow it up."

Linda and Kelly came over and sneaked a look at the vessel.

"I like it," Kelly said. "Going out in *style*."

"Or not." John pointed to the Banshee fighters crossing below. "There's our ride out of here."

Linda studied the Banshee flight for a moment, then craned her neck to look at the huge ship again.

"I see only one problem," she said. "That vessel must be more than twenty kilometers long and hundreds of decks high. Even if the Banshees intend to set down there, we could spend days looking for them."

"We'll think of something," John said. "But if I were to guess, whoever is in those Banshees is coming to *us*."

John led the way back to the cargo sled, and they resumed their advance.

The next facility turned out to be a dormitory, so after blasting their way in, they had to shoot their way across a thousand meters of metal-floored lobby, laying heavy suppression fire on at least fifty Jackals. The aliens were so poorly trained that their idea of blocking an advance was to hide behind the furniture on both sides of the kill zone and lay blind plasma fire in an inadvertent crossfire. They hit each other more than they did the Spartans or their vehicles, and they weren't wearing armor. By the time Blue Team emerged on the other side, Fred was down to two SPNKR missiles, John had just three grenades, Kelly had two, and nobody had more than a single magazine for their assault rifles.

But everybody still had an M6 sidearm with a full magazine, John still had twelve shotgun rounds in his M90, and Linda had fifty-two for her M99. So they were well-supplied for both long-distance combat and close assault. It was just the in-between ranges—where most firefights actually occurred—that would be a problem.

Not over yet, John thought. *We can do this.*

As they rode toward their next firefight, Blue Team spent their time brainstorming plans, and by the time the transit tube began to branch into different forks and levels, John thought they had something workable.

They stopped and reset the fuses on their remaining ordnance—two octas and four Havoks—to two-minute delays, then went to the viewing band and took another look at their final objective: a massive tangle of girders and airtight passageways that probably massed more than all of their other targets combined. Annihilating it would unbalance a whole section of the orbital ring. And the wreckage that *wasn't* vaporized in the blast would be hurled away with immense force, dragging along everything to which it was attached. The entire structure would slide out of orbit and plunge flaming into Naraka's cloudy atmosphere, virtually guaranteeing a severely hemorrhaged Covenant supply chain—a bloody nose John hoped the aliens would not soon forget.

Now that they were almost directly above the space docks, they also had a much clearer view of the vessel itself. Most of the immense ship they'd spied earlier was hidden between the two huge fabrication barns that hung down to either side of its patchwork hull. But the oval bow had already been completely covered. To John, it resembled the head of one of those huge, grinning whales whose pictures he had seen during the Earth module of his human-history classes.

The Banshee flight that he had seen before had already arrived and disappeared into one of the fabrication barns, but John could see a lot of rushing silhouettes in the mouth of a hangar about a quarter of the way down the starboard barn. Given the timing and circumstances, he thought it safe to assume he was looking at the Banshee flight's location. He pointed to the hangar.

"Set that as your waypoint," he said. "Then check the pressure integrity and rebreather status of your Mjolnir."

"I'm going to need some patching," Fred said.

"Who isn't?" Kelly asked, reaching for a cargo pouch. "I just hope we have enough."

"We do." Linda drew two handfuls of patches from her thigh pouch. "I brought extra."

Some of the patches had Black Dagger insignias on the split peel, but John didn't ask. Battlefield scavenging was a necessity for behind-the-lines operators.

A few minutes later, they backed to the far side of the transit tube; then Linda opened fire on the viewing band with her M99. The first round barely dimpled the sturdy material, and the second merely created a cloudy disc. But they had a lot more high-impact sniper rounds than they did SPNKR missiles, so John had her keep trying.

The fifth round created a web of outward-radiating stress cracks. Five more shots around the perimeter of the web produced more cracks—and a high-pitched whistling as the transit tube began to depressurize. John motioned Fred forward.

"Give it a kick."

Fred sprang into a two-booted flying side-kick that shattered the viewing pane and sucked him out into space.

"Like that?" he commed.

No one answered. They were too busy trying to avoid being knocked into a tumble as they were pulled through the breach together.

Once they were outside and began to drift apart, it grew easier to bring themselves under control. They quickly formed into a proper fire-team, with John and Kelly thirty meters from each other in front, and Fred and Linda about twenty meters behind them.

They activated their thruster packs and began to descend toward a small oval of light set amid a vast wall of oval lights. In his mind, John heard Avery Johnson warning him not to lead from the front. Trouble was, when units got this small, there was no place *left* but the front.

Besides, Chavez and Small Bear and the rest of Third Platoon and a lot of other courageous Sierra Force soldiers had sacrificed their lives well. Much of the alien fleet-support ring was starting to fall out of orbit in ruins, two space elevators had been destroyed, and at least one Covenant city on Naraka's surface was now a radioactive ruin. The mission had *already* succeeded.

Whatever happened next, the Covenant was going to know that humans fought back.

The hangar mouth yawned wider as the team drew nearer. John began to see shadows along the threshold. It was hard to tell their species, but most seemed to be dragging hoses and pulling lev-carts—so they were probably just maintenance hands, and not much of a threat in their own right. If John's assumption was correct—that the Banshee pilots were a Covenant special-forces unit assigned to hunt down infiltrators—then the aliens' most capable fighters would be twenty decks above, rushing to intercept Blue Team before they breached the transit tube hatches.

Assuming that everything went according to plan, those unknown hunters would die having never seen a Spartan, when one of Blue Team's Havoks detonated twenty decks below. And that was just fine with John. He didn't feel any need to look them in the eye or acknowledge their courage. All that mattered to him was stopping them, and he didn't much care how he did it.

Blue Team dropped even with the hangar mouth, and John confirmed that his assumption about the source of the shadows had been correct. In the silvery work light, he could see a three-Jackal crew tending each of the Banshees, with a couple of Grunts puttering nearby in an open cockpit. He saw no sign of a security team, though there were plenty of dark corners where a Brute or two might be lurking, and in the back of the large chamber stood a pair of luminous blue columns that he assumed to be alien lift tubes.

"Looks like we're good to go," John said over TEAMCOM. "Everybody ready?"

A trio of status lights winked green inside his helmet. Since he had only twenty-eight rounds remaining in his MA5B magazine, he switched his fire selector to single and hit his thrusters.

John's HUD flickered and dimmed slightly as he passed through the energy barrier at the hangar entrance; then his boots thudded to the deck as the artificial gravity kicked in. He immediately opened fire, concentrating on the left side of the hangar and putting a single round into every alien he saw. The Jackals went down either limp or convulsing, but always with surprise in their eyes. The Grunts either collapsed or exploded as their methane packs detonated.

A couple of breaths later, M99 rounds started to drop John's targets before he could, and Fred's voice sounded over TEAMCOM.

"We're in. Step two."

John and Kelly stopped firing long enough to move over to the nearest Banshees and reach inside, bringing the impulse drives online and activating the instrument consoles. They checked to make sure the controls responded to their touch, then repeated the sequence on the next two.

Assured that at least four of the craft were operable, John said, “Good to go. Step three.”

He and Kelly fired a few rounds to keep the enemy confused and their heads down, then dropped behind cover and removed the last of the Havoks from their magmounts. They opened the control covers, then tucked the bombs under their arms. John looked over to see if Kelly was ready and received a green status wink in return.

“Go!”

Each holding a Havok in one hand and an assault rifle in the other, they jumped up and raced toward the lift beams in the back of the hangar. So far the maintenance crews were either hiding or dying, and nobody opened fire. The assault was going even easier than planned.

So far.

Twenty paces from the lifts, John said, “Initiate.”

“Affirmative,” Kelly replied. “Initializing.”

‘Szatulai stepped out of the gravity lift to find fifty Kig-Yar standing beside the overturned cargo sleds they used to haul scrap away from the *Hammer of Faith*, the supercarrier being built in the huge construction kreche. Their long muzzles were hanging agape, and they were staring after Castor and Orsun as the two Jiralhanae pushed their way up the traffic-choked passageway, bellowing at the drivers to clear the way and flipping their sleds aside when it proved impossible to comply. The passageway curved out of sight before ‘Szatulai could see what was blocking traffic, but he had no doubt that it involved the Spartans.

A trio of Second Blades in black Bloodstar armor stepped out of the gravity lift and turned to follow the two Jiralhanae.

"Wait," 'Szatulai ordered. When the trio obeyed, he switched from the Bloodstar battlenet to his helmet's external speaker, then turned to the nearest sled driver. "Does this passageway not lead to the Ringroad?"

"It does—" The Kig-Yar hesitated, clearly struggling to recall the honorific appropriate to someone wearing the armor of the Silent Shadow, then said, "First Blade. We're scheduled to deliver this load of hull trimmings to The Forge of Faith, but the emergency pressure hatches came down."

'Szatulai's stomach began to churn. "Why?"

"A pressure breach in the Ringroad." The Kig-Yar pointed toward an observation blister about ten sleds up the passageway. "Chardal and Gulo claim they saw four soldiers in strange armor pulled through the hole, but they always claim to know . . ."

Paying no attention to the rest of what the Kig-Yar said, 'Szatulai turned back toward the gravity lift and began to issue orders over the Bloodstar battlenet.

"The demons are going around us," he said. "Back to the hangar . . . now!"

John and Kelly stopped twenty meters from the lift tubes and tucked their assault rifles under their arms, then shifted the Havoks to both hands and pressed the fuse triggers. John's onboard computer commenced a two-minute countdown on the HUD.

A blue glow arose inside both antigravity lifts, and a pair of Elite warriors dropped into view. They were wearing that glossy red-black space assault armor that John had seen several times before, and both were holding plasma rifles.

"Throw and go!" John ordered.

He flung his Havok toward the antigravity lift, using an underhanded pitch and putting his body into it. The device was small but heavy, and it flew only about halfway before dropping to the deck and continuing to roll.

Kelly's did the same, and the two aliens raised their plasma rifles to fire.

The Elite in front of Kelly took an M99 round in the chest and went flying into the bulkhead, overload static still crackling across his cratered torso armor. The alien in front of John simply erupted into a ball of flame and flying limbs as one of Fred's SPNKR missiles hit home.

Two more Elites had already stepped out of the lift, and another pair was following. Had John been in their position, with a couple bomb-looking things rolling toward an elevator that would carry them into the depths of the installation, he would have gone for the damn bombs, would have raced them to the front of the hangar and dumped them into space, and it wouldn't have mattered that the enemy was in his way—because if those bombs went off, everyone was going to die anyway.

The Elites didn't seem to care about the shipbuilding dock. Nor did they seem to care about dying. All they wanted to do was kill the Spartans.

They stepped over the Havoks and brought their plasma rifles up . . . and met the same fate as the first two Elites, this time with one taking an M99 round in the helmet, and the other cartwheeling off in two separate directions after catching Fred's SPNKR missile on his lower pelvis.

The countdown on John's HUD reached 1:45.

"Retreat already!" Fred yelled.

John *was* retreating, and so was Kelly, backpedaling as fast as they could, pouring rounds into the next two ranks of charging Elites and trying to dodge return fire. Neither action was going very well.

John emptied his magazine without taking down his target's energy shields, and while he was switching to the underslung grenade launcher, he took a plasma bolt in the shoulder. It penetrated his armor and screwed up his aim just enough to send the grenade flying off to detonate harmlessly in a corner.

Then the Elite was on him, tossing his plasma rifle aside and bringing up his hand with one of those red energy swords. John blocked the sword with his assault rifle and barely managed to duck out of the way as the crackling blade sliced through the barrel. He stomp-kicked the alien's knee and saw its leg buckle sideways, then sprang away and snatched his M90 off his rear magmount and put a round into the Elite's helmet. Its energy shield finally went down, and mandibles and purple blood flew in every direction.

The countdown on John's HUD read 1:34.

He racked another shell and opened fire on the next Elite, but this one was even more agile than the others and sidestepped the moment John's finger pulled the trigger. Then it leapt forward, bringing its energy sword around in a head-high strike that was a little too obvious. Rather than duck and expose himself for an easy reverse slash, John spun inside the blow and jammed his shotgun up beneath the Elite's helmet.

Again, the alien was too quick, tipping its helmet aside just before John opened fire. But this time, at least the energy shield crackled and went down.

John pumped another round into the chamber, then felt the Elite's free arm snaking around his chest, trying to take advantage of his shoulder wound to immobilize for the coup de grâce.

Bad mistake.

First, pain was nothing to a Spartan but incentive to fight harder. Second, Spartans wore power armor backed up by a neural interface. All they had to do was think, and their Mjolnir reacted. John *thought* about ripping the entrapping arm away, his shoulder erupting in anguish as his hand moved over the top of the Elite's forearm. He clamped tight and shoved downward, using the alien's own wrist to block the energy blade driving up toward his chin.

The Elite's hand fell, severed at mid-forearm, and the blade kept coming. John leaned away and managed to avoid taking the point under his helmet. But he sensed pressure along the side of his neck and felt blood trickling down inside his skinsuit.

John's ears began to drum with panic, and he tried to assure himself it wasn't the carotid. If that had been cut, he would already be falling unconscious.

And he wasn't.

So he jammed his shotgun down on the Elite's foot and fired. The alien's grasp loosened and it began to topple, still holding the sword next to John's neck.

John went with it, jamming his free hand up inside the alien's sword arm and pushing it away. They collapsed to the deck, John still on top and holding the blade at bay. He started to beat the alien's sword arm with his shotgun barrel, so unnerved by his close call that he didn't stop even after the wrist snapped sideways and the energy blade sizzled out . . . not until Kelly stepped up behind him and gently pulled the shotgun from his hand.

She pumped another round into the chamber, then placed it against the badly wounded Elite's helmet and sent brain matter fanning across the deck in every direction.

"You okay, John?"

"Fine." John sprang to his feet and took the shotgun back, then looked down at the mess that had nearly killed him. "Just another friggin' alien."

John glanced around and, fifty meters away in the back of the hangar, saw a pair of black-armored Brutes stepping out of the antigravity lifts. They were armed but confused, their helmets swinging back and forth as they looked from one Elite corpse to the next.

The countdown on John's HUD reached 1:00 and began to flash red.

"Let's get out of here." He turned and started for the Banshees, slapping patches on his armor as he ran. "While we still can."

The four Blue Team members jumped into the nearest fighters, then slipped into the stability harnesses and pulled their canopies down.

Fred's voice sounded over TEAMCOM.

"Heads up. Those Brutes could be trouble."

John put his hands on the controls and felt the Banshee rise beneath him, then turned toward the back of the hangar. The two Brutes were only about thirty meters away and racing forward with surprising speed for their size; but as John watched, they tossed their weapons aside and angled toward open Banshees.

He thought about opening fire on the pair, but the countdown on his HUD was flashing a big red :36, and he had not forgotten what happened the last time he was in a Banshee when a nuclear device detonated nearby. He swung his craft toward the hangar exit.

"We are letting those escape?" Linda's voice was neither approving nor disapproving, just curious. "Why?"

"Remember Etalan?" John pushed his controls forward and led Blue Team out of the alien hangar. "Poor gamma shielding."

The Spartans shot out of the hangar and pulled up, accelerating hard to climb into a higher orbit before the Havoks detonated. John kept one eye on the countdown in his HUD and the other on the Banshee's tactical holograph.

The Banshees carrying the two Brutes departed the fabrication barn at :23 and dived toward Naraka, using the planet's gravity well to help put as much distance as possible between themselves and the impending detonation. They began to pull up at :17 and dropped out of the bottom of the holograph at :12, and John suspected they would enter a stable orbit before the Havoks' gamma pulse knocked out their instruments.

As Blue Team's Banshees continued to climb away, the enormous fabrication barns—and the half-built ship they flanked—did not drift toward the bottom of the tactical holo so much as shrink and shift aft. Other Covenant fighter craft began to flit through the display, and a sporadic stream of alien voices sounded from the cockpit speakers. By the time the countdown on John's HUD reached :10, the image had finally reached the back edge of the display and started to move off.

John couldn't read the alien symbols on the tactical holo, so he had no idea whether Blue Team would be far enough from the detonation point to avoid having their instruments knocked out—or whether there were any prowlers even left to retrieve them.

What he did know was that someday there *wouldn't* be, that even Spartans weren't immortal.

If he kept pushing limits and jumping at assignments everyone else considered suicide, it wouldn't be only the support troops and prowler crews who got killed. It would be him and Blue Team and—eventually—the entire squad.

But what choice did they have?

Operation: SILENT STORM was only the beginning. Naraka was being hit hard, but John had already seen enough from the Covenant to know the UNSC wasn't going to win the war in a single battle. The aliens would recover from the shock of an attack inside their own space and return with a vengeance . . . and when they did, the Spartans would be waiting.

Ready to do the impossible.

They would just have to be smart about it.

The countdown on John's HUD reached :05. John activated his locator beacon, then spoke over the encrypted Sierra Force channel.

"Sierra-117 requesting Blue Team extraction, four members. Repeat: all four members."

Somewhere out there, a prowler acknowledged with a single click.

The Havoks detonated, and the Banshee instruments blossomed into static and died. John popped his canopy and, as the starfighter tumbled, pushed himself out into space. Fred and the rest of Blue Team were doing the same, and they fired their thruster packs, maneuvering themselves into a recovery line with fifty-meter spacing. Below and behind them, a few glowing remnants of the megaship fabrication barns were fluttering away in separate directions, all that remained of a mighty behemoth that would never have the opportunity to terrorize humanity.

John could only guess how many alien workers had perished with the vessel, but the number had to be in the tens of thousands—possibly even hundreds of thousands. For an instant, he was tempted to think of them as innocent victims of the war, much like the millions of people who died every time the Covenant glassed another world. Then he remembered what they had been building here, and he realized there could be no comparison. The workers who had died aboard the fleet-support ring were as much a part of the Covenant war effort as the officers who commanded their fleets and the warriors who fired their plasma rifles. They were *all* working toward the destruction of humanity—and John refused to feel bad for beating them to the punch.

A double click sounded inside John's helmet, and he fired his attitude thrusters, slowly spinning himself around until he saw the dark silhouette of a UNSC prowler blocking the stars beyond, the mouth of its open drop bay a dim purple square yawning ever larger as it swooped toward him.

John tapped his maneuvering jets ever so gently, spinning himself around so that he was oriented boots-down as the bay swallowed him up. The moment he crossed the threshold, a pair of Black Dagger assault troopers stepped into view and grabbed him by the arms, helping him decelerate into the prowler's artificial gravity and guiding him onto the deck.

"Welcome aboard, Master Chief." The voice came over the command channel, and it belonged to Captain Nelly Hamm. "We're packed to the gills, but it'll be an honor to make room for you and your Spartans aboard the *Night Watch*."

EPILOGUE

Ninth Age of Reclamation
36th Cycle, 185 Units (Covenant Battle Calendar)
Fleet of Inexorable Obedience, Assault Carrier *Pious Rampage*
High Equatorial Orbit, Planet Zhoist, Buta System

Seven times Nizat 'Kvarosee had stood in his observation blister watching worlds burn, and not once had he considered that one day it might be the Covenant's turn.

Now, as he watched pieces of the Ring of Mighty Abundance slide out of orbit and plunge burning into Zhoist's atmosphere, he could not imagine why.

Perhaps he had believed the humans too craven to bite at the hand of the butcher. Or perhaps he had been so blinded by faith that he had expected them to submit to the will of the Prophets as humbly as did the Sangheili.

In his shock and shame, he truly could not recall the reason.

A growing hum announced the arrival of the being Nizat wanted least to see. He kept his gaze fixed on the disaster below and did not acknowledge the San'Shyuum's approach. Of course, the Minor Minister of Artifact Survey refused to take the hint.

"How did you let this happen?!"

Nizat turned to see the San'Shyuum coming in his chair, his serpentine neck arcing forward in accusation, and he realized he had never wanted to kill a being so much in his life. And why should he not? He was certain to lose command of the Fleet of Inexorable Obedience anyway. So what difference would it make?

Before Nizat could act on his murderous impulse, his steward, Tam 'Lakosee, caught up to the chair and stepped to Survey's side.

"We did not *let* this happen, Your Grace," 'Lakosee said. "Any more than the humans *let* us cleanse E'gini and Borodan. It is unreasonable to start a war and think the enemy would not fight back."

Survey's eyes widened with indignity. "I can see *you* won't be rising any further," he said. "Allowing infidel boots to defile a holy world is *not* a reasonable loss."

"Neither is losing two of the Ten Cities," Nizat said. The Ten Cities had been a gift left behind by the ancient Forerunners, and the humans had obliterated a pair of them with their hellbombs. "Or the destruction of the Ring of Mighty Abundance. But Tam is correct, Your Grace—what did the Hierarchs expect when they started this war?"

"Not *that*!" Survey flung a three-fingered hand toward the catastrophic scene above Zhoist. "And the Hierarchs won't be pleased to learn you have been blaming them for *your* failure!"

"And what can the Hierarchs do as a form of punishment? Take my fleet from me?"

He started to turn back to the observation blister, but stopped when 'Lakosee gave a polite clack of his mandibles. Nizat replied with a clack of his own, giving the steward permission to speak.

"I have news of the blademaster."

"Ah." Nizat had grown so angry watching the Ring of Mighty

Abundance break apart that he had finally told 'Lakosee to summon Tel 'Szatulai to explain. Now that he had calmed down, however, he was beginning to realize that if anything was going to be redeemed from this catastrophe, it would be what 'Szatulai had learned about the Spartans and their methods. "I hope your news is good."

"I fear not," 'Lakosee said. "He was killed by the Spartans. His Jiralhanae battle chiefs saw him die."

"And since Castor and Orsun survived to make the report, we can assume the Spartans are dead?" Survey surprised Nizat by recalling the pair's names.

"No, Your Grace," 'Lakosee said. "The Spartans escaped in captured Banshees."

"Of course they did," Survey said. "It would be too much to expect Jiralhanae battle chiefs to think for themselves."

"They were fortunate to survive, Your Grace." There was a note of irritation in 'Lakosee's voice. "They barely escaped before the hellbombs destroyed the *Hammer of Faith* in her construction docks."

"And those Spartans are *still* out there?" Nizat began to have a sinking feeling. "In our Banshees?"

'Lakosee's mandibles splayed soundlessly; he finally answered, "As far as we know, Fleetmaster. The search and rescue crews have recovered the corpses of twenty of the humans' Blacksuits and captured eight more, but none were Spartans."

Survey used his gravity chair to push between the two Sangheili. "Idiot," he said to Nizat. "You allow your shipmasters to take bodies and prisoners? After the way—"

A blue energy blade crackled to life, and the Minor Minister's insult came to an abrupt end as his small head dropped into his lap. Nizat and 'Lakosee had to step farther apart to avoid having their feet crushed when the gravity chair lost power and dropped to the deck. 'Lakosee deactivated his energy sword and offered the hilt to Nizat.

"I am sorry, Fleetmaster. I could not allow him to disparage you at a time like this."

Nizat waved the hilt away. "Think nothing of it." He stared down at the San'Shyuum's lifeless body for a moment, watching the red blood dribble from the partially cauterized neck in his lap. "We will incinerate the body, and I will explain to the Hierarchs that he died battling for the Faith."

Which was close enough to the truth that Nizat would not regret the exaggeration. How dark his path had grown, that he would deceive the Prophets so casually—even if it was to save a worthy Major.

'Lakosee's mandibles splayed in shock. "Fleetmaster, I cannot ask you—"

"You are not asking," Nizat said. "And we are done discussing it. There are more important matters at hand."

Which was also true. Nizat's hearts had begun to pound in counterpoint as soon as Survey began to berate him, and not because of the typical San'Shyuum condescension. He could not quite identify it, but there was something alarming about 'Lakosee's report. Why should there only be dead soldiers of one kind? Could the Spartans be so much superior to humanity's other warriors? Or was it just their special armor that made them so ferocious?

It was an answer that Nizat would have soon enough, once he discovered what had become of the schematics 'Szatulai had received from the human traitors. He was uncertain which to hope for—that there was a lineage of human soldiers far superior to the Covenant's own elite warriors, or that the humans knew how to build armor that would make super-soldiers of any of them.

But that was a dilemma to be considered at another time . . . and probably by another fleetmaster. For now, Nizat's duty was to protect what he had not lost already.

"Have the fleet break orbit and withdraw outside the gravity well,"

Nizat said. "And tell me more about these prisoners. Have the interrogations begun?"

"Only the preliminaries," 'Lakosee said. "The prisoners will not be turned over to Castor and Orsun until the capturing shipmasters can send them to the *Pious Rampage*."

Nizat knew what that really meant—the shipmasters were holding the prisoners so their own mind melters had a chance to work on them. But that was to be expected. He had done the same thing more than once as a young shipmaster.

"What of the preliminary interrogations?" Nizat said. "Are the mind melters learning anything?"

'Lakosee spread his mandibles briefly, then said, "That is what is strange, Fleetmaster. No matter how hard the prisoners are beaten or shocked, all they do is what the humans call laughter."

1718 hours, April 15, 2526 (military calendar)
UNSC *Razor*-class prowler *Night Watch*
Libration Point Three, Planet Naraka, Agni System

John would never forget his first Sweet William cigar—he was pretty sure of that. It tasted like an old boot-sock smoked over dung-fire after a two-week march, and his first and only draw had made him cough so hard he popped all eight of the butterfly bandages holding his neck wound closed.

He could not imagine how Avery Johnson took such pleasure in them, especially under the circumstances. They were sitting together in the crew lounge of the UNSC prowler *Night Watch*, which had recovered not only all of the personnel vacced by Ghost Flight when Hector Nyeto fled, but also Blue Team, Green Team, and two Black Dagger survivors of the assault on the orbital ring.

Avery had been the last person rescued at libration point three, and he was wrapped in a heated blanket, having been left floating in space for so long that his suit heaters had failed and he'd nearly frozen to death. He had an oxygen cannula in his nose because he had run out of rebreather time, and there were two different IVs in his arm, as the resulting CO_2 buildup had almost killed him.

They were looking out the viewport toward Naraka, watching flame trails light the planet's yellow clouds whenever a segment of the alien fleet-support ring dropped out of orbit and began to burn up in the atmosphere. Sometimes the flame trails would last all the way to ground and end in the beautiful orange blossom of an impact detonation.

Avery would shout and slap the arm of his chair, then Kelly and the rest of the Spartans would cheer. Fred would find some new way to crack wise, and Daisy would laugh a little too hard, and Linda would shake her head at the two of them. John thought it was probably the best party he had ever attended—though he didn't have much to compare it to—and the celebration was made all the better by the fact that all twelve of his Spartans had made it back.

He just wished the same could be said for the 21st Space Assault Battalion. So far, the three surviving prowlers of Hush and Slipper Flights—the only on-site search craft available—had recovered just eleven more of the Black Daggers who had accompanied Blue and Green Teams up the space elevators, and John had heard that those troopers were having a very different kind of gathering aboard the *Hush Now*. When the opportunity presented itself, he intended to go over and offer his condolences, but he had been told it might be wise to let some time pass. What that implied, he wasn't sure he completely understood.

The chronometer on the wall changed to 1719 hours, and Kurt-051 said, "That's gonna be the Green Team auto-detonation."

Almost instantly, eight blinding points of light appeared near Naraka and swelled into the white fireballs of an octanitrocubane explosion. Unlike Blue Team's previous announcement, six of Green Team's devices detonated about an arm's length above Naraka, in a cluster of blue slivers that were all the naked eye could see of the alien fleet.

An awed silence fell over the compartment as the Spartans honored the sacrifices that went with all those white blossoms—each detonation represented a Black Dagger who had carried a live octa into battle and fallen before he or she could use it . . . yet somehow *still* managed to sneak their devices aboard an enemy vessel.

Once the bright spheres had shriveled back in on themselves and vanished into the nothingness of explosive annihilation, Avery Johnson took the oxygen cannula out of his nose; holding it at a safe distance, he took another puff of his Sweet William.

"Now, that's a beautiful thing," he said. "All those Covenant ships getting blown straight back to hell."

"When you're right, you're right," Daisy-023 said. "But there ought to be three prowlers with them."

"Ghost Flight?" Fred asked.

"You must be a mind reader," Daisy said. "Those bastards killed Colonel Crowther and cost the 21st a lot of good soldiers. I can't believe they're going to get away with this."

"They're not," Fred said.

"What are you gonna do about it?" Kelly asked. "Go AWOL and hunt them down?"

"I'm in," Daisy said.

"Colonel Crowther certainly deserves to have that score settled," John said. And he meant it. Without Crowther's example, he might never have learned the subtle but important difference between being a leader and being a commander. He owed the man a debt of gratitude that he might never be able to repay. "But is that the way to honor him, by doing something he'd really look down on?"

"Whatever it takes," Daisy said. "That's the Spartan way."

"On the battlefield," John said. He could see where this was going, and Daisy wasn't the kind who blew off steam just talking. Neither was Fred, for that matter. "And it's not just Spartans who believe in that. Crowther sacrificed everything—his whole *battalion*—to make this operation a success."

Daisy rolled her blue eyes.

"Don't *do* that," Johnson said. He leaned toward Daisy. "Don't act like getting lucky with Operation: SILENT STORM and destroying a *single* support base means we've won the whole damn war."

Johnson started to continue his rant, then seemed to catch himself. He settled back in his chair and glanced up at John, as though to say *it's your unit,* you *deal with it.*

Which was only right, John realized. It looked like he was going to be leading the Spartans for a long time—at least if he was as good as it seemed like everyone was beginning to think he was—and he needed to set the tone for his command.

"The sergeant is absolutely right," John said. "You can bet Naraka isn't the only fleet support world the Covenant has, so you know they're going to come back at us even harder than before. We Spartans are going to have our work cut out for us from now on, and we'll need to have each other's backs all the way. That's how we honor Colonel Crowther's legacy."

Daisy drew herself up straight. "Understood. You can count on me."

"I know I can." John paused, then smiled and added, "And rest assured, we're *going* to get Hector Nyeto. I promise. The one thing we know about him is this: he *will* come for us again. And when he does, we're going to be ready for him—and we're going to take him out."

Avery Johnson let out a cackle. "I couldn't have said it better myself." He leaned forward and pointed the butt of his Sweet William at John. "Looks like you've got this, Master Chief."

ACKNOWLEDGMENTS

I would like to thank everyone who contributed to this book, especially: my first reader, Andria Hayday, whose suggestions and insights always improve the manuscript at least threefold; Ed Schlesinger for being a great editor and for his endless patience throughout my mother's long illness and death; Jeremy Patenaude for all of his great suggestions and being really, really good at his job; Tiffany O'Brien for making the Halo universe such a welcoming and fun place to work; Chris McGrath for the excellent cover art; Joal Hetherington for copyediting—always the trickiest of jobs; and everyone at 343 Industries and Gallery Books who make writing in the Halo universe such a delight.

ABOUT THE AUTHOR

Troy Denning is the *New York Times* bestselling author of more than thirty-five novels, including *Halo: Retribution*, *Halo: Last Light*, a dozen *Star Wars* novels, the Dark Sun: Prism Pentad series, and many bestselling Forgotten Realms novels. A former game designer and editor, he lives in western Wisconsin.